Honor's Pledge

Rocky Mountain Legacy

◆◆◆◆◆◆◆◆◆◆◆◆◆◆◆

KRISTEN HEITZMANN

•••••••••••••••••••••••••

Honor's Pledge

BETHANY HOUSE PUBLISHERS
MINNEAPOLIS, MINNESOTA 55438

Published by Bethany House Publishers
A Ministry of Bethany Fellowship International
11400 Hampshire Avenue South
Minneapolis, Minnesota 55438
ISBN: 0-7394-0588-8
Printed in the United States of America

To my parents,
Richard and Jane Francis,
who instilled a love for storytelling
and the handling of the pen.

KRISTEN HEITZMANN was raised on five acres of ponderosa pines at the base of the Rocky Mountains in Colorado, where she still lives with her husband and four children. A music minister and artist, Kristen delights in sharing the traditions of our heritage, both through one-on-one interaction and now through her first novel, *Honor's Pledge*.

Abigail Martin jumped at the gunshots, dropped the bolt of blue calico, and hurried to the window. She caught her breath as Blake McConnel, red-faced, shouted threats to Mr. Montgomery Farrel, who stood cool and unresponsive. The gun discharged again, this time not at the sky, but at the feet of the tall gentleman, spewing a cloud of dirt into his face as he leaped backward. Farrel's cool demeanor ignited into fury. Blake took aim again and hollered, "Draw yer weapon and settle it!"

From her vantage behind the small-paned window of the dry goods mercantile, Abbie watched both men: Blake in his worn pants and tousled hair; Farrel in tan breeches, knee-high boots, shirt sleeves, and vest. A pearl-handled Colt hung at Farrel's hip, but he didn't reach for it, nor unclip the leather strap that held it in place. Thankfully he possessed greater self-control than Blake.

With her heart pounding, Abbie rushed for the door but was blocked by the corpulent Bailey sisters pressing their faces to the glass, oozing excitement.

"Will you look at that? It's the McConnel boy steaming like a kettle." Eleanor Bailey wiped the shine from her cheek and forehead with a limp white handkerchief.

Ruth giggled. "Maybe he'll injure Mr. Farrel so's he'll need doctoring."

"I'm afraid that job'll go to the doc, sister. Now that we have one."

Abbie's chest tightened as Blake raised his arm again and pulled the trigger, but the gun didn't fire, and she released her trapped breath. Blake hammered the gun with his hand, then threw it in the dirt and charged Montgomery Farrel, who stood poised to receive the onslaught.

Farrel had the benefit of a longer reach and more years, but Blake was huskier and out of his head with anger. Pressing herself between the two soft bodies, Abbie gained the door and pushed through. The townsmen hollered the fighters on with carnival shouts, but at Blake's next thrust, he was grabbed from behind by Deputy Clem Davis. He contained Blake's fury with arms as thick and powerful as a grizzly's.

Montgomery Farrel bent to pick up his hat from the dusty street. His dark hair no longer waved smoothly but bent into unruly curls down the back of his neck. He slapped the dust from his hat and followed the deputy into the jail, the lines of his face as hard as the rocky bluff for which the town was named.

"Five dollars gold says Marshal Haggerty'll dismiss it," Jonas Roberts hollered.

"Five says he don't," contended old Jake. "Now that the new deputy's got his hands on the young'un, he'll keep 'im awhile."

"All depends if Farrel's a mind to press a charge."

Jonas Roberts shoved back his hat and swiped his forehead with his shirt sleeve. "Anyone else an' they'd have let 'em fight it out. Guess we can't have no one lettin' loose on Montgomery Farrel, now, can we?"

Abbie bit her lip in frustration. *What on earth had Blake been thinking?*

"It's a shame Deputy Davis spoiled the fun." At her glare, Mag French tipped his hat to her with a yellow-toothed grin, then spat.

Abbie turned away. She wished she could throttle Blake herself, then wished he hadn't been hauled into the jail. All this for a few flattering words! True, Mr. Farrel's compliments had slid from his tongue as gold dust from a sluice box, but it was no more than any of the young men in town might have said, given the opportunity. And he had lingered as he bowed over her hand, held on perhaps longer than necessary. Blake had glowered like a ranch dog on a coon.

Even then, things might have been all right if Mr. Farrel hadn't remarked how very much he had enjoyed his visit the previous evening without mentioning at all that it was her father's company he'd shared . . . mainly. Blake had gone off like a cannon, but Abbie had figured that was the worst of it. When he had stormed away, she thought he'd lick his wounds and be done.

She watched the jail door for Blake to emerge, hangdogged but free. He was temperamental, but . . . gunplay! At least the fool boy was alive. Montgomery Farrel had never even drawn the gun that hung at his hip, though a man rarely invested in that fancy kind of hardware unless he could handle it. She shuddered to think if he had.

As the door opened, she clasped her hands together at her chest, but Mr. Farrel came out alone and prepared to mount. Her heart sank. He must have pressed charges after all.

Catching up her skirts, Abbie flew to his side. "Mr. Farrel."

He turned to her and tipped his hat with the slight bow that betrayed his southern breeding. It lost none of its elegance, even though his face was smudged, one sleeve askew, and dust up to his knees. "Miss Martin."

For a moment she faltered. "Blake's in jail?" That much was obvious. He opened his mouth to reply, but she rushed on. "Surely you know he intended you no real harm."

"I'm afraid I know no such thing." He spoke softly in the manner of the South, but his voice was deadly serious. "Had

11

he not possessed an inferior weapon, I might have been forced to kill him. I don't consider gunplay a game."

Drawing herself up, Abbie tightened her mouth into a determined line. "He's just a boy, and I'm certain it won't happen again. If you would just drop the charges against him . . ."

Montgomery Farrel hooked his thumbs into his belt. "And what would lead me to think that it won't? That rascal has a hornet in his hide."

"It's all a misunderstanding. I'm awfully sorry for the trouble. I truly don't know what gave him the notion to behave in such a manner. . . ."

"Don't you?" The ghost of a smile played on his mouth.

She flushed. "Well . . . I . . . if I told him that my feelings are not what he . . . thinks they are . . ."

Montgomery Farrel ran a hand over the sleek sorrel neck of the stallion, loosening the reins from the hitch. "You believe his jealousy can be cured by a dose of truth?" Mr. Farrel smoothed back his hair and replaced his hat under the afternoon sun. His tone was cool but no longer angry.

"I'll speak to him. I'll speak to him right now." She flashed a smile and spun for the jail, her skirts swirling against her legs. Inside, she walked directly to the desk.

"Afternoon, Miss Martin," Marshal Haggerty said. Behind him, Deputy Davis removed his hat with a bearish grin. He dwarfed the marshal, and the tight space smelled of him, like an animal's den.

"Good afternoon. I've come to see Blake."

Marshal Haggerty motioned her by, and she moved to the single stone cell of the Rocky Bluffs jail. Blake sat on the thin cot, head hanging and hands limp on his thighs. He was too old to whip but looked like he deserved it anyway.

His head came up. "Abbie! What are you—"

"I need to talk to you, Blake."

He jumped up and encircled the bars with his hands. "This ain't a place for you."

"It's hardly a place for you, either. What have you gone and done?"

"I won't stand for that Montgomery Farrel comin' in here like he owns the whole darn town, makin' eyes at you with all that fancy talk. I warned him off, but he don't listen."

Exasperation choked her, and Abbie stamped her foot. "This is plain foolishness, and you've no right to be causing him trouble."

Blake's face fell. "You're not taken with him?"

"No, I'm not. But I'm not taken with you, either." She paused, softening. "Oh, Blake, I have great affection for you, but I haven't a notion what made you carry on so. You've been itching over Mr. Farrel since he came. Promise it'll stop now."

"Well, it won't exactly do me no good if you don't care for me anyway. Not that it much matters now."

"I believe Mr. Farrel will drop the charges."

"What charges?"

"What charges! Maybe attempted murder, and I'll wager he knows the law."

Blake cocked his head, shaking the hair from his eyes. "Are you bein' straight with me, or are you tellin' me all this to try to save my neck?"

"I've been completely honest with you."

He sagged. "I was afraid of that."

"Give me your word you'll not bother him again."

"You have it," he muttered.

"Say it, Blake, on your honor."

"I won't mess with Farrel no more . . . on my honor." He grinned, and Abbie squeezed the knuckles that protruded from the cell, relief washing over her.

"You'll find someone else to guard as ardently."

He slowly nodded. "Maybe I will. But it won't be the same."

He slumped down on the hard bunk against the wall.

That settled, Abbie rushed back out and searched for Montgomery Farrel. The narrow street cleaved the twin rows of single and two-story board buildings with false fronts feigning greater stature. Her eyes swept to McConnel's livery, where the smoke and noise of hot metal on an anvil rang into the air.

Only God had kept Wes McConnel from hearing the ruckus and thrashing Blake in the street himself. If Pa had been at work at the newspaper across the way, he might have done the same. She scanned the hardware store, sporting the name of the new owner on the sign: Peterson Hardware. Across the street she searched the General Mercantile and Dry Goods, then the grocer's, where the Bailey sisters were haggling over something.

The walkway by Mrs. Munson's clothier, the post office, and on down to Pa's news office was empty. Turning her head, Abbie gazed the other direction—town hall, lumberyard, bank, school, and the church, still closed up after the untimely loss of Reverend Peale. There were several horses tethered at the hitching posts, mostly before the saloon-hotel, where the men were no doubt drinking off their excitement in the afternoon heat. Mr. Farrel's unmistakable horse was nowhere to be found. With annoyance she realized he had gone, and with him her hopes of Blake's immediate release.

Two

Abbie raised her chin, climbed into her buggy, and started for the Farrel ranch. It was northeast of town, a good step farther than her own family's homestead, and over the prairie with hardly a shrub to shade her way. When the house came into sight, it was like an oasis in a grass desert. She pulled the horse to a stop beneath an arching cottonwood.

The house before her was impressive with a distinctive southern flair. She had not seen it up close before, though the town had buzzed over it for months. Montgomery Farrel had chosen the sight well, availing the shade of the trees already established by the creek that ran behind. Centered on the pink stone face of the lower story was a sweeping portico with white pillars and wide stone steps flanked by matching large-paned windows, and on the west side rose the narrow, arched windows of a room her eyes could only imagine.

Abbie raised her gaze to the white-painted second story, with its curved tower room at one end and five black-shuttered windows. So much glass dazzled her. Even the eaves and arches of the attic had small rounded panes. She was impressed in spite of herself. The house was generally considered extravagant, showy, and improvident, and every mother in town hoped her daughter would live there as the wife of the handsome, cultured Montgomery Farrel. Abbie's chin jutted. She had no such aspirations.

She mounted the stairs and applied the large brass knocker to the door. It resounded hollowly, and Abbie stepped back when it opened almost immediately. She stared into the grizzled black face of a man in a white coat and gray trousers.

"Yes, miss?"

She straightened. "I wish to see Mr. Farrel . . . please."

He stepped back for her to enter, closing the door silently behind. The entry was like a cathedral, all arches and carved wood. She followed him into a parlor that would have held the entire living space of her family's farmhouse.

"Who may I say's callin'?"

"Abbie . . . Miss Abigail Martin."

He actually bowed and backed out. Abbie eyed the low lacquered walnut table and a matching secretary with a marquetry of vines and leaves. She ran her hand over the settee, plush and velvety soft, tucked with buttons and edged with sloping wood, carved into an elegant floral fan at the center. She stroked the fabric again for the pure pleasure of its softness.

Across from the velvet-draped windows, the stone fireplace was crowned by a mantel that held a marble clock and two silver candelabras as well as a daguerreotype of a man in a gray Confederate uniform and a small portrait of a stunning woman in a lace-edged gown.

Abbie drew up close, studying the arching brows and delicate curve of the woman's mouth. In spite of her stiff pose, there was a sweetness in her smile, and she looked very young. Abbie jumped when Montgomery Farrel spoke behind her.

"My father and mother."

Abbie saw the likeness. "Your mother is beautiful."

"Yes, she was." His voice softened. "She died when I was seven."

"I'm very sorry." She turned to face him.

He bowed his head. "This is indeed an honor, Miss Martin." He was cleaned and groomed, as though the afternoon's altercation had never happened. She was certain he would never mention it again if she did not. But then, Blake was sitting in the jail. . . .

Abbie squared her shoulders. "I had expected—hoped—to be able to continue our conversation in town, but you'd already left when I finished at the jail."

The corners of Montgomery's mouth flickered. "I see. I'm sorry to have inconvenienced you. I didn't realize you had more you wished to say on the matter."

Abbie's temper flashed. "You might have considered that I would give you Blake's answer."

"Again I apologize. I failed to understand the immediacy of your concern." He motioned her to the settee. "I presume you told him the nature of your feelings?"

Abbie flushed. Why had Blake taken it into his head to embarrass her so? "Yes. And he's agreed not to bother you in any way. He gave his word and very much regrets his actions."

Mr. Farrel's smile broadened. "He said so?"

Abbie stammered for a reply, realizing he'd seen through her embellishment. They were interrupted by a woman carrying a tray with a pitcher of tea. The scent of the fresh mint leaves filled the room.

"Refreshment, Mastuh Monte." Her skin was like oiled mahogany, her hands large and thick.

"Thank you, Pearl. Set it there on the table."

She obliged and left the room.

"Are they your slaves?" Abbie bit her lip as Mr. Farrel frowned.

"Slavery was abolished with the war, Miss Martin. Although I don't expect you know much about it, do you?" He poured and handed her a glass.

Abbie wrapped her fingers around its chill. "I know what

I've read and what Pa has told me. It's all rather complicated."

"As is all war."

"Pa was sympathetic to both sides but believed we ought to remain a single nation, not divided into warring states."

Montgomery turned to the picture of his father on the mantel, his back straight and firm in his tailored coat. "I think my father believed that as well. But he fought for the Confederacy."

"Why?"

"Because honor demanded it. He knew we couldn't win. Unlike some, he saw that our resources would fall far short if the war prolonged, but our sovereignty and honor were being wrenched from us. For that, he fought."

He faced her, and Abbie saw a fire behind his words. Not only did he believe in what he was saying, he embraced it deep inside. His voice was low, but there was no masking the intensity.

"That is the honor I understand. The ability to do what one must, even when it is against one's heart." He softened. "Do you believe that's the honor with which your friend holds his word?"

At last she had a chance. "Yes, I do. Blake's impetuous, but he's honest through and through." And that was true. Blake would keep his word if it killed him.

Montgomery Farrel stood and leaned against the mantel, sipping his tea. "Where I come from, dueling, though not unheard of, is illegal. On occasion it may be handled privately by arrangement, but one does not accost another on a public street like two mongrels after the same scrap. Here, 'calling someone out' seems an acceptable means of settling quarrels."

Abbie sighed. "It's not so much acceptable as unstoppable. There are few enough who try to block a bullet aimed at another." Abbie could see that the afternoon's event had disturbed him more than she thought. Blake had insulted Montgomery Farrel's honor and made a spectacle of them both. "But truly Blake would never have shot you. And he won't repeat it."

"I'll accept your word for that."

"Then you'll drop the charges?" Abbie breathed hopefully.

His smile was warm and gracious. "I'll drop the charges."

"Oh, thank you!" She clasped her hands together at her chest.

Montgomery Farrel bowed again. "Would you do me the honor of remaining for supper?"

She was caught off guard. "Here?"

"Unless you have a preference."

Abbie glanced about her, absorbing the grandeur. *Clara will be green.* "All right. But I'll have to let Mama know not to expect me."

"I'll send the message to your mother."

"And to town for the marshal?"

He smiled crookedly. "And for the marshal." As he spoke he strode to the secretary, took out two sheets of thin vellum paper, and laid one out for Abbie with a pen and inkwell. She quickly sat and wrote the note explaining her whereabouts to her parents, then blotted and handed it to him. He folded it along with his own and called for James.

After dispensing instructions, he turned back to Abbie. "It's rather close in here. Would you care to walk outside until supper?"

"That's because of the heavy draperies. If you took the velvet off, left the lace, and opened the windows on either side, you'd get a cross breeze and cool it off nicely."

He raised an eyebrow and she added, "But yes, I'd like to walk."

"Well, then . . ." He motioned her toward the door. At the

foot of the stairs, Abbie gathered her skirts in a futile but required attempt to keep them from the dust. Montgomery Farrel clasped his hands behind his back and strolled beside her.

They walked in the shade of the cottonwoods, then turned onto a path that skirted the hill. Long shadows lined the pale, grassy fields. Abbie turned her face to the breeze, letting it scatter the damp tendrils clinging to her forehead. She glanced sideways at Mr. Farrel. The handsome, angular cut of his features, the dark brows and deep brown eyes, the firm, wide mouth all came together in a dashing blend that he muted with his nonchalance.

He didn't flaunt himself, and Abbie quickened to the thought that he had no need to. He was tall—taller than her father, who stood five eleven—and lean, but he moved with an elegance of motion that was as foreign as his slow, lilting speech, and she unconsciously matched her gait to it. Montgomery turned and she dropped her gaze. A sweat bee buzzed her head, then swung in dizzying loops up into the blue expanse.

As they dipped into a small valley, they came again under the shade of a line of cottonwoods and chokecherries spreading their dense branches over a clear stony stream. Hare bells and Queen Anne's lace flowered beneath. She couldn't help but exclaim, "How lovely!"

Montgomery Farrel smiled. "I'm glad you like it. This is my favorite spot on the ranch." He swept his arm forward. "To your right, bald Pikes Peak, and away east, the prairie. But within this little circle nothing seems as stretched and open."

Abbie followed his extended arm as he pointed, then turned back to him. "You're not used to the space yet. It'll grow on you. This place is solid as the rock beneath us. Beautiful, yes. Wild perhaps, but not as a jungle teeming with danger or an Arabian desert hiding its treasures beneath hot, blowing sands. Here you can grab hold of the land and feel its strength." She lifted a chunk of granite, pink and gray with sparkles of quartz and feldspar. "I think God started here and just spread out the rest of the world with what was left."

He was watching her curiously. "Is that spoken from experience, Miss Martin?"

Abbie smiled. "Limited, I guess."

He opened his mouth to respond, but the clanging of a bell broke the evening still. He raised an eyebrow conspiratorially. "That's the signal for supper, and if we value our necks we'll not delay."

As they started back, Abbie asked, "Mr. Farrel . . ."

"Please call me Monte."

"Monte . . ." She tested the name. Yes, it suited him. Outside with the breeze in his hair, it suited him well. "If your pa fought in the war, how is it that you didn't suffer the hardship that's upon the South?" She thought she must have offended him when he didn't answer. His gaze went far out before them.

"Long before the war, my father believed the future of the nation lay out west and filed this land on speculation as well as other pieces farther north. When the war ended, our southern holdings were decimated like everyone else's, but our western investments survived."

"How could he homestead the land without living on it?"

"He outfitted partners to homestead it the three years, and when they had full title, he purchased the plots from each outright. This particular ranch was the best of his stakes with free access to water and virtual control of the water source for miles on the open range. That far extends the original survey."

"Your pa was a man of foresight. Why didn't he come out here with you?" For a terrible moment she thought he might have been killed in the war when she saw Monte stiffen.

"He loved his home. So fiercely did he love South Carolina that he faced unspeakable horrors in her name. And when he returned from the war after being captured and imprisoned by the Yankees, he came back to a land he didn't know. There was no way for him to maintain his plantation without workers, his health was broken, and life as he knew it was changed. Yet he would not desert it."

Abbie tried to imagine how difficult it must have been. "Could he not have sold his holdings out here and rebuilt?"

"He could have, but he wanted this for me. When he died, his last wish was for me to make my life here instead of drudging through what was left of the 'glorious South.'"

"So your pa's gone, too?" Abbie stopped. "Have you no one else?"

"My sister, Frances, lives with her husband in Charleston."

Clasping her hands, Abbie drew in her breath. "I think it was very brave of you to come here alone and start a new life."

Monte smiled. "How old are you, Miss Martin?"

"If I must call you Monte, you may call me Abbie. I'm seventeen. Why?"

"I suspected as much."

"You're not so very much older?"

"Not so very much. But six years can be a great deal, and at times you seem substantially younger."

He was obviously amused, though she failed to see the joke. When he motioned, she preceded him up the stairs.

"Would you care to freshen up before we eat?"

"Yes, thank you."

Pearl showed her to a bedroom where a pitcher and bowl were prepared for her use. The cool water felt good on her skin as she wiped her hot face and neck. She unbuttoned her bodice front and swabbed the cloth down to the edge of her camisole, where it protruded softly before shrinking over narrow ribs.

Her hair was wild, so she picked up the brush from the washstand and ran it through the stubborn tangles, then tucked in the combs and tossed the spiraling curls out behind her shoulders. She reattached her bodice and went downstairs.

Monte ushered her into a real dining room as fine as the hotel, seated her at one end of the long cherrywood table, and took his place at the other. Pearl and James brought dish after dish to the table. Monte must have seen her surprise. "Pearl rarely has the opportunity to cook for company. She makes the most of each occasion." He muted his smile.

Pearl huffed. "I cooks what I wants."

"And in abundance."

"As any gen'leman would appreciate."

She bustled to the kitchen, but Abbie caught her look of satisfaction at having the last word. James offered each dish and served out the portions. Abbie felt four years old with all the attention.

Monte skewered a slice of chicken soaked in wine and cream and had it nearly between his teeth when Abbie said, "Hadn't we better offer a blessing?"

His mouth clamped shut with only a touch of sauce, which was quickly licked away. "I'm afraid living alone here has made me careless in more ways than one. Thank you for the reminder. Have you a special prayer that you prefer?"

"Oh no. Father Dominic at the mission says that it's always best to speak whatever thanks is on your heart."

Monte nodded and bowed his head. "Heavenly Father, I thank you for this food given from your bounty, and for my lovely guest with whom I share it, and for the hands of your servants who prepared it . . . in such abundance." He raised a single eyebrow at Pearl, who puffed out her cheeks and refused to acknowledge him. "Amen."

"Amen," Abbie answered. "Father Dominic teaches the small children the prayers to recite, but he says that when you know the Lord, you should speak to Him personally, with reverence, of course. But, after all, it makes sense. I mean, it's very nice to hear poetry and such recited, but it would be very trying to have someone speak to you that way all the time, don't you think? I mean it's—" She paused suddenly. "Don't you think it's rather difficult to converse all the way across the room like this?" She leaned to the side and gazed at him around the vase of larkspur and daisies.

Monte motioned to James, who immediately came to his side. "Move Miss Martin's place down here, please, James."

"Yessuh." He moved swiftly, carrying her plate and glass, down to the seat beside the head of the table where Monte sat. Abbie reached for her silverware and napkin, but Monte's eyes halted her, and James moved these also. Monte stood and seated her once again.

"I suppose this must be contrary to southern etiquette, but I've never had the misfortune of attending finishing school, so I'm afraid I say what I think and do what seems right."

Monte's mouth twitched. "Two admirable qualities that southern women disdain."

She savored the pork in raisin sauce and roasted potatoes, then dabbed her mouth. "It's strange to think that two areas in the same country would be so very different. I wonder what I would be like had I been raised in the South."

"Southern society would never be the same, I believe." Monte chuckled. "And I shudder to think what my competition would be."

"Why?"

"If there's one thing irresistible to a southern gentleman,

it's a belle who doesn't fit the mold." He skewered a buttered carrot. "Not that he would marry her, of course. He must be conscious of the future generations and choose a lady of impeccable character and lineage who will bear and raise his children according to the tradition and heritage of past generations." He bit the carrot, chewed, and swallowed. "It doesn't necessarily make for happiness, though, and the poor fool spends his life pining for the belle who might have brought him out of all that. It's much freer here."

"That's terrible!"

He startled. "What?"

"That a man would marry for those reasons and then continue longing for someone else."

"Ah, but we're a strange breed. And I suppose it's no worse than the customs of the West such as your bargain brides— women purchased by men they've never met. At least there's a noble cause behind it."

"A noble cause?" Abbie felt her ire rise.

"Preservation."

"Of what?"

"Of what matters."

Abbie laid down her fork. "Did your parents not love each other?"

He wiped the white cloth napkin over his mouth. "I can hardly say from experience, being so young when my mother died. But my father always spoke of her with tenderness and never chose to remarry. I would imagine he loved her very much."

"Then what you said is not always the way."

Monte laughed. "I didn't intend to distress you. Of course people marry for love, or at least affection. But sometimes there are strictures that make doing things you desire impossible."

"And you feel that if I were landed in southern society, I may be quite attractive but certainly not marriageable."

Monte sobered. "I see that my words have been careless. For that, I apologize. I never meant any such thing." He paused. "Although I must admit it's rather a different world, very closed and self-protecting. What's left of it, anyway." He sighed. "I suppose it will soon be like any other place, and none of the things we all thought inviolable will matter anymore."

"That's terribly sad. Has it changed so much since the war?"

"What was once idyllic and gracious is now tired and grasping, the unscrupulous trying to get their hands on whatever they can from the owners no longer able to sustain their family estates."

He gazed across the room. "I was fourteen when my father went to fight. I would have gone, too—I was desperate to go—but he'd have none of it. He insisted I stay and care for my sister, Frances. Aunt Bess and cousin Darcy came to stay with us, and at different times, I had households of women in my care. Father knew what he was about.

"It was not on the battlefront alone that the war was waged. I had my hands full hiding livestock and goods so that we and our neighbors didn't starve. Many a night I trenched the ground behind the houses so that silver and jewelry and heirlooms could be hidden away. Many times I rushed on horseback from plantation to plantation warning that the soldiers were coming.

"There were even times I hid the sisters and daughters of Confederate soldiers in holes in the swamp because if they were seen, the alternative was worse. Everywhere the soldiers came they brought ruin. If they couldn't beat us on the battlefield, for sure they would beat us at home, destroy our property, defile our women, starve, burn, pillage.

"I think it would have been easier to face the bayonets of the Yankee front line than watch my father's property ravaged and looted by marauding Union soldiers wantonly destroying what generations of Farrels had built."

Abbie tried to imagine strangers attacking her home and being helpless to protest. "How did you stand it?"

"What choice did I have? I was charged to protect those in my care. It was a sore trial for a young, able-bodied man to remain home, and there was more than one time I nearly slipped away in the night to find a company and join up. My spirit cried out to fight."

"What kept you?"

"Frances, mainly. She was . . . It was very hard for her. I recall one raid of the soldiers, very early on. She must have been eleven or twelve . . . twelve, I guess. She had a collection of glass horses, very dear to her."

He shook his head. "For sheer cruelty, a soldier smashed them. Not all at once, with an accidental blow, but one by one as we watched through the crack, holed up in the false back of the wardrobe. I think he knew we were there. My rumored presence made our home a favorite target for marauders, a game to tempt the coward southern boy to fight. He did it to bait me, and I had never before exercised such extremity of self-control." His eyes burned. "But I had Frances in my arms."

He sat silent a long moment. His temple pulsed. "For days she didn't speak. She gathered the pieces, sorted them out which piece to which horse, and fit them together, though there was no bond to hold them. It was a terrible sight. Had the soldier returned, I would have committed murder, no matter the consequence."

Abbie felt his raw pain.

"For what?" He shrugged. "If you think for one moment this war was fought over slavery alone, think again."

"Was your pa a slave owner?"

"He was born to it, and the economy required it. But our people were well cared for. Almost family. My father saw to their needs as he did to his own children." He rested his forearms against the table edge. "On the day of the president's Emancipation Proclamation, he wrote to tell our people they were free, though many of our neighbors kept it hushed. Even so, not a half of them left us until his death, and James and Pearl chose to come out here with me. They are, however, compensated."

Abbie cringed. "I'm sorry. My remark was thoughtless. But Pearl did call you Master Monte."

"A title of habit and inflection." Monte motioned, and James served the coffee. "You've lived here long?"

"Since I was eight. Well, not actually here in Rocky Bluffs. Pa came out with Wes McConnel to prospect in Auraria, where building lots were free for the taking. Mama wasn't crazy about living in a mining camp, and Pa wasn't a miner, but I loved it.

"Sadie, she's my sister four years older, she cried and cried. I prayed every day that Pa wouldn't give up and take us back. My memories of Kansas City were the smell of slaughterhouses and too many people. He stuck it out until the twin camps merged into Denver City and grew fast enough to get a newspaper. Pa saw his chance. He signed on with the paper."

"Ah." Monte nodded.

"After two years Pa was feeling crowded. He filed for a homestead near the new town of Rocky Bluffs—more trading post than town—but he saw promise. He bought a press of his own and we moved. I was ten, though it seems I've been here forever."

Monte's smile was indulgent, and she felt suddenly provincial and backward. "But I've read about so many places. My grandfather works in book publishing, and he sends us books about everywhere. Ever since I was small I've imagined seeing Europe and Africa and China. Blake and I..." She stopped.

"Go on ... Blake and you." His tone was smooth, but his eyes were again amused.

Well, she'd started it, so she might as well finish. "Blake's family has been our nearest neighbor from the start, and he and I, both being the youngest, spent much of our time together. I made up games, and we playacted. Of course, he expected me to play the helpless lady trapped in the jungle, and he the hero who came to my rescue." She laughed.

"Perhaps he didn't know it was playacting, and that's why he took it upon himself to rescue you from my attention."

Abbie dropped her eyes. "I suppose that's possible. I wish I'd known he felt that way."

Monte leaned back in his chair and studied her with a crooked smile. "How is it that you didn't?"

"I've always considered him one of the family. He's two months younger, and it was nice to think of him as a little brother. It gave me great license to bully him into giving me my way."

"I don't imagine it took much bullying."

"Maybe not lately, but at first it certainly did."

Monte laughed. "I don't think I'd like to try to withstand your bullying, myself."

"Well, lucky for you I've outgrown it."

"Now that you're all of seventeen."

Abbie's chin came up. "Actually I'm nearly eighteen." She dabbed her mouth with the napkin and pushed her plate away. It was instantly removed by James, whose presence Abbie had forgotten, and she blushed at having spoken so freely in front of a total stranger. Mama was right. She did need to learn to hold her tongue and be appropriate.

But after all, what was appropriate in this house? Monte didn't converse with the servants, except when something was required, and they didn't participate until called upon. Yet they shared a fondness, she could tell, and Pearl had positively glowed when he teased. It was confusing, and she wished she had not said some of the things she had, even to Monte. He seemed to draw her out and let down her guard—not that she had much of a guard, as Mama would point out. "It's getting late. I should go now."

Monte rose and pulled out her chair. "I'll get your carriage." He paused. "What amuses you?"

"The way you say carriage. It sounds like something for royalty to lark about in." Abbie could have bitten her tongue. Who was she to speak so to him?

He replied slowly, softly. "Perhaps I consider you royalty."

Her chest quickened suddenly at the look in his eyes. Then he turned, and she followed him to the door and out into the night. The sky was sugared with stars, and the air smelled sweet. Monte hitched her mare to the buggy and saddled his own horse.

"You needn't ride along. I know my way well enough."

"Although it stretches propriety to be out with you after dark, I intend to drive you back. This is wild country."

"It's really not necessary."

He tied his horse behind the buggy, placed his hands around her waist, and lifted her onto the seat. Sitting beside him in the dark, Abbie fell silent, the night noises creating a sleepy symphony of cricket song and wind in the grass. After the satisfying supper, the rocking of the buggy and the regular *thunk, thunk* of the horses' hooves lulled her. She fought the drowsiness spreading like a warm quilt, covering her senses. "It must be later than I thought," she murmured.

"We did rather linger over supper. I can't remember enjoying a conversation so much. Perhaps it was the table arrangement. I'll be sure to have it set that way the next time you come."

His words caused that unfamiliar jumping inside, and Abbie thought of Blake's remark. Perhaps she was not taken with Montgomery Farrel, but it was not out of the realm of possibility. His stiff shirt brushed against her cheek as her head drooped against his shoulder, and she pulled back.

"Rest if you like." He was perfectly at ease, and she wondered if others had slept on his shoulder.

The thought brought her up straight, and she pulled the shawl close. Even the midsummer nights were chilly. She curled her back into the corner of the seat but still felt him close. Her concern for Blake and the events of the afternoon faded into the darkness.

Three

Abbie threw the cloth into the dishwater when she saw Blake saunter into the yard. "Oh, Blake, you're free!" She ran through the open door to meet him. "You gave me a terrible fright!"

"Came straight over soon as they let me out."

"Didn't Marshal Haggerty get Mr. Farrel's message?"

"He said I may as well spend the night fer good measure." Blake jammed his hands into his pockets. "Come and walk with me."

"I have to finish the dishes."

"I'll wipe." He followed her in and picked up the cloth to dry as she plunged her arms back into the sudsy water, then dunked the dishes in the hot rinse tub. Blake made a cursory swipe and set them on the board.

"I hate to think of you spending the night in that cell on that terrible little bed. I hope it's taught you a thing or two." She handed over the heavy iron skillet.

He grunted. "Wasn't so bad."

Of course he'd say that. He was always in one scrape or another and never admitted the hardship. She doubted very much that any number of nights in the jail would change him, but he'd given his word, and that he'd keep. Abbie wiped her hands on her apron and pulled it off. "There now. We can run off for a bit anyway. Mama's gone to town, so she won't need me yet."

They headed down the path from the house toward the shelter of the craggy vale. The day was dry but hadn't yet worked up the heat of the one previous. No cloud marred the china blue sky. Suddenly, Blake grabbed her hand and took off at a run, rushing down the slope between the mounds of scrub oaks toward the rocky creek at the base. Abbie collided with his chest as he stopped short. Laughing, he did not release her but looked down and grinned. "Tell me the truth, Abbie. Are you my girl or ain't you?"

"Blake McConnel, unhand me immediately!"

"Not till I get my answer."

Abbie made a face. "I told you yesterday."

"But you didn't mean that, did you?"

"I wouldn't have said it if I didn't."

"Yes, you would. I know you would've helped me out any way you could."

Abbie softened. "Well, I guess so, but I really did tell you the truth."

"Are you so sure of that?" He tightened his arms and pressed his mouth to hers.

"Blake!" Abbie wrestled free and shoved at his chest.

He stumbled back, laughing. "Ah, Abbie. Didn't you like it a little bit?"

"I certainly did not. You might be able to get away with kissing Caroline Glazer, but not me."

"I was seven years old when I kissed Caroline Glazer!"

"Well, your manners haven't improved in ten years!"

His face sobered. "Abbie, I love you. I've loved you as long as I can remember."

"Blake, you can't mean that. You're like my brother!"

"Well, I ain't your brother. And soon, I'll be able to file for my own place and make a home for us. If you don't run off and marry someone else, that is."

Abbie tossed her head. "And who would I marry?" She pushed him aside. "Let's not talk about it. I'm going to wade." She sat and removed her high-topped shoes. Blake grinned. Sitting down beside her, he pulled off his own boots and stockings and rolled the legs of his pants. Abbie tucked up her skirts so that her legs were bare to just over her calf. "Don't you tell Mama, now," she ordered, seeing his eyes trail from knee to ankle.

"Aw no." He grabbed her hand and steadied her against the rush of the icy flow. The first minutes hurt as the water tugged at her ankles. She stretched to a flat rock farther out, avoiding its sharp edge and the myriad other stones. Blake leaped over behind her. "Numb yet?"

"Getting there." She lifted her reddened foot, then plunged it back in. A blue dragonfly rode the air on opalescent wings. She reached up to it, slipped, and Blake caught her.

"There, you see how much you need me?"

"Your strong arm is appreciated, but that doesn't mean anything." She watched a leaf spiral in an eddy, then shoot past. The hem of her skirt slipped down and dragged along her calves. She tugged it up again. "I should get back now. Mama and I are replacing the ticking today. She won't want to be held up."

Blake helped her back to the bank, and they held their bare feet up to dry in the sun and breeze. Abbie stretched her toes.

"You sure have purty feet."

She pulled them down immediately and rubbed them with the edge of her skirt, then tugged on her shoes and headed up the slope. Blake scrambled up and followed.

"I reckon I'd better get to the shop myself. Sure hate bein' sweat to death on a day like this, though."

"Your pa just wants you to learn smithing, Blake. You don't have to do it forever."

"That's right. First chance I get I'll be on to better things."

Abbie smiled. "You might find any work just as onerous." She let the word slide glibly from her lips to taunt him.

"Just as what?"

"Never mind."

When they reached the house, he tugged her arm. "You think on what I said, Abbie. It may seem too soon to you now, but I don't want no one gettin' a jump on me."

"And you think of what I said, Blake, and look elsewhere. If you're hankering for a wife, try Clara Simms. She's been gone on you for a year now."

He grinned. "You can't get rid of me that easy. I know you'll come around."

"Think what you like." Abbie turned up her nose.

Blake laughed. "One of these days you'll beg me to kiss you."

"Oh, go away!" she huffed. "You're simply impossible anymore!"

"You think on it," he called over his shoulder.

Abbie flounced into the house. Really, it was intolerable for him to have gone crazy all of a sudden. She had half a mind to ignore him altogether.

Mama was inside, and Abbie unpacked the bolts of ticking and heavy thread and spread them on the floor between them. She almost blurted that Blake was out of jail, but she was still praying Mama hadn't heard he was ever in.

"Was that Blake?"

"Yes. He's off to the smithy." She caught her wet hem under her ankles as she settled to the floor. "Mama? How'd you know you loved Pa?"

Mama took a good long look and removed the needle from between her lips. Then as she applied it to the material, she said, "Well, you remember that your pa worked at the newspaper in Kansas City."

Abbie nodded. She knew this part of the story.

"We'd just come to town and my pa planned to open a general mercantile, so he stopped at the newspaper to learn what was available for sale. He thought he'd get a more honest rundown there than the land office."

"And Pa saw you . . ."

"Do you want to tell the story or shall I?" Mama raised her brows. "Really, Abbie, you must curb your enthusiasm. Never interrupt, and never, never let on that you know something already."

"I'm sorry."

"Yes, Joshua saw me in the wagon and plumb forgot how to speak. My pa couldn't get a word out of him and thought him simpleminded."

Abbie laughed, imagining Pa without something to say. "I wish I could have seen his face!"

"Well, I had no idea he'd noticed me. But he told your grandpa that if he returned the following day, he'd have a list of properties. And he did indeed have a list that he had compiled the night before, naming only the opportunities close to the newspaper. My pa chose one and set up shop, and one day, as I was working the counter, your pa came in, introduced himself, and asked me to marry him."

"Oh, Mama, you must have been swept off your feet."

"I was appalled," she said flatly, not lifting her eyes from her work. "I'd never met this man who brazenly offered himself, and I told him I was sure I'd do no such thing."

"How did he change your mind?"

"He kept at me day after day, claiming he'd never realize his dream if I wouldn't go west with him. He said he'd be forced to keep working for his father, who was not an easy man, unless I consented. He brought me flowers and candies and tokens of his affection and refused to be daunted by my continued refusal, until one day I heard myself agree."

"Had you fallen in love with him?"

"It seemed more that I'd freed myself of a nagging gnat." She laughed, dropping her hands into her lap and tipping her head. "But I realized that little by little he'd worked himself into my heart, and I've never regretted it. Your pa is the finest, most high-minded man I've ever known."

"But . . . didn't you feel just a little crazy for him? I mean . . ."

Her mama grabbed up the fabric again. "I give myself credit for more sense than that. A love that starts from fluttering hearts and moony eyes is seldom one that lasts. I hope you'll find a husband who's intelligent and thoughtful rather than one who sweeps you off your feet."

Abbie tossed her head. "Blake has got the silly notion he'll be my husband."

"He said so?"

She nodded. "He believes he's in love with me."

Mama laid her hands together on the ticking in her lap. "I think that was inevitable, don't you? The way you two have run off together since you were small, and now that you've grown into such a lovely young lady . . . if only you acted like one more often."

"Mama!"

"Do you feel the same for Blake? He's a nice young man, and our families have been—"

Abbie threw up her hands. "You sound like a newspaper advertisement. I think it's a ridiculous notion. Blake is . . . well, he's . . . I thought you wanted me to find a cultured, educated man. Blake was too stubborn to learn more than the rudimentary skills in all his years at school."

"Nevertheless, he's an intelligent boy and well-mannered."

Would she say that if she knew he'd stolen a kiss and tried to shoot a man? And spent the night in jail?

"At any rate, you're young enough not to rush into anything. Perhaps you'll find he's the best choice, or perhaps someone else will come along. There's plenty of time."

Abbie worked her needle in and out. She kept her voice light. "Mr. Farrel's nice, isn't he?"

"Yes. Your pa enjoys talking with him. Lord knows he has few enough men with whom to talk literature. Did you enjoy your supper?"

"Yes."

"How exactly did you find yourself there at that hour?"

"I went to speak with him about a concern."

"Oh?"

"It was nothing really, and I didn't think you'd mind, as we'd been properly introduced and Pa was so fond of him. . . ."

"I'd prefer you not make calls on gentlemen in their homes uninvited, Abbie. You are, need I remind you, a young lady. I know things are not what they were back East, but some semblance . . ."

"Yes, Mama. But did you know he has colored servants?"

"I'd heard."

"They used to be slaves, but he pays them now. They came with him even though they were free not to."

"That speaks well for him. Obviously his family was not one that mistreated the poor slaves in their care."

"It's strange to be waited on like that."

"Many people have servants in other parts of the country." Mama sighed. "There's so much you don't know. If it was possible to scratch enough together, we could send you to one of the schools back East, or even in the South. The women there are taking girls into boarding schools and teaching them the arts of fine society in order to survive, poor things."

Abbie groaned. Finishing school! "Monte thinks I'm unacceptable for southern society."

Mama paled. "Don't tell me you've embarrassed yourself already! Did you forget your manners last night? And how is it you call him Monte?"

Abbie cringed. "He asked me to call him that, and I didn't forget my manners. We were merely discussing the differences between the stuffy old South and here."

Mama rocked back on her heels and pursed her lips together. Abbie knew that look. It was her all-knowing, ferret-out-any-unrevealed-detail look. She imagined God looked at her that way, too. She poked her needle through the fabric.

Her head came up, though, as the clop of hooves sounded outside. A boy knocked on the open door. The horse he rode was too fine to be his own, judging by his scruffy pants and shirt, and Abbie perked up as he told Mama he had a message for Miss Abigail Martin. She took the note, written on the same vellum paper she had used yesterday.

"'Dear Miss Martin, would you honor me with your company for a ride this afternoon? I would call for you at one o'clock. I sincerely await your reply. Montgomery Farrel.'"

Abbie's eyes met her mother's and she giggled. "I told you I remembered my manners."

Mama glared, indicating with her eyes the presence of the messenger boy. "Would you like to go?"

"Can you spare me?" Abbie breathed hopefully.

"I can."

Abbie turned eagerly to the boy. "Tell Mr. Farrel that I accept his invitation."

He stuffed his hands into his pockets. "Don't you wanna write it down?"

"Gracious, can't you remember that little bit?"

He shrugged sullenly.

"Oh, all right. Hold on a minute." She rushed into the house. Their paper was not so fine as Monte's, but she wrote a pretty hand and scribed her acceptance with an extra flourish at the end of her name. She turned as the boy left. "It'll be two hours before he comes for me. If we hurry we can get these done and stuffed as well."

"You're a good girl, Abbie." Mama smiled. "Even if you are overly enthusiastic. But please try to maintain your poise this afternoon. Mr. Farrel is new here and not accustomed to a more relaxed social order."

"Oh, Mama, you worry unnecessarily. Mr. Farrel is perfectly relaxed himself and not at all concerned with the way things were for him." Abbie tossed her curls, and Mama sighed.

Four

Montgomery Farrel read over the note and smiled. "Thank you, Will." Then he strode into the hall, where he found Pearl swinging the feather duster. He coughed.

"I can't stop the dust comin'," Pearl huffed, "but I'll see it don' lay where it don' belong."

"Yes, quite. Pearl, I'll be out this afternoon. Can you locate the basket carrier from Versailles?"

"You havin' that young miss?"

"I am."

She puffed out her lips. "Then I don' know what you be needin' that fo'."

"Oh yes, you do. And don't bother scolding. I don't intend to intoxicate the young lady. Wine enjoyed alfresco is the regular practice in most of the world."

"Most o' the heathen world."

Monte headed to the cellar. He ran his hand over the bottles already collecting dust, chose one, and wiped it with the cloth that lay handy. He carried it up to the kitchen, where Pearl was stuffing the basket with bread and cheese.

"There are only two of us."

"I mean to fortify her against the devil's tool."

"Really, Pearl."

"Don' you gimme them eyes. I knows young men when liquor's involved."

43

Monte laughed. "I would no more compromise Miss Martin than rob a bank."

She shook her head. "Then, I don' know what you needs that wine fo'."

"Drink. Refreshes the palate."

"Water does the same."

"Much less satisfactorily." He slid the bottle into the side pocket and hung the basket over his shoulder. "I can't say when I'll be back. Don't trouble yourself over supper."

Climbing into the carriage, Monte took the reins in his hands and clicked his tongue to Chance. The horse tossed his mane and trotted forth. Unlike last night, Monte did not dawdle across the distance. Whereas having Abbie dozing beside him had given him cause to dally, her absence, and the anticipation of altering that, effected a snappier pace. He was as eager as Chance was fresh.

"Good afternoon," he called as Mrs. Martin stepped onto the porch. She was a handsome woman, but his eyes went directly behind her to Abbie. Was there ever a sweeter sight?

"It's a nice day for a ride," Mrs. Martin said.

"Yes, it is."

"Where were you planning to go?"

"I was hoping Abbie might show me about. I've not had the time to acquaint myself yet."

Abbie took his hand as he lifted her in. "I know lots of places. We'll be up in the hills."

Monte raised a brow, but Mrs. Martin waved them off. Apparently she was accustomed to Abbie's wandering.

As they rode, Abbie played her part as guide, pointing out the landmarks they passed and telling him whatever legend or lore was associated with the spot. Either her teachers had drilled her hard, or she had a head for history.

"At different times this was a meeting place for the Arapaho, Kiowa, Ute, and Cheyenne Indians. Great numbers of them gathered here for their summer festivals or tribal meetings. Don't you wish you could have seen it?" She didn't wait for a reply. "What a thrill to be a part of that and see them dancing to the big skin drums and . . . what's so funny?"

"I'd like to see you dressed up in deerskin hides and dancing to the drums."

"I didn't say be an Indian." She caught the side as the buggy swayed. "But I can't help feeling I missed something. The Sioux and Arapaho, Kiowa and Cheyenne have gone, and with the government reservations . . . well, now there are only the Utes and an occasional band of Comanche."

"I don't think many consider it a loss."

"Well, I do. Can you smell the sage?" She jumped topics with hardly a breath. "And see, that's sumac there and chokecherries. But you have chokecherries at your stream, haven't you?"

"I have, and I'm flattered you remember." Monte edged the buggy through a crevice and steeply up as she directed. He should not have so blindly accepted her lead. "Are you certain this is a trail?"

"I've never actually brought a buggy up, but I ride it horseback."

"It's a good distance from your father's homestead."

"It's no distance at all."

No, of course not. Not when all was distance out here. Cradled by the base of the mountain, one forgot the emptiness of endless grass and sagebrush that made up his acreage. But though this was pleasant, his grassland would prove more profitable. Abbie bumped against him as the wheels took the rise.

"The scrub oaks make it hard to get through, but there's the way ahead." She pointed.

He gauged the width askance, then proceeded on faith as the gnarled, finger-leafed branches scratched against the sides. "You do plan to get us out of here again. . . ."

Abbie laughed. "I've never been lost yet."

"That's encouraging."

"Do you see how the ponderosas are joined by fir and juniper? If we went far enough up, we'd find lodgepoles and spruce and kinik-kinik."

"I see you're a botanist as well as a lore master."

"Not a master of either, but I like to know things."

"Ah, you see? A southern lady would never let on she was more clever than I."

She spun in the seat. "I never said that."

Monte laughed. "You needn't. And don't apologize. I highly value intelligence, even in women. Maybe especially so. Which way, scout?"

"Head over to the right. It levels there, and we can leave the buggy and walk if you like."

Monte unhitched Chance, tethering him to graze while they retrieved the quilt and basket and started up the hillside through the thick growth of scrub oak and mountain sumac.

"Watch for cactus." Abbie gathered her skirts and climbed. "Sometimes the needles go right through your boots, and the yuccas are worse. Spanish Bayonets. They'll slice your leg and give you a terrible itch." Her foot slid on the loose gravel. Like a mountain goat, she skipped onto a rock ledge, but not before he'd glimpsed a length of ankle and shin. If she realized, she made no sign, nor pretense at maidenly chagrin.

He followed. "How far up do you plan to go?"

"Far enough to see out to the pinery, over the bluffs, and all the way across the prairie. Maybe far enough to see the ocean."

"You'd need eagle eyes for that."

"Then I'll imagine it there. Tell me what it looks like." She stopped and turned out toward the east, where the brown and gold grasses stretched unbroken, except where the pinery lapped the hills blackly and the bluffs stood like massive, un-marked graves.

Monte pointed toward the horizon. "If you were standing now on the edge of the shore, as far out as you can see would be the deepest blue right up to the edge of the sky where the blues meet and almost merge. The sun glances off the peaks of the waves as off the facets of a sapphire, and overhead the white gulls swoop on their gray-tipped wings and call, dipping now and again to the water's surface, then winging up into the wind again. And down below, the white-frothed breakers roar in to throw themselves at the rocks encrusted with mussels and smelling of salt." He stopped suddenly, caught by the tears sparkling in her eyes, bluer than any ocean he had seen, with the lashes drooping down in long, graceful arcs.

"Hoh . . ." Her breath released. "You make it so beautiful. How I'd love to see it, really see it."

He felt speechless in the wake of her emotion and the vi-brancy she held within. "It's easy to describe what you know. Were you to tell what you see here from your mind's eye, you'd bring tears even to men." And he didn't doubt it. The way she had spoken of this land the previous day had moved him deeply. What would it be like to show her the places she imag-ined? It was exhilarating to consider.

He made for a cluster of ponderosas at the top of the ridge and spread the quilt in the shade beneath their branches. As he seated her, the breeze bent the pale, golden grasses and nod-ded the heads of the orange Indian paintbrush, yellow lupine, and blue Mertensias that dotted the hillside. Would he notice these if Abbie hadn't quickened his senses?

From the bushy mountain mahogany came the throaty call of a meadowlark. "That's a meadow—" She stopped.

"Yes?"

"I think you're tired of my lessons."

"I think I've never enjoyed lessons more."

"I talk too much."

"Then I'm guilty for listening." He opened the basket and laid out the crusty rye and the white ball of cheese. After their hike, he was glad Pearl had sent it.

"I teach at the mission, and it comes so naturally I forget myself."

"Ah." He took the wine bottle, twisted the coiled screw into the cork, and slowly slipped it free.

"I teach the little ones whenever I can so Father Dominic can drill the older children."

"Sounds like a good arrangement." The goblets were wrapped in cloth. Pearl did her part, no matter how reluctantly. And he couldn't fault her concern. At the end, drink had destroyed his father.

Abbie hesitated when he held a glass to her. "I don't know that I should have that."

"Come. It's a habit I acquired in France. But I promise the wine loses all ability to intoxicate when imbibed in the open air under the shade of a mighty pine."

She cocked her head. "Sounds like Indian lore to me. Some medicinal hocus-pocus."

Monte laughed. "I assure you I have no intention of endangering your senses. You're far too amusing in your right mind."

"Amusing?" She raised the glass to her lips. "Are you so gracious to all your guests?"

Monte laughed. "Of course."

"And I suppose you have plenty of opportunity."

"I've found no shortage of willing parties."

Her eyes flashed. "Are you so smug? Last night I could have sworn I dined with a gentleman. It seems I was mistaken."

"My most abject apologies." He took her hand, well shaped and strong, not soft and pale as others he'd held. He suddenly felt foolish toying with her. She had no coquettish airs. "Can you forgive me?"

She raised her face, surrounded by riotous brown curls only halfheartedly contained by the combs. "I'm not sure how to take you. If you're sincere . . ."

"I am always sincere." Monte had never been more so. He handed her an end of bread and a wedge of cheese. "Peace?"

Abbie smiled and accepted it.

"So." He raised his glass to hers, then drank. She took a swallow and puckered her face.

"Well?"

"Somewhat like . . . cider . . . that sat too long."

He laughed. "It'll grow on you." He drank his own. It was smooth and mellow. A wonderful Bordeaux. What a shame it was lost on her. "I presume your friend was released from jail?"

He surprised the color to her cheeks. "Yes. I appreciate your kindness."

"I'd no desire for revenge. I simply want to know that my person and property are safe from further incident."

She waved the bread in her hand. "Oh, Blake? Why, he's just headstrong and impulsive. He doesn't really have a wicked bone in his body. Though I guess we're a little alike in that we act before we think . . . sometimes."

"I would never have guessed that of you, Abbie. You seem so reserved." When she sighed, he chided himself for teasing.

"Mama wishes I were, that's for certain. And I do try to think before I speak, but sometimes the thoughts just come so fast I don't have time to check them over before they're out."

"That's what I find so refreshing. If there's subtlety in your nature, it's well disguised."

"Mama says I was left too long to my own devices and grew wild romping the hills with Blake. But truly I think the skills I learned will stand me in better stead than all the ladylike things I could have done."

Monte leaned against the rough-barked tree. "And what skills have you learned?"

"Oh . . . how to recognize and track the trail of seventeen different animals. I can whittle a stick and spear a fish and climb a tree even better than Blake."

"Let's see."

She turned to him, surprised. "See what?"

"See you climb a tree."

"I beg your pardon, Monte. I admit I'm lacking in social graces, but I do have a sense of decency. I can hardly climb a tree in this." She pinched up her skirt.

"And what did you wear to climb with Blake?" He watched the blush burn up her cheeks. What was he on to? This was too much fun to let go.

"I was a good deal younger then."

"And?"

"I'd rather not say."

"Oh, come now . . ."

"Really, Monte."

"All right then, I'll be forced to speculate."

Abbie tossed down the bread. "Well, if you must know, I tucked my skirts up. But I was hardly out of pigtails then, though I guess old enough to know better." She turned away.

"I'm sorry." He suppressed the laughter in his throat. "I assure you, your secret is safe with me."

Abbie wove a grass blade between her fingers and didn't respond. She was certainly slow to forgive. What was that intractable streak in his nature that took amusement at her discomfiture?

"I truly do apologize. And I don't think any less of you for it. In fact, I rather admire you. Who knows . . . one day you may need that very skill."

Abbie brushed the grass from her skirt. "I do actually have a number of appropriate skills as well."

"I'm sure you do. But I applaud your adventurous spirit."

"I'm just made that way, I guess. Some people are."

"That's true. I remember Duncan Williams had a similar bent. He was a constant thorn in his father's side because if he didn't find adventure, he created it. I recall the time he put gunpowder in the headmaster's stove. It was rather a more exciting opening to the lecture than we were accustomed to." Monte laughed at the memory. "Thankfully, no one was injured. Except for Duncan, of course, who couldn't sit on his horse for days." He drained his glass and filled it again, then held the bottle toward her.

She shook her head. "Was he your friend?"

"We were never close. The two I call friends are Chandler Bridges and Milton Rochester. Our families have been devoted for generations. There's nothing I wouldn't do for either of them."

Abbie murmured, " 'Thine own friend and thy father's friend forsake not.' "

Monte nodded. "Yes, exactly."

"That's how I feel about Clara Simms. We're nothing alike, but we understand each other, and she accepts my faults without complaint."

"And you hers, I presume."

"She hasn't any. She's perfectly well-spoken, gentle, and sweet."

"That's all well and good, Abbie. But life calls for variety. I'm far more interested in a girl who can track and fish and climb a tree."

"I wish I hadn't told you that."

"I promised to keep your secret. Now you can't think of it anymore." A sudden gust blew through her hair, and he followed her gaze to the sheet of gray looming over the mountain.

"It's going to storm."

"It's only clouds." He didn't want the time to end.

She ignored him and stood. "You don't know how suddenly

the thunderstorms come on." As if called upon, a flash and rumble echoed her words.

Before they had climbed down the slope to the buggy, the first raindrops slapped down, cold and hard, no gentle shower. By the time he hitched Chance, Monte was thoroughly wet. "You weren't joking." He climbed in beside her.

"I've spent enough time outside to know."

The rain was pelting and Chance strained against his hold, snorting as the first hailstones smote his back.

"There." Abbie pointed. "The hogback."

Monte veered toward the sloping ridge of stone and pulled under its shelter, soothing the horse with low tones. "I'll never doubt you again." He winced as lightning seared the sky.

"Mama will be worried. But we don't dare go until it's spent."

Water rushed past in the ravines, red and angry, as the white stones battered the ground and piled up like snow. Abbie shivered.

"Cold?"

"I forgot my shawl."

He retrieved the quilt and wrapped her shoulders. She snuggled into the thickness.

"Look at you, though. You're soaked through," Abbie said.

"It is a bit chilly."

"There's room for two." She held up the quilt edge.

Was she brazen or simply innocent? Nothing in her expression betrayed anything but concern for him. "Do you mind?"

"Sometimes circumstances call for concessions. Just don't tell Mama."

He settled into the folds. If ever there was a time for Pearl's suspicions, this was it. Abbie's thin shoulders almost asked to be wrapped in his arm, the scent of her soap was fresh and wild, and her eyes . . . No wonder Blake had taken a gun to him.

The poor kid was probably smitten senseless, and he could be, too, if the storm lingered.

If Abbie guessed his thoughts she made no sign, but then she was young. Too young. He shifted away, but her warmth stayed with him.

The hail thinned but still the rain drenched the land. Did anything happen gently here? At last the storm slackened. Reluctantly, he pulled down the quilt and tucked it against Abbie's side. "I believe we can make it now."

"It's better to wait."

Monte smiled. "Abbie, I have been driving for some years now."

Chance heaved and strained through the mud and flowing ruts. The flooding was worse than he expected, and their progress abysmally slow. Beneath the ragged fringe of gray, the westerly sun sent a fleeting glow, then slipped behind the ridge. The rear wheel bogged. Chance snorted, backed, and strove against its hold. The wheel stuck fast. Monte chafed, but he wouldn't force the animal. Tossing the reins, he jumped down and surveyed the wheel. "Can you drive?"

Of course she could drive. She could track and fish and read the weather. And he should have listened to her. He shouldered the buggy's side and pushed as she urged the horse. The wheel turned, climbed, and spun back down. Chance balked.

"Shall we both push?"

"Thank you, Abbie, I can manage." He sounded crosser than he should. "Again."

Once more the wheel spun. She jumped down, heedless of her dress in the mud. Monte straightened, but she didn't join him. Instead, she took Chance's head and pulled. The horse strained in the fading light, and Monte threw his weight against the carriage. The wheel caught, turned, and kept turning. As the horse leaped forward, Abbie stumbled but kept her feet, and Chance tossed his head, straining against her.

Monte strode forward and took hold of Chance. Abbie was breathing hard, her dress clung to her legs in muddy streaks, and her chin was smudged. But she smiled doggedly. She was an imp, and for one insane moment he felt like kissing her.

Five

By the lantern light, Joshua Martin hailed them as Monte halted the carriage in the yard. Chance's head sagged, and Monte could only imagine the sorry sight they made, though Joshua's smile was forgiving.

"Looks like you two had a bit of a wet ride." Joshua handed Abbie down. "Come on in, Monte. I'll find you a dry shirt."

Mrs. Martin looked up from the stove. "Goodness!"

"We're fine." Abbie halted her mother's fuss. "The horse bogged down, is all."

"You're soaked to the skin. Get right out of those wet things." She dropped her voice. "And for heaven's sake, Abbie, there's mud up to your knees." She turned. "Mr. Farrel, you'll stay to supper?"

The kitchen smelled wonderful, and he was hungry. "I'd be honored."

"You'll get a taste of Selena's famous Irish stew." Joshua tossed him a shirt. "There's a basin in the back."

In the lean-to off the kitchen, Monte stripped off the wet shirt and washed, then wiped down his boots and toweled them dry. For all its lack of elegance, the Martin house was as clean as any, and he'd keep it that way. He hadn't missed Mrs. Martin's scolding to Abbie, though he rather thought it had more to do with him than her condition alone. He had brought her back in a sorry state, but that was her doing, and he guessed Mrs. Martin knew it.

Monte pulled on Joshua's dry shirt and rolled the sleeves, as the cuffs were too short for his arms. Then, after smoothing back his hair, he turned and went back to the kitchen.

Abbie looked as fresh as he felt. Her dress was changed and an apron tied over, her hair pulled back in a ribbon. Instead of having vapors and bemoaning their ordeal, she was briskly setting out the flatware and plates. A guest appearing now would never know she'd been out in a hailstorm, dragging a horse and buggy from a ditch. She was remarkable. Truly remarkable.

They sat down around the table in the small kitchen, and Joshua offered the blessing. Mrs. Martin dished the bowls of stew, then passed him the rolls, hot and crusty from the oven. In Joshua's shirt, with the heat of the stove at his back, Monte felt more at home than he could remember feeling for a long, long time. He took the cup of coffee Mrs. Martin offered.

"I'm pleased you could join us, Mr. Farrel."

"Monte, please."

She nodded. "It's a shame the weather was so inhospitable for your ride."

"There's no controlling that. I'm only glad we had shelter from the hail or Chance would have had a bad time of it." Monte sipped the coffee. It was rich and mellow, as good a blend as Pearl brewed, and he'd wager at half the cost of the beans he had shipped up from Louisiana.

Mrs. Martin laid her napkin in her lap. "Mr. Farrel ... Monte, I've been wondering, would you know a reasonable girls' school Abbie might attend?"

Abbie's spoon stopped halfway to her mouth.

Mrs. Martin must be more concerned than he thought. He clearly perceived Abbie's pique, but he hid his amusement and chose a formal tone. "I know of several, one in particular that is highly recommended. Mistress Bradley, the headmistress, is my late mother's second cousin."

"What's this?" Joshua tore his roll in two.

Mrs. Martin spoke softly. "I think we should consider a school of this type. There are areas where Abbie's education has been lacking."

"Lacking! She knows more—"

"I don't mean book learning. She's had more of that, no doubt, than she needs. I mean social graces."

Monte watched Abbie's jaw set. Her discomfiture was too tempting. "It never hurts to broaden your horizons. Develop new areas of proficiency."

Joshua shook his head. "You don't have to go halfway across the country to do it."

"There's nothing like that here, Joshua," Mrs. Martin replied.

"What she can't learn here, she doesn't need to know." Joshua spooned the stew but didn't take the bite. "Tell me, Monte, what did you think of Mr. Bridley's journal?"

Abbie's shoulders relaxed. It seemed Joshua had the final word.

"I agreed with a good many of his assessments. But on the Indian affairs, I think he's off the mark." He glanced at Abbie, but she refused to meet his eye.

"How so? Don't you think coexistence with the Indian is not only possible but desirable?"

"Coexistence between men is hardly possible. The War between the States has shown us that. You cannot blend the Indian's world with the white man's. You cannot further the gains of the one without diminishing the other. It'll end up all or nothing."

Joshua shook his head. "I hope you're wrong there."

"Mark my words, there are dark times ahead. The Indian, like the Negro, will find the arms of society do not embrace him. Look at your Sand Creek Massacre for proof. Women and children slaughtered inside the bounds of their reserved lands. And why? For simply being there." He took the slice of pie Mrs. Martin served and nodded his thanks.

"And that's the injustice. But that doesn't mean it has to continue."

"But it will continue. Do you think that because high-minded people raised a cry to free the Negro, they will open their homes and families to him? Do you think that any Indian bureau can erase the memory of scalped children, families brutally murdered in their sleep? I believe there'll be more bloodshed on both fronts before it's over."

Joshua cut his fork into the wedge of blackberry pie. "I'm afraid that's likely. But I can wish it weren't and do what I can to stand against it. I have a voice and it's a powerful tool. I can speak for what's right."

"That's all anyone can do." Monte scraped the last of the pie from the plate and pushed it away.

"Another piece of pie?" Mrs. Martin held the dish, but Monte shook his head and wiped his mouth.

"Thank you, Mrs. Martin, but I've been too indulged already. Joshua's praise of you is well deserved."

She smiled. "Thank you, Monte. And please, call me Selena."

Abbie stood to help her mother clear away.

"You'll want to get back," Joshua said, and Monte rose.

Abbie reached past him for the pitcher, still without a word or glance. Had he gone too far with his teasing? She was certainly quick to take offense, but it didn't sit well with him to leave it at that. He touched her elbow. "A word with you, Abbie?"

Selena nodded, and Abbie followed him outside. The night air smelled of the rain, but the clouds had torn open swaths of stars. Monte breathed deeply, leaning on the railing. "Why do I have the distinct impression you're displeased with me?"

"I'm sure I don't know." She didn't look his way.

"And I'm equally sure you do."

She spun. "You're a traitor!"

He feigned more dismay than he felt. "You have cut me to the quick! How have I betrayed you?"

"All that you told Mama. She'll never let it go now. And what of all that talk about preferring a girl who could track and fish and . . . was that just talk?"

"No, it was not. But I meant what I told your mother, too. There's a place for everything, all kinds of talents, and you ought not limit yourself to those you can't admit in public. Come, Abbie."

"Come nothing. How would you like to be trapped in some place where all you did was swoon and whine?"

He fought a laugh. Her description was more apt than he would admit. "Consider it an adventure, a jungle of sorts."

Her eyes deepened in the moonlight, the lashes casting delicate shadows on her cheek as she looked up. "And who would come to my rescue, I wonder?" Her brows raised . . . enticing him?

Monte leaned close, his breath suddenly tight in his chest. "Perhaps you would find you needed no rescuing. I believe you could conquer the entire jungle on your own."

Abbie tossed her head. "And establish myself as the belle men pined for but wouldn't dare marry?" She laughed. "That's all right. I wouldn't dream of marrying some fancified eastern gentleman with lily white hands, anyway."

That stung. Monte grasped his hands behind his back. "That's rather extreme, wouldn't you say? And whom would you dream of marrying?"

"Oh, someone who didn't care if I could embroider or simper over tea with the proper malaise in my tone."

"Like Blake, perhaps?" He twisted his mouth ironically.

"Perhaps."

"But you don't love him."

"Maybe someday I will."

She was indeed taunting him, the vixen. Monte laughed low. "Well, I wish him the best of luck, then—Blake or whomever you choose. He'll certainly need it."

Abbie's mouth fell open. "Hadn't you better see to your horse, Mr. Farrel?"

"Yes, I suppose I had."

"Good night, then."

"Good night, Miss Martin," he drawled, and she swept into the house without a backward glance.

At least he had evened the ground.

Six

As a funeral cloak on bony shoulders, the clouds hung ominously still over the mountains. Abbie felt the air. Yesterday's hail was nothing compared to what this storm promised, and she hurried with her chores, pulling the clean wash down from the line and tossing it into the large woven basket with less care than was her wont. The chickens were nervous and raced about wildly when she shooed them into their pen and tossed them their feed.

By the time she had the sheep herded into the large, airy barn, the wind, even in July, was chilling her. With one glance at the cow, horse, and hog safely contained, she grabbed her skirts and ran for the house. Abbie could smell the rain coming, and lightning split the sky as she closed the door against the wind behind her. "It's really going to hit us this time!" She found Mama in the front room darning socks. "The clouds are black with malice."

Mama looked up. "I wish you hadn't such a way of expressing things. You put a shiver right up to my neck. I surely hope your father has sense enough to stay in town and not try to make it home."

"Pa's sensible."

"Sometimes. Other times he doesn't think to look up or around him if he has a story in his head or a thought forming."

Abbie looked out. With sudden violence, the storm smote the house.

"Are the sheep in the barn?" Mama asked.

"Yes, and the other stock, as well."

Abbie put her hands to her ears at the growing cacophony of the rain becoming hail. She stared at the ice marbles bouncing on the ground outside that grew to the size of pullet eggs. Never had she seen hail of such destructive power.

Mama dropped the darning egg and came to stand beside her. "Lord, have mercy."

"I'm sorry, Mama. Perhaps it won't be so bad." But Abbie could see her words were false.

"Perhaps," Mama murmured.

◆◆◆◆◆◆◆

Monte dashed for the newspaper office in the wake of an earsplitting crack of thunder. He gained the door and burst through.

Joshua grinned. "You sure do take to this weather, Monte. Haven't you had your fill of the wet yet?" he hollered over the din.

"I have, but I don't seem to have the apparatus to predict it like you folks do," Monte shouted back, shaking himself like a dog. At least Chance was at the livery and would be cared for if he was delayed. He smoothed back his soaked hair. "I thought it was supposed to be dry out here."

"The only thing you can count on is that the weather will never be what you thought. Soon as you get set for dry, it floods, and when you're ready for rain, the ground plum shrivels up." Joshua watched through the window as the rain turned to hail. "Only the good Lord knows what we need better than we do."

"Looks like what we need is a good thrashing." Monte came up behind and followed his gaze.

Joshua shook his head. "Folks are going to suffer from this one."

As he spoke, a drop of water fell from the rough-board ceiling, followed by another, and then more. Grabbing a bucket, Joshua caught the flow. "Sure hope it's not hitting like this at home."

Monte pulled aside the shade on the west window. "I wouldn't count on that. Have a look at those clouds." He hoped Abbie hadn't been caught out again. This onslaught made yesterday's a lark.

As the night drew on, the rain continued, and the street became a young river. "I'm thinking it's foolhardy to try for home tonight," Monte concluded.

"I'm afraid you're right, though my belly has a complaint."

"What do you say I brave the street and fetch us something from the hotel?"

"I'd say you have a taker." Joshua reached into his pocket.

"Keep it." Monte pulled his coat up over his head and dashed out into the rain. Pearl would have something to say about him presenting her another pair of mud-stained trousers, but it appeared she might as well get used to it. The water rushed up to the top edge of his boots with enough force to threaten his footing as he leaped onto the far boardwalk and entered the hotel. He secured a couple of fried chicken dinners, then made his way back.

"You're a good man, Monte." Joshua grinned as he opened the box and viewed the meal.

They talked long into the night. Joshua Martin possessed a keen wit and good humor, but there was also a strength of character that reminded Monte of his own father before the war. He was challenged by Joshua's ideas and found himself wondering what the man was made of, and in turn, what he had passed on to his daughter. Though Abbie favored Selena in looks, he suspected it was Joshua's temperament she had inherited along with the startling blue eyes.

When they had burned the oil low, they set the chairs end to end, and Monte bent himself into the space while Joshua curled up on the bench. It was a comfortable companionship he shared with Joshua Martin, and more. He respected the man and suspected Joshua returned the esteem. He hadn't thought to find that here.

He cradled his head on his arm and shifted one leg under the other. The rain made hardly more than a murmur on the roof as he closed his eyes to sleep.

♦♦♦♦♦♦♦

Abbie's face drew into a long imitation of the sight that met her eyes when she stepped out into the bright morning sunshine. Unlike a morning following a gentle rain, in which everything is fresh and shining, the earth looked ragged and unkempt. Shredded greenery and mud covered everything. Each plant lay trampled and flattened, and the trees were nearly leafless, except for the hearty ponderosas. Even the indestructible yuccas were limp.

She and Mama made their way through to the garden and viewed the devastation. Mama lifted a tiny cucumber from beneath a matted wreck of leaves. She turned it slowly in her hand. There was not a mark on it, and she sighed. "Maybe you and your pa are right. Maybe a place like this doesn't want refinement. Maybe you just have to be able to survive."

Pa galloped through the gate and reined in beside them. Slipping from the horse, he surveyed the battered land, his expression grim. "Well, I guess we can be thankful it wasn't worse. How did the stock fare?"

"Abbie got them all in before the storm hit." Mama tucked the cucumber into her apron pocket.

"Good girl, Abbie." He caressed her cheek. "I know I can count on you to help your mama."

Selena bent and lifted the severed vine that held the remains of two more immature cucumbers. "This is going to set us back. There's not much to salvage, and with the grasshoppers last year . . ."

"We'll manage." Pa looked over the land. "We'll just have to buy our vegetables like the townsfolk do."

Mama didn't argue, though Abbie knew she wondered where the money would come from.

"I'll have a look at the damage." Pa made his way to the barn, and Abbie followed. She needed to milk Buttercup anyway.

The oozy floor showed the extent of damage to the barn roof. "The house is bad, too, Pa. We shored it up as best we could, but it'll need repair." The sheep pressed against her legs as she reached for the milking pail and slid the stool to the cow's side. "I wish Grant were here." She always missed her brother more than her sister, Sadie, but now when Pa needed him, she really felt his absence.

"Well, right now he's reading law at Harvard. You know that's always been his bent."

"I know, but there are times we sure could use him back here."

"We'll make do."

"I'll help any way I can."

"I know you will, and there'll be plenty to do for all of us." Joshua let the sheep out into the yard. "Go ahead and take them to the pasture, Abbie. I'll do the milking."

She kept to the high ground as she led the sheep, avoiding the pockets of wet earth. By afternoon the ground would be dry and in a week parched again, but for now it had slaked its thirst. She wondered if the storm had hit Denver, where Sadie lived with her husband, Joe. Then she thought of the mission in Rocky Bluffs and stopped short. Their roof had been needkins homestead, for one. They'll be packing up within the week and heading back to Missouri."

"I'm sorry for them," Mama said.

"They hadn't the constitution to last out here. You saw the state of their place."

"Yes, but Blanche had her hands full with twelve children."

"Could have had plenty of help if they'd ever trained and disciplined them." Joshua shook his head. "I'm not passing judgment. Just seems like some folks ought to stay where things are easier."

"Sometimes it's hard to know how things can get." Mama laid a hand on his shoulder.

"I'm that sour today, aren't I?"

Mama smiled.

Abbie went out to the garden and made her way up and down the rows, gently mounding the dirt up around the potato and sweet potato plants that were hardly more than a few stems with straggling shredded leaves. The blossoms had already set, and possibly they would come back and produce the tubers, but it wasn't likely. The carrot greens were gone, but the roots were already strong and established. The lettuce, spinach, and chard were demolished, nor was there much she could do for the corn, pumpkins, squash, and cucumbers.

"Afternoon, Abbie."

She turned. "Hello, Blake. It's a dismal sight, isn't it?"

"I dunno. Seems like the purtiest thing I've seen."

"Don't go being crazy again," she snapped. "I'm talking about the garden, you fool boy."

"Is that any way to treat me when I come to offer my help to yer pa?"

"Did you, Blake?" She regretted her words immediately and slipped her arm through his. "Of course not. Forgive me?"

His cheeks were ruddy from the walk and the work he'd already done, no doubt. He flipped the hair from his forehead and grinned. "Maybe we oughta kiss and make up."

She pulled her arm away. "I declare, I don't know what's gotten into you!"

He was laughing, and she turned her back on him and continued down the row.

"Can I help?"

"I thought you were helping Pa."

"He don't need me till he reckons the damage."

"Surely your own garden needs as much work as ours."

"Ma and Mariah are seein' to it."

"Then you can gather the waste for the hog." Through the corner of her eye, she watched him obey and softened. He was as good-hearted as he was vexing. And with Grant away, his help would be a boon. "Thank you, Blake."

He looked up from where he bent and winked.

Seven

Abbie paced the mare, though Shiloh was fresh and eager to run. All around her were signs of the hail, but the prairie grasses were springing back better than the cultivated plants at home. As she approached the mission, she could see its adobe walls had withstood much damage, but she knew the beam and shingled roof could not have. The side building where the children slept looked especially battered.

She dismounted and tethered Shiloh. With a stroke to the mare's neck, she left her and went to the door. Brother José greeted her, beaming to the top of his brown tonsured skull. "*Buenos días.*"

"Good morning, Brother. *Cómo estás?*"

"One is always well in God's hands."

He led her in through the gathering hall where they took their meals and past the open kitchen. Brother Thomas rolled a great mound of dough over the floured board, nodding as she passed.

The children sat along the walls of the schoolroom with slates across their knees, and the empty space in the center showed Abbie what she had come to discover. Tarps and buckets kept the water from the wood plank floor. Father Dominic looked up from the book of Psalms he was reading aloud, and several of the small ones around him smiled at her. The room was impossibly still, though it contained fourteen children and the priest.

"Forgive my interrupting."

Father Dominic smiled. "Time is the Lord's."

"I can't stay today, but I wanted to see about your roof."

"It is as you see it."

Four-year-old Tucker squirmed, nudging the tarp edge with his toe. A rivulet started across the thickness, and Father Dominic caught his eye before the child could wiggle it again. Abbie wished she could gather the little ones out to the yard and work their letters, but she was needed at home. "Shingles may be hard to come by, but I'll see what I can do."

"Your gift is welcome. Labor we have, but few materials."

As she rode home, Abbie wondered how she could find shingles for them. If Mr. Thorne was charging so dearly, people wouldn't spare any from their own use, and Pa couldn't possibly cut more than they required. Maybe she and Blake . . . but that would be slowgoing for the two of them to cut so many. She shook her head. Somehow she'd think of a way.

◆◆◆◆◆◆

Four days later, Abbie perched on the ladder with a pail of water for Pa and Blake as they worked the old broken shingles off the roof of the house. She turned at the rumble of wheels on the drive. A pair of black horses pulled a wagon, and she recognized Chance and another black as like him as a twin. Monte drove them.

Shading her eyes, she made out his load. Fresh-hewn shingles. She caught her breath and hurried down the ladder.

"What's all this?" Pa followed close on her heels.

Monte tipped his hat to her, and she nodded stiffly back, remembering her grudge. He turned to Pa. "I took the liberty of sending to Denver for shingles, as the local mill was committing usury."

"I expect the freight ran you more dearly."

"I sent my own men after them and cut the price by order-ing for two."

"Aha. You're a shrewd dealer. What's the cost to me?"

"Ten cents a bale."

Pa whistled. "That's music to my ears. I'd be weeks cutting this load by hand."

Monte jumped down. "And as it happens, my roof is under control, so I'm offering my hands as well."

Abbie hung in the shadow, still stinging from their last en-counter. But this was a tremendous windfall, and it was good to see Pa so excited. It seemed Mr. Farrel was not afraid to work, and Pa could use all the help he could get.

"Now, there's a fine thing." Pa pulled off his hat and wiped his forehead. "Between you and Blake, I'll be set in no time."

Abbie bit her lip against a giggle as Monte glanced up to the roof. She wished she could see Blake's face right now. Monte's was inscrutable as he strode to the wagon bed and opened the back. Instead of fine trousers, pleated shirt, and vest, he wore a blue cotton shirt and denim pants, with a ban-danna tied at his neck. Even so, he looked every inch the aris-tocrat. Blake would be fuming.

Abbie went inside. "Mama! Monte's brought shingles!"

"Oh my, what a blessing!" Mama cupped her cheeks. "I thought we'd be weeks without a proper roof!"

"There's a wagonful, enough for the barn as well, and ... maybe there'll be some for the mission, too. I mean with all that Pa's cut already..."

"They're welcome to whatever we have. Oh, Monte's a good man. Did you ask him in?"

"He's on the roof with Pa ... and Blake." Now she did gig-gle.

Mama frowned. "What happened between Monte and Blake

is not a lark. I certainly hope you'll not encourage any further trouble."

Abbie cringed. So Mama had heard. "I never encouraged any in the first place. Blake just lost his head. Lucky for him, I saved his neck." She collapsed, giggling, into the chair.

"Abbie, it's not a laughing matter."

But the idea of Blake and Monte together on the roof was altogether too funny to resist. She gave in to the laughter in spite of Mama's annoyance.

Monte wondered at the cause of Abbie's laughter filtering through the open doors. She had been stiff and aloof enough a moment ago. But it was a delicious sound, and he wished he'd been party to the source. He looked up to find Blake watching him. He'd obviously heard, also. Joshua paid no mind, but then he lived with the chance to hear Abbie laugh.

A pounding of hooves brought Joshua's head up. Sterling Jacobs reined up sharply in the yard. "Joshua!"

"What's the ruckus?"

"Paper's been ransacked. I think you'd better come see."

Joshua leaped to his feet but glanced at his companions.

Monte straightened. "Go on. Blake and I will handle this."

Joshua climbed down and ran for the barn.

Blake went to the edge. "Who done it, d'you suppose?"

"They're sayin' in town it was Hollister's gang."

"Why hit the newspaper?"

"Why does anyone do a senseless thing? Maybe they didn't like the column Joshua printed last week. He didn't mince any words describin' them."

Monte sat back on his heels. "Who's Hollister?"

"A two-bit thievin' scoundrel." Blake scowled. "He's been hittin' the stage and unsuspectin' folks for the past year. Has a ragtag bunch of no-goods tryin' to make a name for themselves."

Monte appraised Blake. "He's been at it for a year and not been caught yet?"

"It takes a bit of doin' to round up a gang like that. Too much open space, too much wild country."

Sterling and Joshua set their horses for town. As he watched them gallop away, Monte glanced at Blake. They were alone now, and the boy was clearly uncomfortable.

Blake hunkered down and worked his wedge under a shingle. "I reckon it's as good a time as any to beg pardon for losin' my head."

"No harm done." Monte busied himself with a patch of splintered shingles.

"I guess Abbie gets me a mite worked up."

"Perfectly understandable. She's an awfully pretty package."

"I figured you'd noticed."

"It would be difficult to miss." Monte heaved a handful of broken shingles over the side. "Hand me that hammer, will you?"

Blake passed it over.

"So what are your plans, Blake? Smithing like your father?"

"Not if I can help it. That's an awful hot an' dirty way to make a livin' in my book. I mean to go west . . . soon as I can talk Abbie into comin' along." He glanced up at that.

"Good luck. I don't get the impression Abbie's easily talked into anything."

Blake frowned. "No, she ain't." He yanked hard on a stubborn shingle.

Monte heard the door below, and in a moment Abbie joined them on the roof with the water bucket. Stopping on the flat portion above the porch, she gazed about her. "Sure can see a long way from up here."

Blake grinned. "Good as the old lightning pine, ain't it?" He made his way down to her from the ridge.

"Well, I wouldn't say quite—" She caught herself. "I wouldn't know."

"Sure you would. Remember how it . . ." Blake didn't catch her point until he took the cup of water and faced her glare.

Monte smiled crookedly.

"Lunch is almost ready." She dipped the cup again.

Monte took it, trying to gauge her mood. Was she still holding her grudge? Once the thrill of besting her wore off, he'd regretted it. She pushed a loose strand of hair back and tried to avoid his gaze, but with a will of their own her eyes met his, and he could see a throbbing pulse in her neck. She may be angry still, but she was having a difficult time keeping it. He drained the cup and handed it back.

"Thank you, Abbie."

She spun without answering.

Red-faced and sullen, Blake kicked a pile of old shingles over the side, then sat and yanked on the next row.

Abbie lowered herself onto the ladder. "Mama made your favorite apple dumplings, Blake. Get yourself good and hungry so you'll be sure to have room." She disappeared over the side.

Blake didn't speak again. When Selena called for them to come eat, Monte motioned Blake to precede him down the ladder, then followed. After washing at the pump, Monte went into the kitchen. He eyed the table overflowing with biscuits and corn bread, boiled potatoes with parsley and bacon, fried zucchini and onions, roast venison and cold chicken, and a big pot of Boston baked beans. "Selena, I have never seen a more welcome sight in all my life."

"Hard work builds an appetite." Selena set the milk pitcher on the table and they all sat down. "Monte, would you be so kind?"

"Ma'am." He bowed his head and folded his hands. "Our heavenly Father, we thank Thee for the bounty from Thy hand, and for all the good things that Thou dost bestow. Give us grateful hearts in all things and keep us ever in Thy sight. Amen." As he expected, Abbie peeked up at his formal prayer, and he winked.

She turned away, but not before he saw her amusement. She'd get over her irk. The work had built a hunger and Selena was a good cook, but his appetite died when Joshua stormed into the room in a fine temper. He tossed his hat at the hook on the wall and left it where it landed on the floor. Joshua's face was a mask of fury.

Monte knew before asking. "The press?"

"Destroyed! There's no repairing it." Joshua dropped into the chair and pounded his fist on the table. Abbie jumped. Clearly his temper rarely showed itself. But what man took this quietly?

Monte felt the affront himself. "What possible motivation could someone have for destroying the press?"

"What does it matter? What's done can't be undone." Joshua brushed away the cup Selena held out to him, his fury barely held in check.

This was not the time for guests. Once Joshua's head had cleared, Monte would talk with him, figure things out. But for now . . . "You'll want some time." Monte nudged Blake up and, with a hand on his shoulder, ushered him out. He had him to the porch when Abbie swept by and pressed a parcel into Blake's hand.

"Dumplings."

Blake grinned. "I'll be over tomorrow."

She nodded, and Monte waited silently while she watched him walk away. As she turned, he caught her elbow. "Walk with me."

"But—"

"Your parents need time. Alone." He directed her away from the house.

His jaw was set, his thoughts rushing. Memories of gun

stocks through leaded-glass cabinets ... china crunching underfoot ... ax gashes on banisters worn smooth as silk by the hands of generations of Farrels ... He drew in his breath and forced it to release slowly, evenly. "Tell me about your father's holdings." She jerked at his voice, and he realized her thoughts were as haggard as his.

"I don't know. I don't think we have anything but the homestead and the paper."

Her voice sounded small, and he responded instinctively, tucking her hand through the crook of his arm. God, where was the sense of it all? "Then there's no possibility of a new press?"

"Oh, Monte, I don't know. I can't see how. Things are tight ... very tight."

She didn't resist his comfort, and their feud was obviously forgotten. He could be thankful for that. "Well, this is the land of opportunity. There's always a way." He patted her fingers.

Clouds cluttered the sky, masking and unmasking the sun. She was unnaturally quiet as they walked, no chatter, no lessons from her today. He sensed her concern and searched for words. He'd played this role before, set Frances and cousin Darcy off from feeling the helplessness, the fear, the overwhelming loss. But never completely. "Blake's a good man."

She looked up. He had her attention at least. "A hard worker." He earned a faint smile.

"I was concerned for the two of you on the roof together."

"Did you think he might shove me off?"

"Perhaps."

"And would that trouble you?" He cupped her fingers, but she looked away.

They climbed the rise and came among the sheep. A brown-faced lamb bumped Abbie's skirt. Stooping, she stroked the soft head, burying her fingers in the new wool. The lamb nuzzled her face and grew so persistent he forced her to sit. Monte settled beside her and the lamb found his ear.

Abbie smiled as he pushed the animal away. "He likes you."

"He hasn't very good manners."

Losing interest, the lamb bounded away, and Monte stared out over the prairie. "Look at that empty space out there. With people moving west, this could be a great city."

"I hope not. I like it open as far as you can see and the sound of the wild things at night." Her voice caught. Wrapping her knees with her arms, she rested her chin. "I don't think I can bear it if we have to leave."

"Don't even talk that way. Of course you won't leave."

"I love this place. Can you understand that?"

"You asked why my father didn't leave the South, and yet you know his sentiment. Yes, I understand."

"Did you feel that way for your home?"

"I watched the South die. To stay would have been to live in a past that no longer exists. I have yet to find a love for this place, but I believe it holds my destiny."

Abbie lay back in the grass, her chest rising and falling. Monte wondered if she knew how alluring she was, lying there like that, and guessed not. If she even remembered he was there, it was far from her thoughts. And who could blame her? The loss of the press . . . he knew well enough the setback that would be, but until she spoke of leaving . . . Flashes of faces, hard and leering, blue, brass-buttoned chests, Frances's eyes wide with horror . . . Oh yes, he knew what it was to be forced from your home.

His chest burned as he lowered himself beside her and watched the darkening clouds. A single raindrop struck the side of his head and Monte glanced at her. "As much as I hate to say it . . ." He raised her to her feet.

She smiled. "Now it's you reading the weather. You're an apt pupil."

"I've never been dull, especially with an instructor so engaging. Perhaps one day you'll teach me to fish with a spear as well."

"Perhaps..." She tipped her head. "And what would you teach me?"

Monte reached out and raised her chin. "Were you not a child..." he drew her close, "there is much I could teach you." The skin of her cheek warmed to his fingers.

"I'll have to wait, then," she whispered.

"That's most unfortunate."

She stepped back. "Some things are worth waiting for."

Releasing her, Monte laughed. "Yes, indeed, some things are. Shall I wait, then?"

"That's entirely up to you."

Eight

Abbie eyed the half load of shingles left when the house and barn were repaired. Monte had not returned, but Blake had come each of the last four days and worked beside Pa. She toed a bundle beside the barn. "Have you a use for these shingles, Pa?"

He pulled a nail from between his teeth and placed it. "What are you thinking?"

"The mission was hit hard. They're in a bad way."

He hammered the new board to the barn siding. "Take them and welcome."

"Shall I have Blake drive them out?"

"He can manage the wagon."

Blake groaned when she dragged him back to the side of the barn to load the shingles, but he obliged and hitched Shiloh and Sandy. Abbie climbed up beside him.

"The way I figure it," Blake said as he drove over the rough track, "you owe me a bunch for this."

"God loveth a cheerful giver, Blake."

"Well, sure an' all, but . . ."

"Did you hear what Pa told your pa last night?"

"No. Did you?"

"I wouldn't be asking if I had. I don't like how he looked, all bleak and tired. Your pa was almost as bad, so it couldn't have been good news."

"Well . . ."

"I can't figure it. Pa's always one to discuss. He doesn't keep things to himself. Not like some men."

"That's—"

"But now it's like he's all bottled up. He'll answer if you ask, but then nothing. And today he's hardly said a word."

"Maybe he can't get one in."

Abbie shoved Blake's shoulder. "This is a serious matter. I can't stand not knowing what he's thinking."

"I'm sure he's got his reasons."

"And Mama, too. She hasn't scolded in days."

"Count yer blessings."

"You're impossible," Abbie huffed.

Blake shrugged. "Look, Abbie, if they wanted you to know, they'd tell you. If they ain't said nothin', maybe there's nothin' to say."

"But something has to be done. Pa can't make a living without a press. Our homestead is too rough and wooded to ranch for profit. We haven't the grazing for large herds and . . ."

"You're borrowin' trouble."

She sighed. "Maybe I am."

He reached over and patted her knee. "Ain't nothin' we can't figure out together."

He meant it kindly, so she didn't scold. But she had no confidence in his assurance. Things were being decided, and she was intentionally being excluded.

When they arrived, Father Dominic's face lit like Christmas at the bounty of shingles. "The Lord's miracle."

Abbie had never seen his smile so broad nor viewed his long ivory teeth. She almost believed God had multiplied the shingles, there were so many left over. But then, Monte had ordered an abundance.

The other brothers crowded close as Blake opened up the back. As they rolled the sleeves of their robes and helped him carry the bundles to the wall, Abbie found the children work-ing in the garden.

She groaned. Theirs was as decimated as her own, but they had no funds to purchase vegetables so were salvaging even the pieces. Little Tucker Finn lunged for her, and Abbie scooped him into her arms, then reached for the others. Jeremy and Emmy and Judith . . . even fourteen-year-old Silas stood close.

"We've brought shingles, Silas. They'll be needing you."

He grinned.

"Have you salvaged much out here?"

Felicity waved her arm. "Some. The wall kept the squash and pumpkins safe."

"We got some peas." Tucker squeezed her legs.

Jeremy snorted. "They were beans, knucklehead."

Silas connected a knuckle with Jeremy's head. "How's that for knucklehead?"

"Come now, none of that." Abbie pulled away. "What would you say to hide-and-seek?" She feared their roar would bring the brothers running and hushed them, laughing. "Who should be 'it'?" She never doubted it would be she.

When Blake came for her nearly two hours later, she had Tucker asleep in her lap and the others gathered together un-der the tree for her stories. She handed Tucker over to Felicity and followed Blake back to the wagon. He lifted her in and they started back. "Thank you, Blake."

"Yup."

"You were busy a long while."

"Yup."

She glanced at him sideways. "What—"

"I had a look at the roof."

Abbie slipped her arm through his. "And?"

"And I'll be out there tomorrow."

"Oh, Blake." She squeezed him.

He scowled. "Shoot, Abbie. It ain't nothin'."

She didn't embarrass him further. Blake had his own brand of devotion to God and to the meek brothers who served Him, though he'd never admit it. She knew it was so, but she would not let on, not to Blake anyway. She had come on him talking to the Lord in the woods one day, and he'd near died of embarrassment. Of course, he'd been thirteen and acting awkward anyway.

Besides, her thoughts were too preoccupied again. The children had provided a needed respite from her worry, but as they closed the distance home, all her trepidation returned. As soon as she went inside, Abbie knew Pa was ready to speak his mind. He sat her at the table and spoke softly, but she couldn't believe what she heard.

"No, Pa!" She gripped the table edge.

"Abbie, there's no other way. Grandpa has a position for me, and it's a good opportunity."

She pushed back her chair and jumped up. "There's opportunity here, Pa! That's what this is, the land of opportunity! That's why you came here in the first place. Can't you remember?"

Pa's hand was gentle on her. "I'm sorry. But we have to go. I'm not a cowboy, nor a man of commerce, nor a smith like Wes McConnel. I craft words, and I have to go where I can do it profitably."

"But what about Denver?"

"Yes, I could possibly get on with another paper there and scratch out a living working for someone else, but Grandpa's offered something better."

Abbie swallowed back the tears. She knew what this was costing him. The lump that had lodged in her throat grew hard. Pressing his hand, she forced a smile. "I know you'll do what's right. You always do."

He nodded, but his eyes were dull.

Abbie ran for the barn and saddled Shiloh. It wasn't fair to ride her hard after the work she'd already done, but she needed to release the ache in her chest before she could hope to tell Clara. She tethered Shiloh in front of the grocer's and rushed in.

Clara jumped up. "Abbie, what on earth—"

Abbie grabbed her hand and pulled her toward the stairs to their living quarters. "I have to talk to you."

Clara opened the door to her room. "I'm so sorry about your pa's press. Have they found who did it?"

Abbie shook her head. "They're sure it was Hollister. But that's not what matters. The worst is . . ." She forced the words out. "We have to go back to Kansas City."

Clara's hands flew to her face. "You can't! How will I ever get by without our chats and the way you make me laugh? What will I do?"

Abbie shook her. "It's not you, Clara. You'll marry Blake McConnel and raise up sons for your pa's business. I'm the one being uprooted. Kansas City! I'll suffocate for lack of mountains, open space, or a wild thing anywhere. I'll end up married to a bank clerk with a balding pate and spectacles and soft white hands." She dropped into the chair.

"Isn't there something you can do? Your pa could take out a loan at the bank and buy a new press."

"Pa won't take on a debt. He's never owed a man anything, and he won't start now."

Clara sat and folded her hands in her lap. Neat, honey-blond waves framed her dejected face. "How long do you suppose before you go?"

"I don't know. Pa will have to sell the homestead and whatever he can salvage from the paper. Maybe a few weeks. I don't know." The tears welled up, but she refused to let them fall.

"Does Blake know?" Clara's voice was hardly above a murmur.

"No." Abbie tossed her bonnet, covered her eyes, and cried.

Clara's arms circled her, and Abbie sniffed. "It's all right." She pushed away. "I just had to let it out. Now I'm done."

"Oh, Abbie." Clara pressed her hands. "We can write each other. You can tell me all the new things. You always wanted to see someplace new."

"Kansas City is not new." Abbie slumped. "I should be more careful what I wish for. I may not like it when it happens."

"Shall we have tea?"

"I couldn't swallow it."

"Oh, my dear. You will be here for your birthday, won't you?"

"August fourth is eight days away. I don't see how we can be gone that soon."

"Then I shall have the most sumptuous birthday party for you and invite all the girls. They'll want a chance to say good-bye, and you'll have presents to remember us by. I know exactly what I'll get you."

"No one can give me what I want. No one can give me this place."

"I wish I could, Abbie. I truly wish I could."

♦♦♦♦♦♦♦

Inside the rough cabin tucked against the overhanging cliff, Buck Hollister crossed his boots up on the table. "Second week with no *Chronicle* from Rocky Bluffs. Not bad fer two-bit black-guards."

"Word is he's gotta move back East now."

Briggs spoke low and Hollister eyed him. He looked more weasel than man, and maybe he was, the way he sniffed out news. He wondered how much Briggs kept to himself. "That'd be mighty fittin'." Hollister struck a match against the table and lit his cigar. "If he ain't got nothin' nice to say, he oughtn't say nothin' at all. Ain't that what you learnt in Sunday school, Conrad?"

"Amen." Conrad padded his soft, pink palms together piously.

"Shoot, Conrad . . ." Hollister laughed.

Briggs tugged out a chair and straddled it. "He's got hisself a right purty daughter."

Hollister sobered. Sometimes Briggs made even his blood run cold.

"Maybe he'd sell 'er and buy hisself a new press." This comment from the kid, Wilkins, tickled the men, and Hollister waited for the laughter to pass.

"Per'aps you oughta go an' ask 'im, Wilkins. Offer 'im a good price."

The kid colored like a girl himself and stammered. "I . . . I ain't offerin' nothin for no wench!"

Briggs bit a plug of tobacco and shoved it in his cheek. "Maybe we oughta have a look at the goods first."

"Aw, I ain't paid fer no goods in two years." Hollister dragged on the cigar. "If Wilkins wants the girl, jest take 'er."

"I ain't said I wanted 'er, so shut yer mouth!"

Hollister's gun flew from the holster to his hand. "Who's gonna make me, kid?"

Wilkins cowered, and Conrad sidled close. "The kid's just joshin', Buck."

Hollister kicked the chair aside and went to the door. Staring out into the night, he smelled the pines. "I'm thinkin' it's time to move on."

"Where to?" Briggs asked.

"Maybe down New Mexico."

"Nothin' but Mexicans there."

Hollister bristled. Briggs was the only one with brains enough to worry him. "You got a better place?"

"There's good pickin's up that Injun pass. Them gold digger's comin' through."

Hollister watched the darkness. Briggs had a point. "I'll think on it tonight."

Nine

The dun hide of Buttercup's flank was soft and warm against Abbie's cheek as she closed her eyes and worked her hands automatically on the udder. "Oh, Buttercup, we'll have to sell you and the sheep and everything. . . ." The cow swung her head back, chewing with unconcern. The soft *fitt, fitt* of the milk in the pail marked off the seconds, each precious to Abbie now that her time here would end. As she urged the last bit of milk from the udder, a shadow filled the open doorway, and she turned to see Blake. His hair was slicked, and he wore clean pants and shirt.

"Mornin', Abbie."

Abbie smiled. "You going courting, Blake?"

"I am." He strode over and raised her to her feet. "I'm courtin' the purtiest girl in the whole territory."

"Now, Blake, I already told you . . ."

"But things are different now. You'll be eighteen tomorrow, and in two months I will, too. In four years I can file for land, and until then we could have the trapper's cabin at the edge of Pa's homestead."

"But, Blake . . ."

"If you marry me now, you won't have to leave. We can stay here or go west if you like. Whatever you want, Abbie."

She searched his face, tanned and freckled, pale blue eyes beneath brows that cut straight across, nose broken by a fall from his horse when he was eight. She knew him better than she knew herself.

Abbie hadn't considered marrying him, yet perhaps it could be as they'd played it in their childhood, she and Blake together. His arms came around her and she didn't resist but blushed as he brought his mouth to hers.

A horse in the yard interrupted them, and Abbie drew away, then peered out to see Monte astride a beautiful sorrel with black socks and mane. She lifted the milk pail. "I have to think about it, Blake. I'll give you my answer tomorrow."

Blake balled his fists at his sides. "That man is worse than a plague of grasshoppers!"

Abbie met Monte as he dismounted. "Monte, he's beautiful!" She ran a hand over the stallion's neck. It was arched and proud, and he held his tail like a plume.

"Good morning, Abbie. Is your father home?"

"No." She sagged. "He went to post a listing for the homestead."

"Ah. Then I'll try to meet him on the road."

"Won't you come in?"

"Not just yet, thank you." Monte pulled himself back into the saddle, tipped his hat, and whirled about. The stallion high-stepped, then dug in its hooves and broke into a canter. The yard felt empty as the dust settled behind him.

Abbie dragged inside and set the pail on the table. The skimming bowls were set out, and she poured the warm milk, then rinsed the pail at the pump. "Mama?"

Her mother came in from the lean-to.

"Blake asked me to marry him." Mama's cool fingers lifted her chin, and Abbie felt her scrutiny all the way inside her.

"Is that what you want?"

"I don't know. I want to stay, and Blake is ... Blake. He's always been there, but..." Abbie searched for the words. "I don't know if I love him. I mean, of course I love him, but I don't know if it's the way he loves me. Wouldn't it be wrong to marry him if I don't know I love him?"

"Sometimes that comes later. Sometimes the feelings follow the promise. But you're both so young. . . . What did you tell him?"

"That I'd answer tomorrow."

"Then we'll pray today. When you give your answer tomorrow, there must be no second thoughts. If you tell Blake yes, it's a forever yes."

"I know that, Mama." Abbie's voice quavered. Unexpectedly she remembered Monte, close as he'd been that day on the hill, and her whole being trembled. But that was foolishness. She was nothing more than a child to him. He had said so himself.

She tied up her hair and pulled on her old skirt, then dropped to her knees on the kitchen floor and took up a brush. Sinking it deep into the sudsy water, she applied it vigorously to the floor. Her thoughts swept back and forth like the brush. Could she marry Blake? Marry Blake? Why not? Why? *Swoosh, swoosh, swoosh,* the brush whispered until her shoulders ached and her knees were soaked and weary.

◆◆◆◆◆◆◆

Halfway to town, Monte met Joshua on his way home and raised a hand in greeting. He swung about beside him and ordered his thoughts. Seeing Abbie so shortly before did not aid him in that. But nothing would be gained by jumping in too rashly. Joshua was a keen man and had not made his decision lightly.

"Fine day," Joshua said.

"Yes." Monte matched his horse's pace to Joshua's. "Aren't too many places you can find this kind of clemency with just enough weather to make it interesting."

"You're right there. I admit I'm going to miss it. Just about broke my heart telling Abbie. You know how she feels about this place. But you've got to be practical even in the realm of thought and journalism. Without a press, I can't be much of a newspaperman."

Monte surveyed him. Joshua appeared to have made peace with his decision. He would follow it through if Monte failed to sway him. "As a matter of fact, that's why I was looking for you, Joshua."

"Oh?"

"I've been thinking what a sore loss it'll be for this town without a newspaper. And a good newspaper needs a good editor. I can't think we'll find anyone to compare with you."

"Well, that's kind of you to say, but it can't be helped." Joshua fiddled with his reins, betraying his consternation more than his words had yet.

"I think maybe it can." Monte cocked his head. "I have in mind a business proposition."

"What sort of proposition?"

"A partnership. I'm taking a personal interest in seeing that Rocky Bluffs doesn't lose the best newspaperman west of the Mississippi, and I'm willing to make it worth your while."

"In what way?"

"I supply the equipment and you provide the expertise until such time as you can or desire to buy me out."

"That's a mighty attractive offer." Joshua veered down the gully and back up. "What makes you think it's worth your investment?"

"I told you, I appreciate your abilities. Where I come from, a man who can put into words what others want to think, or ought to think, is more highly respected than many others. You showed great courage in telling us what Hollister is made of and, in a way, cemented public opinion. Otherwise, it'd be too easy for a man like that to become a hero."

"Not if I can help it."

"We need that sort of conscience out here, and men of your wit and wisdom."

"That all?"

Monte raised an eyebrow. "I admit I take perhaps a slightly more personal interest in retaining you . . . and your family."

"Aha! I imagine my journalism wouldn't be so sorely missed as my beautiful, blue-eyed daughter, eh?"

"Perhaps on a more equilateral basis."

Joshua laughed. "Well, Monte, you've given me food for thought. I sure would like to stay if it were possible."

"I've spent the last two weeks adjusting my accounts so that the purchase can be made immediately should you accept."

Suddenly, Joshua smacked his thigh. "By golly, of course I accept! I can't think of a partner I'd rather have." He reached across the gap between their horses, and Monte shook his hand. "What do you say we turn back to town and write us up a contract? I've a mind to cancel my sales notice!"

"Sounds first-rate to me." The satisfaction surprised him and went to his head. Monte wheeled his thoroughbred around and kicked in his heels. Joshua bolted after him, hooted a great 'yahoo,' and spanked the horse's rump with his hat.

♦♦♦♦♦♦♦

Abbie took the horses' reins as Pa and Monte dismounted. "I'll get them watered. Go ahead and wash for lunch." She was glad she had mentioned Monte's looking for Pa. Mama had counted on them returning together. She led Pa's Sandy and Monte's fine stallion to the water together and waited while they drank, then led them to the shade and tethered them.

When she went in, Monte held her chair for her to sit. His face was inscrutable, and whatever business had brought him seemed to have been inconsequential. She bowed her head. Pa offered the blessing with such enthusiasm that she glanced from him to Monte. When he had finished, Pa turned to her.

"You still hoping to stay here?"

Had Blake spoken with him? Was he giving his blessing here and now, feeling a load lifted from him? Her heart sank. "Of course I am, Pa."

"Then I guess we will."

Pa's eyes were laughing, and she turned to stare at Mama, who looked as surprised as she.

"I'd like to introduce my new partner in the newspaper business." Pa waved his hand toward Monte. "We'll be sending for a new press by the end of the week, and by fall we'll be printing our premier issue."

"Pa!" Abbie jumped to her feet and threw her arms about his neck, then turned to Monte and caught herself before doing likewise. "This is wonderful! This is ... I must go tell Clara!"

"We have a guest, Abbie," Mama scolded.

Monte smiled. "That's all right. Abbie would burst if she had to hold it in while we discuss details."

Grabbing her hat, she flew from the room. She heard her mother's sigh like a familiar farewell and covered the ground to the barn in a flash. She heaved the saddle over Shiloh's back, cinched and tightened it, slid the bridle between the mare's teeth, and tossed the reins over her head, then mounted. Throwing her skirts behind her, Abbie dug in her heels.

She didn't bother to smooth her hair before bursting into the store and grabbing Clara by the arms. "We're staying!"

Clara embraced her tightly, laughing and crying at once. "That's the best news! The girls will all be so glad!"

"Except Marcy Wilson." Abbie laughed. "Won't she be green when she hears it was Monte who made it possible for us to stay?"

"Monte? You must tell!"

"And I will." Abbie hooked her arm through Clara's. "Come

somewhere we can talk." They rushed up the stairs to Clara's room.

"Monte and Pa are partners."

"Partners how?"

Abbie opened her mouth and stopped. "I guess I didn't wait to hear that part. I just know that they're going to be partners at the paper, and because of that we're staying. And now I won't have to answer Blake, either."

"Answer Blake?"

Abbie choked. She hadn't meant to tell Clara about Blake's proposal unless she chose to accept it. When would she ever learn to hold her tongue? "Blake asked me to marry him." She took Clara's hands. "I'm sure it was that he knew how much I wanted to stay."

"That's all right, Abbie. I know Blake loves you."

"He doesn't really. He just hasn't looked at it practically. We'd be like two wolves at each other's throats. We're really too much alike."

"What will you tell him?"

Abbie shrugged. "That we've plenty of time."

Ten

Like a promise, the sun crested the ridge, igniting the blush of morning sky. Abbie could only remember one year it had stormed on her birthday. The sunshine was God's gift to her. She rose and dressed and went out. Dew jeweled the grass, and the chickadees chirped from Mama's apple tree. She headed for the pump with a towel and bayberry shampoo. Blake was there waiting.

"Can't a girl even wash before callers arrive?"

"I was up most o' the night. Took all my willpower to wait this long."

A lump formed in Abbie's throat. Why did he persist in these feelings for her? "Blake, I have some news for you."

"I know you do. And I surely hope it's the news I want to hear."

She hung the towel on the hook and set down the soap. "Pa's decided to stay."

"What?"

"Isn't it wonderful? We don't have to go! Monte and Pa are going to be partners, and they're getting a new press and starting over."

Blake frowned. "And what about us gettin' married an' all?"

"We don't have to rush into anything." She touched his arm. "It was gallant of you to ask, though."

"It wasn't gallant, and I ain't play actin'. I want to marry you. I love you somethin' awful, and whether yer pa leaves or stays makes no difference to me." His hands clenched at his sides.

She felt an ache in her chest. "I'm sorry, Blake."

"Hang that Montgomery Farrel anyway!" Blake kicked a clod as he stormed off.

Abbie closed her eyes. It was the right thing, but telling herself that didn't make it better. She hated to hurt him. Rubbing the soap into her palm, she hung her hair beneath the pump and lathered. When she finished washing, she went inside.

Mama caught her chin and raised her face. "Why so crestfallen? Surely a birthday girl must feel more cheerful than that."

"I talked to Blake. He's awfully upset."

"You told him no?"

Abbie nodded. "I'm not ready to be married, and now that we're not leaving . . ." Tears came to her eyes. "I surely never meant for him to care that way. I swear I never led him on."

"Sometimes it just happens."

"He blames Monte."

"Monte! Why on earth?"

Abbie shrugged. "I guess for making it possible for us to stay."

"I hope he shows better sense than he did the last time."

"He gave his word not to bother him again."

◆◆◆◆◆◆◆

The mirror reflected her glowing expression as Abbie viewed herself dressed and primped for her party. For once her riotous curls were contained, and her toilette satisfied even Mama's scrutiny. She pushed thoughts of Blake's disappointment out of her head. She would make it up to him somehow.

Pa lifted her into the buggy and drove her to the town hall, where she jumped down amid the girls who gathered around. "I'm so glad you're staying, Abbie." "Clara couldn't wait to tell us." "Happy birthday, Abbie!"

Ushered to the hall, Abbie gasped to see the room decorated with flowers and paper streamers. All the chairs were arranged against the walls. Clara clasped her arm. "So we have room for the games." She winked at Becky Linde. What was she up to? Abbie searched the excited faces as she was tugged in beside the two tables of dainties and finger foods.

"We all made them," MaryBeth Walker told her.

"You must be expecting an army."

"More like the cavalry . . ." Becky Linde giggled and Clara pinched her.

Abbie turned as Marcy Wilson came in the door. Leave it to her to arrive after the guest of honor. Fashionably late, she'd call it. "It's amazing she doesn't get a crick in her neck," Abbie whispered to Clara. "One day her nose'll stick up there, and she won't see where she's going."

"Shame, Abbie. Not on your birthday," Clara scolded. "Don't let a single thought ruin it for you."

"I'm sorry. That was uncharitable after all you've done. Of course you had to invite her, and I'll do my very best to appreciate even Marcy tonight."

Clara clapped her hands and announced Blind Man's Bluff, and Madeline Foley covered Abbie's eyes so she couldn't see. The girls spun her until she staggered and she heard them scatter, stifling their giggles. It seemed an awful lot of shuffling, and try as she could, she didn't touch a one of them. They must have spread to the very edges of the room, and there was a draft from the door. Were they leaving the room? Was this a practical joke? Clara wouldn't do that.

But what was that? It sounded . . . it was. The fiddle bow on the strings. Abbie pulled the blindfold from her eyes. "Surprise!" The crowd had swollen, not only with the girls, but the young men as well.

"Clara, what . . ."

"Ma and Mrs. Munson are chaperones, and Mr. Peterson's here to keep the boys in line. Everyone wanted a chance to say good-bye, so it was the best I could do."

"I don't believe this," she said as the fiddle started to sing. "Most of these people don't even like me."

"Oh, Abbie." Clara laughed.

Marty Franklin and his brother Burt bowed to them, elbowing each other. With a smile, Clara took Marty's hand, and Burt swept Abbie onto the floor. He was clumsy, but he meant well. Over her shoulder, she saw Mack and Davy McConnel, but not Blake. She guessed he didn't feel like celebrating, but she hardly had time to think about it. Burt surrendered her to Phil Mayes for the next dance, and he in turn to Will Stoddard.

Laughing as Will spun her to the closing chord of the quadrille, she found Monte at her side. She had seen him enter, but as a moth to a flame, Marcy had fluttered to him . . . then clung like a leech. He bowed. "May I have the honor before someone else commandeers you?"

Abbie laid her hand on his warm, firm palm. "It's that the girls are so outnumbered."

"I doubt very much that's it at all." He led her out to the center and placed a hand on her waist. "I took the liberty of providing the score for this dance."

"Oh?"

"It's a waltz that is quite fashionable abroad." He drawled "abroad" and smiled.

Around them the dancers paused as the fiddlers took up the three-four beat. Monte led her through the step until she was comfortable, while the others watched and then followed. "You have it?"

"I think so."

"Then follow me." He swept her in glorious circles, his motions smooth and graceful, but strong enough to guide her without error. "What do you think?"

She knew he could see her delight. "I hope it never ends."

"Would that were in my power."

"It feels wonderful to spin and step this way. Where did you learn it?"

"Vienna."

"Oh, Monte, you've seen the whole world!"

"Not quite." He smiled. "There's enough left to show you."

Abbie could not tell by his tone if he was teasing. She knew well enough how his tongue would slide as easily over a barb as a compliment, but he looked sincere.

"I'd be happy to see even a little piece now that you vouchsafed our staying. I'm so indebted to you."

"It was strictly selfish, I assure you. How else will I learn to track and fish and . . . climb trees," he whispered wickedly.

Abbie pulled back. "Don't you dare breathe a word of that!"

He laughed as they passed through the opposite couple, then joined hands again. "Surely you don't think I'd reveal your wild ways to all these fine ladies, do you?"

"That would be the end of me if Marcy Wilson got wind of it. Mama would send me off at the first opportunity."

"Then I'll guard your secret with my life."

His hand on the small of her back sent shivers up her spine. They faced a new couple, and he released her to be turned once by the alternate gentleman, then rested his hand beneath hers as they turned in a right-hand star, then a left. That part was familiar. She knew it from the Spanish waltz and others.

Then Monte's fingers were again on her back and clasping hers at her shoulder. He moved her with such skill she hardly felt the effort. The fiddlers stopped playing, and he bowed over her hand so closely that his breath and perhaps his lips warmed her skin. Abbie stood perfectly still as he surrendered her to Milton Fiske. She felt transformed.

Milton asked her something, but she didn't hear. She didn't even care that Marcy rolled her eyes and slandered her to Nora Thorne. Scarcely noticing, she curtsied to Milton and caught sight of Blake in the doorway, searching the crowd.

"Excuse me, Milton, I . . . excuse me." She pressed her way through. "Oh, Blake, I'm so glad you've come! I thought . . ."

Grabbing her hands, he pulled her outside the door. "I've come to say good-bye, Abbie."

Her chest convulsed. "Good-bye?"

"I'm leavin' with Mack in the mornin'. We're headin' to the mountains fer gold. Up Gilpin County. I know there's more to be found and I mean to find it."

Abbie fought for words. "You can't be serious!"

"I am serious, Abbie. And maybe I'll come back rich enough to buy you a fine, fancy house and all the things Montgomery Farrel would give you."

Abbie's hands fell to her sides as a hard knot gripped her stomach. "You think that's what I want?" Tears stung her eyes.

Blake faltered. "I know what you're tellin' me, Abbie. I just don't know what to do with it. Maybe when I come back you'll feel different, an' that's my hope. But either way I gotta go."

The tears slid over her lids. She felt as if a part of her were being torn away, and Blake wrapped her in his arms.

"Don't cry, Abbie."

"Oh, Blake . . ." She couldn't tell him to stay because she could promise him nothing. Why did things have to change for them? Why couldn't they still be friends? Pressing her face to his chest, she cried, and Blake held her without speaking. At last she looked up, and he kissed her tenderly.

"Good-bye, Abbie. I sure do love you."

Through the tears she watched him walk away. The wild thought of running after him and accepting his proposal filled her, and her feet almost obeyed, but it wasn't right. Maybe one day it would be different, but for now her love was not what he wanted it to be.

She heard a step behind her and knew without turning that it was Monte.

"What is it, Abbie?"

"Blake's going prospecting. He's leaving because I wouldn't marry him."

Monte turned her. "If you don't want him to go, why don't you tell him to stay?"

"Because I can't promise what I don't have to give him. I can't marry him if I don't love him." She turned away. "But I feel so wretchedly awful."

"Blake's his own man. You're not responsible for his decisions. Maybe you just helped him with his timing."

She closed her eyes.

"Abbie." He raised her chin and made her look at him. "You're eighteen years old tonight, and there's a whole roomful of people here to honor you. Come in and dance."

"I can't."

"Yes, you can. In a small way it's doing what you must, even if your heart's not in it. It's honor, Abbie."

Drawing a deep breath, she wiped the tears from her eyes.

"That's better. And since I found you, I'll claim this dance. Then you'll be all over your sniffles with no one the wiser."

"I'm not as good at conquering jungles as you thought."

"Perhaps I don't mind playing the hero on occasion."

He led her in on his arm. Marcy was hovering near, probably waiting for him to reappear, and her expression soured. Abbie wondered what she had overheard, but Monte winked and led her to the floor. By the time their dance ended, she had contained her tears, though the ache in her heart remained. A quick search showed her that Mack McConnel had gone as well, and she sighed.

"Chin up, now," Monte breathed in her ear, then left her to Clara. The chaperones were clearing the floor, and Mrs. Simms had the girls cleaning up the tables.

"Let's slip away," Clara said, taking her hand. They crossed the street to the store and hurried up the stairs. Inside her room, Clara closed the door behind them and went to her wardrobe. She pulled a small box tied in ribbon from the drawer.

Abbie took it and sat on the edge of the bed. Pulling the ribbon free, she opened the box and lifted out a necklace of small blue beads. Clara dropped down before her. "It's made by Indians, Abbie."

Abbie stared at her. "How did you get it?"

"You remember Mag French and his awful son Travis? Last time they were through, Travis had a whole string of these, and I remembered that he sold several to Mrs. Linde. She wanted to send them to her nieces in Boston. She had only this one left, and I convinced her to sell it to me for you." Clara smiled triumphantly.

Abbie looked at the beads and tried to imagine the Indian woman stringing them. Perhaps she had a papoose on her back and feathers woven through her hair. "You don't know how much this means to me. Thank you."

"Now let's get changed for bed."

They undressed and climbed into the covers side by side. Clara turned down the wick of the lamp and rolled to her side. "All right, out with it," she whispered.

"Out with what?"

"Whatever it is that made you cry tonight. I know you too well to be fooled by that smile you pasted on when you came back in with Monte. What happened? Did he—"

"It's not Monte." Abbie bit her lip. "Blake's leaving."

"Leaving?"

"He's going to the mountains to hunt for gold with Mack."

Clara was silent.

"I'm so sorry, Clara."

The words seemed flimsy. As she slipped into the cusp of sleep, Abbie felt Clara's shoulders shake and heard the quiet tears. She couldn't remember feeling so empty.

Eleven

Monte sat his horse as well as any man out there, but he was less sure what to do with a herd of cattle, especially these bony-looking, long-horned brutes that moved sprightlier than any cattle he'd ever seen. He'd opted for the Texas breed after learning their suitability to the Colorado pasture, but these looked more like something fit for the wild.

Well, he had hired the men to deliver the four hundred head of cows and heifers, and this they'd done and were well paid for the job. Now it was up to him. He watched the cowboys circle the herd, whistling and shouting, keeping them moving, keeping them contained. He would need more men than he currently had.

Riding up beside him, Cole Jasper tipped his hat. "Well, Mr. Farrel, here's yer herd and they're a fine bunch. You'll want to get them branded right away, 'fore any rustler gits an eyeful."

"They look a little rangy."

"If you mean they're long-horned and long-legged, you're right. That's the Texas cow. But you'll find they're good feeders. They're quick and produce a hardy calf. You get yerself a couple Durham bulls and give 'em run o' the ladies a few years, you'll develop a superior breed in no time."

"Thank you, Cole. Your men have done a good job."

"Guess we'll be movin' on then."

105

"Before you go, you wouldn't know any good hands looking for a position, would you?"

"Who's yer foreman?" Cole cocked his hat back and wiped the grime from his face with the back of his arm.

"Well, it seems I am."

"Nope. Don't know any cowboy worth his salt's gonna work for a tenderfoot who ain't got a foreman. No offense."

Monte considered the man's insight. He'd watched the way Cole handled the men, obviously well respected yet not taking any guff when it came time to work. Sizing up the man, he guessed him to be early or mid-thirties, though the sun and air had leathered his skin. Ruggedly handsome, tough and wiry, he looked as though he'd been born on a horse at the backside of a herd, and Monte liked his honesty. "How would you like the job of foreman yourself?"

"I ain't lookin' fer a change."

"What are you paid now?"

"Well, I ain't a foreman, just a trail boss. I git eight dollars a week."

"I'll make it sixteen. I have a good bunkhouse, a handful of men, and you can hire as many more as you need. The only condition is you teach me what you know."

Now it was Cole Jasper who scrutinized him. "You won't git in the way?"

"Not until I know as much as you do." Monte smiled.

Cole grinned back. "That'll be the day. All right, Mr. Farrel, I'll take it." Monte held out his hand, and Cole shook it firmly. He wheeled his horse around. "Hey, you lame-dog, good-fer-nothin' scoundrels! Anyone wanna stay and work for Tenderfoot here? You'll be answerin' to me."

Several of the men looked at each other and there were a few unsavory comments, but, surprisingly, not a one rejected the offer. Cole was indeed the man he needed. Monte turned Sirocco back to the house.

◆◆◆◆◆◆◆

The branding proved his shrewdness in acquiring Cole Jasper. Monte watched the men rope the new cattle from horseback, then leap down, yank the animal to its back, and immobilize the thrashing legs. The acrid reek of burnt hair merged with the smell of the herd as the hot iron was applied. Then the steer or heifer was released, sporting the half moon bar over the star that showed the animal belonged to his Lucky Star Ranch. With jovial if disrespectful amusement, Cole showed Monte how to use the rope and how to throw it, but he wouldn't allow him near the herd while the men were working. "We got a job to do, Mr. Farrel."

Monte suspected Cole was testing the waters, keeping him to his pledge of noninterference. He held his tongue and returned to the house. After sliding the rope from the saddle, he weighed it out in his hand, opened the loop, then gripped and spun it over his head. Shooting his arm forward, he aimed for the fence post. The rope fell useless at his feet, snagged by his shoulder. He kicked it and left it lying.

Cole could work the ranch and report to him at the end of the day. He strode forward, worked the pump lever, and splashed in the cold water, colder still in the chilly air, then smoothed back his hair and straightened. Maybe he'd go see Abbie. Nothing would cheer him more, nor so effectively take his mind off the cattle business. He looked in the direction of her homestead.

He hadn't seen her since her birthday three weeks ago when they'd danced. That had been a night of revelation. She was no longer Joshua Martin's pretty daughter. She was important to him in her own right. He shook the water from his hands. Two things about that concerned him greatly.

One, Abbie seemed set on delaying her maturity and was not the least interested in being romantically courted, and two, her tears at Blake McConnel's departure had revealed a far deeper attachment than he had believed present. If she cared so deeply for Blake, it wasn't prudent to pursue a relationship. She needed time to sort out her feelings. Practically, it was easy enough to meet with Joshua at the newspaper office. Personally, it took all his strength of will not to ride over to see her.

He entered the house and went to his study. The ledger lay open on his desk, and he looked over the start-up expenses. Four hundred cows and heifers at ten dollars each. That was an outlay of four thousand dollars already. But he'd taken Cole's advice and sent for a pair of prime Durham bulls, five hundred dollars each, and on his own initiative scouted a herd of Shorthorn. He'd buy fifty Shorthorn cows next year and put some beef on his breed. He might not be able to rope a steer yet, but when it came to business, he knew how to turn a profit.

✦✦✦✦✦✦✦

Abbie walked the mare up through the scrub oak turning from green to multihued reds and oranges, clothing the feet of the mountains in color. Above, bright flashes of yellow displayed the aspens' glory, sharply contrasting with the rich dark hue of the evergreens. Of all the seasons, she loved autumn best and breathed deeply the cool September air.

These last weeks had been solitary. Clara was hurt and angry about Blake's leaving, and Abbie had spoken truly that most of the girls from town were not close acquaintances. She and Blake had schooled at the mission, and she was never one for many friends if she had one or two dear. Without Blake, she was left to herself. This, too, she wouldn't have minded, except that she didn't know herself anymore. Too many feelings conflicted.

Again Blake's absence ached inside her as she turned the mare's head up the mountain. Did the land miss him as she did? No. It was nothing but stone, and yet there was an echo of all the times they'd spent here. Only God knew where he was now. She wondered for the hundredth time if she'd done the right thing. She tried to imagine herself setting up a home for Blake. Maybe it would be in a tent in a mining camp somewhere far away. She saw him coming in the flap, taking her in his arms . . .

She shook her head and kicked in her heels, and the horse bounded up the steep incline over the trackless ground. The trees thickened, oak and pine and spruce, and she strained to see the summit of this first ridge. Arching her head back, she murmured, " 'I will lift up mine eyes unto the hills, from whence cometh my help.' "

The woods were silent but for the soft thud of a cone striking the brown, brittle carpet of needles. Had even God tired of her?

Monte and Pa had printed the first edition of the new expanded *Chronicle*, adding a literary column reviewing the best and newest works, a fashion column written by Marcy's mother, Judge Wilson's wife, and a weekly contest. Pa and Monte were pleased with the enterprise, at least according to Pa. She hadn't seen Monte since her birthday. Abbie frowned, skirting a towering moss-covered boulder.

In the pocket of her skirt, the pistol banged her thigh. Since the fires south of them had driven hunting parties of Comanche and Jicarilla Apache into the area—two historically antagonistic tribes—Pa insisted she carry it. She knew how to shoot. He'd taught her when she was twelve. She touched the weapon concealed in her skirt but was not concerned. The Indians had been peaceful and kept their distance. Sightings, but no incidents, were reported.

Abbie had seen none. As though in answer to her thought, from around the rocky projection through the trees came a Comanche brave astride a paint mustang, followed by four more.

Abbie pulled up her mare and sat perfectly still. The stern, black-haired men scrutinized her, and she in turn, them; their buckskin leggings and bare chests, their hair braided with fur strips and feathers, and on their backs the long slender bows and quivers. They looked magnificent. There was something so wild yet indescribably noble in their bearing.

She wondered if she should be frightened, but wasn't. Perhaps her admiration showed, because after a long moment the leader lifted his arm in salute to her, and she smiled in return. Just as swiftly, they turned and vanished back into the shadows, and Abbie released a thrilled breath.

She wished they had spoken. Not that they would have understood each other's words, but she longed to have communicated something. Perhaps she had. Like her, they were part of this place, and perhaps the love of the land had connected them. The look in the brave's eyes as he saluted her had been one of respect. She descended the slope cautiously until she was free of the trees, then gave Shiloh her head and cantered toward town.

She burst into the store. "I have to talk to you, Clara."

Clara hurried behind. "What is it? You look like you've seen a ghost."

"Do I?" Abbie laughed. "No, but I did see a hunting party of Comanche as close as that door."

Clara's eyes widened. "Tell me!"

"I was riding in the hills and had just gotten to the edge of the trees when they came out of the shadows, not making a sound. Five of them, all dressed in feathers and buckskin, and we all stopped and looked at each other—"

"You mean they saw you, too!"

"Yes, and then the leader raised his arm like this and saluted me, and then they were gone. It's the most exciting thing that's ever happened to me!"

"Abbie!" Clara dropped to the chair. "You could have been

killed or worse—captured and carried off!"

"Nonsense! They were no more interested in harming me than I was them."

Clara shook her head, then turned away.

"Are you angry with me, Clara?"

"Why would I be angry?"

"Because of Blake."

Her shoulders sagged. "It's just . . . we're so different. It's no wonder Blake could never see me. You're . . . it's like being a very dim star next to the moon."

"No, Clara . . ."

"I know it's not your fault. It just hurts so much that he thought there was no one else worth staying for."

"Maybe it'll be different when he comes back."

"If he comes back."

"He will. I know he will. Blake is as much a part of this place as I am. He just needs to work out the trouble, and then he'll be back."

"I don't know."

"Oh, Clara, I've questioned myself over and over. What could I have done differently? How could I have kept him from leaving? But in the end, Monte was right. Blake alone is responsible for his decision."

Clara walked to the window. "Have you seen him lately?"

"Who?"

"Monte."

"No. Pa says he got in a herd."

"Judge Wilson's had him out to supper twice this last month. I know it's Marcy's doing. I saw them out on the porch together last evening, and she fairly hung on his arm."

Abbie was surprised how that rankled. "If Monte's foolish enough to fall for her, he deserves her."

"Her father is a judge."

"So what. Monte's hardly a fortune hunter. Not that

Marcy's any great treasure. Oh, that was unkind. You would never have said that."

"I might have thought it." Clara suddenly laughed. "Oh, Abbie, I've missed you. I'm terribly glad those Indians didn't steal you away."

Abbie hugged her. "I have to run. Mama will be looking for me."

"Come again soon."

"I will." Rushing outside, she nearly collided with Monte.

"Why, Abbie, what a pleasant surprise." He removed his hat.

"Is it?"

"Indeed."

"I suppose you've been busy."

"I've been converting my ranch into the real thing and trying to learn how to run it. There's more to being a gentleman rancher than at first appears."

"I imagine there is. Lucky for you Marcy Wilson can provide a distraction from your labor."

Monte's eyebrow raised. "Why, Abbie, I believe you're jealous."

"What a ridiculous notion." She pushed past him and loosened the reins from the post.

"Won't you stay and have supper with me? At the hotel?"

"I'm sorry, Monte, but I prefer my invitations premeditated."

He stared. "Are you turning me down?"

Abbie sweetened her smile. "I need to get home. Mama will worry, and it'll be well nigh dark before I return as it is."

"And you shouldn't be out alone at all. There are reports of Comanche in the area."

"Yes, I met them earlier." Abbie tucked her foot in the stirrup.

"Met them?"

"I saw them in the woods when I was riding. That's what I came to tell Clara."

Monte frowned. "Well, thank God they didn't see you."

"Oh, but they did. Actually they saluted me. I think we understood each other." She pulled herself up.

He grasped the reins. "You wait for me, Abbie. I'm going to escort you home."

Abbie laughed. "What's the matter? Do you think I'm going to run off and live in a tepee?"

"I think you have far less sense than I suspected."

"Well, thank you anyway, but I'm perfectly capable of seeing myself home. Doubtless the Comanche would not have saluted me at all if he'd seen your sour face beside me."

She tugged, but he refused to release the reins. "I'm asking you to wait for me to get my horse."

"Oh, all right."

Monte let go and returned in a moment on the black-socked sorrel.

"You'll miss your supper in town, but maybe Mama will ask you to stay."

"Acquiring supper's not my purpose."

"Then what is your purpose?" Abbie clicked her tongue, and Shiloh stepped out.

"To inform your father of your experience and suggest he not allow you to ride alone until these Indians have left the area."

Abbie pulled up sharply. "You wouldn't!"

"Oh yes, I would. You have no idea of the danger you placed yourself in."

"I was in no danger at all! And I had my pistol if there had been trouble. But they were as noble and honorable as you." She urged Shiloh ahead. "Monte, if you tell Pa not to let me out, I'll never forgive you."

"If I don't say anything, will you promise not to go up into the woods until we know they're gone?"

She considered his offer. "Well, I won't go into the woods."

"Abbie, I mean stay away from any place the Comanche might be. A successful hunt just might include you, too, and you might not think them so wonderful if you have to share a tent with one. I'm sorry if that offends your sensibilities, but you have no idea what that salute meant. It could just as easily have been marking you. Is it possible you don't know what the Comanche do to female captives? How they are tortured and disfigured?"

"I've heard. I'm not a child you need to scold."

"No doubt they noticed that, too. And when they'd made sure you'd never be fit for white society again, they'd no doubt have their way with you."

The idea of being wife to one of those men was not as exciting as simply seeing them in the woods. But Abbie was sure that had not been their intent. Something unspoken but true had passed between them, something Monte didn't understand.

"I think you're wrong, but I'll stay away from the hunting ground. Only don't tell Mama or she'll never let me out again." Digging in her heels, she called, "I'll race you to the bluffs!"

Monte overtook and passed her, the long, smooth strides of his thoroughbred cutting through the prairie. Abbie lay down close to Shiloh's neck and urged her to more speed, shortening the gap but not catching him. Drawing near the bluff, he slowed and brought the horse around. "Better luck next time." Monte smiled. "But you should choose your races more wisely."

Shiloh choked and dropped her head. Abbie knew how she felt. The stallion held his neck arched and back-stepped in Monte's hold, submitting to his master, but only just. She thrilled at the sight and wondered if Monte would ever consent to her riding him.

"I've never seen such a horse! If you raced him he'd be un-beatable!"

Monte dismounted and rubbed the stallion's neck. "He is unbeatable. His sire, Rahjim, was one of the finest."

Abbie slipped down beside him. "What's this one called?"

"Sirocco. He comes from the desert where the siroccos blow hot across the sand."

She stroked the bony head and muzzle. The horse seemed barely contained, as though wild dreams of hot desert nights burned in him still. Solid, sweet-tempered Shiloh had no chance against him. Abbie looked past his head to Monte. "Why haven't you been out to see us?"

"Have I been missed?"

"Of course. Pa enjoys your company, as he has so few well-read friends, and Mama, too."

"And?" The corners of his mouth twitched.

"Well, the chickens haven't really made your acquaintance, nor Buttercup, either, but the little lamb you met on the hill has been bleating dreadfully." Abbie swiped a spiral of hair from her face.

Monte stopped and grabbed her hands. "Are you ever going to grow up, Abbie?"

She smiled impishly. "I suppose it'll happen one day."

His voice grew husky. "Did you miss me?"

"Yes," she whispered.

Monte straightened. "Dusk is drawing on. We'd better go."

Twelve

It felt like the walls were closing in, and the silence, usually welcome, only made her want the breeze and birdsong of the mountainside. Abbie chafed. Why had she promised not to ride? Monte did not understand. He didn't see the Indian affairs as she and Pa did. He was mistaken about her danger; she knew he was. But she had given her word.

She went outside and headed for the line where the clean sheets puffed like roosters' breasts. They smelled of sage and wood smoke. Working quickly, she folded them into the basket, then, while she was near, she gathered the chickens into the pen and locked the door.

Back inside, she peeked into the oven at the sweet rolls, her peace offering for worrying Mama last night. Even Pa was on edge when she'd returned late, though he appreciated Monte's escort. And Monte hadn't breathed a word. In a few days she would be out again, with Mama none the wiser.

The rolls were rising nicely but hadn't begun to brown. She grabbed a shawl and made her way to the slope where the sheep carelessly uprooted the grasses, an irritation to the cattlemen whose herds had the sense to bite the grass off and leave the roots. But she liked the gentle animals even if they were dull-witted, and she called to them as she climbed through the fence for the shortcut. The sheep recognized her voice and pressed against her legs. She pulled open the gate and led them through. Ever since their old dog Rip had died, they'd had to lock them up in the barn for the night or the coyotes would have their way.

They pressed together in the enclosure, and she secured the gate. Pa had the team, so she filled Buttercup's box with fodder and went out. She froze at the door. Five Comanche braves stood directly before her on their mustangs. Monte's words flashed to her mind. Had they marked her for capture? Across the backs of the spare horses were deer and antelope, as well as braces of rabbits, some skinned and some not. They seemed out of place here in her yard, and not at all as they had appeared in the woods, somehow larger, more menacing.

They were nearly motionless, but suddenly the paint tossed its head. Without thinking, she reached up and stroked it, and a curious expression passed over the face of the leader. After a moment, he reached down, untied a brace of skinned rabbits, and handed them to her. Abbie received them. "Thank you." And then with a sudden thought, she added, "Wait," and hurried into the house.

Pulling the hot rolls from the oven, she wrapped a good portion of them in paper, then went back out and handed them up to the brave. He smelled the paper, then nodded and handed the package to the other braves to smell also. The last slipped it into a pouch. They never spoke but wheeled their horses and rode away. Why had they come? Had they been looking for her? Had they felt that same oneness she had experienced yesterday?

In the kitchen she washed the rabbits and prepared them to roast. Mama would have convulsions when she learned she had received them from an Indian right here on the homestead, but Abbie would not disdain his gift. She seasoned them with thyme from the garden and basted them with a little melted butter, then tucked them into the oven to bake. Mixing up a corn bread batter, she poured it into a heavy iron skillet smeared with bacon fat and placed it beside the rabbits. That finished, she wiped the counter and washed out the cloth, then dried her hands on her apron and untied it.

She curled up in the window seat with a book, and soon the aroma from the oven filled the house. What did their gift mean? Had they counted her as one of their own, not a stranger or a threat, nor a usurper? She wanted to believe that. She hoped Monte was wrong and that the government reservations would soon be unnecessary. But she'd heard talk and knew that in one thing he was right. People did not forget the horrors, of which there had been plenty, and as long as fear drove their decisions, there would be no joining of worlds. She jumped up when Pa pulled open the door.

"Why, Abbie," Mama said. "What's that cooking?"

"Come and see."

"Rabbit? Where did you get rabbit?"

"They were a gift." Abbie turned to Pa and explained. Mama's face paled.

Pa patted her shoulder. "It's all right, Selena. We'll likely never see them again, and Abbie was right to treat them with respect. Not only was it the safest thing for her to do, but they're God's children, too, even if their ways are different from ours."

"But think what could have happened!"

"Whatever could have, didn't, so we'll enjoy this meal. Give me a hand in the barn, will you, Abbie?"

As soon as the door was shut behind them, he turned to her. "Did you have your gun?"

Abbie shook her head. "No, Pa. I was right here. I only take it when I go away from the house."

"Abbie, I have great respect for the Indian Nations. But your mama's fears are justified. I don't want you to take this lightly."

"I don't. But I know they wouldn't hurt me."

Pa laid a hand on her shoulder. "Don't let respect replace caution."

Abbie enjoyed the meal more than many she'd had, and as she knelt beside her bed that night, she thanked God for the braves and the people they would feed from their hunt. "I don't expect they know you, Lord, as we do, but somehow I think You know them."

As she lay in her bed to sleep, she saw in her mind the Indian brave and felt again the excitement of what had passed between them. She couldn't wait to tell Monte she had been right.

◆◆◆◆◆◆◆

"But you should have seen his face! Even Pa understood and said I did right. I tell you, Monte, it doesn't matter what people say about the Indians being savages. These men were honorable, and they paid their respects as nicely as any southern gentleman." Abbie set her chin stubbornly, and Monte frowned.

"I don't know that I appreciate the comparison."

"Well, you ought to."

Monte shook his head. "I don't suppose I have a chance of convincing you otherwise, so I won't try. I'm just glad they got their game and left the area."

Abbie brushed the hair out of her eyes as she strolled along beside him. His reaction was far less satisfying than she had anticipated. "How is it coming with your cattle?"

"I understand why your father has sheep."

Abbie laughed. "Not going so well?"

"I made the best investment ever in hiring a foreman. I admit I'd be lost without him and not continue the enterprise."

"What would you do instead?"

"I don't know. There's mining opportunity. But that's a

rough lot, and I've never been a gambler. What I'd really like is to raise thoroughbreds. Arabians."

"Why don't you?"

"I don't think there's a market for that sort of horse out here."

"Well, you could send them back East."

"Not until the railroad comes through."

Abbie frowned. "Do you think it will?"

"Of course it will. It's only a matter of time, and I wouldn't think much time."

"Oh, Monte, it'll spoil everything!"

"Honestly, Abbie. I think you're an Indian at heart. Having the railroad will bring commerce and culture. Freight will no longer be carried tediously by wagon and oxen. It'll enable people to come and go great distances with ease."

Abbie plucked a reddened leaf from the gray knobby branch of a scrub oak. "I suppose there is a positive side."

"Indeed there is. Why, you could easily travel to all sorts of places just to see them."

She smiled. "I'd like that."

"Yes, you would. There's a whole world out there that you haven't begun to experience."

"Only in my imagination." She laughed.

They arrived back at the yard as Pa pulled up in the wagon. "Ah, Monte. Come and help me unload this meat."

Abbie looked into the bed at the slabs of meat from the hogs that Pa and the McConnels had butchered together. She hated the idea of raising the animals just to slaughter them, but the hogs would provide meat all winter and through the spring until they acquired another weaner and began the process again.

Monte pulled himself into the wagon. "If you're interested, Joshua, I could show you how to build a true southern smokehouse and you'd have the best mouth-watering hams and chops you've ever tasted."

"That just might be worth the trouble." Pa took the slab Monte handed down and carried it to the shed.

Two days later they finished the smokehouse back behind the barn. Abbie watched them hang the slabs of meat inside and start the slow wood-smoking. They laughed, coming out grimy and hot, and splashed in the water from the pump. Pa clapped Monte on the shoulder as though he were family. She wondered if it helped fill Monte's void.

The October evening was cold, and the soaking at the pump had the men pressing close to the stove to warm themselves. Abbie smiled as she reached around Monte to gather the dishes.

"Well, Selena," Pa said, crowding into the kitchen as he buttoned his cuffs. "You'll have yourself some fine meat this year."

"Are sure the coyotes can't get at it? I'd hate to give them more of an invitation than before."

"It's safe as can be. Unless they can figure that catch Monte rigged better than I can." He leaned over the pot of corn chowder simmering on the stove. Mama shooed him from the trout browning in the skillet.

"A feast fit for a king tonight," he declared. "Abbie, if you learn to cook half as well as your mama, you'll make some lucky man mighty happy."

She squeezed past and laid the checkered cloth napkins around the table. "Oh, Pa, most men'll eat anything."

"Now, there's a fine attitude."

Mama pulled the johnnycake from the oven. "She already cooks well, as evidenced by the job she did on those rabbits."

Monte frowned. "Well, if it's rabbits Abbie's needing, I hope we can find a better way to provide them. I'll hunt them myself if need be."

Abbie opened her mouth to protest, then relented. How could she explain? Monte was honestly concerned for her welfare, and that gave her a warm satisfaction that rivaled any emotion evoked by the braves.

Thirteen

The first frost dusted the ground as Abbie hurried beside Mama down the boardwalk to Pa's office, but he burst out to meet them with Sterling Jacobs behind him. "How bad is it?"

"They're coming in just now," Mama said. They made their way back through the crowd as the marshal rode to meet the crippled stage. Gus held the team of four with one arm while the other lay bloody in his lap. Riding alongside, then cutting off in front, Marshal Haggerty brought the horses to a stop.

Pa pushed forward. "Where's Crocker?"

"Inside," Haggerty said. "He wasn't as lucky as Gus."

"God have mercy." Pa pulled open the door. Abbie was pressed into the crush as people pushed forward to see. The body lay across one seat, and the two faces across from it were nearly as pale.

"All right, everyone back off!" Marshal Haggerty spread his arms and nudged them back so Gus could climb down from the seat.

Abbie stepped away as Pa escorted a heavy woman with a handkerchief to her nose. Red streaks ran down each cheek and her eyes were puffed. Abbie could hardly blame her.

"Oh, my dear!" Ruth Bailey squeezed through. "Who would have thought..."

"Aunt Ida! Thank the dear Lord!" Eleanor pressed her aunt's hand between her palms as Ruth led her off. The other man in the stage stepped down, straightened his vest, and looked around him.

Abbie watched the muscle in his jaw tense. He was probably as frightened as the Baileys' aunt, but he wouldn't show it. Poor man. He was thin and balding, with the hands of a clerk.

She turned as Pa asked, "Any guesses who did this?"

"Don't need to guess." Gus staggered and leaned against the stage. "It was Hollister."

"So he's added murder to infamy." Pa's tone was as cold as the air.

"And we'll hang him now." Marshal Haggerty led Gus through as Doc Barrow took his other arm.

Deputy Davis galloped in, sliding to a stop before them. "Trail's cold, but there's somethin' to start with." He leaped down and rifled under the driver's seat. "They got the deposits and the post dispatch."

"Actually, we regathered the post dispatch," the passenger spoke. "It's inside, somewhat the worse for wear."

The deputy eyed the loose pile of letters scattered on the floor of the stage, then shook his head. "Someone give me a hand with Crocker."

Wes McConnel shouldered through, his face as ruddy as the thick red muttonchop sideburns. They hauled the body out.

"Someone get them letters."

Abbie stepped forward. With a deep breath, she climbed into the stage and gathered the mail. On one letter she recognized Blake's handwriting and tucked it into her pocket, then hurried the rest to the Post Office.

Back outside, she tore open the envelope.

Dear Abbie,

We're doin' fine. Found some gold but ain't much of it. Mack had a fever, but he's better now. Some of the men get drunk a lot, but we're keepin' our money in our pockets and bringin' it home. Hope you miss me, cuz I sure miss you. Hope you ain't married to Farrel yet.

Love forever,
Blake

Abbie clutched it to her chest and breathed a prayer of thanksgiving. Running directly to the grocer's, she burst in on Clara. "Blake's safe!" She waved the letter and crushed Clara in her arms. "They've even found some gold. And they're keeping their heads. That'll be Mack's doing."

Clara slipped free. "Could I . . . would you mind if I . . . saw the letter? I know it's written to you. . . ."

Abbie handed it to her. Clara read, then looked up. "Married to Farrel? Montgomery?"

Abbie waved her hand. "Blake has gotten that fool notion into his head from the start. Remember when he tried to shoot him?"

"Is Montgomery Farrel courting you, Abbie?"

"Of course not. We've had a picnic or two, and he comes to the house mainly to see Pa. We do walk on occasion, but there's nothing more than that." Abbie felt her cheeks burn.

"Why, Abbie Martin, I declare you're sweet on him!"

"I'm not, either. Monte's nice, and I enjoy his company, but I'm in no rush for romance, I assure you. I've had enough of the whole business for a long while."

Clara handed the letter back. "I have to remember you're younger. I'll be nineteen next week and . . . I'm beginning to want a home of my own and . . . Marty Franklin's been calling on me."

Abbie's mouth dropped open. "Are you saying you're not going to wait for Blake?"

"Oh, Abbie, you read it yourself. Blake loves you. He always has, and even if you never marry him, he'll still love you. I want someone who sees me first, not as a replacement. And Marty is sweet and funny and kind."

"But this is so sudden."

"It doesn't matter. He . . . asked me to marry him last night and . . . I accepted."

"You accepted?"

"Yes. And we're going to be married next month, and as soon as the house is ready, I'll have you to my own home for tea."

"I guess that means you won't slide down the banister anymore."

Clara grabbed her arm, laughing. "Hush! You want Ma to hear?" Then she squeezed her hand. "Besides, Marty's building a loft."

Abbie smiled. "I am happy for you, dear Clara."

But as Abbie rode home in the buggy beside her mother, she felt more dismay than pleasure for Clara. How could Clara marry Marty when she had loved Blake so long? Did she just put away her feelings like linens in a drawer? She helped Mama carry the flour and beans inside, then stood at the window, her wrap over her arm. Mama bustled around her, then took hold of her shoulders.

"Abbie, go have a walk. You're in too much of a fog to help me here."

"Yes, Mama." Abbie pulled her wrap from the hook. As soon as she was out of sight of the house, she broke into a run and rushed across the grassy slopes, the crisp air making her lungs ache until she at last collapsed on the ground and lay back. Her bonnet had flown off, and her hair lay loose, snagged on the dry grasses. She closed her eyes and tried to imagine Clara as Mrs. Marty Franklin. There was nothing wrong with Marty. He was nice as Clara said. But she couldn't believe that Clara loved him, and marrying for any other reason was unthinkable. The cold air carried the scent of woodsmoke, and Abbie felt the changing of the season deep within her. Suddenly a twig snapped and her eyes flew open.

"I'm sorry I startled you." Monte stood over her. "Please don't get up. You're absolutely enchanting lying there in the grass as though you've taken root."

Abbie sat up and pulled the grass from her hair.

"I called at the house, but your mother said I'd find you out here."

"And you have." Abbie smiled. "In total disarray." She untied the strings to the bonnet hanging down her back and lifted it.

"Don't put it on, Abbie. I like it just the way you are right now." He settled to the ground beside her. Abbie dropped the bonnet.

"So tell me, what were you thinking so hard about?"

"Clara's getting married."

"That bothers you?"

"How can she marry someone else when she's loved Blake so long?"

"It happens more often than you know."

Abbie frowned. "Next thing, you'll be telling me you're marrying Marcy Wilson."

His eyebrow raised in humorous surprise. "I will never tell you that. I give you my word of honor."

"It just doesn't seem right."

"You have a fairy-tale notion of marriage, Abbie." He pulled a grass blade from the hair behind her ear. "It's not always the way you want it to be . . . true love ending in lifelong marital bliss. I've no doubt Clara will make a good wife for her husband and be happy in the process. Familiarity breeds affection, and affection can become love."

She shook her head. "Then why does God give us the capacity to fall in love in the first place? It doesn't make sense."

Monte chuckled. "Are you questioning the good sense of the Almighty?"

"No. Just your interpretation of it. I don't believe God plays some divine game of heartbreak. I think He intends us to love with our whole being."

His voice thickened. "I wish that were always so, Abbie," he said, his eyes traveling to her face. "But then, who could ever be joined, short of finding that perfection?"

"I don't know. Maybe people settle for less before they find the one they were meant for."

"You would never settle for less, would you." It was a statement, not a question.

His finger traced the line of her jaw, and Abbie raised her eyes to him. "I hope not."

He turned away. "I came to tell you I'll be going home for a while."

"Why?"

"My sister's husband has been working with our solicitor to sell the plantation, and I'm required to conclude the transaction. I don't know how long it will take and . . ." He smiled. "I didn't want you to think I was avoiding you."

Abbie sniffed. "Why would I think that?"

"You did the last time when you were jealous of Miss Marcy."

"I was never jealous! With whom you choose to spend your time is of no concern to me."

"None at all?" His mouth still smiled, but his eyes deepened.

"I told you I missed you."

"You might miss an old dog or a favorite book as well. Tell me truly, Abbie, will you think of me while I'm gone?"

"Yes, I suppose I will."

"You suppose?"

"I will," she whispered.

He leaned close, and her heart crescendoed. "You'll never be far from my thoughts, Abbie Martin. Nor have you been from the first time I met you."

A strand of hair blew across her face and he reached up to brush it back. The touch of his fingers on her skin awakened her senses, and she caught her breath sharply.

"Perhaps when I return, I'll find a young lady ready to be courted in earnest, instead of a tomboy girl more interested in Indian braves than a gentleman who seeks her affection."

Abbie forced her voice to steady. "But you've no idea how long you'll be gone. Perchance another gentleman will make the discovery first."

Monte grasped her arms and pulled her against him. "Then remember your own words, Abbie, and don't settle for less until you know what I would give you."

She trembled as his hands slipped from her arms to encircle her. "Monte, I . . ."

His lips found hers with passionate determination, and Abbie surrendered. His hands on the small of her back pressed her close, and she felt the firm muscles of his chest. Her fingers slid over his shoulders and caught in the waves of hair on the back of his neck. Gently, he kissed her again, then released her.

"Think of me while I'm gone, and know that every waking moment and every dream I dream will be consumed with you, my darling. Nothing will keep me a moment longer than must be, and when I return . . ." His finger traced her eager lips. "Well, we'll see when I return."

Abbie sat still, her chest rising and falling with ragged breaths. The thought of his leaving now was terrible. Tears burned her eyes, and he gathered her in a soft embrace.

"Now see what I've done?" he whispered. "I should have left

you in childish oblivion, but selfishly I drew forth your womanly response. Forgive me?"

She nodded, laying her head against his chest, and he held her again.

"I'll miss you dreadfully, Abbie."

"I'll miss you, too . . . far more than an old dog."

He threw back his head and laughed, pulled her up, and spun her. Planting his hand on her waist, he waltzed her on the hillside to the music of the wind, then kissed her hand. "Good-bye, Abbie."

The lump in her throat made it impossible to answer, but as she watched him go, she knew that she loved him as perfectly as she had ever dreamed.

Fourteen

Blake looked up as Mack dropped the small bag of gold dust onto the rough table and sank into the chair. "We're barely payin' our way." Mack fondled the measly bag, then tossed it aside. "We'd make better use of our time smithing or workin' any other job than this. Face it, Blake. Whatever gold there was to be found has done been found, and it ain't been us that done it."

"I ain't goin' back broke."

"I should've never brung you in the first place." Mack sounded more regretful than bitter. "And I ain't goin' back without you. But, Blake, you gotta realize when we're whooped. We ain't gonna make it big. We prob'ly ain't gonna make it at all."

Blake ran a finger over the jagged edge of the table. "If you wanna quit, then go on back. I ain't leavin' without gettin' what I came for."

Mack shook his head. "Can't you see it's a lost cause?"

"Ain't no such thing if you work hard enough. I mean to find gold."

Sighing, Mack jabbed his fingers through his hair. "You're just past yer eighteenth birthday and as stubborn as an old mule! We got enough for one more month's provisions. If we ain't no better off when that's done, we're goin' home ... both of us ... if I have to tie you to my horse an' drag you."

"One more month." Blake grinned. He already had two inches on Mack. It'd be a sight for Mack to haul him anywhere.

Blake was up almost before the sun the following morning. The one thought that got him out of bed, that made him keep on when his back was burning with the effort and his hands were raw, that drove him to continue searching, was already consuming his mind. Abbie. He would find what he needed to be able to provide her with everything she desired. He pictured her in his mind, imagined her waiting for him, anticipating his return. Her tears when he left had been all too real. He knew she cared for him even if she didn't know it yet herself, and nothing would stop him from returning, triumphant, to claim her.

Mack stumbled out of the shanty that kept off most of the rain—if very little of the wind—when they slept, then groaned. "You at it already?"

"Yup. It's fixin' to rain, and I intend to use whatever time we got left."

"Want some coffee?"

"Sure." Blake kept sifting the sluice waters. "Bring it out here, okay?"

"Yup."

When Mack went in, Blake stood, leaning back to stretch his tired muscles. The air was cold and the sky dark and threatening. It might be more than rain this time. Could easily snow, being October. He caught his wrists behind his back and rotated his neck. As he did so, his eye skimmed the mountainside above him and snagged on a dark recess he hadn't noticed before.

The rains that caused last week's flash flood must have opened it up. He squinted. It looked to be a sort of narrow crevice. Grabbing the lantern from the porch, he started up the mountain and scaled the ridge. When he estimated he was over the crack, he let himself down and landed close to the opening.

Inside yawned black, and he stooped to light the lantern. It burned with a poor grade coal oil that smoked badly but served its purpose.

Pressing himself sideways into a crack scarcely wider than his chest, he held the lantern before him and squeezed through, ducking to avoid a low projection. After some twenty steps, the passage broadened considerably to the span of three men, and his torch sent flickering shadows across the walls before shining on the prettiest vein he'd ever laid eyes on.

He closed his eyes and prayed. "Thank you, God. I know you gave me Abbie now. I mean to do right by her an' You, all the days of my life." Then quietly and carefully he climbed out and made his way down the mountainside. God had directed them to this claim that contained this cave and led him up here this morning. He would continue to provide.

Mack was standing, annoyed, beside the sluice box holding his coffee when he returned. "You gotta go halfway up the mountain to relieve yourself?" he asked.

"That ain't what I was goin' for." Blake took the steaming cup and swigged the bitter brew. "Mack, I found us a gold mine."

◆◆◆◆◆◆◆

Abbie sat with Tucker leaning on one side and Jeremy the other. At her knees, Emmy and Pauline held the reader as Pauline sounded out the words, her finger inching over the page syllable by syllable. "Long 'I'," Abbie said.

"'Find ... a ... h—ome.'" She looked up. "Like us. The pup ain't got a family."

"Doesn't have. The pup doesn't have a family. But you do. You have one another and Father Dominic and Brother Thomas and Brother José."

"It ain't the same." Emmy lisped her "s" through the gap in her teeth.

Abbie folded her hands in her lap. "It's not exactly the same, but it's a home with people who love you."

Tucker stroked her hand with his fingers. "We ain't got a ma."

Abbie's chest constricted, and she closed the little fingers inside hers. "Well, you have me." As he pressed in closer, she wrapped him in her arm. "And you have Jesus. Remember He told his friends, 'Suffer the little children to come unto me, and forbid them not; for of such is the kingdom of heaven.' Emmy, you have a turn now."

Emmy slid the reader closer. " 'All night the storm ... raged. ...' "

Abbie looked at the faces around her, so young, so trusting. She hated to think what these children might be like were it not for the brothers' care. How the mission came to be there was still a miracle as far as she was concerned. It was there before the town, an outpost of Christianity for the Indian tribes. Father Dominic had come after his predecessor was lashed to a tree and burned by the Indians he came to serve. Now they served the children.

Emmy stammered, "Vor ... vor ... a ..."

"Voracity. It means greed, gluttony. Because of the other dogs' greed, the pup went hungry."

She went on, her lisping voice even. " 'He found a ... place away from the pack and lay his head on his paws.' "

"Thank you, Emmy. And now I have to go." Abbie stood. "But I'll see you all tomorrow."

She pulled on her cape and found Shiloh ready in the stable. Brother José had given her mash, then saddled and bridled her. Abbie led her out. Starting back across the brown prairie, she remembered the one time Reverend Peale had suggested the town families adopt the children. Though no one had openly reproached him, he was bad-mouthed behind his back. Not only were the children foundlings, but they had been raised thus far by Roman Catholic priests, which was not actually true, as only Father Dominic was ordained to the priesthood.

That hadn't mattered so much until one faction headed by Mildred Beatty set up an outcry of contamination, as though the children were tainted by smallpox or worse. It was the first time Rocky Bluffs had been torn by divisions. Previously people took religion as they could get it, from one denomination or another, and mostly considered themselves lucky to have both the brothers and Reverend Peale. It shook Abbie to see people choosing up sides, when all Reverend Peale had intended was to give homes to children in need.

That was the year Mama suffered pneumonia, and so even in the Martins' Irish Catholic family, no orphan came to stay. Reverend Peale never repeated his call, but he spent a good deal of time and strength seeing to their needs and providing the brothers with medical supplies and clothing. And on Sundays he called the townsfolk to charity and faith in the Savior who provides even for the sparrows.

Abbie wondered if the children weren't better off where they were, in the direct hand of God. When her family attended mass at the Mission on Sundays, she would come to tears at the sweetness of the children's voices raised in song and repeating the Latin mass parts, lisps and all. Surely God wasn't divided as they were. She had seen His hand on Reverend Peale as surely as it guided Father Dominic. It was their own limitations that fenced in God, even in a place where people needed one another to survive.

She tightened her grip on the reins. Her hands were cold, her nose and cheeks nipped as she set her face into the wind. With the days so short, she'd be hard pressed to make it home before dark.

Fifteen

Smoke spewed from the stack as hissing steam shrouded the wheels grinding to a stop. The station was amass with people as Monte stepped off the train, stiff and sore from inactivity. The smell of salt air hit him immediately even through the drizzle. He sought and found his sister, Frances, coifed and elegant beside Kendal Stevens. Her husband looked as dandy as ever. How Kendal managed to keep them in their finery, he didn't know.

Frances leaned her cheek forward to receive his kiss, and Kendal pumped his hand, saying, "It's good to see you again . . . great to see you again, although the Wild West seems to agree with you."

"That it does." Monte looked around him at the crowd. They were a queer assortment. Worn-out gentry, gauche new arrivals flaunting ill-gained riches, white trash who had allied with the Federals suddenly raised in status, carpetbaggers come to take their pound of flesh, Negroes with frightened, angry, or sullen eyes thrust into a world they didn't know.

Monte shook his head, forcing a bright tone. "I don't recall seeing so many people in the same place at once. We're rather more spread out in the Colorado Territory. Decidedly sparse, you might say."

"And you must tell us all about it." Frances slipped her arm through his. "But let's hear it someplace warmer."

The cold drizzle soaked his coat as he grabbed his bags and climbed into the carriage that looked as though it had seen much use. It creaked forward as Kendal giddapped the horse, an animal Monte would not have looked at twice. Still, they were riding, which was more than many of the old guard.

"We've found a new place," Kendal told him. "More suitable for a family."

"Is that an announcement?"

Kendal laughed, puffing his chest. "As a matter of fact, yes."

"When?"

"Next April." Frances smiled, but not with the enthusiasm he might expect.

"That's wonderful news. Congratulations!"

"You might experience the same if you ever settled on one woman." Kendal fingered the waxed end of his mustache with a crooked grin.

"Monte's head is too much in his business." Frances brushed the moisture from her skirt. "He hasn't time for romance."

Monte smiled. He needn't verify nor discount either statement. The carriage rolled through the muddy ruts toward a black-shuttered, white brick townhouse, tall and narrow, but more than sufficient.

"Here we are, then." Kendal reined in.

Monte leaned out. "Very nice, Kendal. You keep my sister well."

"It isn't the plantation house. . . ."

"It's better this way." Monte felt the stirring of resentment. How slowly those feelings die. "The place was falling to ruin. You'd have had a time maintaining it. A new start is best."

"Perhaps."

Monte followed Kendal up the front stairs and into the hall. "Very nice indeed. I see Frances's hand everywhere I look."

"Oh yes, I insisted she decorate exactly as she wanted."

Monte nodded. "A wise choice. Not only as my dear sister has impeccable taste, but as you'd never hear the end of it." He winked at Kendal and Frances huffed.

"You'll never change, will you, Monte? Always the tease."

"Would you have me otherwise?"

"I might." She raised her chin. "Now let me show you the rest of the place." She led him upstairs.

Kendal followed with his bags, and Monte asked, "Where's Rawley?"

"Passed on," Kendal said. "Hard to replace a darky like him these days. They're a shiftless lot and expect more than they're worth."

Monte didn't reply. Kendal's flaw was his disparagement of the Negro. Probably better that he have no manservant. Not that he mistreated them; Frances would never condone that, but he didn't consider them as people at all. Monte had seen their humanity very young, and though the reshuffling of the societal order had brought the demise of all he had treasured, he could not dispute the justice. So one built new dreams. His father had been right to send him west.

"I expect you'll want to retire early after your travel." Frances opened the bedroom door and waved him in.

"It was tedious."

"Shall I have your supper sent up?"

"No, no." He took the bags from Kendal. "I'd rather catch up on your affairs."

"Then I'll have supper served, and we'll all make it an early night."

"Frances . . ." Monte caught her arm as she turned to follow Kendal out. "Are you feeling all right? You look pale."

"I'm fine, Monte." She stroked his fingers on her arm. "Always the concerned big brother."

"I don't want my stay to tax you . . . in your condition."

"I've been longing for your return."

Monte paused. Her eyes were shadowed, not so as to raise concern, yet ... there was something. "Well, an early night will do us all good."

◆◆◆◆◆◆◆

Monte stepped out with Kendal from the solicitor's office the following day. Kendal closed the door behind. "Mr. Bernhart is handling this as a personal favor. His fees—"

"Will be paid from the proceeds." Monte started down the walk. "Clarence Bernhart was Father's solicitor. He does not work for the Farrels pro bono."

"Yes, but ..."

"Come, Kendal, let's have an end of it. We'll turn some profit, and that's more than others have done."

"Well, of course. Anyway, we've several weeks before the money clears and everything is completed."

"Yes, I expected as much." His breath fogged in the frigid air as he stepped down into the street, crossed, and remounted the walk.

Kendal kept step beside him. "Frances will be pleased. She was afraid you'd slip in like a shadow and be gone the next day without a chance for her to show you off to her friends, old and new."

"I'll admit I'm eager to return. But as long as I'm here, I'll see everyone I can."

"And satisfy Frances. Thank heaven for that. You've no idea what I had to endure once she learned you were indeed coming. But then it's no secret between us who comes first in Frances's heart."

Monte shifted uncomfortably. "Come, Kendal. Don't speak foolishness. Frances feels she must order my life, as she does yours and anyone else who will let her. Motherhood, I'm afraid, will only accentuate that trait." He was gratified to see Kendal puff again with the shift in conversation. The last thing he wanted to face was Kendal's old envy.

They only had time to wash and dress before supper. As Monte lathered himself in the bath, he fumed again at Kendal's presumption upon Mr. Bernhart. To expect a man to work for nothing when you had even a penny to pay was despicable. No one with integrity would consider it, but Kendal...

He sighed, pouring the pitcher of hot water down his back. Well, Kendal was different. He rubbed himself dry and dressed in his black long coat and tan breeches, wiped his boots up to the knee, and tied on his cravat. He checked himself in the mirror, straightened the gray quilted vest, and went downstairs.

Kendal's other guests, two business associates, were already in the study, and Kendal held out a hand to him. "Ah, gentlemen. Here he is, Frances's illustrious brother and western entrepreneur."

Was the glint in his eye the touch of brandy or something else?

"Montgomery Farrel; Elias McDonald and Frederick Glenn."

Monte didn't recognize either name. He shook their hands in turn and bowed. "I'm honored."

"Certainly the honor is ours," McDonald said. "We've heard nothing but praise of your accomplishments."

Monte waved a hand. "I've merely seen to what was at hand."

"Ho. Methinks he doth protest too much." Glenn laughed and sipped his brandy.

Kendal handed a snifter to Monte and offered the candle to warm it. Monte shook his head and instead held it cupped in his palm, slowly swirling. "Tell me, Kendal ... brandy *before* supper?"

"Things are changing, Monte."

"Ah. And what has my sister to say for that?"

Kendal stroked his mustache, smiling. "Your sister has much to say about everything."

Monte sipped. "He that has ears to hear, let him hear."

McDonald and Glenn laughed rather too raucously, and Monte studied them. Something nagged. They were too smooth . . . too elegant. But then, didn't Kendal look the same? He sipped again. His purpose here was not to monitor his brother-in-law. Probably chasing ghosts anyway.

They were served at supper by a Negro house girl and an older woman . . . ah yes, Dilcey. Monte nodded to her as she filled his glass and she smiled. He turned to find Kendal watching with an ill-disguised smirk. Let him. Monte had thrashed him once on the subject; he'd do it again.

Glenn and McDonald were decidedly vague about their business. Once again Monte bit his tongue. Kendal was having a hard enough time of it with the horrors of reconstruction all around him. He was entitled to run his affairs his way, and Frances seemed none the worse for it. She sat at the end like a beautiful sculpture, ordering everything impeccably. No sign of weariness tonight. She glittered with jewels.

Monte imagined Abbie in just such a sapphire necklace. His chest constricted. No, better he not think of her yet. The ache of longing quenched his appetite, though the fare was superb.

After the meal he declined Kendal's offered cigar but accepted another brandy. The men were growing tedious with their constant questions about his western concerns. Monte drained the last of his brandy and smiled. "Forgive me, gentlemen. But it's been a long day and I have engagements tomorrow."

Sitting at the escritoire in his room, he slid out a sheet of paper and the pen. *My dearest Abbie* . . . His eyes came up to the wall, and he held the pen poised. He could almost smell the scent of her still. What insanity had induced him to behave as he had with her on the hillside? Such insanity he would never do without again. He had almost thought to claim her, but honor refused. His heart rushed. As soon as he returned he would speak for her. The thought alone was ambrosia. His pen returned to the paper and the steady *scritch, scritch* transferred his thoughts to words. Soon he would return. Soon.

Sixteen

Chandler Bridges crowed when Monte strode into the stable. He was a creature of habit, so Monte had expected to see him right where he was and had the element of surprise in his favor.

"Monte, you look incredibly good considering you've been so long from polite society. You've even kept your scalp."

Monte laughed. "I have indeed, though I notice yours is rather diminished."

Chandler stroked his fair hair, then sparred good-naturedly with him. "I heard it rumored you were back. Shame on you for taking two weeks to show up."

"Frances has commandeered my every moment with friends whom I was obliged to entertain with tales of the West."

"Any worth telling?"

"Only the ones I fabricated." Monte chuckled. "I fear my sister will never visit me."

"Then, shame again. You've not grown out of your roguish ways."

"Ah, but I have. I'm a man of commerce and a gentleman rancher."

Chandler shook his head, grinning. "Care to join me on my rounds?" He tightened the cinch under the horse's belly.

"Certainly. I haven't seen the old place in ages. But you

147

must give me a fresh horse. Kendal's nag is near death from the journey here."

"Good horseflesh is dear if you can come by it at all."

"So it appears."

As they rode, Monte noticed the careful patchwork that replaced true maintenance, the fields left fallow. "How do you manage it?"

"It's a bit of a balancing act, but the soldiers never hit us like they did you. Too out of the way, I suppose. Father has had to place himself in a bit of jeopardy with a loan this last year. Rather a sizable one I'm afraid."

"I'm sorry to hear that. But the land is still profitable?"

They rode into the dim November daylight. "It is if we can figure out the labor problems and file all the necessary forms to use our workers . . . and barring any natural or man-made disasters."

"I admire you, Chandler. You and your father are the fighters. You won't allow the Yankees to master you."

"We're all changed, though. Even those who didn't fight the war have been scarred and even maimed, though not physically. It's as though the North is not content with tactical victory but must rip out our soul as well."

"I'm sorry." Monte clapped a hand on his shoulder. "Being removed from it all these months, I almost forgot how it is here." He let his gaze settle on the hazy horizon beyond the gray fringe of barren trees. This place had been as much a home to him as his father's plantation, the families as thick as true relations, and closer now with the debt of honor that lay between them.

Monte never forgot that Chandler's father had saved the life of his own in the battle of Seven Pines when the Confederate forces were driven back. Nathan Bridges had stood between Monte's father and enemy fire as he dragged him, injured, from the field. Monte sighed. "I must say it is a different life in the Colorado Territory, new and exciting to be so free and prosperous."

"I'm glad for that. But don't get me wrong, there's plenty to celebrate still, and we never miss an opportunity if we can help it. As a matter of fact, we're having a bit of gaiety tomorrow night in honor of my sister's engagement."

"Which sister would that be?"

"Aileen."

"And who has the honor of her hand?"

Chandler sent him a sidelong glance. "Whom would you guess?"

"Surely not Duncan?"

"The very same." Chandler laughed.

Monte whistled with surprise. "I thought your father swore never to give the hand of his daughter to that prankster."

"She'll have none other, and Father hasn't the fight left in him. Besides, for all his faults, Duncan is of the old guard and a far superior choice to any of the new rabble who would seek her hand." He frowned. "Aileen is the least of our worries. It's Sharlyn who's really causing concern."

Monte reined in. "Not meek, sweet-tempered Sharlyn, who wouldn't say boo to a horsefly?"

"I'm afraid she's too gullible for her own good."

"How so?"

"It's rather an involved situation that goes back to Father needing the loan. There's a certain blackguard who would get his hands on our land by any means. He first tried to buy it outright for an insulting price, and when Father sent him packing, he began to make trouble with our people—the workers, I mean.

"Learning of the loan, he then tried to purchase the note, no doubt intending to call it immediately and force the sale. Thankfully, Mr. Rochester at the bank would never stab an old friend and refused to turn over the note for any profit."

Monte's anger flamed.

"Failing to achieve his ends, this scoundrel began to pay court to Sharlyn."

"Your father received him?"

"No, indeed. But, Monte, things are different now. Let's face it, if a girl wants to see a man, she'll find a way whether or not it's approved by her family."

"I can't believe that of Sharlyn."

"She's bewitched."

"She must be. How can she go against her father in this?"

"She doesn't realize the intricacies, and Father cannot bear to break her heart by revealing the mercenary nature of his attention. We're hoping the fool will betray himself before we must lay her heart open to the reality. As it is, she'll hear nothing against him. Perhaps your coming will prove a great boon."

"How so?"

"Sharlyn was always inordinately fond of you."

"Fond? More afraid than fond, I think."

"That was not fear, Monte; it was awe."

"Well, whatever it was, I rarely got a word out of her. But then she was young."

"Not so very. She's twenty, you know. Just seems younger, being so petite and shy." Chandler nickered to the horse and it stepped forward and Monte's followed. "As a matter of fact, I thought I'd have a brother of you by now."

Monte quirked an eyebrow. "How so?"

"Your pledge, man."

"What pledge?"

"To marry Sharlyn."

Monte threw back his head and laughed. "Good heavens. I'd forgotten all about that." He shook his head, sobering. "It comes back clearly enough, though. I recall the expressions on our fathers' faces. I'd never seen them so long, so filled with angst, yet trying with all that was in them to hide it. I tell you,

Chandler, I'd have signed anything. I wonder what happened to that note."

Chandler shrugged. "I'll wager Father holds it still."

"Well, at fifteen, and with the war starting, marriage to anyone was the farthest thing from my mind."

"What about now? Twenty-four is none too young to consider it."

"And I may yet. But we both know Sharlyn would faint dead away if I ever approached her with it."

Chandler chuckled. "She's grown up a bit, you'll see." His smile faded. "Too much, maybe."

Monte was quiet. "Well, I'll be glad to talk to her if you think it'll help."

"Do that, Monte. If she'll listen to anyone, it would be you."

"You far overestimate me."

"Not where it comes to the ladies. And don't bother contesting that. I've known you too long ... and heard you claim hearts with words alone. The worst of it is, you did it without trying."

Monte laughed, glad that Abbie was not there to hear. The thought of her sweetness put away all previous ventures. He was closer to matrimony than Chandler knew, but until he spoke for Abbie, he'd keep that to himself. He turned the horse's head. "Well, I may surprise you yet."

◆◆◆◆◆◆

Abbie stirred and gazed out the window. The snow lay deep on the fields and another storm threatened. It seemed this would be a wet year. Sometimes they went a full month or more between blizzards, but already this month it had stormed three times. She hated being confined to the house and hadn't been able to get to the mission for over a week.

Closing the book that lay across her knees, she sighed. If only Monte would write again. The letter he sent just after arriving in South Carolina had been filled with details of all that he was seeing, things he knew she would love to hear, as well as veiled references to his affection. Already, it was limp and ragged from being opened again and again each night and clutched to her heart. She missed him so much! Would he be home for Christmas? Oh, gracious! How would she survive the time until he came back?

When Pa came home, he winked and pulled an envelope from his coat pocket. "A little something from Montgomery Farrel, I'd wager."

"Thank you, Pa." She reached for it with studied nonchalance.

"What does he have to say?"

Mama poked him. "Don't tease, Joshua. Abbie can fill you in after she's read her mail in privacy."

Abbie went to her room and carefully worked open the envelope.

My dearest Abbie,

I spoke more truly than I knew in saying I would miss you dreadfully. Not a day goes by that I don't wish I was at your side, there or here it matters not. How I miss our chats and all the quaint ideas you share so candidly. More painfully, I miss feasting my eyes upon your sweet and glowing face, and the feel of your delicate fingers tucked into my arm. I cannot close my eyes without seeing you lying in the grass, your hair in wayward disarray. If I continue like this, I'll go mad; therefore, I shall now describe to you how I occupy my days.

There are suppers and parties at which I see as many of my old friends as possible. It is strange how time does not separate friends, don't you think? I have not seen Milton Rochester for three years, since he went to medical school and I moved west, but when we were reunited last night, it was as though no time had passed. And, of course, Chandler Bridges is like a brother to me still.

The sale is nearly completed, and I have only a handful of other concerns before I'm free to return, but I feel honor bound to spend some time at least with my mother's relations and various others who have been kind over the years. Still you must know that each moment away is bittersweet. Had I the courage I would have taken you with me in spite of propriety, but then I would not damage your reputation, which has remained intact in spite of the interesting array of skills you have acquired.

Abbie could almost see the crooked grin and the teasing glint in his eyes as he wrote that, and she caught her breath as the longing rose fiercely within her.

I must close now, and as I will be traveling from place to place the next few weeks, I will reluctantly not ask you to write back, but will anticipate instead the response you will prepare for my return.

My greatest affection,
Monte

Tears stung her eyes as Abbie clutched the letter to her chest. What a remarkable ability he had to make her heart sing and ache in the same moment. If only he would come home!

Seventeen

Aileen Bridges' gala was well attended, Monte noted, and he nodded to those he knew. It had been some time since he was surrounded by such grace and class as assembled there. And he was not unaware of the figure he cut and the eyes upon him. It recalled him back to the days before the war. Even then he'd been aware of his stature and attractiveness, but in the years that followed . . . the growing into manhood through the madness . . . he'd set aside less serious thoughts than those of commerce and survival.

Now, with his love for Abbie awake in his breast, he felt everything more acutely. The beauty of the women, the music of the orchestra . . .

"Ah, here you are, Monte." Chandler pumped his hand and lowered his voice. "Come, let me present you to Sharlyn. She's in a state since Father refused to allow Denman to escort her tonight."

Monte followed him to where Sharlyn sat on the plush settee. She had changed very little from the delicate girl he remembered. Her eyes lit with surprise and delight as he bowed over her hand. She trembled. Poor, shy girl. "How very nice to see you, dear Sharlyn, and how lovely you look tonight."

She blushed but surprisingly answered quite calmly, "Thank you, Monte. This is a tremendous surprise."

"I'll leave you two to get reacquainted." Chandler bowed.

Sharlyn flipped open her fan, for the storm outside and the fires at either end made the crowded room stuffy. "I didn't know you were back."

"Only temporarily. I had business to attend."

"It matters not the reasons that bring back an old friend," she murmured.

He stared. "Forgive me for asking, Sharlyn, but when did you learn to speak?"

Her sweet laugh tantalized him. "Oh, I suppose it came on me gradually."

"May I?" He took the seat beside her, recalling Chandler's words. She wasn't despondent now. Perhaps he could distract her after all. "How is it that I find such a delightful creature unescorted tonight?"

Her cheeks flamed. "The gentleman who would have done so was not admitted."

"Not admitted? Why?"

"Father wouldn't have him."

Monte handed her a glass cup of punch from the tray offered him by the servant. "That seems unlike Nathan Bridges to deny you anything." He waved the man away.

"I can't understand it. From the start, Father has taken a dislike to Robert Denman." Her eyes were like cool green pools as she glanced at him and then quickly away. Monte wondered if he'd ever seen them directed to him before.

"Surely he must have his reasons. But whatever the case, Robert Denman's misfortune is my advantage. Would you do me the honor of a dance?"

He led her out to the floor among the other dancers. All the gentility of this place settled upon him as he danced. He found her a far more sanguine companion than ever before. What had been crippling bashfulness was now demure reserve. She was pleasant company, and he commandeered her for the next dance as well. If his thoughts were really a thousand miles away, and his heart as well, he didn't let on.

"Tell me about Colorado." Sharlyn arranged her skirts as he returned her to the settee in the alcove by the window.

"It's wide open, rough and broken and dry, mainly gold and brown until you come near the mountains, which seem to erupt from the prairie like a mighty wave, causing the land all about to ripple into scrubby wooded hills. There are very few trees outside of the mountains, mainly one variety of pine, but there is a rugged beauty that is incomparable, unless it is to South Carolina you compare it."

"And the town in which you live?"

"Rocky Bluffs is a busy place for the area, but you'd laugh to see what distance there is between the homesteads, some an hour apart, others even more. The cultural activities are somewhat limited, though there is talk of an opera house. Only talk I imagine. Unlike the mining camps that sport cheap imitations of theatrical arts, Rocky Bluffs maintains a surprising discrimination. Because of that they have no theater at all." He laughed. "But the businesses are multiplying as more people seek the opportunity of the West."

"And what is your business, Monte?"

"I have pokers in several fires. But the newest is cattle ranching."

Her eyes widened. "Is it really the way they portray it with the cowboys and the cattle?"

Monte smiled. "I don't know how you've seen it portrayed, but the cowboys are a singular breed. I have over a dozen working for me, and there is no end to the distraction they provide."

Sharlyn folded her hands in her lap. "And the ladies?"

"Western ladies are a hardy lot, yet surprisingly genteel as well." He thought of Abbie's graceful bearing contrasted with the image of her lying in the grass the day he had kissed her. "They're like thoroughbred horses, delicate to behold yet strong enough to ride the wind."

Her eyes were shining.

"I know one who can track seventeen different animals, which by the way is more than I know, and catch a fish with a spear she whittles herself."

"Please tell me more. What's her name?"

"Abigail Martin. But she's known as Abbie. She met a whole band of Comanche warriors in the woods one time and was not in the least afraid, but thought it a great adventure. And that, even though she's two years younger than you."

"How fine that sounds. You must be very happy there. I hear it in your voice."

"I admit it agrees with me."

"You'll return soon?"

"I'm not sure when I'll have things wrapped up here, and I intend to visit as many friends as possible. I would imagine I'll see out the end of the month, but I want to be home by the holidays at least." He imagined a Christmas proposal to Abbie.

"Katherine Devereaux will be holding her annual Christmas Eve gala. It's a pity you'll miss it."

"Perhaps by then you'll be allowed to spend it in the company of your Mr. Denman." Monte watched her reaction.

Blushing fiercely, she whispered, "Yes, I hope so." But her eyes flicked up to him again and retreated.

"Tell me about this lucky young man. What's his business?"

Sharlyn hesitated. "I . . . I don't really know. It all seems quite mysterious, but I believe he doesn't want to tire me with unromantic details."

"More likely the poor devil finds he can't think straight when caught in the gaze of your lovely eyes."

Those very eyes stared up at him in surprise, too astonished to look away. "Well, I . . . I don't know about that. . . ."

"Oh, come now. Surely he's mentioned the spell he must find himself under whenever you turn his way?"

"Monte . . . I declare I don't know what to say."

"My apologies. I didn't intend to make you uncomfortable. Whatever sweet words of his have captured your affection, it's none of my affair. Please forgive my impertinence."

Her gaze fell demurely to her hands still folded in her lap. "There's no need at all to apologize, I assure you," she whispered. He bowed over her hand and felt her tremble once again.

✦✦✦✦✦✦✦

The message was vague, but its urgency unmistakable, and Monte hurried down the stairs to find Frances. "There's some trouble at the Bridgeses'. I don't know if I'll return by the supper hour, so please don't wait on me."

Frances glanced up from her sewing, some lace thing for the baby, no doubt. "It's not even noon. What possible trouble could keep you from supper? I've planned tonight's company for two weeks. If you're not here to escort Mary Saunders . . ."

"Frances, I don't know what's happened. I only know I'm urgently requested."

"Well, you're urgently requested here, too."

Her pout reminded him not to push. For all her twenty-one years, she seemed not a day over eight. That was partly his fault. Father hadn't the heart to chastise her after the war. In fact, he'd hardly noticed her. It was to Monte she had turned for everything, wheedling and simpering, then fuming and pouting until he gave in, as he inevitably had.

Once again, he buckled. He kissed her cheek. "Set my place, dear. I'll do my best." He hired a cab to take him out to Willowdale. He was admitted and shown to the study, where Chandler paced. "What's happened?"

Chandler gripped him by the arm and pulled him in, closing the door behind them. His face was haggard as he took a note from his pocket. "We intercepted this on its way to Sharlyn from Denman."

Monte took the note and read.

My Darling,

The time has come for us. I cannot stand another day away from you and will no longer be put off by your impossible hopes of convincing your father to let us be wed. He will and must accept it when the deed is done. You have promised to trust me in this, and I tell you that we must steal away this very night. I shall await you at the normal hour.

Yours passionately,
Robert

"Good heavens. The man's determined."

"The man's dead."

"What?" Monte searched his friend's face.

Chandler took back the note. "When Father found this, he flew into a rage such as I've never seen."

Monte had witnessed the rages of Nathan Bridges. He could well imagine this one.

Chandler crumpled the note. "Monte, Denman didn't stand a chance."

"You're not telling me Nathan . . ."

"Denman was skulking in the barn, waiting to see that his missive was delivered. I saw none of it myself, but Isaiah reported it all. He swears Father gave him time to prepare. . . ."

"Then that will stand at the inquiry."

"There won't be one."

"What are you saying?"

"I ran when I heard the shots. Besides Isaiah, I was the first one to them. I thought Denman's bullet had also found its mark, but . . . Father was struck down by a hemorrhage in the brain. Doctor Brown can't say he'll recover."

Monte stood incredulous.

"He's barely able to speak, and his strength is dwindling. He asked me to send for you."

"Why?"

Chandler shook his head. "I don't know. Will you come up?"

"Of course."

The room was dim, but even so, Monte was shocked by the sight of Nathan Bridges, always imposing and proud, now lying limp and pale. He was a man of fiery temper, and Monte had often wondered how he could have produced such mild-mannered offspring. Nathan raised a trembling hand, and the doctor nodded.

Monte sat in the chair beside the bed. He tried not to notice the drool from Nathan's sagging mouth.

Almost inaudibly, Nathan Bridges spoke. "Your father was my best friend."

Was the man wandering? Monte nodded. "He felt the same for you, sir."

Swallowing, Nathan worked his mouth. "I have little time left. Listen now."

Monte drew up closer to hear him.

"Sharlyn must never know what's happened this day. She could not live with it. . . ." He drew a ragged breath. "Your father and I spoke of a match between you and my daughter. You recall the pledge?" His eyes probed.

Monte began to sweat. "It was a wartime oath . . . in the event you didn't return. . . ."

"It was a pledge. I am asking you now to honor it. Marry Sharlyn."

Monte's throat turned to sand.

"Take her away from here. She's loved you since she was a child. She'll accept your proposal." He closed his eyes, and at first Monte thought he had no more to say, but then the man gathered his strength. "It is God himself who brought you back here in time." The breath left his chest in a low wheeze, and he raised his hand faintly again. "It must be today . . . now . . . before she learns . . ."

Again Monte wondered if Nathan was delirious, hoped it were so, but the eyes suddenly cleared and burned into him.

"Will you do this for all that our families have been to one another, by your honor as a gentleman and your father's son?"

Oh, God! Nathan called upon his honor. What of Abbie? What of the life they would have together, the love that even now burned so fiercely in his chest? *Oh, God! How can I turn my back on that?* He recalled his own words to her. *"The ability to do what one must, even against one's heart; that is the honor I understand."* Monte shuddered. He had never meant the words prophetically.

But he suddenly understood what was being asked of him. He was bound by honor, by the debt his family owed this man, and by his own pledge. A noble cause, he had called it. Preservation of what mattered. He closed his eyes.

What would Sharlyn do if she knew her father had killed the man coming for her and himself in the effort? How would she live with it, she who could bear to hurt no one, who could scarcely face praise, let alone this shame. There was desperation in this house that for reasons known only to the Almighty, he alone could ease. All that Nathan Bridges had stood for, fought for, all that Monte's own father had believed in, was wrapped up in the honor that required him to accept.

"I will." His voice was blank, but it was done. His pledge given once again, and Abbie lost to him.

Nathan Bridges sank into the pillows and smiled thinly. "Go now and find your bride."

Monte held himself straight as he walked out.

"Monte, I had no idea. . . ." Chandler faltered outside the door. "Sharlyn is a wonderful girl . . . I think she'll make you a fine wife. . . ."

Monte nodded. He had to get his mind cleared in order to accomplish what he must. "Do you know where she is?"

"In the garden. She knows nothing. Father insisted he speak with you first."

Monte wished Chandler would not look so closely. He knew him too well.

"We'll hold the ceremony immediately in Father's room, as he desires."

Again Monte nodded. That was good. Get it accomplished before he had time to think of what it meant.

"Give me a moment, will you?" Monte slipped into the office before going to the garden. There was one thing he must do before he saw Sharlyn. He would not fulfill his pledge without first bringing an end to whatever expectations he had put in motion before coming, lest he prove faithless and false to both Abbie and Sharlyn.

With a hand he barely kept steady, he took paper and pen. He had intended to write Abbie tonight, but, God help him, not like this. Just seeing her name in ink on the paper made him want to crush and throw it away, to run upstairs and refuse. Nathan would understand. He would have to. Sharlyn . . .

Monte closed his eyes, and the pain in his heart seared like a branding iron. Yet he had known Sharlyn too long to deny the wreckage this would make of her spirit. It was not in her to bear guilt. He gripped the pen with grim resolve. *Dear Abbie, Do you recall our first discussion, when we spoke of honor and its purpose? You know—*He refrained from adding "my dearest"—*that I must follow that honor wherever it leads. Therefore, for reasons which I cannot disclose, I am married to another. Please know that I remain ever your faithful servant, and my heart will think of you always. Most sincerely, Monte.*

It was inadequate. Wholly so. He concealed the paper in the envelope and recorded the address. Then he took another sheet and hastily penned: *My dear sister and Kendal, Events have transpired that have changed my—*He almost wrote "life"—*plans. You will rejoice to know that I have taken Sharlyn Bridges as my wife* *and plan to leave immediately for a European excursion. I will send for my bags. Please see that the letter included is posted to Rocky Bluffs, Colorado Territory, at your earliest opportunity. This is important. Wish me well, Monte.*

There. He would not need to face Frances or withstand her scrutiny. His secret was safe. He scrawled the number and street and stepped into the hall. "Here, lad."

"Yessuh?" The young Negro boy came close.

"Take the letter to this number and see that it is delivered directly into the hands of Mrs. Stevens."

"Yessuh."

Monte pressed a coin into the boy's palm, then setting his face, he strode toward the garden. There he found Sharlyn with her white blond hair and lashes, green eyes, and flawless rose-petal complexion seated like a beautiful fairy amid the leafless trees. He slowly drew in his breath. Sharlyn must never know that his request was insincere. Forcing a smile, he approached.

"Monte!" Her smile was instantaneous. "How nice of you to come."

He bowed over her hand, beginning the role he would play from then on. "You are the fairest rose in the entire garden."

The color went clear to the roots of her hair. "There are at present no roses in the garden."

"The season matters not. Were it summertime with every bush in full bloom, still you would be fairer." He sat beside her on the cold stone bench and heard her indrawn breath. Forcing himself not to think of the consequences, he spoke gently. "I have two things to tell you. One, I fear, will bring you grief, and one, I pray, great joy."

Her smile faded. "Why, Monte, what is it?"

"I'm afraid your father has suffered a hemorrhage and will perhaps not have long to live."

Her hands flew to her face.

"Therefore the decision that's upon you must, and I apologize, be made in haste."

"What decision?" Her voice was tremulous.

He lifted her tiny hand in his, noting how soft and fragile it appeared. The hand of a child. "It's your father's wish that . . . you and I be wed. I would consider it a tremendous honor if you would consent to be my wife." Monte was satisfied that his tone was sincere, and he hoped Sharlyn could not detect the agony those words had caused him. How many times he had dreamed of saying them to Abbie! How would he ever make Abbie understand? Could she ever understand?

Sharlyn stared.

Bringing her hand to his lips, Monte kissed her fingers. "I know it's someone else you hold in your heart . . . but I'll try to be all that you hoped for. . . ."

"Oh, Monte, you're wrong. It's not that way at all! I just never dreamed that you would ask me!" Tears started in her eyes as she whispered, "I have loved you forever."

The irony clawed at his heart, and he felt compassion for her as he gazed on her tearstreaked face. "And you accept?"

"Oh yes!"

It was done. Part of him had hoped, had dared to believe that she would refuse him, but she had not. He stood and raised her to her feet. "I must prepare you; your father is not as he was. But his desire is that we be wed immediately in his room. Are you able to face that?"

"I can face anything now," she murmured, allowing Monte to lead her upstairs to her father's bedchamber. She ran at once to his side, bending low, the tears streaming down her cheeks.

Nathan smiled weakly. His color was gray, and it was clear he was fading fast. When her weeping persisted, he mumbled, "Not supposed to be sad. You'll marry Monte?"

"Yes, Father. Gladly."

"And you'll leave tonight."

"No. I couldn't leave you."

"You'll leave tonight." He addressed himself to Monte. "Take her abroad. Be frivolous."

Monte barely had time to nod before the minister arrived and was ushered into the dim, still room. It was a brief ceremony and subdued, and when instructed to do so, Monte leaned down and kissed Sharlyn gently, seeing at once the radiant joy in her eyes. Nothing would ever be the same for him again, and he prayed God would give him the strength to accomplish what honor had demanded.

◆◆◆◆◆◆

Frances threw the letter to the floor. How could he! Monte married? And to Sharlyn Bridges? Why, she was no more fit for Monte than . . . than . . . Oh! She clenched her fists at her sides. And to go off secretly without so much as including her in the ceremony. How like Monte to shun the pomp his wedding should have held. But to exclude her altogether . . . And the dinner guests would be arriving any moment. She kicked the envelope, and it slid to Dilcey's frightened feet.

"Take care of that trash. And here . . ." Frances scooped up Monte's note and crushed it without reading further. She didn't care what apologies he made. She now saw very clearly what place she had in her brother's life.

Kendal came in the front door and nearly stumbled over Dilcey. "Good heavens." He glanced at Frances. "What on earth are you . . ."

"Mizz Frances, there's a letter in he'ah. . . ."

"Burn it! Take it to the stove right now and burn it!"

"Frances." Kendal took hold of her shoulders.

"Burn it!"

Dilcey rushed for the kitchen.

Frances worked her mouth to voice her hurt and outrage to Kendal as he gripped her shoulders in alarm, but her thoughts grew fuzzy, and she collapsed into his arms.

Eighteen

When Christmas had long passed and all of January as well with still no word from Monte, Abbie fretted. Where could he be? He had said he would be visiting relatives, but this was too long! Taking her cape, she wrapped it about her. "I'm going out, Mama. I won't be long."

"It gets dark early, Abbie."

"I'll be careful."

She hurried Shiloh over the brown, frozen ground to Monte's house. She had not been here since the first time they dined together. Instead, Monte had become a regular in their home. She dismounted and approached the door. James answered her knock as he had before. "Yes, miss?"

"Can you tell me please when Mr. Farrel is expected to return?"

"I couldn' say, miss. But maybe Mr. Jazzper, he knows."

"Where can I find him?"

"He'd be in the barn or the bunkhouse."

"Thank you." Abbie found Mr. Jasper as he strode from the barn almost into her arms.

Startled, he steadied her and apologized. "Pardon me, miss. I'm not lookin' where I'm goin'."

"That's all right." Abbie smiled. "Mr. Jasper I hope?"

"That's right." He pulled off his hat.

"Could you tell me when you expect Mr. Farrel to return?"

"'Fraid not. Haven't heard from him in some while."

Abbie sighed.

"Is there anything I can do for you? I'm handlin' things while he's gone."

"No, thank you. It can wait."

"Would you care to leave yer name?"

"Abbie. Abbie Martin."

"I'll tell him you called, Miss Martin."

"Thank you."

She felt Cole Jasper watch her mount and when she turned, his eyes were still on her. He replaced his hat as she kicked in her heels.

◆◆◆◆◆◆◆

After dickering with Clara's father over the eggs she had brought him, Abbie made her way to Pa's office. February had passed without Monte's return, and still no letter had come. No matter how hard she tried to put him from her mind, she couldn't. She felt dull and empty without him.

As she pushed open the office, warmth enveloped her. Pa looked up from the press, his fingertips black and a smear on his cheek. "Aha. Just the sunshine we were needing."

She handed him the basket. "Mama says for you to share and not make Mr. Jacobs beg."

Sterling Jacobs looked up from the table where he was sorting letters into the type boxes, assisting Pa and learning the business. Pa peeked in at the muffins and breathed deeply. "Tell your mama she's lucky I'm a Christian man, or he'd not have a crumb." He winked at her.

Back outside, she stopped short and gripped the post as the stage pulled up in a cloud of dust. Her heart nearly pounded her ribs when Monte climbed down, resplendent and even more handsome than ever. With her breath catching in her throat, she refrained from rushing forward and throwing herself into his arms, but before he saw her, he turned and helped someone out of the coach behind him.

Abbie stared at the delicate creature with emerald eyes and hair so pale it was almost colorless. She was dressed in a green velvet cape with a fur-trimmed hood. Could this be Frances? She didn't resemble Monte at all.

As he tucked the dainty girl's hand into his arm, Monte looked up. His face revealed for an instant an inexpressible emotion, but it was swiftly veiled and he smiled. It was not the smile she had dreamed of all these months. It was indescribably vacant and mirthless.

He turned to receive the bags and trunks being handed down to him, then called to a boy and paid him to load the baggage into a wagon. His companion's gaze found her, and Abbie felt herself recognized. They approached.

"Monte," Abbie breathed.

"Hello, Abbie." He took her hand and bowed over it stiffly. "May I present my wife, Mrs. Sharlyn Farrel."

For a terrible moment, Abbie thought she might faint as the blood rushed from her face. Lungs that had never failed her before suddenly refused to breathe, and she stood like a statue, inanimate and stone cold.

She forced a greeting, not sure what she said to the tiny person who was Monte's wife, and then she left them behind, moving one foot in front of the other until she reached the mare, mounted, and dug in her heels. Clinging by sheer reflex, she flew across the plain, the angry sobs exploding from her like a torrent bursting a dike. "How could he! Oh, God, how could he?"

Abbie swiped the tears from her eyes, but they filled again. She kicked her heels in, and Shiloh lunged and panted, nostrils flared. The frozen air hung in droplets from her muzzle as her sides began to heave. Abbie paid no heed to where she was, the tears blinding her. Suddenly a windbreak loomed, and the mare veered. Abbie landed hard. Pain shot through her head, then a welcome stupor covered everything as the first dry pellets of snow began to fall.

At first the places being probed seemed disconnected from her body, but then she recognized the pressure on an arm, a leg. When the hands reached behind her neck, she forced her eyes open. The man smelled of leather and tobacco. His breath fogged over her face as he leaned close to examine the swelling at the back of her head. She tried to speak but only managed a moan.

"Don't be movin', now, till I see nothin's broke." His fingers moved across her collarbone to the shoulder on each side. "I reckon I can lift you."

Abbie tried to place him. She had been close to him before; the eyes, the weathered skin . . . Cole Jasper. Monte's foreman. She panicked. Where was she? She struggled to see past his shoulder as he lifted her, but her eyes would not focus. "Please . . ." Why wouldn't the words come?

"Don't fret. I'll git you home."

She relaxed. As he thrust her onto the horse, the pain in her head surged and waves of sickness rolled over her.

Cole pulled himself up and held on firmly. "All right?"

She tried to nod, then lay against his chest. He shielded her from the snow all the way to the homestead and carried her to the door. Mama thrust it open.

"Took a fall from the horse, ma'am. Don't seem to have nothin' broke, but she's mighty cold. I'm thankful I was lookin' fer strays, or no one mighta been out that way fer a long while."

"Oh, dear Lord . . ."

Cole laid Abbie on the sofa. "I'll fetch the doc. I don't reckon you want to leave 'er."

"You're so kind, Mr. . . ."

"Cole, ma'am. Cole Jasper." He tipped his hat, then swung back into the saddle.

Abbie felt like a rag doll as her mama removed the wet clothing and dressed her warmly. Rather than clarifying, everything seemed to be dimming, a confusing hodgepodge of motion and shadow. Of course it was a dream. A terrible, impossible dream. She slept and woke. Men's voices. Mama's cool hand on her cheek. Then sleep again.

•••••••

Monte turned as Cole was shown into the library. "Where have you been?"

"Mr. Farrel, if you wanted a welcoming party, you shoulda said when you'd be comin'."

"The other men checked in hours ago."

Cole fingered the brim of the hat he held. "I've been doin' a bit o' rescuin'."

Something in Cole's manner caught Monte short. "Oh?"

"That young Miss Martin that come lookin' fer you the other day took a fall out round Templeton Gap."

Monte stood as though Cole had struck him.

"Got a good knock and purty near froze. I fetched the doc."

"What is it, Monte?" Sharlyn's skirts rustled as she entered.

Monte's mouth felt like chalk. "Cole, this is my wife, Mrs. Sharlyn Farrel."

His eyes widened. "A pleasure, ma'am."

"And for me, Mr. Jasper. Monte's told me wonderful things about you."

"That right?" Cole cocked his head.

Ordinarily, Monte would have come back with something cutting, but his temple was throbbing and he gripped the brandy decanter.

"Monte?"

He turned to Sharlyn. "You remember the girl you met in

173

town this morning? Cole found her unconscious in the snow."

"Is she all right?" Sharlyn faced Cole.

"I reckon so. But it's lucky I wandered up that way or she'd be a goner by now, I guess."

Monte winced. "Well, thank God you were there. We'll discuss business tomorrow."

"Yes, sir." Cole tipped his hat to Sharlyn on his way out.

Monte recoiled at Sharlyn's touch on his arm, then caught himself. "I'm sorry."

"Poor Monte. You're so fond of her."

He swirled the glass cupped in his palm. "Abbie's father is my partner, as you know. He's a fine man." Sharlyn's eyes rested on him. He could not avoid this, but how could he speak of Abbie? "They were the first to welcome me here, and Abbie ... she's like this place. Fresh and strong and uncorrupted. She..." The brandy burned in his throat.

Sharlyn was perceptive. Not too perceptive, he prayed. Even these few words conjured memories and desires he must restrain. What he had expected to feel at his return was nothing near the terrible reality. Not to saunter over to the Martin homestead and sit at their table, sharing a meal and lively banter, nor to stroll the hillsides with Abbie, nor to see the look of anticipation in her eyes when he arrived....

Instead, he would endure the memory of her shock and condemnation. He had expected disdain, though part of him had hoped she would understand and accept the message in the letter he had sent through Frances. But the wild look of incredulous pain ... Had she refused to believe his words? Had she hoped the letter would prove some cruel trick?

And now she lay injured, as much as by his hand. He wanted to tell her everything, to explain what had happened and why, but that would betray Sharlyn. The depth of his loss left him hollow.

Sharlyn waited.

"I am concerned for her," he said simply.

She nodded. "I pray she'll recover soon. She must be very special to earn such respect from you."

Monte's jaw tightened, and he reached for her hand. "You're special, Sharlyn."

Her color rose up. "You make me so happy."

◆◆◆◆◆◆◆

Cold, darkness, sweat, and shivers. Abbie's head was thick. The darkness lessened, and faces appeared. One face, pale and smiling, so delicate . . . eyes like mossy pools . . . Sharlyn, Sharlyn Farrel. She jolted awake. The room was dark, but she could make out the shape of a man slumped in a chair in the corner. Monte! No, too thick to be Monte or Pa. A medicinal odor accompanied him. Doctor Barrow. Her eyes closed again.

◆◆◆◆◆◆◆

"I believe she's past the worst of it now." Doctor Barrow's voice filtered to Abbie. "Pneumonia is a threat with a chill like this, but her constitution is strong. I'll check back day after tomorrow."

Through the thickness she saw him gather his things. What day was it? Why must there be a tomorrow? A pain worse than her head gripped her inside. She had been foolish to ride so carelessly, but she was worse than a fool to have trusted Monte with her heart.

Mama saw Doctor Barrow to the door, then returned to her side. Abbie recalled waking at odd times, the lantern in her eyes, the smell of Doctor Barrow's fingers. She must have hit her head hard, but things were clearing now. She wished they weren't.

Mama made no small talk. "I'm sorry about Monte. I know

it doesn't seem possible, but it will pass. 'To everything there is a season, and a time to every purpose under heaven.'"

Closing her eyes, Abbie nodded. Did Mama know how it hurt to think God had allowed this, after all?

Nineteen

Abbie took her shawl and stepped outside, breathing in the smell of spring, even though it would still be some time before the green returned in earnest. Though in other places March meant spring, here it was a crazy back-and-forth affair between the wet, heavy snows and warm, dry days.

A magpie called as Abbie headed for the hills through the scrub oaks, bare with the buds still encased in bark. She was amazed how shaky her legs were, but then it had been so long since she was up and about. The magpie launched into the air, its white breast and shimmery blue-black wings rising high above her. That would be something to experience. If she could fly, she would go far, far away, away from the memories, the places that called out Monte's name to her, the sights that brought his face to her mind. She looked from the bird into the wide open sky and wondered how she had failed.

A cottontail darted out of hiding and scampered across her path. She remembered telling Monte how she could track and fish and climb trees. No wonder he hadn't wanted to marry her. He wanted a proper lady for his wife, but the cruelty of his empty promises was not diminished. *Please God*, she prayed. *Please help it not to hurt so. . . .*

She bent and parted the stubby winter grass to reveal a wild crocus just opening its petals to the sun. She ran her finger over the fuzzy bloom. It looked as fragile as she felt—she who had prided herself on her hearty constitution, on her ability to take whatever came. Well, face it she would.

Two weeks in bed with a concussion and pneumonia had sapped her strength, but she could feel it returning. She breathed the scent of smoke and sheep dung and sage, then turned her steps homeward. An unfamiliar horse was tethered to the post, and at the table with a cup of coffee sat Cole Jasper. Abbie smiled as he stood.

"Abbie, this is Cole Jasper, who found you in the storm," Mama said.

"Yes, I recall. I hoped I'd have the chance to thank you." She could not have sought him out at Monte's ranch. Not even the debt of her life would bring her there.

"That ain't needed, Miss Martin. I just came to see that you're on the mend. Mr. Farrel was askin', as well."

Abbie raised her chin. "You may let Mr. Farrel know that I'm completely recovered. I haven't been thrown since I was very small. I'm lucky you happened by when you did." Cole looked too restless and windblown for the kitchen to contain him. His green eyes and riotous blond hair belonged on the range.

"Well, I'll just be on my way. Thank you fer the coffee, ma'am." He nodded to Mrs. Martin.

Abbie walked him to the door. "Thank you for everything, Mr. Jasper. I owe you my life."

Cole pulled the hat down on his brow. "I'd be obliged if you'd call me Cole."

"Very well, Cole. Give my regards to Mr. and Mrs. Farrel." Abbie said the proper words with the proper tone.

"I will, miss."

"Abbie," she corrected.

"Miss Abbie." Tipping his hat, he left.

"That was kind of him to come, wasn't it?" Abbie knew her voice was flat. Even she didn't recognize it.

"Yes," Mama replied, looking long at her.

♦♦♦♦♦♦♦

The thawed ground was soft beneath the buggy wheels, and the baby leaves of the scrub oak, sumac, and mountain mahogany were unfurled as Abbie passed through on the way to town. Stopping before the grocer's, she nodded to Clara's pa, then went inside. "Why, Clara! What are you doing here?"

"Now there's a greeting."

Abbie laughed. "I'm sorry, but here you are behind the counter . . . and in your condition."

"I'm filling in for Ma today, who's poorly, and it's I who should be surprised to see you. It's been ages since you've come to town!" Clara tipped her head. "How are you, Abbie? But for this baby I'd have come . . ."

"I'm strong as a horse. You know that." She handed Clara her list.

"Have a licorice." Clara pulled the flour sack from the shelves behind her.

As Abbie took a licorice drop from the jar, the door opened, and Sharlyn Farrel came in. Abbie's chest lurched.

Sharlyn's face glowed, her hair a pale halo, her smile angelic. "Miss Martin! I'm so glad to see you've recovered. I've wanted to visit, but Monte said it was too far for me to go alone."

Abbie heard Clara's breath catch. Sharlyn's words stung, but she made no sign. Of course Monte would not escort her over, though it was little farther to her homestead from his than the trip Sharlyn had made to town. At least he had the decency to keep his distance. "Yes, I suppose it is far when you're not familiar with it."

"So this is fortuitous. Could you . . . would you come to tea this afternoon?"

Sharlyn's cheeks flushed, and her face was so hopeful that Abbie bit back the instant rejection that had risen. She was aware of Clara behind her, who knew her so well she would read her expression, hear the falseness of her lie. She hesitated.

"Monte's with the men for roundup, and I'm longing for company." Sharlyn seemed to shrink into herself with this admission.

"Thank you. I'd be delighted." Abbie gripped the box that held her order. "I'll wait outside." She couldn't bear to have Clara watching her another minute. The bell on the door jingled as she pressed through and slid the box into the buggy. Her eyes glanced toward the church with the notice on the door. *Pastor wanted.* As though some reverend wandering by might see it and stay.

She sighed. She felt very much like a lost sheep. She had begged off the Sunday morning trips to the mission, claiming the distance too much for her yet. But it wasn't the distance across the land. It was the gap between her heart and God that kept her home. She tried, but she felt parched like the cracked stream beds awaiting the spring runoff.

Shaking her head, Abbie drew herself up. *What's done is done. I'll not be pitied.*

Mr. Niehman, the postmaster, stuck his head out the door of his tiny office. "I've a letter for you, Miss Martin. Came on the stage today."

"Blake," Abbie breathed. She dropped the box and ran to fetch the letter. "Thank you." She worked it open and slipped out the paper within.

Dear Abbie,

   We did it! We found gold and we're comin' back. Now I can give you everything you want. Mack an' me sold the mine and we'll be packin' up soon, so you wait for me. I love you, Abbie, and I shore hope you feel the same now.

Blake

Abbie stuffed the letter into her pocket. Picking up her

skirts, she burst back into the store. "Blake's coming back! He and Mack found gold, and they're coming back!"

Clara clapped her hands. "Oh, Abbie, I'm so glad!"

"Blake?" Sharlyn asked.

Abbie had forgotten her. "A friend. A dear friend."

She wished she could go somewhere alone and sort out her thoughts, but she had accepted an invitation. James drove Sharlyn's buggy and Abbie followed with her own. It was wonderful news that Blake was returning. Surely it was wonderful. Then why did it fade and leave her so empty?

It was more painful than she imagined to walk into Monte's house, and Abbie wished she hadn't come. She had never coveted his wealth, nor did she envy Sharlyn her grand home. Only Monte had mattered. But if they were all to live in the same town, she would have to get past the hurt, and she prayed silently to be able to start now.

Sharlyn was at ease with the servants, and bitterly Abbie realized that she had been born to that. Monte had chosen a woman bred in his heritage and traditions who would raise up his children properly. The ache gripped her. It had turned out exactly as he had said. She wondered if he pined for her. Well, she would not. She would get past this pain if it took all her strength to do it. She replaced her humble prayer with hard resolve.

They sat together in the parlor, and Pearl brought them the tea tray. Lifting the pot, Sharlyn poured out the steaming liquid into the fine china cups and handed one on its saucer to Abbie. "I'm so glad you could come. From the start I've wanted to meet you. You were the first person from Colorado Monte told me about."

"I guess he'd have to start somewhere." Sharlyn's eyes flicked to her, and Abbie changed her tone. "I imagine you're used to many more people."

"Yes . . . I miss my friends and family, though I've never been one for crowds. I think if I were more like you . . ." She blushed.

Abbie forced a smile. "And what am I like?"

"I shouldn't speak of what I don't know. Of course I . . . I can't say. . . ."

Abbie softened. "You don't have to worry. I'm the worst for saying inappropriate things."

"I don't believe that."

"Well, you don't know me."

Sharlyn twisted her hands. "I would like us to be friends. When I was younger I was painfully shy."

Abbie felt Sharlyn's discomfort and wondered what had changed.

"You're all the things I wish I could be. Brave and strong and adventurous."

There was a cold sinking in Abbie's stomach.

"Monte spoke with such enthusiasm. I couldn't hear enough. I was as excited to meet you as to see my new home."

The girl's southern accent, so like Monte's, gave her voice a soft lilt that sweetened her words. Sharlyn couldn't be mocking or baiting her. She was almost childlike in her honesty. Was it possible she had no idea what had been in Monte's heart? But then, what had? Lies and dishonor—nothing he would reveal to his wife.

"That's very kind." It sounded false and patronizing. "Had I known Monte was bringing you, I . . ." Abbie's throat constricted. She couldn't lie to the guileless woman. "It's a surprise, of course."

"It was sudden. I keep pinching myself." Sharlyn pressed the skin of her arm between her fingers, leaving a rush of pink on white. "But please, tell me about Blake. Is he your beau?"

Abbie paused. "I don't know what he is. Just Blake, I guess. He taught me woodcraft and hunting and . . . things I don't suppose a lady needs to know."

"Why not? When Monte told me the things you could do, track and carve a spear . . ."

Abbie's anger flared, incensed that Monte had told Sharlyn all the personal things she had shared with him. What right did he have to reveal her soul to this stranger, this usurper? She wanted to run and scream and tell Sharlyn that it was she whom Monte had held in his arms, her lips he had kissed!

A sudden flush burned Sharlyn's face clear up to the hairline. Her voice quavered. "I've offended you."

Forcing down the resentment, Abbie willed herself to remain seated. "Not at all. Did Monte tell you about Blake?"

"Not a word."

"Well, when Monte first came to town, Blake tried to shoot him."

"What?"

"He was a bit overprotective." There, let that sink in. But to her surprise, Sharlyn laughed, and Abbie found herself laughing, too, the sudden release like sun after a storm. The parlor door opened and Monte stood there. Abbie's laugh died in her throat.

Sharlyn turned. "See who I have here, Monte?"

"Yes." His eyes were on Abbie alone.

"I was just leaving." Abbie stood up stiffly. "Thank you for tea."

"Must you go?" Sharlyn wilted.

"I'm afraid so."

Abbie had brushed by Monte and made it down the porch stairs before he could reach the front door. "Abbie, wait!" he called, but she threw herself onto the wagon seat and took up the reins.

"Ha!" Shiloh jumped and Abbie did not look back.

◆◆◆◆◆◆◆

Monte lay in the dark. How would he survive this? He

closed his eyes, and her face appeared behind his lids. Silky brown hair springing from her soft skin, eyes that made him weak when the lashes drooped just so, and the soft mouth that had responded so richly to his ardor. He flung his body onto his side, and Sharlyn stirred.

He looked at her lying like an angel in her white gown. He could almost imagine wings sprouting from the thin shoulder blades beneath the fabric. What man would not be thrilled to have so exquisite a creature beside him as his own? She was his wife for better or worse until death. He reached out a hand and stroked the fair hair twisted into a braid behind her back. Sharlyn's eyes opened, and he kissed her.

Twenty

Abbie ran her fingers through the long grasses as she sat on the hill beside Sharlyn. Monte had given in to Sharlyn's urging and shown her the way here, and she now made regular visits. For all her demure bashfulness, she seemed stubbornly determined to befriend her, and as a child picks a scab, Abbie let Sharlyn's talk of Monte rip open her wound again and again.

But looking at her now, sitting in the grass with her skirts circled about her, Abbie found that, even more than Clara, Sharlyn had connected with her heart. Was it because they loved the same man? Or was it just Sharlyn herself? Abbie drooped the chain of black-eyed Susans over Sharlyn's pale head like a crown. "There now, you're a nymph holding court. What will you decree?"

Sharlyn touched the blossoms. "I wouldn't have any idea. What would you?"

Abbie leaned back, feasting on the springtime around her. "I decree that the wind blow us an adventure."

Sharlyn laughed.

Abbie sat up again. "What shall it be?"

"Let's not have Indians."

"Why not?" She gestured up the hillside. "Right up that ridge is where I saw the Comanche braves. It was the most indescribable thrill when they came out of the woods on their mustang ponies, all dressed in beads and feathers."

"Were you really not afraid?"

"It wasn't a fearful thing at all. It was as though they were part of the mountains and I was, too."

"Have you seen them since?"

"Not since they brought me the rabbits. But I've looked." Abbie's eyes went up to the ridge. "Perhaps in the fall they'll return. Some bands still come through, and the Utes live up the pass south and west of here." She shook her head. "I've never been moved as I was by that hunter, and I hope . . . I believe he lives free, somewhere."

"I should like to see him, but I would not like him to see me."

"He'd think you were a vision from the Great Spirit."

Laughing, Sharlyn asked, "Why would he think that?"

"Because you're so fair and tiny." Abbie turned to her. "Perhaps he would think you were sent to lead them to a new hunting ground, unviolated by settlers who think their ways are savage."

"Are they not, Abbie?"

"Sometimes. But then so are ours. Even the ways of southern gentility can be cruel." Abbie spoke without thinking.

"Is that why you and Monte are no longer friends?"

Abbie bit her lip. "Why do you say that?"

"Isn't it so?"

"Of course not."

Sharlyn pulled the flowers from her hair into her lap. "I believe he's hurt you . . . and I know it grieves him."

Abbie turned away.

"I've known Monte since I was a child, and he can't bring trouble to anyone, especially one who was once, and must still be, dear to him."

Abbie wanted to shake her. How dare she defend Monte? "Really, Sharlyn. You think the oddest things." She pointed.

"Look, there's the eagle that nests on the bluff! Just look how magnificent!"

The bird circled below them, dove suddenly and grabbed a rabbit in its talons, then mounted up with powerful strokes toward the bluff. Life and death in one act. Life for one, death for the other.

Abbie stood and replaced her wide-brimmed hat. Sharlyn rose behind her. "Shall I come tomorrow?"

"I'll be at the mission."

"The mission?"

"The Franciscan brothers run an orphanage school." Abbie spoke as she walked. "Blake and I attended there. Blake hated it, of course. It's one of the only ways we're different. He was a naughty boy and wouldn't learn his lessons. Repeatedly, Father Dominic applied the rod and made him recite his lessons alone since he hadn't followed in class. I'd wait, and when he came out, he'd whistle like nothing had happened and then take my hand and run until he had worked out all the shame of it.

"I think I loved him best then, because he was so brave not to cry or rage or even complain. But then the next day or several days later it would be the same all over again. He never did learn much. He was too stubborn."

Sharlyn sighed. "I wish I could learn better. As hard as I try, I can't seem to decipher the words. They look different every time I see them."

Abbie stopped. "Are you telling me you can't read?"

"It's very difficult. That's why I like it so much when you and Monte tell me about things and people. It's like reading a story."

"I'll read to you if you like. I have ever so many books."

Sharlyn pressed her hand. "Would you, Abbie? Sometimes Monte reads aloud, but it's different kinds of things, and I think it frustrates him."

"Does he know your trouble?" She knew how highly Monte valued literary skills.

"I have alluded to it, but . . ." She sighed.

They entered the house and Abbie led the way to the study, opened the door, and relished the smell of the leather bindings. This was her favorite room in the house, and she silently thanked the Lord that He had not afflicted her like Sharlyn. "Would you choose one or shall I?"

"You choose, Abbie."

"Then I'll read you *Jane Eyre*. Have you heard it?"

"No."

"It's terribly tragic. Just like the author herself. Charlotte Brontë was sent off to a dreadful school for clergymen's daughters along with three of her sisters, and two of them died early, possibly because of that. Charlotte herself died in childbirth."

"Like Monte's mother," Sharlyn mused.

"I didn't know it was childbirth."

"Yes, and the infant son with her. Terribly sad."

"You've known him a long while." Abbie spoke half to herself.

"All my life, though I never dreamed he saw me. He was so . . . full of life and humor. And I . . ." She waved her hands. "Listen to me running on."

Abbie curled her feet under her in the window seat, willing the hurt to subside. The next three hours, she read aloud as Sharlyn sat enraptured by the tale, eyes glowing and mouth drawn up in a smile. She was surprised when Pa came home from work.

Sharlyn jumped up. "Can it be that late! What will Monte think?" She rushed to her feet, and they reached the door just as Monte rode up stern-faced in the buggy. What had it cost him to set aside his pride and come? How deeply he must care for Sharlyn.

"Thank you ever so much!" Sharlyn squeezed Abbie's hand.

Monte handed Sharlyn into the buggy. Then, climbing up beside her, he grabbed the reins. Abbie had her back to him before he said his stiff, "Good evening, Abbie."

✦✦✦✦✦✦✦

Abbie thought of Sharlyn as she listened to the young voices forming the sounds from the first primer. "No, Jeremy." She ran his finger back to the word he had mispronounced.

"Re ... si ... st."

"Good." She let him read on. Could she help Sharlyn? Part of her took a wicked delight in Monte's disappointment. Sharlyn's inability to study and discourse with him must be a thorn in his happiness. But a look into Jeremy's round face filled her with remorse. Would they trust her if they knew she was capable of such wicked thoughts? "That's enough. Pauline, read now."

Abbie knew little about Sharlyn's difficulty. She had read of studies on brain conditions that made learning difficult. She was not qualified to work with something like that. Perhaps the best she could do was satisfy Sharlyn's longing by reading aloud as she had. It was little enough.

Twenty-One

Blake led his gray mare close as Mack pulled a rope tight and grunted, "Sure am tired of strikin' camp." He checked the ropes again on the three mules loaded with provisions and gold coin, the proceeds from the sale of their mine. "Ready?"

"Yup." Blake mounted. "I can almost smell Abbie's cookin' already." He threw his head back and sang the chorus of "Oh, Susannah," but substituted "Oh, my Abbie."

Mack shook his head. "She'll be cryin' for you all right if you mean to keep up that noise."

Blake laughed. "Sure wish we were there. I got me a longin' down in my chest that ain't gonna give me peace till I take her in my arms. . . ."

"Yeah, yeah. I know all about that burnin'. But we ain't there yet, so cool it down."

Blake was sore and saddle weary from toiling over the Rockies. But every mile was one mile closer to home. The sun beat down, sapping his strength. "Sure am glad it ain't August." He wiped the grime from his forehead.

"Yup. It's already hot 'nough to singe a rattler."

The mountains were dry tinder waiting for a spark, except at night when the chill drove the heat away. It wasn't so much the heat but the sun bearing down on them without a cloud to thin it.

The regular plodding of the horse lulled Blake into silence.

It was funny. Here he was rich, and he didn't feel any different at all. Except he was a whole lot surer Abbie would have him. He wished she could have written him back, but he hadn't had an address for a while, tucked up into the slopes. He and Mack had kept clear of the busy camps, most of which housed the already producing mines. They hadn't the money for that kind of operation and weren't looking to work for someone who did. So they stuck with the old tried and true panning and sluicing, trying areas not already worked.

At least that had been the plan. Mack was right, though. They never would have got much that way. Finding the vein had been their redemption. Of course, that meant money to set up, machinery, men ... and a whole lot more know-how than they had. Once they'd picked clean all they could get at, it was time to hand it over to someone else. It took less than a day to find a buyer, and the deal they cut wasn't half bad. How Abbie's eyes would shine when he told her.

But they had ground to cover yet. In a day or so, depending on the mules, they'd be headed down the Ute pass, then skirting the base of the foothills along the eastern slope to Rocky Bluffs and home.

The sun finished its lazy arc and sank to the earth. Blake's back ached something fierce by the time they stopped for the night. He climbed out of the saddle and groaned. "I been too long doin' this."

Mack tipped back his hat. "That makes two of us."

They unpacked and watered the mules and horses at the creek they'd followed for the better part of the week. Mack stretched out against his pack. "You want a fire?"

"Nah. I'll jest fill my belly with jerky and sleep like a baby." Blake climbed into his bedroll and shuffled until he was comfortable. "See ya at midnight." Curled into the blanket against the cold mountain air, he watched the moon shrink from an amber globe to a small white disk as it climbed the sky. Overhead an owl whooshed and disappeared into the trees. Blake closed his eyes and imagined Abbie in his arms. Soon . . . soon.

When morning came, they broke camp and packed up the meager provisions they had left, redistributed the bundles on the mules, and started out again. To break the tedium, Blake urged his horse beside Mack. "You know the first thing I'm gonna do when I get back and marry Abbie?"

"Yup. The first thing any man does when he marries."

"I mean after that." Blake grinned.

"What?"

"I'm gonna take her up top of the lightning pine and have her pick whatever piece of land she wants, and I'm gonna buy it for her."

"Abbie's eighteen years old now. You ain't gonna git her to the top of the lightning pine."

"Wanna bet?"

"I bet you one hundred dollars you don't get her anywhere up that tree."

"Easiest hundred bucks I ever made." Blake laughed. "Abbie ain't worried what people say. She'll make it to the top, and I'll be right there beside her just like we used to."

Mack shook his head. "You always were a pair of wild ones."

"I couldn't imagine it any other way. Who'd want to marry someone who didn't do nothin' but cook an' clean and whimper all the time?"

"Nothin' wrong with cookin' and cleanin', Blake. If you plan to live in a house, that is. But maybe you and Abbie will just perch in some tree, eh?"

"No chance. I mean to build Abbie the finest house in all Rocky Bluffs. Finer even than Farrel's. What're you gonna do when you git home, Mack?"

"Take a bath."

◆◆◆◆◆◆◆

The lumberyard was filled with eager faces as the fiddlers stroked the strings and tuned, and Monte led Sharlyn past the tables laden with punch and cider, apple Betty, fruit and confections. In spite of his resolve, he searched the room for Abbie. She stood fresh and beautiful in a gown the color of her eyes, her hair pulled into thick sausage curls except for the ever present tendrils that teased around her forehead.

"Shall we join Abbie?" Sharlyn tugged his arm, following his gaze.

Jarred from his thoughts, he patted her hand. "You go ahead."

He watched them embrace in greeting. How ironic that the person who stood between them should be welcomed so warmly, while Abbie refused even to look at him. At first he had welcomed the distance. Being near was too painful. But now he hungered for something of what they'd had. Some small connection. Some indication that she felt more than loathing for him.

Laughing, she glanced his way. His chest lurched, but she turned her back so as not to repeat her error. He released his breath.

Joshua nodded, and Monte returned the gesture. No welcome there, either. You don't jilt a man's daughter without paying a price. He eyed the punch with disdain. Whiskey would be in better order, but the women's temperance were up in arms for every town function, Founder's Day included. Fortunately, Sharlyn wasn't militant about drink, as it had become a consolation. Of course, it was impossible to imagine her militant or even passionate about anything, except Abbie maybe.

What quirk of fate had knit them so closely? Did Abbie use Sharlyn to torment him? Did she encourage her to run on continuously over everything she said and did? No, that wasn't possible. Sharlyn was oblivious. He masked the need that fed on her recounting, but it was worse to have Abbie translated secondhand and know that were he present, she would grow cold and silent. One day it would drive him mad.

The caller climbed onto the crate and ordered the gents to find a lady to do-si-do. Monte waited until Abbie was claimed before he found Sharlyn and swept her into motion.

"Oh, Monte, we haven't danced in so long."

He felt a stab of remorse. She was lovely and eager to please. Sister to his closest friend, bound to him by honor . . . and love. It shone in her face and rang in the lilt of her voice. They bowed low to pass under the arms forming an arch above them and stepped backward, clapping, before he hooked his arm through hers and spun. Sharlyn was grace itself, as light as air on her feet. Had she set her hat for anyone, she would have had him. But she was his.

The square dances were lively, working off the exuberance of the gents, and, as Abbie once said, more like a stampede once the cowboys hit the floor. Near at hand, he watched as Cole claimed her.

"I declare, Cole, I hardly recognize you." Abbie curled her arm through his.

Cole ran a hand over his trimmed mustache beneath the slicked and parted hair. He was playing the part well. "I meant to git a dance with the purtiest girl in the room."

"I'd have danced with you anyway."

"I was hopin' it wasn't a beholdin' kinda thing."

"Of course not."

Monte frowned. What did Cole think he was doing, dancing with Abbie like that, his hold on her as sure as his confidence in anything else. The music came to an end with the two couples at arm's length. If Abbie noticed he was near, she hid it well. Cole stayed right beside her, not releasing her arm. "I've a mind to keep hold of you fer the next one, Abbie, if you'll have me."

"Well, I . . ." One of Monte's cowboys came up eagerly.

"Git lost, you mangy critter." Cole stepped between them. "Abbie ain't changin' partners."

Monte expected Abbie to protest, but she seemed amused. "Cole, that was terrible."

"I don't hear you complainin'." He swung her to the floor again.

Monte tightened his arm on Sharlyn. "Cole's making a fool of himself."

"Why shouldn't he dance with her?" Sharlyn asked, more aware than he suspected. "He's nice enough, and a good dancer from the looks of it."

"She's eighteen years old. He's probably twice that at least."

"Surely not."

Sharlyn rarely disagreed with him, and Monte raised an eyebrow. "Close enough. And he's not in her class."

"I thought everyone was equal here, that there were no class differences."

"Well, you're wrong. Abbie is . . ."

" . . . qualified to decide for herself."

Monte was at a loss. This was the closest to argumentative Sharlyn had ever come. Was she defending Abbie to him?

"If you're concerned," she added softly, "why don't you ask her to dance yourself?"

He quelled his anger, feeling suddenly empty. "She'd not have me."

Sharlyn's hand rested on his arm. "Why not, Monte?"

"Suffice it to say I'd be the last person with whom Abbie would dance."

Thankfully she didn't press him. He settled her with a cup of punch, then found Cole at the end of the long table. "Miss Martin's too young for you."

Cole turned, surprised. "What's got yer hackles up?"

"It has nothing to do with me." Monte frowned. "You could

be her father, for heaven's sake."

Cole grinned impudently. "I'd'a had to start awful early fer that. Besides, I don't hear Abbie complainin'."

Monte wanted to cuff the smug smile from his face. Where did he get off . . .

Sharlyn slipped her arm through his. "Let's get some air, Monte."

He let her tug him. Any more of this and he would come to blows with Cole Jasper. The man was a cocky scoundrel. The cold air felt good. Overhead, the stars were brilliant in the sky.

Sharlyn clasped her hands at her throat. "I've never seen so many stars in all my life. Why do you suppose there are more here?"

"There aren't more. You just see them more clearly through the thinner air." He said it gently, but Sharlyn's cheeks flared. He wished she were not so sensitive. He had to constantly watch himself. And as hard as he tried, he couldn't get past her simpleness.

He liked to be challenged, and Sharlyn was anything but challenging. He looked at her now, downcast and silent, and brushed her arm with his fingers. "It doesn't matter how few or how many. In the starlight you're lovely." He kissed her forehead.

"Oh, Monte, you're so kind."

Her words burned him. He would pay dearly for his falseness.

Another couple stepped out and walked a little way, barely visible in the shadows. Monte leaned on the railing and breathed the night air. Abbie's laugh caught him by surprise as her partner spoke something too softly for him to catch the words. But he caught her into his arms, laughing. "Jest as easy as ropin' a steer." It was Cole. Of course.

"You wouldn't dare." Abbie's voice held the playful tone

that Monte remembered so well. He watched as Cole immobilized and kissed her.

"Cole Jasper!"

He released her. "Next time don't dare me."

"I never did!" There was indignation, but not enough to dissuade a swagger like Cole Jasper, and when he leaned close to repeat his offense, Abbie put up little resistance. Monte's fist curled involuntarily as his teeth clenched together. His chest felt squeezed as he stiffened, grabbed Sharlyn's arm, and turned her back in.

Passing through the lighted doorway, he caught her expression, and his chest went cold. He could only guess what she had seen revealed in his face. He led her to the floor to the strains of a waltz. She was like a child in his arms. "My darling," he whispered into her hair. Sharlyn said nothing.

"Are you feeling well?"

"I'm tired."

"I hope you weren't chilled."

"No. Not at all. But . . . I'd like to go."

He gathered her wrap about her and settled her into the buggy. It was his responsibility to care for Sharlyn. And he did care, though he never declared a love he didn't have for her. Was it honor not to dishonor her with a lie?

They drove in silence. Soft lights glimmered from the windows of their home as he drew up near the entrance and stopped. He lifted her down from the carriage and led her inside. She was silent and pale, and he knew he had hurt her. He must be more careful not to betray his feelings. He would put Abbie from his mind. He must, God help him.

As he watched Sharlyn ascend the stairs, he handed her wrap to James, then went to the library and poured a snifter of brandy. The aroma rose up, and he allowed it to warm in his palm before it coated his throat. He stared at the wall. What had been between Abbie and him was past. One day someone else would claim her. Again the brandy coursed down his throat, and he closed his eyes. What if it were Cole? No matter. It would not be he. He refilled and drained another glass, then went upstairs to Sharlyn.

She was in the bed, eyes closed, but she did not look asleep. He undressed. Sharlyn was warm and still as he climbed in beside her. "Sharlyn?" he whispered. She didn't answer. He rolled over and slept.

Twenty-Two

Looking down the pass from the summit, Blake surveyed the narrow trail winding down Ute pass. It looked a wild, undisturbed country, the pines densely clothing the slopes on either side of the trail. His hand went to the pistol at his side, there, ready, should he need it. "Last leg, Mack. Let's make it a short one."

Leading the mules down the narrow, winding way, Blake kept his senses alert. Even so, when the rough, burly man lunged in front of them he was surprised. His horse shied, then steadied as he held tight to the rein.

Three more horsemen surrounded them from the woods, blocking the trail forward and behind. Blake's muscles tensed.

"Well now . . ." The swarthy man spoke. "You boys must be near tuckered out haulin' all that stuff over these here hills, I'd wager."

Neither Blake nor Mack said a word, and the pink-faced man beside the first chuckled. "You reckon we oughta give 'em a hand with it, boss?"

"Seems it'd be only neighborly. All we ask is a proper thanky kindly." He hooked his thumbs in his belt over the twin revolvers. "See, boys, we're gonna help you with them mules. Kinda take 'em off yer hands awhile."

Blake's temper flared. "We don't need no help."

Mack shifted in the saddle but didn't speak.

The man on foot looked up to the horseman behind him. "You hear that? This boy don't need our help."

"Don't seem neighborly to me," the pink man replied.

A voice from behind said, "Jest shoot 'em, Hollister."

Blake stiffened. He had already guessed as much, and he'd fight before he'd let Hollister have his gold.

The swarthy man glared. "We don't shoot no one we don't have to, Wilkins. Round here we hang 'em."

The pink-faced man flitted his eyes. "Look, kid, jest let go the mules and ride out."

Hollister spun on him, and he backed off. Then turning back, Hollister snarled, "Now, boy, you owe me an apology. An' then you kin ask real nice fer help with yer mules."

In the fiery rush of his rage, Blake reached for his gun. A shot blasted before his hand found the trigger, and Mack lurched in his saddle, then tumbled out. Blake froze as the shock registered.

"Mack!" He leaped to the ground.

"You done killed yer brother, boy."

Crouched in the dirt, Blake turned Mack and held his head in his lap.

"Don't fight 'em," Mack groaned. "Abbie don't need yer gold." Mack gripped his hand, face contorted, then he grew limp.

White-hot fury seared Blake as he lunged for Hollister. The impact of a bullet sent him sprawling to the dust. First the sting, then pain filled his side as nerves and blood vessels found the damage. He moaned, feeling the blood soak into his shirt. Opening his eyes, he made out a pair of boots and slowly raised his face. *Oh, God, forgive my foolishness. And make Abbie think well of me. I loved her the best I could. You know that, God. You know.*

The shot exploded through the quiet woods and echoed down the rocky canyon.

✦✦✦✦✦✦✦

Side by side with Clara, Abbie strolled the boardwalk.

"I feel like a hen," Clara said.

Abbie laughed. "You have a reason for your girth, dear Clara. At least you're not foolish enough to clamp yourself into a corset."

"Doc Barrow won't allow it. Any woman in his care caught wearing a corset past the fourth month is charged double."

Monte and Cole stepped from the saddlery before them. Cole tipped his hat, grinning broadly. "Mornin', Abbie, Mrs. Franklin."

"Good morning, Cole, Mr. Farrel." Abbie caught Clara's arm and pressed on.

"Abbie, how could you?" Clara whispered. "You were cold as ice."

"I was perfectly cordial." Abbie stepped into the street. Before she could cross, a wagon rolled past, driven by a man she didn't know, but with a start, she recognized the gray horse with three white socks and off-center blaze tied to the back. She gripped Clara's arm. "That's Blake's horse!"

As the wagon stopped before the marshal's office, Abbie rushed forward, but the driver stopped her before she could get close. "No, miss, you won't be wantin' to look in there. A couple o' boys got killed in the pass an' I'm bringin' 'em in."

Abbie's knees jellied. "What boys?"

"By their bill o' sale, Mack and Blake McConnel."

Blood pounded in her ears and a choking scream gripped her throat. Both Monte and Cole ran over, but it was Cole who reached out and pulled her to his chest. People rushed in as the news spread, and Marshal Haggerty's voice rose above the hue. "All right, everybody keep back. We'll be makin' a posse soon enough."

Abbie felt cold as Cole held her until Pa cut through the

crowd. She pushed free of him and of her pa and fought toward the wagon bed.

"Don't let her do that! They been dead fer some days."

Pa grabbed her back.

"I don't believe him, Pa! It isn't Blake. It can't be!"

He kept a hold. "You stay right here. I'll have a look." He reached in and lifted the canvas, and his face set as he let it fall. "Where's Wes?"

"He's been fetched."

Abbie's fists clenched at her sides. "Pa?"

"I'm sorry, Abbie."

Deputy Clem Davis was barking orders. One group would ride with him and one with Marshal Haggerty. Cole turned to Monte. "I reckon I'll ride out with the posse."

Abbie raised her chin. "I'm going, too." The men turned to her.

"No, you're not," Pa said.

"I am, Pa. I'm going to find who did this."

The crowd grew quiet. Cole circled his hat in his hands.

Marshal Haggerty strode over. "We gotta ride long and hard, Miss Martin."

"I can ride as well as anyone out here."

"Look, I got a job to do, and I can't do it lookin' after you as well. Joshua?"

"Come on, Abbie. The men will find them." He reached for her arm, but she pulled it away.

Her chest rose and fell. Tightening her jaw, she swung around, her skirts swirling behind. The crowd parted to admit Wes McConnel, looking suddenly old, and grew silent as hats were removed. Abbie wouldn't look at him, wouldn't view his grief. She would fight back. An eye for an eye.

She made her way to the stable. The buggy could stay, and she would use whatever saddle was at hand. Her limbs seemed to work of their own volition, because her mind had gone numb. She would not think of anything but finding Blake's killer.

She had the buggy unhitched and the saddle on Shiloh's back when Monte walked into the shadows. She didn't look at him but reached under the horse's belly for the cinch. He took the reins.

"Don't try to stop me."

"I have to."

She pulled the cinch tight and tested it, then reached one foot up to the stirrup. Monte grabbed her arm, and Abbie yanked against him. "Let go! If they won't let me go with them, I'll go myself!"

"You can't."

She tried to pry his hand off, but Monte grabbed her other arm as well. "Abbie, you'll only make it harder for them. They need their strength concentrated on the business at hand."

"I don't need their help!"

"Whether you need it or not, they can't help giving it. You'll only keep them from doing what they must."

She struggled against his grip. "Let me go! You can't stop me!"

"You can't bring Blake back, and endangering yourself won't prove your love." His voice was calm and cruel.

Abbie's mouth fell open. "How dare you!"

Monte held his grip. "I'm sorry, Abbie. I'm truly sorry."

She trembled. "Well, don't be. Don't be sorry for me, ever, do you hear?"

"I'll see you home."

"You won't."

"I promised your father."

"What's a promise to you? Kindly remove your hand, Mr. Farrel."

"Not until I have your word that you'll go home."

Abbie felt her defenses starting to crumble. *Dear God, don't let me cry in front of Monte.* "I'm going home." She swung into the saddle, slapped the reins, and the horse lurched forward.

Out in the open, Abbie turned the horse's head to the hills. If they had shot them down in the pass, would they make their escape to the west, away from the town and pursuit? But that would be expected. What would a twisted, wily mind do? She gazed back over the plain, crisscrossed by gaps and ridges. That's where a snake would go.

The horse was fresh, but she had no provisions. It could be hours before the posse was ready to go. What could she do alone? She could track them. She could track as well as any man out there, thanks to Blake. No, don't think of him. But she heard his voice, *The trick is to walk gentle. Don't mar what's left for you to see.* They had crept together following scratches so faint, a bent twig, crushed foliage. A pack of horses would leave much more.

Abbie raised her head. Once past the town, she would traverse the plain until she found the track. *Can't rush off half-cocked.* She had laughed at that. Blake telling *her*, when he was the one blowing off at anything. But in the woods or on the hunt he was like a wild thing himself, sly and still and wise. She would need water. But going to the homestead would seal Pa's orders.

She swung wide to the Maccabee cabin. With luck, old man Maccabee would be sleeping one off. Dismounting, Abbie looked cautiously about. Only a nest of wasps droned in the corner of the porch roof. She crept forward. The door rubbed against the rough floor as she made a space just wide enough to press through. Inside smelled stale and sour—sweat and whiskey and smoke. Her eyes grew accustomed to the dim. The single room was empty.

On the wall hung a pair of canteens. Two would be better than one, but Maccabee would more likely believe he'd misplaced one than both. She pulled it from the nail. This was almost too easy. Back out in the sunshine, she squinted. The mare stomped one hind leg. Abbie dipped the canteen past the rotting shelf of the well and brought it up soaked and filled, then hung it around her neck and mounted.

Stealth and speed together. Stay close to cover. Well, there wasn't much cover where she was going until she reached the gullies. So speed for now. The horse responded, leaping into a canter, and the wind brought tears to her eyes. She declared it was the wind. Her hair whipped her face. Skirting the farthest outbuildings of Rocky Bluffs, she held the horse to a canter and began crossing the plain in a series of passes. She concentrated on the southern reaches since the Ute pass lay that way.

Sweat spread between her shoulder blades under the noon sun as she kept her face to the ground. Mourning cloak butterflies flew up on black wings and a prairie dog scuttled to its hole. As the sun arced toward the mountains, she drained the last of the water and flung the canteen across her back to keep it from banging her chest. Her neck and shoulders ached. She had stopped twice to rest the mare and walked her frustration off. Herds of antelope, rabbits, coyotes, and varmints had left their mark, but no sign of horses.

Abbie kicked the dirt. Had she guessed wrong? Had they gone over the mountains after all? There was more cover that way, more danger and difficulty, but it was too obvious. An animal on the run switched back. She urged the mare farther south. Suddenly she reined in, pushing up in the stirrups. The ground was torn and trampled. She dropped to the grass. Hoof marks as deep as her second knuckle; the front edge dug in sharply. They were moving fast.

Her heart pounded in her chest. The marshal would be gone. They were starting at the pass, hoping to get the trail there. Maybe they'd follow it here, but how much time would be lost? Could she catch up to them? If she cut directly to the pass ... but Shiloh was spent. Even now her head hung and her gait was rough. Abbie turned for home. The horse smelled the wind and perked her ears.

"Last effort," Abbie whispered and urged her past a trot to a canter. They'd make it to the homestead before dusk if she could keep this pace. Then ... if Pa would not allow her to go ... But someone would go when she told them what she'd found.

Before she reached the homestead, Pa met her. His face was drawn, but he said nothing when she burst upon him. "I found tracks."

"Your Mama needs you home."

A cold weight settled in her chest. "But, Pa ..."

"The men are riding, Abbie. Women have another call."

"But ..."

He turned his horse about. Pain washed over her. Hadn't she as much right to vengeance? What awaited her at home? Blake? No. She had sent him away, called him a fool boy for loving her. The mare plodded behind her father's gelding.

When they reached the homestead, Mama was on her way to the McConnels'. Abbie slipped off the mare and climbed into the buggy. Turning to Pa before he led Shiloh off, she said, "I found the track, Pa. They're not in the mountains. They're south of here and east, out across the plains."

He nodded. She and Mama rode silently.

Abbie entered the house where Blake had been raised and now awaited burial. She viewed the scene as from a great distance. Blake's sister, Mariah, stood with her hands against her face by the table that held the bodies. Mary, her mother, was removing the boys' clothes. Abbie's eyes found Blake, lying beside Mack. Blood crusted the side of his shirt, and part of his skull was gone. A trembling began in her spine, and the ache crushed her chest with iron bands.

She stepped forward once and again until she reached his side. The stench was foul, their bodies blackened and corrupt, but Abbie took a towel from the vinegar water that stood in the tub by the table. Slowly she wrung it out and rubbed it over Blake's face, over the sunken eyes and the lips that curled back. Behind her, Mariah sobbed and rushed from the room. Abbie mutely dipped the cloth and went on washing.

A strange and senseless act. This wasn't Blake. Blake wasn't here. Beside her Mary McConnel and Mama likewise tended Mack. The oldest and the youngest McConnel sons, together in death; no, not death. Abbie forced her arms to rub, her eyes to see ... but her mind would not believe.

When they had been washed, the bodies were draped. Wes and Pa came and stood in the doorway. Wes slumped heavily in the jamb. Davy, the only remaining son, stood behind them with Mariah under his arm. Abbie brushed her finger over Blake's as she stepped back, her farewell unspoken.

◆◆◆◆◆◆◆

The bright morning sun cut sharp shadows from the mourners across the holes in the earth. Father Dominic in his brown hooded robe closed the Holy Scriptures and reached up in benediction. No one looked askance at the Latin, though many had never had any traffic with the brothers. Their grief united them, and their mute prayers reached heaven together.

Abbie stood silent and dry eyed as the pine boxes were lowered on ropes into the ground and Wes and Mary and Davy and Mariah dropped handfuls of earth into the depth. She watched them huddle together, felt her parents like sentries beside her, yet inside was nothing. Sharlyn came forward. "I'm so sorry. If there's anything..." Abbie nodded without really seeing her or Monte beside her. Sharlyn squeezed her fingers and passed by. Others murmured, touched, pressed her hands. They felt foreign and unreal.

The McConnels were gathered back to their home. Abbie walked, spoke, and responded through no effort of her own.

If she thought hard enough, Blake would walk through the door with his crooked smile and tell them all it was a mistake. *I'm home*, he'd say, tossing back his hair. If she thought hard enough she could see it. The waiting was terrible. If not today ... when?

Pa told her word was sent of the track she'd found. No word said they'd heeded it. Everyone guessed it was Hollister they sought, and they knew the odds. With the newspaper Pa called them to war in their hearts and minds against the evil that lived and breathed within the shell of humanity that was Buck Hollister. But the men returned, robbed of vengeance and justice, like wolves that found no satisfaction for their hunger.

••••••

Buck Hollister watched as the single rider sped over the rough terrain, doubled back through a crevice, and up over a ridge before turning into the gulch. He stood at the opening of the cave in the rocky wall, gun ready in his hand. He could smell the nerves of the men behind him. Recognizing Briggs, he relaxed and holstered his gun.

Briggs jumped from the animal. "Posse's gone home." He shoved a newspaper his way. "Thought you'd be interested in this."

Hollister stepped out into the sun and leaned against the rocky wall. His mood darkened as he read. The breath eased past his teeth in a low hiss. "No one calls me a coward. No one."

"We takin' 'im out?" Briggs asked.

He gazed out toward the blue ridge of mountains and the town of Rocky Bluffs nestled at their feet. "You recall that daughter Wilkins spoke of?"

The cold look in Briggs' eyes showed their thoughts matched. Hollister stretched a slow grin and found it returned.

••••••

Abbie dropped to the ground on the grassy hillside beside the gravestones. Blake would never again appear in her doorway or walk at her side, his unabashed affection worn clearly on his face. Too soon, her feeble thoughts had given in to the truth.

In the two weeks since his death, memories of their days together had both tormented and comforted her, and she had found her way here repeatedly to sit beside the graves. The May sunshine warmed the slope through the needles of the pines above her, and a jay scolded from their branches.

Looking up, Abbie could almost hear Blake's voice calling to her from the top of the trunk. *That's it, Abbie. Grab that branch, take my hand . . . ain't this a view?* Was it all because she didn't love him well enough? Even now, she imagined him only as the friend he had been to her, but she hoped that now he understood.

"Oh, Blake," she murmured, "I miss you so. I wish we could have stayed children together. There are so many more trees to climb and streams to wade. And you never did tell Mama, did you? You kept all my secrets better than I did and loved me with all my faults." Her voice faltered. "Please forgive me for driving you away. I never meant it to come to this." Her shoulders shook with the sobs that finally broke through her hard denial.

What was God about? What manner of sovereign was He? Somewhere Blake's killer lived and breathed. Somewhere her love loved another. She shook her head. Her child's faith would not bring her into womanhood. How confident she had been in the providence of God. Was she wrong? Was it all a grand deception? Was Blake at peace? Was there peace?

Not here, nor hope. And yet, not to hope was to despair, to turn her back upon the Lord. Were dreams made only to be broken? Even if her dream were laid before her now, she would not take it up. To hope, to imagine, to love held more pain than she could stand.

Still, life pressed on, moment by moment, and she was a pawn to God's purpose. So be it. She would neither rebel nor embrace. What would come, would come. Rising to her feet, she walked down the slope to the McConnel house and tapped on the door.

Mary McConnel hugged her. "Thank you for coming, but I'm managing."

Abbie nodded. They were all just managing, going from one task to the next, one thought to the next. "I went up to see Blake. I hope you don't mind."

"You go anytime you like. He loved you so." Mary's rough palm brushed her cheek. "I thought you would become my own daughter one day. Even though Blake is gone, I consider you so."

Laying her head on the other woman's shoulder, Abbie wept again, but this time with relief. Her heart would not have been Blake's, had he returned. She was wrong to think they could have stayed friends. She would have destroyed this woman's hopes as surely as she had Blake's. She was not fit to love. She had given her heart wrongly, and God had condemned her.

Twenty-Three

Abbie walked the street, transformed by banners and swags of red, white, and blue, past the bandstand beside the square. People stood shoulder to shoulder along the walks as she pushed through. Sharlyn caught her sleeve. "Abbie, watch here with me."

She hadn't planned to watch the race, but Sharlyn looked so hopeful. They had been strained these last months, and she knew Sharlyn was hurt by her distance. Reluctantly, Abbie settled beside her as the men on horseback took their places behind the chalked line. Nine horses stomped and snorted, tossing their heads and straining against the bit. Cole caught her eye and winked, and she waved her good wishes. Beside him, Monte glanced up, then returned his attention to Sirocco, the black socked Arabian that stood hands taller than the others. Monte's horse was the swiftest, she knew, but it remained to be seen if he could run the course as well as the others without being disqualified.

Sharlyn clung to her arm, breathless with anticipation as Ethan Thomas lifted his arm and the gun shattered the morning. The people cheered as the horses leaped forward, vying for position down the rutted road and off across the plain. The crowd scattered.

"Where shall we go to watch?" Sharlyn asked.

Abbie shrugged. "I'm off to see Clara and the baby. You go

ahead." She wouldn't view Monte's triumph. Sharlyn gave no argument, and Abbie took the lane to the two-story frame house Marty had completed.

Clara was radiant. Beside her the round-cheeked infant dozed, and Abbie quickened at the sight. "Oh, Clara, he's beautiful. How proud Marty must be!"

"He is." Clara beamed. "He's like a cock crowing constantly."

"And with good reason."

Clara cupped the baby's head in her palm. "It was no easy thing bringing this one into the world, but ever so worth it."

Abbie dropped down beside her. "Just look at his tiny fingers. Have you ever seen anything so small? And to think they'll grow into great, strong man hands."

"Well, Marty's not of such great stature, nor his hands so large. Not like Blake's . . ." Clara's voice faded as she stroked the baby's downy hair. "I think of him still. Not as I used to before Marty, but . . . he was fine, wasn't he?"

"Yes. He was fine." Deep within, the memories gnawed. Too fine. She had not deserved him. But Blake would laugh at that. *Go on, Abbie*, he'd say. *You're my girl, ain't you?* No, Blake. I'm nobody's girl. I never will be.

"I'm so sorry for you."

Abbie startled. "You needn't be. Blake's a part of me. Sometimes I feel him here still. Maybe it's better that way."

"He loved you, Abbie. You would have been happy."

Abbie smiled. It was easy. Clara no longer knew her.

The baby made a tiny bleat, and Clara set him to her breast. Abbie turned away as voices outside broke the quiet. "Go, Abbie. Tell me who wins!"

She trudged heavily to the square, where people were already packed for the finish of the race. The sound of hooves reached them, and then a rider, far outdistancing the next two, came into sight. "It's Farrel!" someone yelled, and the cheers rose up. Abbie watched, but not with satisfaction, as Monte's steed flew over the finish line a full minute before the next horse. He did not rein the animal in but allowed its pace to slow and swung around, then walked it back into the midst of the hollering crowd as the other horses galloped through.

"Did you ever see a horse like that!" Marv Peterson called.

"Runs like a devil and strong." Ethan Thomas shook his head and whistled.

Perhaps Monte would find his market after all, Abbie thought. She watched him search the crowd and find Sharlyn like a sweet flower awaiting him. He led the horse there and lifted her in one smooth motion to its back. The cheers and laughter sounded hollow to Abbie. Pounding hooves raised the dust as the stragglers reined in and walked off the strain.

When all the racers had returned, the crowd shifted to the park and Monte climbed the platform.

"Ladies and gentlemen." Judge Wilson raised his arms for quiet. He held up his chin and put on an orator's voice. "One cherry of a race!"

The crowd cheered lustily.

"I say that in sincerity, even though my own Alabaster hadn't a chance against this foreign Sirocco." Laughter. Monte was probably the only one who could have merited that allowance from the judge. "Montgomery Farrel, you're a credit to our town." He presented him the trophy and the eighty dollar prize.

"Not that he needs it," someone muttered behind Abbie. She watched Monte give the trophy to Sharlyn, who had been pushed forward to stand beside him. He bent to kiss her cheek.

One man hollered, "He'll give 'er the trophy but not the prize money!" Monte made great show of pulling the bills from his pocket and placing them in Sharlyn's tiny hand. She blushed fiercely. Abbie made her way out of the crowd and back to Clara's home.

"Monte won. There was not another horse even close, but that's what I expected. His horse is unbelievable. He looked as though he could have gone on forever, hardly panting at all." She wouldn't say that Monte had sat strong and proud on his back, windblown and dirty, and still more handsome than any other. "They come from the desert, you know. Incredible animals."

"Did they present the trophy?"

"Yes. He gave it to Sharlyn."

"Abbie." Clara reached a hand to her arm. "You can't hate him so. It'll only hurt you."

"I don't hate him," she said flatly. "I feel nothing but the greatest disdain for him, and I pity Sharlyn for loving a man so false." Her own words surprised her. When had her longing become contempt?

Clara drew in a long breath. "Maybe he had a reason...."

"Of course he had a reason," Abbie snapped. "Who does anything without a reason?"

"Then you'll give him the benefit of the doubt?"

Abbie smiled. "My dear Clara. Always the peacemaker."

"It's you I'm afraid for. Bitterness doesn't suit you."

"And there, you see? I'm not bitter. Aren't Sharlyn and I the best of friends, just as you and I?"

Clara sighed. "As you say. But, Abbie ... God has His ways...."

"Of course. But I won't keep you. You and little Del will nap now, I think." Abbie kissed Clara's cheek and went out. The last thing she desired was to return to the Independence Day festivities, but Mama and Pa would expect to see her there. They watched her now with furtive glances and wordless concern. For their sake she put on the face they hoped to see.

The booths were filled and the judging nearly finished. Martha Atwater had won the pie contest as always. The grand prize ribbon adorned her gooseberry pastry. Who else could win with gooseberries? And Granny Breck's quilt had beat out Althea Thorne's. Good for her. Althea could come down a peg or two.

Cole Jasper matched his stride to hers. "Lookin' purty today, Abbie."

"Thank you, Cole. You too." She giggled. "I can't help thinking so whenever you've slicked your hair like that."

His jaw dropped. Reaching up, he rubbed his hair ferociously, setting the curls free. "Better?"

"Yes." She laughed. "A cowboy may as well look like one."

"If I'd known you felt that way, I wouldn'a wasted my time slickin' it."

"What I think isn't important."

Cole swiped a bee from her hair. "You guess I give one wit what anyone else thinks? 'Course it was fer you. And then you go an' tell me I'm purty!"

Abbie laughed again. Cole had a knack for lifting her spirits. "I'm sorry. It's just I don't believe in people trying to be something they're not. I like you better when you've just ridden off the range than when you're trying to impress me."

Cole cocked his head. "Well, it's like this, Abbie. I never figured on givin' two hoots what any lady thought of me. But . . . you make it matter somehow."

Abbie stopped. "Don't get ideas, Cole. I don't mean to be unkind, but I'm not looking to be courted. I hope I haven't given you the notion I was."

Cole paused. "You been through a lot lately. Fergive my impert'nence."

"Not impertinence. You've been very kind. But . . ."

Directly before them, Marcy Wilson strolled beside Nora Thorne, tossing her head as she passed. "Seems since Abbie couldn't get Montgomery Farrel, she'll settle for anyone. Imagine, Abbie with a trail boss!" Nasty laughter followed in their wake.

Abbie gasped. "Oh, Cole. It's nothing like that at all. It has nothing to do with you. . . ."

"Don't fret."

Abbie swallowed her rage. "And . . ." She dropped her gaze to the ground. ". . . it has nothing to do with Mr. Farrel, either."

Cole raised her face to look at him. "I know what kind of lady you are." Then tipping his hat, he left her.

Abbie closed her eyes, fighting the angry tears. Did people think that she had set her hat for Monte and lost? Was she not even left her pride? Grabbing up her skirts, she rushed from the park. The street was bare but for a piebald mongrel and a pair of crows. Flying around the corner of the stable, she collided with Monte, and he caught her fall.

"Abbie!"

Raging tears came to her eyes as she wrenched herself away from him.

"Abbie, please let me talk to you."

"We have nothing to say," she hissed, her breath coming raggedly, her fists clenched at her sides.

"There's something you need to understand. My marriage to Sharlyn was a matter of honor."

"Do you imagine it's of any importance to me why you married?"

"A matter of honor, Abbie." Monte's eyes were fierce.

"Honor?" She struggled against his hold. "Honor is a word you use to excuse your dishonesty. Please unhand me. I find your touch singularly loathsome."

Monte released her arms. Lifting her skirts, she ran. She ran as long and hard as she could through the empty street and on over the plain, her lungs crying for mercy and her legs shaking with the effort until she collapsed on the ground and lay gasping. After some minutes, her breathing slowed, and she closed her eyes, regretting her cruel words and the disclosure of her heartache. What was she to do?

She should go back, apologize to Monte, and pretend everything was going to be all right. Lying in the grass, she allowed the silence to sink into her being. Once she would have prayed and imagined God cared. Clara was right. She had grown bitter, and it ate at her, claiming more and more of her spirit with each insult, each disappointment. Had she ever loved Monte? Or had she been a child, dazzled by his suavity? Could she hate him so deeply if she had not loved him equally so?

She grew still, thinking of Monte's words. What was he trying to tell her? What did he mean, a matter of honor? She draped her arm against the westerly glare.

What was done was done. Sitting up, she pulled the grass from her hair and shook out her brown curls, smoothing them with her hands. She stood a long moment, then walked away from town. She needed to be alone. Only the land could comfort her.

Monte's soul stung with the venom of Abbie's words. *"Your touch singularly loathsome . . . a word to cover your dishonesty . . ."* What of his honor to her? Had his decision been wrong? What if he had told Nathan Bridges that he was already committed to someone? He would not have been expected to go through with it. But then what would have become of Sharlyn when she realized she was the cause of such destruction?

No, he had chosen as he had to, even though it cost him everything. Of the two, Abbie was stronger. She would recover in time. And the price he paid would be his silence. Allowing her to believe the worst of him would free her to care for someone else. But did he have the strength? No. He had already failed miserably. For the first time, he turned to heaven with something near desperation. "Oh, Lord . . ." But he fell silent, struggling for control.

Through the war, through the desolation that followed, he

had become a man. He had given God his due, but he had not surrendered his strength. And he had begun again, made a new life, forged his way. Must he admit now that he had failed . . . failed Abbie, failed Sharlyn, failed Nathan . . . failed God. . . . He left the stable and returned to the park.

There he sought Sharlyn and tucked her hand into the crook of his arm. Even as he endured the hatred of the Yankee soldiers during the war to protect those in his care, so now he would endure Abbie's hatred to protect Sharlyn. Her face flushed with pleasure at his appearance. How many times he had neglected to give her the attention she deserved. He would do better. He would fulfill his honor even if Abbie believed him incapable of it.

Twenty-Four

Hearing the hooves, Abbie turned to the solitary rider. She didn't know him from town, though something about him was familiar. Slightly disquieted, she gathered the skirt that she had let drag and felt the empty pocket. No revolver. Suddenly another man emerged out of the gulch before her, and she stopped short. The rider behind kicked in his heels and was upon her in a moment, while two others came up from the road. She froze, and the swarthy rider dismounted.

"Miss Martin, I believe?"

"Who's asking?"

"Yer pa run the newspaper?"

Abbie straightened. "That's right."

"You're an awful long way out by yerself. S'pose I give you a ride. . . ."

"No, thank you." She kept her voice steady and started walking again.

Swiftly he lunged, grabbed her from behind, and covered her mouth with his hand. Twisting in his grasp, she bit down hard. He yelled and wrenched his hand away. She tried to run, but another of the men was instantly before her, and from behind the man struck her once, and then again.

♦♦♦♦♦♦♦

Monte pressed Sharlyn's hand in his. The reddening sky

221

blushed her cheeks, or was it his touch? How sweetly she responded to him. How uncomplicated her devotion. The evening cool was calming the air as the smoke from the barbecue rose.

"Hungry?" she asked.

"Famished."

"You've worked hard today."

"I've played hard."

Sharlyn smiled. "Does your body know the difference?"

"Probably not."

A scuffle caught Monte's eye as two youngsters broke through the tables. "Marshal Haggerty!" The girl clutched her side, obviously winded.

A boy caught up to her and bellowed, "It's Abbie . . . Abbie Martin."

Monte stiffened.

The marshal stood. "What's this?"

"Someone's got 'er! Out on the prairie. They hit 'er an'—"

"Whose got her?" Joshua pushed forward.

"Four men, maybe five. One of 'em had a white horse with one brown leg."

"Hollister." Marshal Haggerty's hand went to his gun.

Monte felt rooted, his whole body going cold.

Sharlyn's fingers trembled on his arm. "Go!" she whispered.

As though released, he ran for his horse with the others not far behind.

♦♦♦♦♦♦♦

Abbie banged against the chest of her captor, each jolt shooting pain to her head. Her thoughts screamed, but the speed of the horse and the number of men kept her silent. She controlled the urge to thrust her head back into his face. It would gain her nothing but pain.

All around them stretched the eastern prairie, broken by

smaller bluffs and arroyos. They dipped, and his arm closed around her. Abbie shoved it off, steadying herself with the saddle horn.

"Feisty little thing, ain't ya?"

"Why are you doing this?" She jolted and gripped more tightly. "Who are you?"

"We'll have us a chat shortly." He veered to the right and cut down into a dry, rocky bed, his horse struggling over the sharp, unsteady surface with the other riders close behind. Abbie feared for the horses, but they kept their feet and thrust themselves and their riders up the far bank and on again. The animals' sides were heaving, and she wondered how much farther the men would force them.

Approaching a cut, they thundered up to the edge, then veered sharply to the left. She saw that it was not a single gulch, but a series of deep, treacherous cuts. Her captor reined in, and she got a good look down the sandstone draw before he swung from the saddle, pulled the reins over the horse's head, and started leading it down. The horse's knees were stiff, braced against the decline as they descended, and she expected its hooves would slip loose any moment and they would go tumbling down. It was one thing to hide tracks, altogether another to die doing so.

But they reached the base without incident, and she saw a low cliff wall beneath the overhang, and in that, a narrow cave opening. It was hardly visible until you were upon it. From any distance away, this would be nothing more than a dry, stony gulch.

Only one rider entered with them, a fat man with the pink spider-webbed skin of a drinker. Were the others splitting off to confuse the searchers? Her chest lurched. Would there be searchers? Only Monte knew she had left, and he would think she'd gone to lick her wounds. It would be hours before the dancing and fireworks wound to a close.

They approached the crack in the wall, and her companion handed the reins to the other man, then yanked her from the saddle. She landed eye level with his grimy chest. His lip curled up.

"We ain't been properly interduced." He took off his hat and grinned. "Buck Hollister, at yer service, ma'am."

Abbie felt the bile rise in her throat. This was the man who had murdered Blake. Her throat constricted—not in fear, but in such an intense hatred that she could hardly contain it. She fought back the invectives that rose to her lips as Hollister directed her into the cave. The light was dim, but as her eyes adjusted, she saw a shaft far up in the ceiling that admitted some light and ventilation. Around the walls were piles of stores and loot, she guessed.

Hollister rubbed his chin. "You're as purty as I was told."

"What do you want with me?"

"Can't a man invite a purty woman over?"

"I'd hardly call bashing my head and abducting me an invitation."

"I see you're as mouthy as yer pa. But we're gonna see to that, ain't we, Conrad?"

Conrad snorted.

Abbie forced her thoughts to calm. "I don't suppose you'd offer a drink of water?"

"Now where's my manners?"

Hollister went to a barrel near the back and filled a tin cup. The water was stale, but Abbie was thirsty and drank it all. Now she knew where the water was, and her eyes found the canteens against the back.

Hollister jutted his chin at Conrad. "Git 'er somethin' to eat."

Conrad went to a rough crate and pulled out canned beans and jerky.

She hadn't eaten since that morning, but the thought

turned her stomach. "Thank you, I'm not hungry."

"Siddown." Hollister shoved her shoulder, and she dropped to the crate. His countenance darkened as he tossed the newspapers onto the rough table in front of her. "I reckon you kin read."

"Quite well." She matched his gaze.

"Then you'll no doubt recall thet yer pa said some dirty things 'bout me an' the boys."

"My pa records the truth."

"Yer pa slandered my name." He scowled. "That's a big mistake."

Abbie stared. "What do you think you are, a hero? You shoot down innocent boys and rob and steal!" Her anger took control. "You're no hero. You're not even a man."

His fist crashed against her cheek, and she fell to the floor, stunned.

"Tie 'er up," he rasped, then stomped outside.

◆◆◆◆◆◆◆

"We won't find anything in the dark, Joshua." Marshal Haggerty reined in.

"It's not completely . . ."

"If we pass something we may not find it again, and no tellin' what we'll muck up without knowing. Think with your head, man."

Joshua stared across the darkening land. How could he go home to Selena empty-handed? How could he leave off searching when Abbie wasn't found?

"We'll make a new search tomorrow. I'm sorry, Joshua."

He'd known when they'd mustered that time and darkness would be the enemy. Hollister had a good jump on them before they'd even got word. The sky was already reddening when they'd set off, and even though they had picked up the trail, it was soon confused and too dim to read. Marshal Haggerty was right. It would do them no good to miss something in the dark, but his heart wouldn't let go.

He raised his eyes to the night. "Oh, Lord, who are mighty in all things, protect and sustain the child you entrusted to me." With sinking heart, he turned his horse slowly back and followed the other men.

Tears streaked Selena's cheeks when he returned. "Where could she be? Why would they take her?" She covered her face and wept.

"They spoiled the press most likely because of what I wrote. I imagine now they've taken Abbie for much the same reason." He slumped in the chair. "I'd have never said a word if I had known."

Selena grasped his hands. "How could you not speak, Joshua? It's who you are."

"At what cost?"

✦✦✦✦✦✦✦

By the end of the second day, Monte rode home, weary and disheartened. Sharlyn met him in the yard. He caught her hopeful glance and shook his head. "Last night's rain obliterated any trail." He dismounted, handing the reins to Will, the stable boy. "We're shooting in the dark now, riding miles of rough, wild country that could swallow her up and leave no trace at all." He climbed the stairs, entered the house, and Sharlyn nodded for Pearl to bring refreshment. He sank to the sofa. "God help us, Sharlyn, we might not find her."

"I'm sorry, Monte. I know she means so much to you."

He looked up blankly. Everything was confused. What was Abbie to him? Hadn't he purged her from his heart? Hadn't she spurned his very presence in her life? Then why was it killing him to have her lost?

"I know what she means to you, too, Sharlyn." He straightened. "I don't want you going away from the house while I'm gone. Not for any reason."

She shook her head. "I won't, Monte. In fact . . . I'll likely be staying close to the house for some time now."

He watched the blush dawn on her cheeks.

"What would you think of Nathan Montgomery if it's a boy?"

Even in his distress, a thrill passed through him and with it a rush of compassion and tenderness for his wife. "Sharlyn! Are you. . . ?"

"I saw Doctor Barrow this morning."

He crossed to her, bent low, and kissed her cheek. "My darling wife."

Her breath caught, and tears sparkled in her eyes. "Oh, Monte. Are you happy?"

"How could I not be?"

She clutched his hand and laid it against her cheek. "I want to make you happy."

"And you do, Sharlyn." God help him, he would be happy.

◆◆◆◆◆◆◆

Abbie was shaking from lack of sleep, hunger, and a growing fear. She had underestimated Hollister's cruelty. After striking her, he had left her tied hand and foot for two days, letting her out only to relieve herself. Each time, Conrad removed the ropes from her ankles, then tied them again when she returned. At no time did they let her out of their sight.

When she refused food a second time, he did not offer it again, and she wouldn't ask. Her lips were parched, though Conrad brought her the tin cup of rancid water. After the first day, the hunger wore thin, but she knew she was getting weak. She looked around the cave—about noon, she estimated by the angle of the sun shaft through the opening in the roof.

The movement of her head caught Conrad's eye. Without a

word, he rose and brought her water. Even the brackish taste refreshed her now, and she drained it, but shrank back when Hollister stepped into the cave. He strode directly to her, wrenched her to her feet, and shoved her to the crate at the table. "Write."

With her hands tied at the wrists, she took up the pencil as he tossed a paper before her. In crude handwriting at the top was written: *Fer Mr. Martin to print ef he wants to see his dotter agin.*

He began to dictate. "Ain't no one hasn't heard the name of Buck Hollister, fastest gun in the territory. This here's the story of his life. At fourteen he robbed a stage and got clean away with no help from no one. Didn't kill no one cuz one look said he meant business, and no one tried fer his gun.

"It was easy as takin' candy from babies, and he hit three more stages the same year. 'Fore long men come askin' to sign up. Wanted posters don't do justice to his likeness no matter how they try."

At this the men laughed, and Hollister joined in with a cocky guffaw. Though insults rose to her lips, Abbie said nothing. Her wrists burned from the rope and she ached, especially her jaw, still tender from the blow. She wrote exactly what he said, though her stomach turned at the writing.

"It takes a man of unusual courage and smarts to outwit any number of sheriffs, marshals, and posses. In that, Buck Hollister . . . what's the word means does best?"

"Excels." Abbie spoke between clenched teeth.

"That's it, excels. Buck Hollister's the fastest, deadliest gun in the territory. Ain't no one he can't face, and no one dares face him. But certain acts of defense been charged against him as murder with no proof of such. Charges of cowardice are outright lies. This here's to set the record straight." He growled, "Sign it."

At the bottom of the page, she wrote her name, and he took

up the paper and read, then shoved it at the boy. "Take it, Wilkins."

Abbie looked at Wilkins, scarcely older than she, but he wouldn't return her gaze. What caused one so young to cast his lot with men like this? She watched him walk out in silence.

Hollister pulled a knife from its sheath. Slowly he thumbed the edge, turning it back and forth. Abbie jumped when he leaned close.

"I reckon you've learned to keep a civil tongue." He worked the blade under the ropes on her wrists. The skin rubbed raw and bloody before the ties fell free. She closed her eyes when he yanked up her skirt and hacked the rope from her ankles.

"Just so's you know, I ain't killed a woman yet."

If he expected an accolade he was disappointed. She looked away and drew a shaky breath. "When my pa prints this, you'll let me go?"

Without answering, he walked out. She could hear him through the opening. "You give it to the newsman, then git out."

"Maybe Briggs . . ."

"They got Briggs on a poster, bonehead. Now ride!"

Abbie glanced at Conrad. Of them all he was the least threatening. At least he saw to her needs the best he could. Now that her hands were free, he brought a plate of beans and a decent end of bread. She wondered if Hollister would rage if he saw, but she ate anyway. She was completely at their mercy and needed her strength. Hollister's shadow fell over her from the crack, but he only grunted and stepped back out again.

◆◆◆◆◆◆◆

Monte could hardly stand what he saw on Joshua's face as they sat across the fire in the moonlight: raw fear, yet dogged determination in spite of the pain. Once he would have reached out to the man, gripped his shoulder, and shared his despair. Now the wall between them kept him silent.

Only Cole and Wes McConnel shared the fire with them as night fell for the third time since Abbie's disappearance. He knew there were other fires scattered over the prairie, other bands of men gathered for the night, waiting for the dawn to light their way again. Would it matter? He fought the thoughts that said no. From the darkness, a horse approached.

"Joshua? Joshua Martin?"

The voice was Ethan Thomas's.

"Here, Ethan." Joshua stood.

Monte likewise jumped to his feet. Had they found her?

"We got word, Joshua!" Ethan pulled up. "Jacobs got a letter left for you at the paper. It's got Abbie's name on it!"

"She's safe?" Joshua demanded.

"That's all I know. They're passin' the word, tryin' to find you."

Monte stepped forward. "I'll ride in with you, Joshua."

Joshua nodded, snatched up his pack, and saddled Sandy. Beside him Monte turned Sirocco, and they started for town. Monte felt the silence between them. "Joshua . . . I feel I owe you an explanation."

"I'm sure you had your reasons."

"I can't tell them without violating the trust placed in me. But I want you to know that I never meant to bring Abbie grief. I truly never did."

"I believe that, Monte," Joshua said, then rode in silence.

Twenty-Five

Abbie looked up as Briggs entered the dim cave and tossed the newspaper onto the table before Hollister. From her place on the floor, she could see the flick of his eyes her way and pressed into the wall. He made her quake as much as Hollister.

Hollister took up the paper and pressed flat the front page. He read aloud the words she had written, the words Pa had faithfully recounted. How he must have cringed to put them into print, but she could see his jaw set, his fingers nimbly doing their work, and doing it well. He would not put principles above her life.

Hollister wrapped up his accolades and looked straight at her. "Listen up, girl. Yer pa's gonna beg." Then he read, " 'To Mr. Hollister.' "

The men laughed raucously. "Mr. Hollister, sir!"

"Shut up an' listen! 'As you have shown yourself interested in preserving your name, I trust you will not stoop to harm my daughter. I am asking you to return her to us. This will go a long way toward restoring your reputation, and I will personally be in your debt. Joshua Martin.' "

Tears stung Abbie's eyes. What had that cost her father to write? "Now will you let me go?" She bit her lip against her breaking voice.

Hollister eyed her but said nothing. Closing her eyes, she

fought the desire to beg. She had to get away! But how could she? Someone was always on watch, and she could not overpower any one of them.

The light from the hole faded, and not even moonlight replaced it. She lay restless, clutching the filthy blanket to her as the men took their places around the floor. Soon the snores marked their positions in the darkness of the cave, but she wasn't foolish enough to hope they all slept. Over the last few nights, she'd realized one was always awake, and they split the night in half shifts.

Still, she lifted her head. Movement at the opening revealed Conrad's attention. She dropped back to the floor. Tears threatened again, but she forced them away. This was not the time to quail; she needed to stay strong and alert. Closing her eyes, she forced her breathing to slow. She would need all the rest she could get.

It was mostly the smell that woke her, even before the rough, sweaty hand came over her mouth. Her eyes flew open as the man's weight pinned her. His hand groped over her clothing. Briggs. She tried to scream through the palm that was choking out air as well as sound and thrashed, freeing one hand and raking it across his face. He gripped her wrist and ground her arm into the stone wall. A shadow appeared above them, and she heard the cylinder of a gun turn as it cocked against Briggs' head. He froze.

"Git off," Hollister's voice rasped.

Briggs rolled to the side.

"Touch 'er agin and you're dead."

Abbie gripped her arms about her and tried to stop her shaking. She forced herself not to think, fighting the sob that rose in her throat. If Hollister hadn't stopped him ... She pressed her eyes shut. It was small comfort to have Hollister as a protector. Only God knew ... Drawing a shaky breath, she drew her hands away from her mouth. Did God know? Did He care? Everything in her cried yes.

"Oh, God," she whispered. "Help me now. I can do nothing without you." The shudders stopped, and though she couldn't sleep, she felt the ache of fear releasing.

She sat up with the dawning and remained calm, even when Briggs awoke and caught her in his steely glare. The red welts from her nails had raised up on his brown cheek. Hollister stood and kicked Wilkins awake. "Git the horses."

Abbie's heart lurched. For once she was left alone in the cave, and she pulled herself up. She could hear them just outside. Conrad came in and filled canteens. Were they taking her home? Again she was alone. "Dear Lord," she murmured, "Though I turned my back, you have not forgotten me."

Hollister came in and took her by the arm. Outside he mounted and pulled her up in front. As his arm went around her, she felt a dreadful loathing. The touch of a murderer.

"You sit still, and you stay free. You try anything, and I'll tie you up agin, got it?"

She nodded. At the back, Conrad took hold of a remuda of spare horses. Had they obtained them since bringing her there, or had they been tethered somewhere out of sight? And what was their purpose? To ride hard and far with plenty of change horses? They started out, keeping to the gulch until it ended, then turned and followed a narrow path up the side and onto the plain. Abbie could tell by the distance of the mountains that they were far from town and not heading that direction. Her spirit sank.

"Please take me back. You got what you wanted. Just let me go. I'll find my way."

"'Fraid I can't do that." His tone was cold.

"But my pa . . ."

"You're gonna see yer pa, all right. He'll come fetch you. But I reckon you may as well know . . . Nobody calls me a coward an' lives."

Abbie's whole body went weak. "Please, please don't hurt my pa. He was only doing what he thought was right." For Pa, she would beg. She would do anything.

Hollister didn't answer.

They changed horses several times, resting only a short time at each break. Abbie saw that they were circling the town in a wide loop. Were there searchers out there? Was there anyone to see them? By nightfall they neared the foothills and stopped beside a smaller bluff that rose up from the prairie. Tucked against the wall was a cabin. Conrad crept forward alone, then returned, nodded shortly, and Hollister dismounted, pulling Abbie with him. She made herself limp in his arms, staggering a little as she landed. It wasn't hard to act it. She felt almost that weary.

Furtively she searched her surroundings. She'd never been this far south, but she had her bearings now, and if she was going to help Pa, she would have to break free before he walked into the trap.

Inside the cabin, the others slept while Wilkins kept watch. Abbie saw him sitting at the edge of the stoop directly outside the open door. She slipped off the rough bunk they had given her and made her way across the room. Startled, Wilkins spun, but before he could make a sound, she stepped outside and whispered, "I'm not feeling well. I need to . . ." She indicated the patch of trees where they had allowed her to relieve herself.

Wilkins grunted, "Be quick about it."

"I'll do my best, but . . . I'm feeling poorly. Please be patient." She made her voice faint and plaintive. He shrugged and looked the other way. Thank God it was Wilkins. Abbie slipped into the shadows. Except for the fringe of trees at the base of the bluff, the land was open all around with little shelter but gullies and rises and occasional clumps of scrub oak and mahogany.

By the light of the fingernail moon she could just make out

the silent form of Wilkins on the porch and counted on his embarrassment to give her time. With a shaky breath she hitched up her skirts and pulled off the narrow hoop. This she hooked over her arm and slipped around the back side of the tallest ponderosa. In the daylight it would not have been dense enough to hide her, but she was praying that the darkness would prove sufficient.

Stretching, she grabbed the highest branch she could reach and pulled herself silently up, tucking her foot in the notch. The first branch was the hardest because she had to swing her whole weight up. She reached for the next. Hand over hand, she scaled the trunk until the branches thinned. She didn't want to lose their cover, but she had to be high enough that no breath, no move would alert anyone.

Through the branches, she could see Wilkins straining her way. He unfolded his legs and stood, stretched, then strode a little way toward the trees. "Hey, you!" He kept his voice muffled. "Hurry up, ya hear?"

Abbie didn't answer.

"I'm talkin' to ya." His voice was louder this time.

No answer.

He exploded with an angry curse, ran for the cabin, and banged through the door. "She's run off!"

"Oh, dear God . . ." Abbie whispered. "Hide me now." *Hide me under the shadow of thy wings. From the wicked that oppress me, from my deadly enemies, who compass me about . . .* Within seconds they were out the door.

"Spread out," Hollister bellowed. "She ain't gittin' far out here."

She clung motionless when Conrad passed directly under the tree. Hollister cursed loudly. "How much head start did ya give 'er, bonehead?" He gripped Wilkins' collar.

"She said she was poorly!"

Hollister spat. "Poorly! She's as strong and twice as smart as you!"

Wilkins cowered.

"Git the horses!" Hollister cuffed his head. "She's gonna git more'n a taste of my fist this time."

Conrad hurried back beneath the tree, but his focus was ahead. He helped Wilkins with the horses, and Abbie strained to hear Hollister's directions. If they scattered now, her work would be harder . . . but to her relief they all fanned in basically the same direction. North toward town.

Abbie let herself down from the tree, ignoring the scrape and tear of the bark against her palms. She pressed through the foliage to the wall of the bluff and climbed. Her legs were shaking by the time she reached the top and started across the surface through the windblown trees and underbrush. She crept with as much haste as she dared while trying not to alert anything that would give her away by a sudden flight.

The daylight was growing before she reached the base of the far side. She pressed on, praying they hadn't already captured Pa. Once in the foothills, she felt the familiar lay of the land and wound her way up and north, wishing she could have taken a canteen. Well, there would be a stream or spring somewhere along the way. Her skirt caught on a branch of scrub oak and she tore it loose, then hurried on. It would not be long before they realized she was not on the prairie heading for town. They were smart enough to know she couldn't fly, and their search would not go farther than she could feasibly get. Would they guess she had gone over the bluff?

Her lungs began to ache as did her legs. To the east, the sun rose like a great glaring eye, gracing the earth with sight. Leaning against a tree, she caught her breath, then pushed on.

◆◆◆◆◆◆◆

Hollister reined in and squinted over the broken, treeless

land. He took off his hat and smeared his hand across his face. "She ain't gone this way. I shoulda knowed right off."

Conrad pulled up beside him. "What now?"

"Cut over to them hills. I'm thinkin' she got herself some cover."

"Git the others?"

"Yeah, an' tell Wilkins ef he wants to live through this, he better find 'er quick."

Twenty-Six

Abbie had to rest. The afternoon sun baked the land, and she wiped her arm across her face, then dropped into the shelter of a spruce, its bed of pointed needles pricking her legs through her skirt. There were a hundred places she could hide. But that wouldn't keep Pa from coming to the trap. Closing her eyes, she moaned, "God, please help me! Please don't let them find me or hurt Pa! Please, please help me!"

She forced herself on and nearly cried out when she stumbled against a root, lost her footing, and came down hard on her knees. She stayed there a long moment as the pain ebbed. No words came, but her heart reached out for God, and she found the strength to go on. Coming at last to a small rocky stream, she fell to her knees and splashed the cold water over her face, then drank. Around her were only the wild sounds of the mountain. Had the men turned to the hills?

She had to keep going, had to push on. Thinking of Pa, his humor and wisdom, his quiet strength, gave her courage. She had to get word to him. Suddenly she came upon the wide base of a trail and looked up the mountain. Was this the pass where Blake was killed? A terrible pain stabbed her, and she stifled a scream. *Oh, Blake . . .*

The pass seemed to echo his voice. *I'm comin' home, Abbie.* She could hardly force herself into the open. It seemed to hold her back. Drawing a deep breath, she swiped at the tears and went through. Just as she reached the trees, Briggs stepped out before her, and she shrieked.

"Lost yer way back?" He sneered.

Hollister came from the woods with murder in his eye, both hands curled like claws.

Abbie froze.

"You're causin' me trouble."

In the wake of her pain, Abbie's fury flamed. "I guess I could say the same. But you can't see past yourself, can you? You're so mired in your own filth you can't even smell the rest of the world. You're an animal!"

His fist sent her into the dirt and she scraped her face as she fell. He yanked up her head and slapped her so hard she was stunned. "An animal, eh? We'll see about that!"

He crushed his mouth to hers, and Abbie fought as he pinned her down. With all her strength she forced him back, and he raised his hand to strike. She cringed, but he stiffened, hung there still and stunned, then fell to the ground beside her with three arrows in his back.

The others ran, screamed, and fell. Wilkins landed only inches from her face, and as she watched the life leave his eyes, a brave straddled him, yanked up his head, and sliced off a piece of scalp. Blood rushed to replace it. A few feet away, Conrad moaned, then grew still, his own face running with blood from the slash across his crown.

Briggs tried to escape into the shelter of the trees, and Abbie shuddered as a war club split his skull. The brave who wielded it leaped onto Briggs' back and uttered a war whoop that rang against the rocky sides of the pass. Abbie covered her face with her hands.

Then it was silent. Her breath echoed in her ears. Slowly, she removed her hands and looked up into the face of the Comanche brave. His eyes still held the fire of the kill, something raw and ancient. There was blood splattered on his bare chest and forearms, and a smear across his jaw. A bloody pair of scalps hung from his belt. Conrad's and Hollister's, Abbie guessed, shuddering. But he held out his hand, and she took it.

Riding saddleless on his mustang, she leaned weakly against his back, letting the rhythm of the horse lull her. How long had it been since she slept? Her body no longer felt like her own, but a weight of baggage only. Her eyes were already closed when the brave dropped her to the ground. She lay where she landed and slept. The sun was sinking when she woke beneath a hide suspended on poles. She sat up.

There was no sign of the braves. Two women tended a fire roasting what looked like rabbit or squirrel. One of them saw her and brought a waterskin. Abbie drank, then handed it back. The woman returned with a basket of flat bread baked with berries. Abbie felt her stomach grumble. The bread was tough and bitter but had a wholesome smell. She finished it.

The other woman was thicker and worked a fresh hide—mule deer from the looks of it—with a sharp-edged stone. Seeing Abbie watching, she indicated the ground beside her, and Abbie came and sat. Both women treated her with deference, though she could only wonder why. Was she captive or friend?

Abbie knew well enough the usual treatment of a female captive by Comanches. She had heard the stories of torture, rape, and disfigurement. She knew also that it depended on the temperament of the particular chief of the band. If the brave who had brought her in was chief, she had hope he would not harm her. But would he set her free?

At any rate, even if she were captive, she was in better hands than before. She shuddered and felt her stomach turn. Swiping a hand over her mouth, she ached to be clean of the kiss of Blake's killer.

The younger woman removed the meat from the spit, wrapped it in cabbage leaves, and laid it on a board. She had ground corn into meal with a pestle in a stone mortar, then mixed it into a watery gruel. This she poured into a hide suspended over the fire and dropped hot stones from the ashes into the mixture.

Abbie looked up. The braves had returned, stepping their ponies silently into the clearing. They swung their legs over the horses' backs and leaped down. Abbie stood and waited for her rescuer to approach. He stopped an arm's length from her, then reached out and pointed to her scraped and swollen cheek. He barked something, and the woman who had been tending the hide came forward with a bowl of ointment. She applied it to Abbie's face. It was smooth and soothing, though something in it stung, and she guessed it had medicinal qualities.

The brave spoke. "Men gone."

Abbie's mouth dropped open. "You speak my tongue!"

"White men speak. Gray Wolf hear."

"You saved my life . . . Gray Wolf. Thank you."

He touched her forehead. "You . . . wise one. Not afraid." He turned from her and spoke to the women in Comanche, then sat on the ground. The other braves sat with him. Abbie backed away, feeling dismissed but uncertain what to do. She sat again in the shelter of the hide on poles. The squaws served the men meat and corn mush in bowls. Then they brought it to Abbie. She sat alone and ate with her fingers.

The women sat together across the fire from her. As they ate, they spoke in low voices, seemingly careful not to disturb the men, who laughed and chattered, waving their arms and gesticulating. By the motions, Abbie guessed they were describing the fight and relishing their victory.

All of Hollister's horses were now added to the Indian ponies, including the remuda left at the shack when they rode off to search. Abbie guessed the braves had raided the cabin after leaving her. The horses were laden with Hollister's supplies and his weapons. It had been a successful raid, indeed, and she still didn't know whether she was part of the plunder.

As she mopped the bowl with her fingers, she thought of Monte's fears for her, his warnings against these very same Indians. It all seemed so long and far away. She was not even the same girl anymore. She drank from the waterskin and set aside the bowl.

Her body ached and fatigue overcame her. It had been too many fear-filled nights, too hard a trek. She lay back on the blanket and closed her eyes. Her breathing slowed and the languid warmth of sleep stole over her. The last thing she remembered was the soft caress of fur against her cheek.

The morning sun warmed the blanket under her face, and she woke. A soft fur had been laid over her, and she was tempted to snuggle down again into its thickness, but she saw that the others were up. The smell of the fire and frybread called her even more strongly. The younger woman brought her a loaf and she ate, then quenched her thirst with water from the skin. Had anything ever tasted so good?

She made her way to the stream below and washed with a soft hide and a root, which she guessed to be yucca, that made suds when rubbed against the hide. She dared not remove any clothing but pushed up her sleeves and scrubbed her arms, neck and face. The ointment had helped her face immensely. Though the scrape remained, it had not swelled or festered.

Looking up, she saw Gray Wolf astride his mustang. He motioned, and she crossed the water. Without a word, he pulled her up behind him. The mustang wore no saddle, only a thick woven blanket with patches of fur, and a halter-type bridle. She noticed the horse's split ears, a Comanche marking. That, and its gaunt condition, told her this horse and rider had been together a long while.

Gray Wolf swung the horse around, expecting her to maintain her own balance. Abbie flashed back to Hollister's hold on her and shuddered. But he was dead. They were all dead.

She had no idea where Gray Wolf was taking her or what his intentions were, but she felt little fear. If he had meant to harm her, surely last night would have shown it. Though she sensed his closeness, he didn't intrude. Like her, he was part of a larger plan. Who but God could have placed him there like an avenging angel? Had the very ground cried out with Blake's blood? Had violence bred violence? She was surprised to feel relieved but not elated. Vengeance was, after all, God's.

The sun caught the dew on the needles of the trees. Everything seemed brighter, greener, more vibrant. She drew a long breath, feeling deeply, richly alive. A bird trilled from a treetop as they passed beneath. It echoed her spirit.

They kept to the foothills and maintained a moderate pace, not the bone-jarring rush of the previous day, but steady. Was it only yesterday she was fearing for her life and Pa's? Only a handful of hours since she was so desperate to escape that she hatched a reckless plan and scrambled up the tree? Only a sun's setting and rising again since the men who murdered without guilt were themselves cut down in their own blood?

When the sun centered above them, Gray Wolf halted in the shade of a mossy crag. He swung down but didn't reach for her as a white man would. She didn't mind. She slid off and sat where he indicated while he led the horse to water and left it loose to graze. From the pouch at his side, he took strips of dried meat and offered her one.

It had a peppery tang and was a gamy meat. She hoped it was venison or buffalo and not dog or any of the other critters she'd heard Comanches ate. Still it was heartening and her appetite awakened. She chewed eagerly. They drank from the skin, then started out again. Gray Wolf didn't speak, and she dared not question him, though her heart beat faster the farther north they went.

As the western sun ignited the sky, Abbie caught sight of

the homestead nestled into the lower hills. Her breath caught as her heart swelled. Gray Wolf reached behind and pulled her arms around his waist, then the horse leaped forward at his word. The wind rushed in their faces. Had he sensed her need?

They stopped at the yard, her own yard, her home. With one arm, he swung her down. She stood speechless. How did one repay a life?

Slowly, he raised his hand. "Wise one."

She repeated the gesture. "Gray Wolf." Her voice caught as she watched him spin, dig in his heels, and gallop away.

Mama stood in the kitchen swinging the broom as Abbie rushed in. "Mama!" She threw herself into her mother's arms. The broom smacked the floor.

"Abbie! Oh, child." Her voice broke.

"Mama, please, don't cry." Abbie squeezed her tighter. "Where's Pa?"

"Looking for you. When writing the article didn't bring you back, he and Cole and Monte took up the search again. Oh, Abbie! What..."

"Please don't ask. I don't think I can tell it twice." She pressed her mother's hands. "But, Mama, I know now that nothing is beyond God. I doubted...when Monte...but who else but God could have brought me through?"

Mama placed a hand to her cheek. "Who indeed?"

◆◆◆◆◆◆◆

The light was soft through the white organdy curtains as Abbie opened her eyes to the familiar blue feathered wallpaper. The warmth of her own bed was a piece of heaven. She ran her hand over the quilt she and her mother had pieced when she learned to work a needle. How much she had taken for granted. The aroma of hotcakes and bacon wafted in. Her stomach tightened. She swung her legs over the side of the bed and went to the washstand.

Last night she had bathed. Even the memory was delicious. Now she dipped a cloth in the bowl and rubbed her face and neck, then hung it to dry and brushed out her hair. Horses in the yard brought her to the window, and with a gasp she spun and ran outside. "Pa!"

"Abbie!" He caught her against his chest so tightly her breath stopped. "Abbie, how . . ."

"Oh, Pa, I was so afraid! It was a trap. They wanted to kill you, and I had to get away before . . . But then Hollister . . . Oh, Pa, I can't tell you how dreadful he was. And the others . . ."

"Abbie." He squeezed her close again, then glanced up at Cole and Monte still astride their horses. "Give us a minute to wash. We've been out all night."

"I'm so sorry, Pa." She looked past him. Monte's face was haggard, his white shirt limp and dirty. Why was he here? Had Pa asked his help? Surely he could have refused.

Cole swung down and slapped the dust from his pants. He might have just come from the range. His eyes weren't haunted like Pa's and Monte's. He looked almost amused, and she felt a smile inside. He probably thought she got home single-handedly. "Mama's making breakfast."

Pa released her. "We'll wash first."

They gathered at the table, and Pa prayed. Tired as he was, he couldn't keep the tears from his voice as he thanked God for His goodness. He looked right at her as he said, "Amen. Now tell us."

"It was Hollister, Pa. He took me to get you. He said no one calls him a coward and lives. He meant to kill you after you printed his letter." She rolled her eyes. "Oh, heavens, Pa, did you ever hear anything like it? It turned my stomach to put it in writing. I can imagine how you felt. . . ."

"Abbie." Pa laid his hand on hers. "Tell us what happened. Where were you? How did you get home?"

"First they took me to a cave in a gulch on the prairie. It

was full of stuff. Must have been a regular hideout. We were there . . . I'm not sure of the days . . . three maybe." She rubbed the red rings on her wrists, then caught Monte's eye and dropped them to her lap. "After I wrote the letter, I thought they'd let me go. But they took me to another hideout south of here a day's hard ride. That's where they meant to bring you. I had to get away before they sent for you."

Cole leaned forward. "How'd you manage that?"

"I fooled the boy into letting me out. I had just time enough to climb into a tree before they started looking. Don't frown, Mama. Some things are good to know. I went over the bluff to the hills and all the way to the pass. . . ." She drew a long breath. "That's where Hollister found me. I don't care to think what would have happened if Gray Wolf hadn't come."

"Gray Wolf?" Monte's voice was low.

She looked directly at him. "The Comanche brave I met in the woods." It was too difficult to hold his eyes. She turned away. "Hollister's dead, he and his men. The Comanches killed them. Then Gray Wolf brought me home."

Cole whistled. "Now that's a tale. I can see the Comanches fightin' for ya, but I don't get them settin' you free on yer own doorstep. You musta had some powerful medicine over that brave."

"I don't know about that." Abbie pushed him the hotcakes. "Now eat. You look as hungry as I feel."

"You reckon they got the McConnels' gold in that cave?"

She froze. A sudden ache seized her. "I hadn't thought that . . . some of those things might be Blake's and Mack's." Tears surprised her eyes. "I know murder's wrong, Pa, but I can't help the satisfaction I feel after what they did to Blake. . . ."

Pa laid down his fork. "I guess the Lord'll forgive us this one. Had they been caught, they'd have hung anyway. I suppose the Comanches just saved us the trouble."

Abbie was surprised how well she remembered the nightmare ride to the cave. She could almost smell Hollister behind her as she rode. She glanced at Pa on Sandy. Behind them rode Marshal Haggerty and Wes McConnel. Abbie turned toward the cut down to the cave in the gulch and led them through.

She heard Marshal Haggerty whistle. "Hollister knew this land like a wild coyote." He spat and dismounted.

"The cave isn't deep, and everything's packed in the back." She stood outside with Pa. "Not for anything will I go in there again."

Pa closed her shoulders in his arm. Wes McConnel dragged a crate and barrel out, and Marshal Haggerty followed with more. Abbie dropped to the earth and pulled open one of the packs. It held no gold, but clothing and a roughly bound journal. She opened the cover.

Mack and Blake McConnel. This here's to account for our time prospecting. . . .

The writing was Mack's, neat, methodical. She flipped the pages and found one written by Blake: *Mack's gittin' discouraged, but I ain't goin' home without what we come for. I mean to bring Abbie all I promised her.*

Tears blurred her eyes. Why, Blake? Why? Only one other entry was his.

We're settin out for home tomorrow. Mack's tired of hearin' how I miss Abbie. He said don't dare write it, but I never listen to him much. I'm comin home to her. How's a man keep that quiet? I feel like hollerin' it all across the country. Abbie, I'm comin' home!

Abbie pressed the cover shut and wiped her hand across her face. She found Wes at the entrance. "Mrs. McConnel will want this." He took the journal in his big hands and nodded.

Pa took her elbow. "The men'll finish here. Let's go home."

"What'll Mr. McConnel do if they find the gold?"

"I reckon he'll put it to good use."

Abbie shook her head. "Is it worth it? To lose your life for gold?"

Pa took her hands. "I reckon it was more for a dream than the gold itself. Give Blake more credit than that."

She turned away. "Then it hurts too much."

"I reckon it does."

Twenty-Seven

Abbie tethered the horse outside Monte's house and pushed her hair back from her damp forehead. She didn't want to be there. The heat was oppressive and her nerves were ragged. The memories connected to this day made her tense and sad ... last year's dance in her honor, Blake's proposal, his good-bye, Monte's waltz ...

It was hardly a birthday mood. But she couldn't refuse Sharlyn's invitation, not with Mama hovering over, looking for any cause to worry. And not after Monte had searched so long and hard.

That thought only confused her more. Why had he been there at her homecoming? Why had it been he who saw it through with Pa? Yes, Cole had done as much, but why Monte? Why had his face revealed an angst and weariness that pained her to see? She pressed her eyes shut and banged the brass knocker. James showed her in.

"Abbie." Sharlyn swept toward her, elegant in a rose taffeta gown with empire waist. The lace overlay trailed inches behind her. "Happy birthday! I'm so glad you could come."

"Thank you, Sharlyn. It was kind of you to have me." She felt and sounded stiff. Where was the easy love she had for this woman? Doctor Barrow had warned that her moods might be unpredictable for a while, but until today she had scoffed.

Sharlyn ushered her into the parlor. There were the pictures of Monte's parents on the mantel, the marble clock and candlesticks, the claret velvet curtains over the lace. The air felt thick and cloying. If she could gracefully turn and run she would.

Sharlyn sat and patted the sofa beside her. "Pearl's oiling the morning room, so we'll have tea here if that's all right."

It wasn't all right. Unexpected emotion choked her. "Of course." Abbie sat.

"I can't tell you how good it is to see you." Sharlyn lifted the cozy from the pot and poured the tea.

"And you, Sharlyn." Abbie took the cup, wishing it were iced—something she could pour down the ache of her throat.

"Are you . . . are you all right? Oh, Abbie, Monte was so worried for you. If you could have seen him . . ."

"Of course, I'm all right. It's been over a month now." Vaguely she wondered why Sharlyn hadn't come to visit. It was unlike her, especially as involved as Monte had been.

"We'll catch up now." Sharlyn smiled, sipping her tea. Every movement was dainty and soft, like that of a butterfly. She loved watching her. Why today did it make her cross?

"Have you heard of my brother, Chandler Bridges?"

She had. The one to whom Monte was devoted. But she hadn't made the connection to Sharlyn before. "I've heard mention."

"He sent us a letter. He's getting married to a lovely girl, Maimie DuMont. Monte's not met her but I have. She'll be so good for Chad."

"That's wonderful news."

"How I wish we could be there. He wanted Monte for best man."

Abbie shrugged. "Well, you could, you know. By stage to the railhead."

Sharlyn blushed. "That's not possible. Not now." She folded her hands. "You see I'm . . . I'm expecting . . . a baby."

Monte's baby. The words were like a knife, burning Abbie's chest and abdomen, proof of his devotion to his wife, proof of their love. The emotion she had seen in his face at her return was nothing but artifice, deception. Abbie's throat felt tight, and she forced her breath through, hardly caring to shield Sharlyn's seeing.

"Please listen, Abbie. I asked you here because Monte won't let me ride now that the baby's coming. He's terribly protective, and I don't fault him it, but I had to talk to you." Her eyes were pleading. "Your friendship means so much to me. Without our time together my days would be so lonely."

Your nights are not lonely. Abbie was ashamed of the thought. Surely she didn't carry the hurt still, surely all that had happened had purged the smallness from her. The last weeks had held a halcyon sweetness, a peace and thankfulness to be alive and home. Even the pain of finding Blake's things had been kept at bay, not reaching inside where she was vulnerable.

Sharlyn's voice softened. "Abbie, I know of your affection for Monte . . . and his for you."

The room closed in. She wanted to run. Was Sharlyn blind, stupid not to see what she was doing to her?

"I've seen it in his face, heard it when he speaks your name. I know he didn't marry me for love. But I will try to make him happy, because I love him. And he is very good to me."

"Why are you telling me this?"

"I feared that when you learned of the baby, you would not bear my company. I know it's painful. . . ."

Something snapped inside. Abbie clenched her fists. "How do you know? What have you ever suffered to understand my pain? Have you lost those who meant the most to you in all the world? Have you lived with the rejection of someone to whom you trusted your heart when it was new and able to dream? What do you know of pain, Sharlyn? Nothing! You know nothing!" Abbie flew from the room and through the doors.

The heat hit her as she fled across the yard, leaped astride and kicked the startled mare, then galloped for home. Shame and remorse filled her, but she rode on until she reached her own barn and unsaddled the horse, turned her out to pasture, and stormed from the barn to walk the land. She felt little and mean and wretched. Sharlyn had begged her understanding, but she had not understood. How could she? She dropped to the grass and gave vent to tears of frustration.

♦♦♦♦♦♦♦

Through the window, Monte watched Cole take the porch steps two at a time. In a moment the knock came at the door. "Come in."

Cole removed his hat as he entered.

"What can I do for you, Cole?"

"Well, Mr. Farrel, it's like this. Tomorrow night I'm askin' Abbie to marry me, and I'm needin' to know if that'll risk my position here."

He wasn't surprised. Cole had spent many evenings out, of late. It wasn't hard to figure where. "No, Cole. It won't risk your position." His voice was steady. "But she won't have you."

"Why not?"

He took up a decanter and poured the brandy. "Abbie has a dream that, perhaps, no man can fulfill. She won't settle for less." He handed Cole the snifter. "She's very young, Cole."

"She's nineteen. That's old enough to decide if I can make her happy." He swallowed the brandy like a shot. "Seems to me, Mr. Farrel, and no disrespect, but you had yer chance."

Monte swirled the liquor in his palm. "I suppose you're right."

Cole replaced his hat and left. Monte sipped the brandy. He was prepared to let Abbie go, but only for her happiness. What kind of life could Cole give her? What kind of love, sixteen years her senior? Would she marry Cole to spite him? She was headstrong enough that it was possible. But what could he do? She'd taken after him like a she-wolf the last time they'd spoken alone. Still . . .

Taking his coat, he stepped out into the cool evening air. Sirocco high-stepped until Monte kicked his heels. The path was well worn between their homes from first his and then Sharlyn's comings and goings. He reined in and tethered Sirocco.

Abbie pulled open the door and stepped back. "Pa's in town with Mama."

"It's you I came to see." His throat was tight. "Will you walk with me, Abbie?"

"I'd rather not." Her voice was soft, not cruel. "Come in if you like."

Monte stepped into the front room, and Abbie offered a chair, but he shook his head. "I don't know how to begin. There's so much I would say, and so much I cannot."

She said nothing. Once she would have coaxed and demanded what he withheld. Now she merely waited. How much she had changed. Did he even know her anymore? Had he ever?

"Cole's coming tomorrow to ask for your hand." He saw the flush of anger in her cheeks.

"What has that to do with you?"

"Abbie, I know well what you think of me, and I don't blame you for it, though there's much you don't understand. But you must know I want for you to be happy."

Her chin came up.

"Cole's a good man, but . . . I don't believe you love him."

She stiffened. "What can that possibly matter to you?"

"You know it does. I can't bear the thought of you in a loveless marriage. Not when you had such hopes, such a dream . . ."

"That dream is dead—and good riddance." She stalked to

the window. "What does it matter if it's Cole or anyone else?"

"Abbie, please . . ."

"I'm sorry, Monte. I've not yet acquired that subtlety in which you found me so lacking and pretended it didn't matter . . . before you went home to find a proper wife."

"Is that what you think?" Monte gripped the chair back.

"It doesn't matter what I think."

"It matters more than you know."

"How dare you come here and speak so? Are you happy only when you think I'll long for you to my grave? I swear I will not!"

"I don't want you to! But think, Abbie, what it would mean to spend your days with someone for whom you have affection, perhaps even tenderness, but not love. You need more."

"You no longer know what I need, Monte. Nor do I." She softened. "Thank you for your concern. I'm sure you're sincere."

"I am sincere." He willed his arms to remain at his sides. "I want you to be happy. I truly do." He picked up his hat and left. He had done what he could. The rest was up to her.

When he had gone, Abbie sat alone in the dark. Why had he come? Did he mean to keep her from marrying Cole? She sighed. She had allowed Cole's visits, enjoyed them even. He asked so little. He made her laugh, and she truly liked him, but she had hoped . . . allowed herself to hope that it was nothing more for him. Why had she believed he was not courting her? Because she had wanted to. She had needed to.

Why had Monte come? He with the expecting wife? She closed her eyes. "Please, Lord . . ."

♦♦♦♦♦♦♦

Cole arrived the next evening, clean shaven but for the trimmed mustache. Thankfully, though washed, he had not slicked nor dressed for the occasion. Abbie met him on the porch. "I'm afraid you're too late for supper, Cole."

"I already ate. I was hopin' we could talk."

She pulled the shawl from the hook and joined him. The night was warm for September, but she felt chilled.

He set an easy pace. "Sure is a purty night."

"Yes."

"Nice ta spend it with you."

Abbie forced a smile, dreading what would come next. But maybe Monte was wrong. Cole wasn't nervous, nor overly eager. They wandered a bit as always, enjoying the air, the scenery.

He stopped walking. "I ain't real good with words fer this sorta thing, so I'm just gonna say it." He reached for her hands. "I love you, an' I want you fer my wife."

Even though Monte had warned her, she was touched. She didn't think Cole was a man to say that lightly. She wished he hadn't. It would change things, and he didn't deserve the rebuff. She tried to be gentle. "It means so much that you would ask, Cole . . . but I can't. I can't pretend something I don't feel."

He looked past her. "That's about what Farrel said."

"Monte spoke to you?"

"More like I spoke to him. I needed to know where I stood if you accepted."

"Cole . . ."

"No, listen. I know I ain't Farrel, but I'd do my best fer you, Abbie."

The tears stung her eyes. "I know you would. You've already done so much. . . ."

"I wasn't meanin' that."

She drew a shaky breath. "Cole, I don't know what I expected from life, but . . . I can't marry you. I can't marry anyone. It wouldn't be right."

"You weren't meant to be alone."

"There are worse things. Being alone doesn't frighten me. Maybe one day it'll be different, but..."

"I'll be gray by then."

She smiled. "Thank you for asking, Cole."

Cupping her face in his hands, he kissed her. "Sure you won't change yer mind?" He kissed her again.

To be held by a man again, kissed, cherished ... "I can't."

Watching him walk into the night, Abbie wrapped herself in her arms. With any encouragement, he would be back. So would any number of others, but she would not marry one she didn't love, and Monte had known that. He had come to remind her of herself.

She stopped on the hill and lay in the grass, watching the clouds scud across the stars. Her thoughts ran back through the past year, touching every good and painful memory alike; Blake's devotion, his death, her capture and rescue, Gray Wolf, and lastly ... the awakening of love in Monte's arms, in the sound of his voice, the touch of his lips, and the pain of his betrayal.

Was it betrayal? Had he been false? She touched the memory. He had promised nothing. Never had he spoken for her, nor broken a pledge. He had done what he must, chosen as he was born to choose. It was done, and she must forgive. But why had he not even told her? If it was a matter of honor, why had he not explained? Did he think her too petty to understand, too small to forgive?

She was too small to forgive. Look at the time that had passed, time she had used to feed her grudge, time that had made her bitter. What was his offense? Finding her attractive and letting her know? The pain lashed out inside.

Yes, there was offense, betrayal, trust broken. Yes, he had urged a love from her, then turned his back on it. Perhaps his reason was compelling. Would she have listened had he told her? Would it have lessened the hurt?

But the wound had been bound long enough. It was time to let it heal, and that wouldn't happen while she washed it in the poison of unforgiveness. Abbie sighed. She hadn't the strength.

But God had proven more than strong enough. What had Father Dominic told her? *Where the heart is willing, God will provide the strength.* She pressed her eyes shut, saw in her mind Monte's earnest face.

He regretted her unhappiness. She believed that. He had concern for her. Maybe that was all there had ever been, concern and caring. She'd been wrong to expect more. *Oh, God, help me.* She dropped her face into her hands, but no tears came. Perhaps a lightening of spirit, perhaps her heart was less pinched ... With a strengthening of her will, she drew a long, painful breath and released him.

◆◆◆◆◆◆◆

Abbie folded Tucker's hands behind him and straightened his shoulders. "Okay. Try it now."

"'All things bright and ... beautiful, All creatures great and small ...'" He worked his mouth around the Ls, but it still came out *smaw.* "'All things wise and wonderful ... the ... Lord God made them all.'"

She smiled. "All right. That's good for now. Whom shall we hear next?"

As she listened to them recite, she felt the bond that connected them—the rejected and unfortunate, children of affliction, maligned and forgotten. But not here. Here they found a haven, and her soul fed on being part of it. They were bright, eager, and affectionate, and they tugged at her heart as no one else.

The night was deep when she unsaddled Shiloh in the barn, and Pa joined her with a lantern. "You're coming in pretty late these days."

"I have so much to do. Father Dominic's given over the middle students to me for reading, letters, and history, and I've started recitation for them all." She heaved the saddle over the rack. "Even Silas."

"Don't you think you're pushing a little hard?"

"They enjoy it. You should hear them. I can hardly make them stop when I have to leave." She filled Shiloh's box and slipped through the stall.

"I meant you."

"I love the work, Pa. You understand that." She blew out her lantern, and he lifted his from the rail.

He pulled open the barn door. "Abbie ... Monte's not the only man."

A shadow touched her. "Of course not, Pa."

Twenty-Eight

A buggy was leaving toward town as Abbie crested the rise over the Farrel ranch. She hoped she had not missed Sharlyn, but then she doubted Monte would allow her out in her condition with it threatening to storm. She'd spoken with neither for the last two weeks, hoping Sharlyn would visit, but it was a vain hope. Sharlyn had said Monte would not allow her to drive. Besides, it was not Sharlyn's duty to right things.

She left Shiloh at the stable with the boy and fought the wind to the porch steps. Monte had the door open before she could knock, and his face was haggard.

What now? "I've come to see Sharlyn."

"I'm sorry. Doctor Barrow said no one's to be admitted."

"What?"

"Scarlet fever."

Abbie stared. "Sharlyn? Scarlet fever's a disease for children, Monte."

"Perhaps, but not in this case." He looked away. "She . . . the baby's gone."

"Oh, Monte!" She gripped his hands without thinking. "I'm so terribly sorry! Truly I am. Oh, I must see her."

"You can't come in. We can't risk it."

"I must see her, Monte. I must!"

"Please, Abbie . . ."

She pressed past him and, picking up her skirt, hurried up

the stairs. Pearl carried a tub and towels from the large bedroom in which the massive four-poster dwarfed Sharlyn like a tiny doll, a crushed blossom. Her eyes had an unnatural brilliance as she turned, and her skin was crimson and peeling. "Abbie..." she whispered.

"Dearest Sharlyn, can you ever forgive me?" Abbie dropped to her side.

"Yes, Abbie, of course."

Behind her, Monte hunched against the doorframe.

"I'm so very sorry for my awful words. I'd take back every one if I could."

Sharlyn smiled faintly. "You spoke only the truth. You shared your heart with me at last, and I'm so grateful."

Abbie took the fiery hand and pressed it to her lips. "I'm sorry about the baby. But there'll be others, and when they come, I'll be so happy for you. And as soon as you're better, we'll walk and read together. See, I've brought Tennyson, and if you like I'll leave it with Monte."

Sharlyn breathed, "Oh yes, I love it when he reads."

"Of course you do." She tucked the book under Sharlyn's hand. "Then I'll leave it and check back tomorrow. Rest now." Sharlyn's eyes were already closing.

Monte walked her out, shielding her from the wind. "I can't see you home."

"I'll be fine."

"Abbie, you mustn't come again. Doctor Barrow will be back soon, and he won't admit you. I'll stay by Sharlyn and read as she likes."

"I told her..."

"I'll explain."

"But—"

"Abbie! Must I beg?"

She sagged. "I'm sorry. You'll send word?"

"I'll come for you myself."

After watching Abbie ride away, Monte returned to the bed-chamber. Sharlyn lay holding the book against her chest, and he sat by her side. Gently, he took it from her but did not open the cover. "Sharlyn dear, there are so many things I should have done for you, so many ways I've not made you happy."

"No, Monte. You've been so kind."

"I brought you here away from all you knew, away from your family, your friends . . ."

"You're my family, and I have new friends. You gave me Abbie, Monte. And I love her, even as you do."

He winced.

"I know what was between you. Though in your kindness you would keep it from me, I can't help but see." She drew a ragged breath. "I guessed long ago that it was at Father's request you chose as you did. Yet I realize that this in itself is love, that by your honor you were bound to me, but you never revealed the cost. You've loved me well, Monte. Better than you know."

Her hand burned in his, and he feared for her. "Darling Sharlyn, when you're strong again, we'll start new, no secrets between us. What was will no longer keep us apart. I swear it. You are my wife and will bear my children, many children for the one we've lost."

Sharlyn closed her eyes and nodded. Monte opened the book and did not leave her side until she slept.

◆◆◆◆◆◆◆

Why did Monte not come for her? Abbie knew with severe cases of scarlet fever it could be weeks before the patient's strength returned, and even then only if pneumonia didn't set in. But surely the contagion was passed. If not for his desperate appeal, she would ignore her promise and go. "Lord, speed Sharlyn's healing and make her strong again."

She actually ached to see her, to make good her promise.

Her heart longed to comfort Sharlyn in her loss. She thought of stories she could read to take her mind from the baby as she gained back her strength. Any number of hours in Monte's house would be worth even one of Sharlyn's smiles. And somehow Sharlyn's knowing the truth had removed the last vestige of a wall between them.

Now they could be wholly friends, devoted not just by the good times they shared, but by a shared and understood pain. And even the pain seemed to have diminished. It would fade and pass away, but their affection would thrive. Abbie longed to tell her this. If only Monte would send for her.

She started back across the street for the smithy, where she'd left Shiloh to be shod. Clouds masked the September sun, bringing a chill and midday gloom. As she came upon the clinic, Doctor Barrow climbed down from his buggy, and she hurried to him. "Doctor Barrow. How is Sharlyn Farrel, and when may I visit?"

Slowly, Doctor Barrow turned to her. "I'm sorry, Miss Martin. Mrs. Farrel has passed on."

♦♦♦♦♦♦♦

Monte stood, hands folded in front of his long black coat. Before him yawned the hole, chiseled from the ground that welcomed the small coffin being lowered. Wes McConnel and Joshua Martin barely strained with the weight. The Reverend Winthrop Shields presided at his first official duty. Monte glanced at him as he stood with the Bible now closed in his very thin hands. The casket came to rest with a final grating thud.

Slowly Wes pulled the rope free, and Monte stepped forward. Reaching down he lifted the cold earth into his hand and allowed it to filter through his fingers onto the casket, then turned away and started for the house in silence.

He had instructed Pearl to lay a meal for the townspeople,

but he didn't join them. He went instead to his bedchamber, opened the wardrobe, and pulled out two large carpetbags. These he loaded with clothing and personal items, then he slipped out the back and went in search of Cole.

As he guessed, he found him alone in the bunkhouse.

Cole stood. "I'm real sorry, Mr. Farrel."

Monte nodded.

"I saw you slip away and figured you'd be wanting a word."

"I'm leaving for a time. The ranch and my affairs, I'm placing in your hands."

"Yes, sir. You mind my askin' where yer goin'?"

"Charleston. I'll be staying with my sister."

"You'll be stayin' awhile?"

"I don't anticipate my return." He pressed his hat brim and returned it to his head. "Rather, I'm not certain at this time of my plans."

"Mr. Farrel . . . does Abbie know yer leavin'?"

He drew a long breath. "No. I left a letter for Joshua in town."

Cole kicked the toe of his boot in the dirt. "I ain't plannin' ta run this place forever."

Monte felt a ghost of a smile. "I'll keep you informed."

♦♦♦♦♦♦♦

Jostling in the stage, Monte was glad to travel alone at least to the next stop. Solitude was a gift. He wouldn't inflict himself on anyone with such dark thoughts as filled his mind. Even Sharlyn's gentle words could not purge them. It was better to be alone.

The thought of Frances's ministrations made him cringe, but she was most insistent he come. And perhaps she was right. Every room in his house condemned him, and none more so than his own bedchamber. There he had taken of Sharlyn's sweetness, then in his sleep dreamed of another and wakened with longing. And in that bed, Sharlyn had died.

Perhaps his actions had been kind, and he hoped this was so, but his heart had been false. He bumped against the side and shifted over. In the letter to Joshua he had included the legal note to their partnership. With that dissolved and the ranch in Cole's hands, he could stay away.

He thought of Sharlyn's words. How long had she known? How had she borne it? Hers was the honor, to give love in return for his lack. In the end her heart proved as strong as he had believed Abbie's to be.

Abbie. At the funeral they had stood silent and separate in their grief. Though he no longer sensed her contempt, he felt the distance between them. It was better to go. He needed to find where, indeed, his honor lay.

Twenty-Nine

Pa caught her at the kitchen door. "Hold on a moment, Abbie."

She buttoned her coat and reached for the milking pail. "What is it, Pa?"

"Monte left a letter. He's gone to Charleston."

She waited. Pa's eyes said there was more.

"He returned full ownership of the paper to me."

"Then he's not coming back."

"I don't know that. He's not sold out, but he left the ranch in Cole's charge."

She nodded and took up the pail. In the barn, Buttercup chewed placidly as Abbie ran her hand along the bony ridge of her back. She tried to imagine Monte gone. Even married to Sharlyn, he had been part of the fabric of her life, but perhaps it was best he didn't return. She had released him from her heart and would not dare invite him in again.

Walking back with the warm milk frothing up a steam into the cold air, she set the pail on the cupboard.

Mama glanced up. "I'm hoping to dye the last of the wool today, Abbie."

"I'll help." She poured the milk into the skimming trays. "But after that I'm going to the mission."

"It's so far to go every day, Abbie. And dark before you return."

"I know my way blindfolded. Besides, I'm working on a Christmas benefit recitation. They're in need of so much. All the children are learning some little thing, and some of them a good deal."

She took up a cloth and wiped the drops of milk from the table. "The new reverend is a kind man, but I'm not sure he's suited to exhorting the tough hides of his western flock, even if he'd the notion. Not like Reverend Peale. No, we'll have to come up with our own ways to remind people of the orphans' needs. And the recitation is the first. I know it will move folks."

Mama shook her head. "I don't doubt your success. I just worry...."

"Well, don't. There's no need. Now, shall I get the pot to boil the dye?"

"I'd rather you went now to the mission and returned before dark."

"Can you manage?"

Mama laid a hand to her cheek. "Wrap warmly. There's snow in the air."

As she drove to the mission, Abbie tested the feel of Monte's absence. With the loss of Sharlyn, it was only one more ache. At least somewhere he lived. His roots had not gone deep enough to keep him here, in the place he had thought had held his destiny. She looked over the endless spread of grassland, brown field after brown field.

The land remained, oblivious to their losses. People came and went, but the world remained. She passed a fence post, broken and sagging. Perhaps it would collapse, perhaps a range rider would find and repair it. Either way, in a hundred years it would be gone, as would the rancher who now claimed the land.

One day even the land would pass away. Nothing was forever. The weight of hopelessness bore down upon her. What was the use? She felt the smooth leather of the reins in her hands. Why continue on? Why trudge the prairie to the orphanage when its charges would soon be grown and gone, its brothers grown old, its buildings barely withstanding each onslaught of weather? What was the point?

She imagined Tucker's face each time she came, felt the pressure of his little arms around her. He was the point, he and all the others. Their needs were real, if only for the day. If for one day she could reach out, broaden their minds, build their spirits, touch their hearts ... then that day had not passed in futility. No matter how small, how fleeting the life of every person, it must mean something.

Maybe she didn't understand it. Maybe she never would. Sharlyn so young, so good. But there had to be a purpose. A purpose larger than herself. And that drove her on through the wind that indeed smelled of snow. It wouldn't be much this early in the year, and the ever greedy ground would receive it, leaving hardly a trace. But it would have done what it was sent for. Roots that were shrunken would swell and pump life into stem and branch.

The mission buildings came into sight, the bare trees weeping the last of their leaves in the wind, the juniper mounds bowing like tired green sentries. The mission was small in the vastness of the plain, but it clung to the earth with the tenacity of the sagebrush, unmoved by the wind, undaunted by Indian fire, unbeaten by killing hail.

Here was her strength, that what God had established would not fail. Though their numbers were small, though their original purpose to bring Christ to the Indians had passed, as long as there was need, there was purpose. And with purpose came hope, with hope determination and assurance of God's provision.

To fill the children's minds with thoughts beyond themselves and enable them to think for themselves meant as much as filling their stomachs. To that task she would commit her energy. She reined Shiloh in and slipped from the mare's back. The blast of wind that sucked away her breath couldn't keep her from the warmth that waited within.

♦♦♦♦♦♦♦

Icy pellets rattled against the window panes of the town hall as the children shuffled nervously behind the makeshift curtain drawn across the room. Abbie held the small ones against her skirt. Silas stood aloof, but she could tell by the flush of his cheeks that his nerves were as tight as any. She nodded to Ben and Michael, who pulled the curtain.

Little Tucker Bates stepped onto the riser. The room hushed. "'The Creation,' by Cecil Frances Alexander, as recorded in *Hymns for Little Children*." He hooked his hands as she'd shown him. "'All things bright and beautiful, All creatures great and *smaw* . . .'" His voice was sweet and clear in the packed room. People who never thought of the orphans' needs had come to hear them perform. There was little enough entertainment, especially in the cold winter months.

Abbie silently congratulated herself. Father Dominic hadn't been easy to convince. Only their need for medicines and warm clothing had won him over, and even then he refused to charge a ticket fee, but agreed to accept donations. She had collected a twenty-five-cent donation at the door from every adult and a nickel from the children. That she had posted the minimum donation amount in the previous week's newspaper with the notice of the event, he didn't have to know.

The room erupted with applause for Tucker, and he bowed a second and then a third time before she snagged his shirt and tugged. Pauline took his place, and then each child in turn. Abbie bit her lip, smiling, as Silas rendered Edgar Allen Poe's *The Raven*, making his voice gravely at, "'Quoth the raven, Nevermore.'"

At the last, Felicity Fenham took the stage. "The Christmas

story as recorded by St. Luke in the Holy Scriptures." Turning her serious eyes to the crowd, she quoted the nativity passage, then closed, saying, "And all the good things we do are to honor the child born that night, for it is in this that we find joy."

Abbie felt the collective breath before everyone clapped, rising to their feet. Behind the curtain, she silently locked her hands across her chest in congratulations as they did on real stages and opera houses. A rush of pleasure and relief flooded her. As the curtain opened again, she pushed the children forward, and they all bowed together. Then Silas reached back and pulled her up with them.

She faced the crowd. Marty and Clara with baby Del sat directly in front. She didn't see a sour face anywhere. "I'm so glad you enjoyed the evening's entertainment. Much work went into each one of the presentations, but we had a lot of fun as well. Next spring, we'll be challenging any and all to a debate night. But be warned, if the arguments they use to escape their lessons are demonstrative of their disputation abilities, you'll have your work cut out for you!" She laughed, and the crowd cheered again.

She was heady with success as the Franciscan brothers loaded the children into the two ox-drawn wagons and covered them in wool blankets. Abbie waved. "You were all wonderful!"

Father Dominic smiled. "A true charitable event." He waved back with the newspaper, and Abbie caught her breath.

Beside her Pa chuckled. "It's hard to pull one over on a man of God."

The children's voices raised in hymns as they drove into the night through the falling snow. Abbie watched until the darkness hid them.

"Well, Abbie, you did a splendid job of that." Pa squeezed her shoulders, then handed her into the buggy beside Mama.

"I had no idea the children would do so well!"

Mama pressed her knee. "They had a good teacher."

"Well, I did keep them excited. But really, I think I enjoy it all more than they do."

"That's the sign of a great teacher," Pa said and clicked his tongue to the horse.

"I was thinking that if Mr. Pemberton is going back to Ohio at the end of the term, maybe the board would consider me for the Rocky Bluffs school."

Pa cocked his head. "I'd guess after tonight they'd more than consider you. You'd have the job hands down if that's what you really want."

"I'd have to know the mission children would be accepted there."

"I don't think that's an obstacle you can't face."

Abbie laughed. "Well, heaven knows I'm not qualified for many other things, unless you want to give me a job at the newspaper."

"I just might at that. But let's think on one job at a time, shall we?"

◆◆◆◆◆◆◆

After Abbie disappeared behind her bedroom door, Selena turned to Joshua and sighed.

"What?" he asked.

"Abbie's no longer a little girl."

"No, she's a fine young lady."

Selena hung her wrap. "How I worried about her. She was so carefree and enthusiastic, overly so."

"She's still enthusiastic. Look how she tackled this night."

Selena dropped into the chair. "Yes, but there's a difference now. The dreamy, spirited girl has become a pragmatic young woman." She looked up. "I can't help hoping the Abbie of old lingers somewhere inside."

Thirty

Monte stood at the window watching the traffic on the street. The mud bogged down the carriages, and the people on foot raised their legs like cranes. It was almost comical the pains they took to avoid the puddles, only to slip through the sludge instead.

"Goodness, Monte." Frances hurried down the stairs. "Didn't you hear the door?"

"I wouldn't presume."

"Presume, presume! This is your home, too." She pulled open the door.

"A message for Mr. Montgomery Farrel."

Monte took the note and recognized Chandler's writing. "Looks like the honeymooners are back." He pulled it open with mixed feelings.

> *My dear Monte,*
> *Imagine our delight to return and find you still among us. Maimie and I would enjoy your company for supper at your earliest convenience.*
>
> *Most sincerely,*
> *Chandler Bridges*

"It seems I'll be offering congratulations in person."

"Not tonight surely. It's dreadful out, and I've planned..."

"No, not tonight, but soon." Monte folded the note.

Kendal burst in through the back door. "Incompetence!" He slammed his crop onto the stand. "I'm surrounded by incompetence! Frances!"

She turned.

"I've let that worthless darky go. Sent him packing on his backside."

"Not Moses!"

"Not Moses," he mimicked. "Of course Moses. How many darkies have we to let go? Ah, Monte. Pour me a whiskey, will you, while I wash. It's a hog bath out there."

Monte poured a pair of whiskeys and waited for his in-law. Of late, he'd limited himself to one, though Kendal had no such restrictions.

Kendal reappeared in clean breeches and knee-high boots. "I tell you, Monte, there's a time for the whip."

"You used your whip?"

"Crop actually."

"What was the offense?" He handed Kendal the drink.

"The horse stood for three hours after the rain with no cover nor rub. Do you know where I found him? In the tack room, reading."

"The horse was reading?" Monte cracked a wry smile.

"The groom, man. The groom was reading. Reading!"

"What was he reading?"

"You ask? I threw the book to the fire. I don't pay him to read."

"I wonder where he learned."

"In hell for all I care." Kendal dropped to the chair.

"Come, Kendal. Find yourself a new groom and be done. I'll ask about if you like."

Kendal frowned. "I'll ask about myself."

"As you like. Though I doubt you'll find many leaping for the chance. You're making a name for yourself."

"As you're quick to point out." Kendal poured a refill and downed it.

Monte said nothing. Kendal's labor problems were his own. Frances managed with Dilcey, baby Jeanette's mammy, and the young maid, Rilla. It shouldn't prove too difficult to replace a groom ... though he did wonder if Kendal's finances were quite what they seemed. Else why hire Negroes when he felt a white groom would better suit?

Frances was clearly piqued. At the table she returned Kendal's comments crisply and offered none of her own. Monte looked from one to the other. Their sparring was growing tedious. Kendal held forth on the ills of the ignorant, freed Negro. He didn't consider that it was his particular Negro's lack of ignorance that had so infuriated him.

Monte didn't point it out. Frances's eyes held a dangerous glow, and he didn't want to be caught in the cross fire. He wiped his mouth with the linen napkin and tossed it in his plate, then smiled as Dilcey removed it. "Very good as always, Dilcey." He jumped when Frances threw her fork onto her own plate and faced Kendal.

"You shouldn't have relieved Moses without consulting me. I depend on him."

"Well, I'll replace him."

"As you replaced Rawley? And Joseph? Am I to harness the horse myself as I answer the door?"

"Rilla can answer the door."

"And saddle the horse? Or will you be in the stable to do the honor?"

Kendal pushed his chair back. "Have a brandy with me, Monte."

Monte glanced at Frances as she fought to contain herself. She waved him away. He followed Kendal to the library and watched him pour two fingers into the snifters.

Kendal handed it over. "You see how she fusses?"

"Now, Kendal, she is my sister."

"And that's the bite, isn't it? To be held up and compared to her impeccable brother. *I'm* her husband."

Monte swirled the liquor. "Perhaps I've worn my stay thin."

Kendal took the wing chair and stretched his legs before him. He shook his head. "Forgive my deplorable manners. It's been a rot of a day."

Monte raised the glass. "That . . . I understand."

✦✦✦✦✦✦

The roads had dried considerably when Monte made his way to Chandler's plantation. Kendal's contrition had extended to use of the carriage for the night, and he'd not had to hire a rig. He left the horse at the stable and crossed the spongy ground to the house. Chandler himself opened the door, with a frowning Benton behind him. "Forgive me, Benton."

"Yessuh. I must be too old to ansuh the do'."

Chandler smiled. "I'm scolded in my own home. He would never have spoken to Father that way."

"Mastuh Bridges knew his place." Benton turned his back.

"Come in, Monte." Chandler showed him to the study. "What can I get you?"

"Nothing, please. I'm nearly sloshed every night keeping up with Kendal."

"Good, then I'll not, either. I think my veins are running wine after six weeks in Italy."

"Ah. My deepest congratulations."

"Wait till you meet her, Monte. She'll be with us shortly. She's making herself beautiful."

"Really, Chad." Maimie swept in, a compact package in green watered silk.

"Monte, may I present my beautiful wife, Maimie. My dear, my incomparable friend, Montgomery Farrel."

Monte bowed low over her hand. "I'm delighted."

"And I. Chandler's told me so much about you."

"My reputation will never stand it."

"On the contrary. But you two have catching up to do. I'll see to supper." Her skirts swept the floor behind her.

Monte watched until the door clicked. "She's a prize, Chandler. I congratulate you again."

"As you have in excess. Your wedding gift was far beyond generous."

"Nonsense. It was opportunity only. I trust you've made good on it?"

"And more. With those profits and the modest profit the tobacco is turning, I'll have Father's loan paid off by the end of the month."

"That's very good news. Your father would be proud of you."

"And of you." Chandler came around the table. "If not for you, who knows how things would have turned out for Sharlyn, for any of us."

Monte frowned. He wished the conversation had not so soon turned that way, yet he had expected it, avoided it, put off coming as long as he could.

"My family and I are forever in your debt."

Monte's chest felt tight. "It's no more than any of us would do."

"Isn't it?" Chandler went to the desk in the corner. "Here, I've something to show you." He pulled out an envelope that Monte recognized as Sharlyn's stationery, monogrammed with her initials S.B.F. He held it out.

Monte reluctantly took it and removed the letter within. The writing was painfully deliberate, and he realized just how severe her affliction had been.

Deerest bruther,

I am overjoyed by the news uv your impending marrige. There is no happyer state, I assure you, for I am most sublimely content even though I hav discovered, not by Monte's telling nor by any action on his part, the nature uv his proposal to me. Did you know, I wunder, that he loved another? For I dout he made menshun uv it.

But you see, by his sacrifice, I am made doubly preshus, one that he wud accept Father's request, and two, surrender his own hopes in order to save me, I am guessing, from the truth of whatever happened that day. Do not be surprised that I know, tho Monte never revealed the reason. There must be one or why ask such a thing of Monte?

But he is kindness itself to me, and I love him better for knowing than I did before. There is no man born uv higher honor. I tell you this in the hopes that your marrige will be uv the same kaliber of joy to you.

Lovingly,
Sharlyn

Monte stared at the page trembling in his hand.

"And so you see, my dear friend, I know what you did for my family." Chandler laid a hand on his shoulder. "And as I recall, I saw it then in your face, though I failed to understand. Why didn't you speak, man?"

"I thought I saw my way."

"How dark it must have looked."

"Not so dark as I made it."

Chandler's grip tightened on his shoulder. "What is it that keeps you here? Is this person lost to you?"

Monte shook his head. "I don't know. She was grievously hurt and believes I betrayed her. After . . . Sharlyn's death, I thought it best to sort out our feelings separately." He handed the letter back. "In truth, I ran. I needed to know if indeed I am a man of honor or if I deceived even myself."

"That's not what I read here." Chandler held up the letter. "Sharlyn was deserving of so much."

"And received so much . . . at your hand, Monte." He reached into the drawer again and pulled out a paper folded once and sealed. "Do you recognize this? I found it among Father's things."

Monte waited as Chandler slit the seal and opened the paper, then held it out. He saw what he expected, the sprawling script of Nathan's hand and signature, his father's beneath it, followed by his own. He remembered the solemn responsibility he had felt as he penned his name that day.

Sharlyn's name did not appear on the pledge. She wasn't party to the arrangement. Monte had not stopped to wonder whether she would accept if the time came. It was simply a pledge to do the honorable thing if called upon, his word given as a man, though his voice had only just settled into its baritone the summer before.

He drew a long breath. "I could not love two at once."

"No, you could not. But Sharlyn's words are true nonetheless. Love is bound up with honor, that serves without reward. You have fulfilled your pledge, Monte. You've kept it well."

Monte was silent. Perhaps that was so. Perhaps.

◆◆◆◆◆◆◆

As he lay sleepless, Monte turned and eyed the paper lying open on the stand beside the bed. His immature hand had penned his name with no idea the impact it would have on his future, only that he had felt called upon to serve, even as his father and Nathan Bridges were called. He had even been proud of it. And what had it gained him?

He fought the memories, each stricken expression of Sharlyn's when he was sharp or impatient, each painful encounter with Abbie, every guilty longing. He had thought to choose truly and follow his honor, but in the end proved powerless.

He had tried in his strength to do right but had not surrendered to the one who held life and death, love and sorrow.

"Oh, Lord . . . I'm a sinner and a fool. All that I do goes awry. But I surrender to you now, not in shame without honor as one man to another, but as one coming to my senses. The war's already been fought, the victory won by your blood on the battlefield of the world. Please take what I am and bind up what I've broken."

He took up the paper, ran his eyes over it in the moonlight, then folded it twice and tucked it into the pocket of his nightshirt.

Thirty-One

Vestiges of snow clung still in the shady crevices, but the ground gave off the rich earthy scent of spring. Beside the grave a cluster of wild crocus put up its heads to the May sun filtering through the tall ponderosas that overlooked the hill. Abbie was glad Monte had chosen this place to lay Sharlyn to rest. It was like her, filled with a quiet beauty and dignity.

She sat on the grassy slope beside the grave and looked at the fairylike angel on the tombstone that resembled Sharlyn in form. The words beneath were more than words to anyone who knew. *Love beareth all things.*

Since Monte had gone, she was free to come to the grave as often as she liked, though only now had the weather permitted her to stay. Closing her eyes, Abbie listened to the chirping of the chickadees and finches hopping about the branches of the trees. It was the sound of spring, of new beginnings, of awakenings.

Sensing the shadow that crept up behind her, Abbie opened her eyes but didn't turn.

Monte spoke low. "I tried to love her. I tried with all that was in me."

She remained still. "I know you did."

"She deserved to be loved. She was . . . very good."

"You made her happy, Monte. You have nothing to regret." With her eyes, Abbie sought the mountains, hazy in the late afternoon light, their tips enshrouded by clouds. Had she known he would return?

He took one step and stood over her. "I hope that's so. But it seems regret has become my constant companion. Each moment holds myriad choices, and one that seems right may never be remedied. Who can say what might have been had the choice never been made."

"I don't know." She looked up. He was thin, even a little gaunt. "Do you remember when you moved my place to the wrong end of the table, and I told you that I say what I think and do what seems right?"

A smile touched his mouth. "I remember."

"I think that's all any of us can do."

"And let God pick up the pieces." He raised her to her feet. "Abbie, would you do me the honor of staying for supper?"

Shaking her head, she laughed bleakly. "I think I'm coming to hate that word . . . honor."

"We have to have honor, Abbie. We can't live without it. It is the backbone of all that is right and just and good."

"Can you say that still?"

"I must say it, or everything I've done, all that I've been is for naught." His voice thickened. "On my honor, Abbie, I love you with all my heart. Do you think you could ever care for me again?"

Abbie heard his words as from a long distance, removed and muted. "I don't know, Monte. I honestly don't know."

He smiled wryly. "But you no longer despise me."

"No, I don't despise you."

He hesitated. "Then I may call?"

"If you like. Pa would enjoy that, and Mama as well. They've both missed you, I know. But the little lamb on the hill is all grown up now and doesn't bleat anymore."

"Yes, I see that."

Abbie walked over to the mare and mounted. "Good afternoon, then."

"Good afternoon, Abbie."

He watched until she was out of sight around the bend of the slope, then dropped his gaze to the gray marble stone and ran his fingers along the delicate carved angel. Silent, he stood, then spoke softly. "I hope you understand, Sharlyn. . . . You always did."

♦♦♦♦♦♦♦

Monte made his way over the once familiar and cherished ground between his home and Abbie's. Only two nights had passed, and probably he was a fool, but he went nonetheless. Sirocco tossed his head as he pulled up to the house, and Joshua came out to the porch.

"Come on in, Monte. We heard you were back, and you've been too long a stranger."

"Thanks, Joshua." He swung down. "Abbie said I might call."

"Good. She's been too long a stranger, also. It's time she came back to life, I'd say."

Monte shook his head. "I don't know that I'll have a part in that. I must tell you, her invitation was less enthusiastic than I'd hoped."

"Well, the good Lord knows His plans; it's our part only to obey. You're welcome in our home, Monte, as you've always been. And if Abbie sees fit to entertain you, so much the better." He gripped Monte's hand powerfully. "But I'm afraid if you want to see her first, you'll have to find her in the hills somewhere."

"That, sir, I am accustomed to doing."

Abbie saw him coming, his tall figure cutting across the

field toward the hill where she sat. Something stirred inside her at the sight, and she sat quietly, exploring the emotion. She looked up as he strode to where she sat, towering over her. "May I join you?"

"You may."

He dropped to the ground beside her. "It's a lovely evening to delight in such beauty."

"It is beautiful at this hour with the shadows so long and the sun kissing everything one last time before it goes."

"It was your beauty of which I spoke." He drew closer. "And I could wish I were the sun if that is its prerogative."

Abbie smiled in spite of herself. "You're ever the silver-tongued suitor, aren't you?"

"Only when it's true." Taking her hand in his, he brought it to his lips. "Have you considered my words from the other day?"

"I've thought some."

"My intention was to give you more time, but my will is not what it once was, and my heart led me here, perhaps prematurely."

"Perhaps."

"Surely, Abbie, you can tell me if I have reason to hope."

Again she felt the stirring. "So much has happened, so much changed."

"One thing that has never changed is my love for you. I know it seems that I was false, but I swear I never intended it that way."

"I know that, Monte."

"Shall I tell you why I married Sharlyn?"

"No. Keep it in silence as it's been. I believe you were bound by the honor that is in you."

"Do I guess correctly that you have forgiven me?"

"I have."

He grabbed her hands to his chest. "You don't know what that means to me!"

Abbie smiled. "I only hope you've forgiven me as well."

"There's nothing to forgive."

"Oh yes, there is."

"Then I'm unaware of it."

She laughed. "I won't enlighten you. Suffice it to say there were thoughts in my mind that Father Dominic would give severe penance for. I felt not kindly toward you, as I know you were aware."

"Then I forgive you every one, and I'd gladly suffer the penance in your place if only . . . you'd give me one small indication that my efforts are not in vain."

"And what might suffice to convince you?" Abbie felt a quickening within.

Monte's fingers caressed her cheek, then cupped her face and lifted it to him. "Perhaps . . . a small demonstration of your affection. . . ."

"Such as?"

His lips drew close and lingered, anticipating the touch.

Abbie's heart sprang into a mighty dance as his mouth came home to hers. The dream that lay dormant, but not vanquished, quivered within.

"Oh, Abbie, will you suffer me to court you?"

"Monte . . ."

"Say yes, I beg you."

She felt the strength of his arms, the pounding of his chest. "I . . . suppose I could think on it." She couldn't stop the giggle that he quenched with a kiss, then crushed her so tightly she could only laugh harder. Cool, reserved Monte.

Overhead a crow scolded from the branches of the ponderosa, and he looked up. His smile pulled wickedly. "What do you say we see who can get to the top of this tree first?"

"Not on your life." Abbie sniffed. "I'm not going up unless you go first, and only if you promise not to tell Mama!"

Acknowledgments

Though it is impossible to name all those who encouraged, critiqued, and cheered this work, I would like to thank my family for their patience, my daughter, Jessie, for her unwavering belief, my husband, Jim, for his honest editing, and my three boys, Devin, Stephen, and Trevor, for understanding ". . . not now, I'm writing."

I would also like to thank my editor, Barb Lilland, whose hard work and excitement exceeds my own, and all the people at Bethany House Publishers who had faith in this work.

Most of all I thank the Blessed Savior, from whom all gifts come, the Holy Spirit whose working enables me, and God the Father, author of life.

Honor's Price

ROCKY MOUNTAIN LEGACY
◆◆◆◆◆◆◆◆◆◆◆◆◆◆◆

Honor's Pledge
Honor's Price
Honor's Quest

KRISTEN HEITZMANN

••••••••••••••••••••••••••••

Honor's Price

BETHANY HOUSE PUBLISHERS
MINNEAPOLIS, MINNESOTA 55438

Honor's Price
Copyright © 1998
Kristen Heitzmann

Published by Bethany House Publishers
A Ministry of Bethany Fellowship International
11400 Hampshire Avenue South
Minneapolis, Minnesota 55438
ISBN: 0-7394-0588-8
Printed in the United States of America

To Jim

through it all
you're always there...
one flesh

KRISTEN HEITZMANN was raised on five acres of ponderosa pine at the base of the Rocky Mountains in Colorado, where she still lives with her husband and four children. A music minister and artist, Kristen delights in sharing the traditions of our heritage, both through one-on-one interaction and now through her bestselling series, ROCKY MOUNTAIN LEGACY.

One

Abbie Martin pressed her face to the rough ponderosa pine bark and clung to the branch with all her strength. Thundering hooves shook the trunk as the rushing force of the herd, crazed and murderous, parted in a wave around the tree. Transfixed, she stared down at the rush of bony spines, heaving sides, wide eyes, and flared nostrils.

Suddenly one longhorn hooked the buggy below and smashed it against the tree. The buggy crumpled as the cow went down, bawling when those behind trampled over it. Abbie pressed into the trunk, trying to shut out the noise. Thank goodness Monte had unharnessed the horse to run free.

She tried to see him below her in the tree, but tears stung her eyes. The dust choked the air from her lungs. She had to get higher. She reached for the sticky branch above. But the tree was slammed and she slipped, caught onto the trunk, and clung.

Abbie scrambled for a foothold, but again the tree was struck, and again. She pressed her fingers into the bark, willing her muscles to stay tight even as they cried out for release. Slowly the ground stopped pounding, though her head and heart continued. She choked, gasped, then breathed. The dust was settling.

She felt Monte grip her ankle and secure her foot on a branch. Then he climbed up behind her, warm and solid. She slackened against him, her back to his chest, her muscles spent. His breath on her neck was strained as they perched like a pair of bedraggled crows in the only tree in sight. But it was over.

"Are you all right?" He spoke into her hair.

Abbie nodded, then turned to see him. His shirt was torn and he had cut his cheek, but it was nothing to his grim face. She had never seen him look so angry; not when Blake tried to call him out nor when she shouted vile insults Monte hardly deserved. His dark eyes were ablaze with unquenched fire.

She cleared the dust from her throat. "Was it the shots that spooked them?"

"I can't think otherwise."

Abbie followed his gaze. The prairie was empty, utterly still. A brown haze of dust lingered—she could feel it on her teeth. She felt the tree sap on the side of her face where she had pressed it to the trunk. Funny how the bark smelled sweet, not pine.

She was suddenly assaulted with poignant memories of real and imagined adventures shared with Blake during her girlhood. Tree climbing for no other reason than to leave the earth behind. As she looked out across the land, she could hear his voice and unconsciously imitated it. "Ain't this a view?"

Monte raised an eyebrow.

She smiled dimly. "I can't climb a tree without finding a part of Blake up here with me."

He drew a long breath. "Here I was fearing for your life, and you're reminiscing over past loves."

"He was not my love, Monte. Even had he returned alive, I could not have cared for him as other than a friend." She knew that to be true. His death had sealed him in her heart as his return could not have.

Monte rubbed his forehead with the back of his sleeve. His hat was gone, and his dark hair tousled into unruly waves. "Can you make it down?"

"Yes." Abbie watched him lower himself to the ground. Even angry and disheveled he was dignified. How was it he always looked so . . . well-bred? He was well-bred, like the horses he kept, like the house he kept, ordered and run by former slaves who chose to come west and serve him still, though now they were recompensed.

She understood their loyalty. Montgomery Farrel commanded devotion, though you could not put your finger on what exactly he did that made it so. He didn't flaunt himself, yet you noticed him all the more. His handsome features, easy, confident bearing, and soft southern drawl were potent, yet it was something more, something deeper that drew one to him irresistibly.

Even in the depths of her bitterness, he was in her thoughts. And now . . . She felt an awkwardness that had never been there, not even when she had first ridden to his ranch to accost him on Blake's behalf after the fool boy had called Monte out for flirting with her.

If she had known what would come of that day, would she have gone? Had she anticipated the heartache, would she have run doggedly to the home of the man who would claim her heart, then reject it? He landed on his feet and looked up at her. Her heart turned over. Yes. She would have gone. She would have done it all to be received into his arms now as he eased her down beside him.

For all his claims of devotion, this was their first outing together since his return from South Carolina. He had three times supped with them, but Pa had commanded his attention, as starved for Monte's conversation as Abbie herself. She was willing to sit back and listen, to watch his expressions, to hear the laughter in his voice, to quicken when the glance of his eyes met hers and lingered. Yet she had felt more uncertain of her feelings than his . . . until he had kept away for three full weeks.

When today's invitation had arrived via Will, his stableboy, she had half a mind to refuse. The old feelings of betrayal and distrust raised their ugly heads and made her cross. More than cross. The thought of turning him down felt almost as good as receiving his note. But she had accepted, and here she was, shaking as much from his touch as from the stampede.

He let her go. The ground was trampled and cluttered with the wreckage of the buggy and three cows, one of which lay with eyes rolling and its massive tongue working the ground. Streams of blood ran from its mouth and nostrils. The wheezing gurgle became a bawling moan.

Without a word, Monte slipped the Colt revolver from its holster and fired. Abbie jumped. The bullet hole was squarely centered in the cow's forehead. Its eyes glazed, the tongue sagged to the earth. Abbie stared from the animal to Monte.

He held the gun silently, the pearl handle gripped in his palm. She had never before seen him use it. His face was hard, his jaw tensed. He suddenly seemed a stranger, a man she didn't know, had never known. *He had to do it. The cow was suffering, yet . . .*

A rider galloped toward them. The shot must have brought him. The cowboy dismounted almost before the dust settled. "Mr. Farrel! How'd you . . . we didn't know . . ." He swallowed hard, no doubt at the look on Monte's face. "Someone got at the herd, sir. We circled round to head off the stampede from the house, but no one knew you were . . ."

Abbie stepped away from the tree.

The cowboy's mouth fell open as he took in her bedraggled state and the crushed buggy.

Monte's voice was terribly controlled. "Did you see who spooked the herd?"

The cowboy kicked the toe of his boot into the dirt. "I didn't, sir. I don't know 'bout the others. It was unexpected."

Monte drew himself up. "Take a look at these cattle, John Mason." He swung his arm over the fallen animals. "Take a good look. I trust this sort of trouble will not again be unexpected."

"No, sir." John replaced his hat. "I'll ride to the ranch fer a wagon."

"Just bring Sirocco and another. Miss Martin can ride."

"Yes, sir."

As John rode off, Abbie held back. This was a Monte she had not seen. He had always been the gentleman, even as a businessman, though in truth she had never seen him conduct business. But certainly she had never heard him speak in such a strained, heavy-handed manner. There was more here than a chance stampede.

Monte holstered the gun and looked at the fallen cows. "What a waste." He lifted the edge of the buggy top with his boot, then kicked it away.

"I'm sorry, Monte."

"So am I. This isn't exactly what I'd planned for today."

"Our best-laid plans." She spread her hands. "God has His way of—"

He turned with controlled fierceness. "I don't consider this His way."

"Of course not. But do you think I planned to be abducted by outlaws, then rescued and set free by Comanche braves? His hand was in that even if I didn't see it. It's just ... life isn't easy to figure."

Monte showed a ghost of a smile. "No, I guess not. Why is it that in your company life seems wilder than anywhere else?"

Abbie cocked her head. "Does it?"

He reached for her arm and drew her close. "You know it does, and I think you like it that way. I could even suspect at my expense."

"Monte."

"I believe you'd see the end of whatever southern ease remains my own." He wrapped his arm around her back.

"What an absurd notion."

"If you were a belle, yes. But we both know..."

"Don't you say it. If you bring up tracking and spearing fish..."

"And tree climbing."

She frowned. "As though that isn't what saved our necks just now. How would you like to have dragged me up there, swooning and blushing?"

He threw back his head and laughed, suddenly the Monte she knew.

She laughed with him, though once again it was directed at her. "You were going to tell me why you brought me out here instead of into the hills."

His eyes deepened, and the laughter calmed. "Yes. Well, it'll have to wait. I'm not of a mind to pursue it now."

"Pursue it?"

"You'll not wheedle it out." He pulled a sticky twig from her hair and released her. He turned and searched through the rubble. She could smell the new leather, paint, and varnish. The flawless seat fabric was now shredded, the stuffing in filthy clumps on the ground. His new factory-made buggy had withstood the stampede no better than his hand-built one could have.

Abbie's throat felt like both drought and grasshoppers had descended upon it. She wished they'd brought a picnic, but then it would now be demolished with the rest unless they'd hauled the basket into the tree.

The sound of hooves preluded John Mason's return with Monte's black-legged sorrel Arabian and a bay mare. "Here y'are, sir. I alerted them at the house that you'd be comin'."

"Any sign of Cole?"

"No, sir. I reckon he's still roundin' up the herd."

"Chance?"

"Back at the stable. Will's rubbin' him down."

Monte nodded. "Then you'd best see where you can be of help."

"Yes, sir." The cowboy tipped his hat to Abbie and kicked in his heels.

Monte gave her a hand to mount, then swung into Sirocco's saddle.

"My, Mr. Farrel. What a genteel outing. Race you back." Abbie dug in her heels and the mare sprang forward. She had no illusions of winning, not after witnessing Sirocco's raw speed, but she wanted to feel the rush of wind in her face and know that she had survived.

◆◆◆◆◆◆◆

Monte waited on the porch as Cole Jasper approached. Dust billowed from every step and clung to the kerchief at his neck. He looked as ragged as Monte felt, and well he might. The sun had set some half hour before, and he was only now coming to report.

Cole slapped his hat on his thigh and perched one foot on the second step. "I figured there'd be trouble." That was as near "I told you so" as Cole would dare.

"Did you get a look at anyone?"

"Not so's to recognize 'em. Three men, maybe more. Nothin' to mark the horses by, just normal stock. Far as I can tell they came up the gulch. Abbie all right?"

Monte's jaw hardened. Word traveled fast. It chafed more than it should that Cole felt justified in questioning him about her. But then it hadn't been long since Cole Jasper had been inclined to marry Abbie himself.

"Abbie's fine."

Cole replaced his hat. "Reckon I'll get some supper."

"How many men are on the herd?"

"Six."

Monte nodded. Inside, he made his way to the study and paced. If this were the first time the stock had been threatened, he could excuse his being caught unawares. Cole had suspected. He had said they were losing more animals than he could attribute to nature.

But Monte had spoken with his neighbors carefully and shrewdly, lest he say more than he intended. None had expressed any concerns, and surely no losses. In a land where men depended on honesty and cooperation, he would expect someone else to indicate trouble if there were any.

So he had considered Cole's remarks premature. But if Cole suspected, he should have been alert, watchful. How did men get close enough to spook the herd—in open country with tumbleweeds for cover, gulch or no gulch?

Monte shook his head. He couldn't blame Cole. He lifted the glass globe paperweight from the desk and cradled it in his palm. He simply wasn't convinced that rustlers were to blame. Rustlers didn't spook a herd in daylight unless they were strong enough to ignore the herders or just plain inept.

Who then? He pictured in his mind the other ranchers: Dunbar, the nearest to the east, Hodge, and Ephart. They were small, running less than one hundred head and half that in sheep. Gifford stocked three hundred head and made use of government land. He'd made one short appearance at the roundup, but they hadn't spoken.

The others didn't seem too thick with Gifford, either, but that meant nothing as he was the newest comer, setting up headquarters only that spring. Faringer and Bates got along well with Cole. Hadn't Faringer worked with him in Texas?

Monte replaced the globe. No one could have known he'd be in the draw with Abbie. It was happenstance that sent the herd their way. He rubbed the back of his neck. Maybe he was wrong to suspect his neighbors. Likely Cole did know a sight more than he, as Cole never hesitated to remind him.

He wished he had an answer that sat well. Other than Gifford, the other ranchers had been running cattle longer than he had, though his father's land claim was one of the first filed. And one of the best.

Despite its appearance, the grass—Sand Drop Seed, Buffalo, and Gramma—was as excellent as the lush green pastures of the East. The ground could be trenched to irrigate, and under Cole's management they'd fenced a choice pasture and made use of natural boundaries to provide shelter and windbreaks on the open range.

Monte had virtual control of the water source on this stretch of prairie, but he allowed sufficient runoff to satisfy ranchers downstream, such as Dunbar. He'd seen that no complaint could be made against him. Too many cattle barons took advantage of people until they had more enemies than friends and lived with their backs to the walls. Not he.

The roundup had proven a good companionship between the camps, who went as far as to share each other's chuck wagons. He had learned over the past year that the best way to keep his help was to hire a good cook. His cowboys had no complaints, and to make sure he never wanted for extra help, he gave word for the cook to feed any herder too far from his own camp during the roundup.

Though Monte had not taken part in the roping and branding

of the new calves, he had rubbed shoulders with the men and shown his interest. Despite Cole Jasper's doubts as to his abilities, Monte intended to run his cattle business from the ground up. He'd make the Lucky Star the best cattle ranch in the territory.

He flipped open the ledger book. Eight hundred head, one-fourth ready to be driven to the railhead in Denver, then freighted east to the beef markets in Chicago or Kansas City, whichever offered the better price. Freight was higher to Chicago but the market larger.

Monte figured he was a choice mark for rustlers or jealous neighbors alike. Perhaps even range pirates—men running cattle without owning land—though their biggest concern was to use the land without getting kicked off someone's plot. The two men they'd come upon during roundup had claimed to be doing just that, and no brands were recognized in the small herd, so they warned them off filed lands and sent them on their way.

Well, he would not again be caught unawares. The risk had been too great to himself and to Abbie. He closed his eyes and heard her again. *"Ain't this a view?"* The slang word had stood out like a taunt. Moments after a brush with death, clinging to the paltry protection of the single tree, she had sized up the situation and come out with that remark. No tears or clinging to him, no shivering need.

Monte sighed. The stampede had certainly distracted him from his intentions. Maybe it was for the best. Perhaps it was too soon to think Abbie had put past wounds behind her. And why not?

Had he not awakened a first love in her, then been forced by God and circumstance to honor his pledge to marry another? Would Abbie ever respond to him again with an unveiled heart? Hearing her name on Cole's lips made him want to rush over there even now and speak for her.

But with Abbie, Monte never knew what to expect. One wrong word, one push too soon and he'd rather wrestle a mountain lion.

His heartbeat increased. It was that same element that got into his blood and made him want her so dangerously much. He closed the ledger. He would bide his time. When the opportunity was right . . .

Two

$\mathbf{A}$bbie pressed her back to the wooden pew. The cadence of the Latin sung by Father Dominic and the voices of the brothers chanting in response stirred her. It had an unearthly beauty that belonged to the cool serenity of the small adobe chapel at the mission. She breathed the incense, imagining the smoke rising to the throne of God. She raised her eyes to the carved figure of the crucified Christ.

His agony reminded her of the first priest who built the mission to bring truth to the Indians. He had been lashed to a tree and burned. But Father Dominic had followed and remained, serving now the orphans and Catholic settlers rather than the Indians, though some still came for food. They were never refused.

Abbie looked over the heads of the orphan children. They were fed in more than body. Here at the mission their minds were formed, their spirits nurtured. She loved working with them. She understood the privilege it was to teach the little ones their letters, the older ones literature and recitation while Father Dominic drilled arithmetic and scientific reasoning. Brother Thomas taught them the cultivation and use of herbs, and Brother José the care of animals.

While some looked upon the children as foundlings and hopeless souls, she saw children rich in promise. She fondly remembered her own days of schooling here at the mission. She had thrived on the learning, though Blake had found it too tedious.

Pain seared her chest at the unexpected memory. Would the ache of her grief ever pass? It was less constant, but no less severe.

Here in the chapel Abbie and Blake had stolen glances and wicked giggles on many occasions: when Blake had released a horned toad in the aisle, when Brother Thomas had fallen asleep and snored. . . . She seemed to feel the ache more here. Maybe he was closer since he now abided with Jesus in heaven. Abbie glanced at the cross again. It was important to remember the sacrifice but even more to know there was hope beyond death.

How else to bear the memory of Blake's face blackened and swollen, his skull shot away by the outlaw Buck Hollister? Blake and his brother Mack. She turned and saw Mary McConnel beside Wes. Did they sense their sons closer here, too? Davy and Mariah sat silently beside their parents. Abbie turned back. She was fidgeting.

Mama nudged her, and she returned her attention to the mass. Father Dominic intoned the words in a clear tenor voice. She would have guessed him a bass or a baritone. He looked too stern to be a tenor, but then his gentleness was a surprise, as well.

Abbie tried to focus on the worship, but . . . what trouble was there at the Lucky Star? That was no chance stampede—Monte's face had shown her that much. Was that why he had been scarce before and again this past week? But no gossip had reached town other than the usual grumblings of a disgruntled cowboy or two.

She could get answers from Cole if she dared, but ever since his marriage proposal, he had not come to visit. *Visit.* He hadn't been visiting, he'd been courting, and she had put an end to that. On the occasion or two that they met in town, he was cordial enough, and she hoped he didn't bear her ill will. She didn't think so. That wouldn't be like him.

But what was Monte hiding? And why wouldn't he tell her? There was a time when they had spoken freely together, too freely maybe. Monte had shared some of his past, but had he ever really told her of his doings? It wasn't natural for him to include her. His was a society of masters and slaves, men who owned men, and women who feigned weakness to please men who desired them that way.

Monte wasn't like that. Abbie knew he admired courage and

strength in women. But there were areas, business particularly, where he excluded her. Well, what right was it of hers to know his business? Even Sharlyn, his wife, had been excluded. Monte had thought her simple, and in book learning she had been.

But Sharlyn had possessed more raw wisdom and strength than he had realized. And Abbie was anything but unlearned. She wasn't about to pretend she couldn't grasp the intricacies and demands of life.

Abbie squirmed, eager to get out this morning. She had tied Shiloh to the wagon in order to ride the plains a bit after mass and see for herself what might be brewing. Monte would be furious, of course, especially if there were troublemakers about, but he needn't know. By the time he came for her tonight, she would be washed and fresh, and he none the wiser.

She startled when Pa nudged her to go kneel at the wooden altar rail and receive the Holy Eucharist. A guilty twinge twisted her stomach when she realized how little she had prepared. In silence she offered her apology as she dropped to her knees on the stone floor, and Father Dominic laid the unleavened bread on her tongue. Surely God understood her shortcomings by now. She remained penitent through the benediction and forced her feet to a restrained pace as she made her way into the sunshine.

After a quick hug for Mama, Abbie unwound Shiloh's reins and mounted, heading south across the grassy expanse. At the draw she saw the start of the land Monte had fenced. He used fences not to contain the animals on the open range but to barricade them from dangerous sections and mark off choice grazing.

Several pastures he had fenced nearer the house to contain the horses and calving cows. She had to admit the fences were few and far between and didn't truly hinder the coyotes, rabbits, antelope, and other wild things. She kicked Shiloh to a gallop, lay down close to the mare's neck, and jumped the fence.

What were the ranchers' concerns? Rustlers, certainly . . . as well as drought, disease, and disputes over water rights and boundaries. There was little she could do about the latter, but as for rustlers . . . Well, she could track as well as any man in town, thanks to Blake. If someone was causing Monte trouble, she'd find out.

After riding some distance with the mountains to her right and the fence line on her left, she angled southwest. If there were rustlers in the area, they'd try to hide evidence of their presence. An uncleared camp probably belonged to the cowboys in charge of the herd. A camp scattered and brushed meant stealth. She saw no sign of either.

There was a triangular piece of shade beneath a cut, and she made for that to lunch. Dismounting, she slid the saddlebag from Shiloh's back and allowed the mare to wander free and graze. The pork sandwich was from the end of last season's smoked meat and tasted wonderful in the open air. Once again she was thankful for Monte showing Pa how to build the smokehouse. . . . Was it only two years ago?

It seemed she had been a child watching Pa clap Monte's shoulder at the completion of the smokehouse and wondering if her family filled Monte's void. She had been brimming with dreams and questions about the wonders of life. And she had not yet discovered the mystery of love that Monte alone awakened.

But that was before. Before he married Sharlyn, before Blake was murdered, before she was taken by Hollister . . . before Sharlyn was taken in death. Abbie had made peace with God, forgiven Monte, and resolved to make her own way. Then he had returned and begged to court her. He had roused hopes and emotions with which she no longer felt comfortable.

She shook her hair back over her shoulders. No matter. The sun was shining, the air was fresh, the day was new, and she had a task ahead. She drank from the canteen, then popped the last of the dried apples into her mouth, relishing the satisfaction of a simple meal.

She gathered Shiloh's reins and remounted. A profusion of pronghorn marks crossed her path, and she guessed at least forty traveled together. There were mule deer, coyote, and fox tracks. A cottontail darted from one clump of sagebrush to another, but beyond that the land was still.

The sun was high, and until it made its descent toward the mountains, most of the wild things rested. She could hear grass-hoppers and bees, the call of a lark bunting, and the squawk of a starling. A quail flushed out of the growth beside her and flut-tered clumsily into the air.

She crested the low rise. Just ahead, a herd grazed lazily—Monte's, she guessed. They were Texas longhorn. For all the dis-paragement the longhorns received, she thought they looked the most natural to the plain. With their long legs and horns and their high bony backs, they were a breed suited to the territory.

Abbie hoped Monte would not attempt to crossbreed them again with the slower, beefier cattle. When he'd tried before, the shorthorns had succumbed to the Texas fever. Cole said it was carried by a tick the longhorns could withstand, but not other breeds. She'd had the distinct impression Cole had tried to tell Monte that, but Monte had gone ahead with the venture and reaped the results.

She raised her head at the sound of hooves. A cowboy cantered toward her. Abbie bit her lip. She hadn't meant to draw attention from one of Monte's men. The cowboy drew up, and she saw it was the same man who had come upon them after the stampede. She could tell he recognized her, too.

He swiped his hat from his head. "Howdy, ma'am."

"John Mason, isn't it?"

He blushed to the fair roots of his hair. "Yes, ma'am."

Another cowboy reined in beside him. *Wonderful.* Any moment now, she'd have a whole contingent to escort her to Monte's door. The new cowboy tipped his hat but didn't remove it. He had sev-eral years on John. "Afternoon, ma'am. Name's Breck Thompson. What can I do fer you?"

"I . . ."

"This's the lady ridin' with Mr. Farrel when the herd stam-peded last week."

Breck glanced at John, nodded him back to the herd, then returned his attention to her. "I reckon you're lookin' fer Mr. Far-rel?"

"No, I was just riding. I didn't mean to come so close to the herd." She was actually a good step from the farthest fringe. They must be watching sharply indeed.

He turned and spat tobacco juice to the far side of his horse. "Well, ma'am, it'd be better if you kept a good distance. As you saw the other day, if somethin' sets them off, they're a chore to stop."

Abbie recalled the demolished buggy, the crushed and bleeding cows. "Any idea what made them spook?" Since she was already seen, she would just make the most of it.

Breck's face might have been stone. "No, ma'am." He jutted his chin. "The house is up that way."

"Thank you." She knew very well which way the house was and had no intention of going there. She urged Shiloh into a canter and continued west, skirting the herd. What had she thought to accomplish? Maybe if it had been Cole on the herd . . . but she suspected she'd get no more from him.

Perhaps the men wouldn't mention her coming. Perhaps they believed her, although they had to realize she'd jumped the fence. At any rate, Abbie would hurry home and be sweet innocence by Monte's arrival.

She urged Shiloh to a gallop with pressure from her knees and eased into the motion. She breathed easier after she'd put a rise or two between the herd and herself, but she did not slacken her pace. Suddenly the horse stumbled.

Abbie leaped free as the mare went down. She rolled to break her fall, then got to her knees, a little shaken, but she seemed sound. Nothing hurt . . . much. She stood as Shiloh staggered up, as well. Abbie brushed the dirt from her dress and sleeves. She was all right. Was Shiloh?

The horse held up the offending hoof. The shoe hung by one nail. From the looks of things, she'd be walking back. Abbie closed her eyes and dropped her forehead to the mare's neck.

Was this penance for her meddling, or perhaps God keeping

her honest? She winced. He certainly had a way of turning her from sin. But she hadn't meant to deceive Monte, only to . . . avoid being confronted. Well, yes, she had intended to learn things he chose to keep from her, but . . .

She sighed. Running her hand down Shiloh's leg, she felt for damage. A small swelling already bloomed at the ankle, and the knee was scraped. She yanked the shoe from the hoof, and Shiloh tried her weight. It held, but painfully. Shiloh tossed her head and snorted. It would be slow going.

Abbie took the reins and led the horse forward. At this rate Mama would have searchers out for her . . . and with good reason. The last year she'd seen trouble enough. Pa and Cole and Monte and most of the townsmen had searched day after day for her when Hollister and his outlaws had abducted her. She could still remember the hollow weariness in their eyes.

And she could just imagine Mama's face when Monte arrived for her this evening to find she hadn't yet returned. Oh, what a commotion there would be! She plodded on. The dust climbed her skirts, and she kicked at a young yucca plant not yet sporting the sharp, stiff spikes of the others in her path.

Abbie swiped the beading perspiration from her forehead with her sleeve. The sun was well on its descending arch and the baked land radiated the heat. Maybe she should have made for town. If she had continued southwest instead of heading directly for the spur of mountain, beneath which her father's homestead nestled . . . She heard hooves from behind and hardly dared to turn. Was it Monte catching her in the act? *Thank you very much, Lord.*

The rider came alongside, and she looked up to find Cole Jasper astride his palomino. He tipped his hat up with his fingertips, releasing a riot of blond hair beneath, and grinned. "Afternoon, Abbie. Lamed yer horse?"

"She threw a shoe."

"And you, by the looks of it."

"I jumped clear, thank you."

"And took a roll. Yer hair's sportin' sagebrush."

25

Abbie reached a hand to her hair and found the sprig. She tugged it free and tossed it.

"You hurt?"

Abbie swallowed her pride. After all, Cole had found her unconscious and nearly frozen as a result of her last fall. "No. I'm not hurt."

Cole dismounted and bent before Shiloh, feeling the leg. "Bit sore, is she?"

"Yes."

"Why don't you leave her with me and take Scotch."

"How will you get back?"

"Breck's just behind me. He'll be along soon enough." He stood. "What're you doin' out here?"

"I . . ." Abbie expelled her breath. "I wanted to know what's going on."

His green eyes sobered. "This ain't the time to meddle, Abbie. If you're lookin' to git yer pa a newspaper story . . ."

So there *was* something happening. "I'm not. I just wanted to know."

"Ain't nothin' to know yet. Just watchin' and waitin'."

"For the rustlers to make their move?"

Cole removed his hat and scratched behind his ear, then replaced it and appraised her. "I don't know what Mr. Farrel's told you."

"Precious little."

Cole hung his head and grinned. "Well, now, Abbie, I am in his employ."

"Oh, Cole. You won't hold back on me."

He shook his head. "Ain't nothin' certain yet. Maybe rustlers, maybe not. Sure wouldn't be the first time. Once word gets out there's a profitable herd . . ." He swung his arm. "Lots of empty country round about."

"Have you seen them?"

He hesitated. "Might've."

"At the stampede?"

He narrowed his eyes, and she didn't give him time to deny it.

"Monte asked if the men had seen anyone. I guessed if you were on the herd . . ."

"Look, Abbie. Like I said before, ain't nothin' certain. You keep quiet on that stampede. Mr. Farrel's of a mind to watch and wait, keep his cards close to the vest."

"So I've seen."

"Well, in this case it's wise. Don't want to tip our hand till we got somethin' fer sure."

"But you think it's rustlers."

"Now, there you go trippin' me into sayin' more than I should. Look, here's Breck comin' now." He held out his hand. "Climb up on Scotch. He'll git you home."

Abbie mounted. The horse was a good two hands taller than Shiloh and broader, too. She took the reins from Cole as he slid them over the horse's head.

"I'll git yer mare back soon as she's able."

"Thank you, Cole." Abbie nodded to Breck who came alongside, then clicked her tongue and heeled Scotch. He responded immediately. Short of any further catastrophe, she had a chance of beating Monte to her homestead. But she knew not to count on it.

Three

Abbie arrived home as the sun reached the still snow-streaked Pikes Peak. The sharp brilliance forced her to avert her eyes. Once it sank beneath the ridge, the sky would burst with color, each string of cloud set aflame in hues of gold and orange, then blushing pink, as though ashamed of calling such attention to themselves.

She had made good time on Scotch and silently thanked Cole for his consideration. But for his happening upon her when he did, she'd still be trudging the plain and tonight's plans would be ruined. She didn't want to think how often she narrowly escaped ruin.

Abbie led Scotch to the barn and stabled him in Shiloh's stall. Cole's saddle must outweigh hers by twenty pounds. She struggled to slide it from the horse's back and hook it over the rail. Scotch tossed his huge head when she removed the bit and filled his box with fodder. She blew the curling tendrils of hair from her forehead as she quit the barn and started across the yard.

Monte was just driving Chance and the old buggy through the gate. As Abbie slipped unnoticed into the kitchen from the lean-to, Mama spun around. "Abbie, where on earth . . ."

"Shiloh threw a shoe. And Monte's at the gate. Have you some water heated?"

"Yes, and I was about to add the beans." Mama sighed. "Well, take it and get washed. I'll have Pa keep Monte."

"Thank you, Mama."

"Toss your dirty things outside the door."

"Yes, Mama."

In the small lean-to, Abbie poured the pot's contents into the metal tub and added two pails of cold, as well. She quickly shed her dusty, bur-covered outer clothing and dropped it outside the door and onto the kitchen floor as Mama had directed. She dropped her underclothing into the water to wash with her, then she stepped into the tub. With more haste than care, she scrubbed herself with the sweet bar of chamomile soap, then rinsed her hair with lavender water.

She stepped out, toweled her arms, legs, and head, and panicked. She had neglected to get a change of clothes before bathing. She could hear Pa's laughter in the front room and guessed Monte's wit was the cause. She cracked the door to the kitchen. Mama was nowhere in sight. Neither were her clothes. "Mama?" she whispered.

No answer. Monte was praising Pa's editorial on education in the Rockies. She pushed the door open further. "Mama?" Nothing. She retrieved and squeezed out her wet chemise and drawers, then pulled them on.

Mama was still not there. She crept out onto the smooth wood floor. With her arms wrapped tightly around her wet chemise and her drawers running streams down her legs, she tiptoed across the kitchen, nearing the doorway to the front room.

Pa was laughing again. "And if I put that in print I'd have half the territory on my neck."

"That hasn't stopped you before."

"All depends what I mean to accomplish. Leading folks to a higher place is one thing, pointing out the planks in their eyes is another. I don't mind taking on a splinter or two, but you have to lead into the bigger things little by little."

"I suppose you're right. If there's . . ."

Abbie streaked across the doorway and rushed for her room. She closed the door behind her and felt the laughter boil up from her chest. She clamped a hand to her mouth and took deep breaths. Monte's expression was one she would not soon forget. She should be appalled, humiliated, but his face . . .

Not that he got much of a look, but all the same. Heavens, if Mama found out! Abbie shivered. Stripping off her wet under-things, she tied on the corset she rarely wore, pulled on the bustle she detested, and dressed in the blue cotton dress she'd been fit-ted for last month. Monte hadn't seen it yet, and he was taking her to town.

She brushed her hair up at the sides and held it with combs. The bulk she left loose down her back. It would dry as they rode. Drawing herself up, she took a quick survey in the mirror. In stockings and leather slippers, and with her breath constricted by the corset, she felt like a lady. Both Pa and Monte stood when she entered.

"Pretty as a picture," Pa said.

"Thank you, Pa." Abbie walked calmly over to Monte. "I'm sorry I kept you waiting."

He bowed. His white gabardine shirt with pleated yoke and ivory buttons, gray trousers, and matching vest were impeccable. Her heart skipped a beat when he reached for her hand and brushed her fingers with his lips. "It was well worth the wait, I assure you." His voice softened with the drawl.

Monte curled her fingers into the crook of his arm and led her out. The sky's fire had passed. Lavender deepened to indigo in the east and paled to pink over the mountains. The peaks themselves were a flat silhouette, like a paper cutting stood up inside the bowl of sky. "Oh, Monte, isn't it lovely?"

"It is. The western skies rival anything South Carolina could produce and make up for much of the dry expanse."

Abbie laughed. "It's creeping in."

He helped her into his older buggy. "What is?"

"This place. You said you have yet to find a love for it, but it's starting, I can tell."

Standing beside her as she settled in, Monte laid a hand on her knee. "Were it not for seeing things through your eyes, Abbie, I doubt I would ever come to it." He walked around and climbed up beside her. Clicking his tongue to Chance, he flicked the reins.

Abbie held her breath, waiting for him to mention her wet

dash. She didn't know whether to laugh or deny it. But it seemed he would be the gentleman tonight. He said nothing about it at all.

An owl hooted in the dusk from a clump of scrub oak as they passed. Monte searched for it. "That's a singularly lonely sound, isn't it?"

"Plaintive, yes. But I don't suppose he's any lonelier than the other wild things. Do you think animals long for companionship?"

"I don't know. Some more than others, I'd guess. Pack animals, for instance."

"Is it companionship they desire or simple need that keeps them together? Protection and survival."

Monte laughed softly. "I don't know. Take cattle, for instance. They huddle together and move as a herd, but I'll wager with the exception of cows and their calves, they haven't really an inkling the others are there. Nor a thought for those who aren't. It's enough to fill their bellies each day and lie safe each night from prowling coyotes and wildcats."

"Birds and creatures that mate for life, though—there might be something there."

"There might." He rounded the bend and flicked the reins lightly to return Chance to speed. "But still, you can't attribute human commitment to animal nature."

"Some humans can't be attributed even animal nature."

Monte glanced over. "I'm afraid that's true. That's why we strive for honor."

Abbie half smiled. She would not debate the merits of honor with him tonight. "Yet the wild things have a code of their own. A code we violate without a thought."

"In what way?"

"By fencing the land and overrunning their homes."

"Oh yes, the poor mangy coyote and the lithe pronghorn that leap fences in a single bound."

"And the great herds of buffalo and the Indian tribes, driven off to make way for settlements."

"Of course, you'd rather live in a tepee than have a ranch and a fine upcoming town such as Rocky Bluffs. Perhaps you'd prefer a savage brave to a southern gentleman seeking your favor. How many horses are you worth, Abbie?" He reached over and raised her chin. "Let me see your teeth and feel the meat on your bones."

He squeezed her arm. "Hmm. Not much extra to get you through a thin winter. Still, you might be a good breeder."

"Monte!"

He shrugged. "Be careful what you wish for."

"I wasn't wishing." Abbie settled her skirts around her. "What are we doing tonight?"

"Don't tell me you haven't heard?"

"Heard what?"

"Is it possible I'm possessed of knowledge you've not acquired?"

"How can I say when I've no inkling what you're talking about?"

"Why, the whole town was buzzing over it today."

"I wasn't in town today."

"No, you weren't, were you?"

Abbie bit her lip. How cleverly he had led her along, trapped her up in her enthusiasm. She tried to hide her discomfort. "I was riding."

"So I heard."

"Did you?"

"Don't play the innocent with me, Abbie. When three of my men feel compelled to report your presence, I pay attention. You couldn't have come near the herd without jumping the fence."

Abbie winced. All three of them. Had Cole told him her purpose? "Well, you know how I feel about fences."

He reined in and turned to her. "Fences can be for protection."

"Goodness, Monte. I was in no need of protection."

"Then you learned nothing from being stampeded by four hundred head of raging cattle?"

Abbie slouched. "You needn't scold. Nothing worse came of it than Shiloh throwing a shoe."

"Yes, I left Cole tending her."

"How is she?"

"She'll mend." He leaned forward and took her shoulders. "I want the truth, Abbie. Why were you canvassing my pastureland?"

"Canvassing?"

He gave her a little shake. "Though both Breck and John believed you'd gone astray, I know well enough your propensities. And Cole was amazingly vague for a man who can detail to me every action of the men in his charge."

So Cole hadn't told him. Somehow his keeping her secret made her feel twice as guilty. "If you must know, I was looking for the rustlers."

"The deuce!" Monte dropped his hands from her shoulders. "Who said anything about rustlers? And if there are rustlers, the last person I need involved is you."

Abbie shrank from the intensity in his eyes. "Monte, I . . ."

"Don't say it, Abbie. Whatever excuse you offer is worthless. I want to know you will desist from any such activity. Give me your word."

"What am I pledging? That I won't ride free and keep my eyes open?"

"Do you live to plague me with concern for you?"

Something in his tone quenched her indignation. "No, I . . ."

"Then promise me you'll not interfere."

"All right, I promise, but . . ."

"Nothing more. Only your word given. I trust you'll keep it."

She bristled. "You're not the only one to honor your word, Monte."

His silence was a worse reproof than any retort. She should not have flung that at him. They both knew what keeping his word had cost them.

"Well, then, shall we?" He took up the reins and the buggy lurched forward.

Abbie stung with his rebuke, though she had brought it on herself. What had she thought to accomplish? To satisfy her curiosity? Did she think there was anything she could do against a gang of rustlers, men reckless enough to risk being lynched for their actions?

Still, Monte hadn't needed to be so ... heavy-handed. He hadn't given her the chance to explain. Explain what? That she deliberately defied what she knew he would want? It hadn't seemed wrong at the start. It was so confusing. It seemed her very nature betrayed her.

Monte spoke low. "Forgive my ire, Abbie. I had intended this evening to be ... congenial. I'm tired of sparring with you."

"I'm sorry, too, Monte. I didn't mean to worry you."

"No. You meant to keep it from me entirely."

Abbie started to protest, then stopped. He was right.

"I've had enough of secrets. I can't live that way."

His tone held both hurt and weariness. It reminded her of what he had suffered the last year and awakened her own loss: the two people precious to her heart who had died. Blake and Sharlyn. She pictured Sharlyn's face, white blond hair, delicate rose petal skin, green eyes as lacking in guile as a newborn babe's. "I mourn her, too, Monte."

She spoke without thinking, and he turned, started to reply, then closed his mouth in silence.

"I thought when you brought her here as your wife, I would hate her. But I couldn't. I loved her so."

"You did so better than I." In the gathering darkness, his face revealed an ache she could almost feel.

"No, Monte. You were faithful and kind."

He reined in. "Faithful and kind. Is that enough, Abbie? Enough to make up for what I felt for you, for the nights I closed my eyes and imagined it was you in my arms?"

Abbie felt her chest tighten. What was he saying? That all the time she had so resented his loving Sharlyn, he had thought of her? Felt some measure of the loss she knew? She recalled the burning of his eyes when she would catch his glance, then coldly turn her back. Something inside had known how that would pain him. Yet how could it, unless he still cared?

Had he spoken the truth—that his love for her had never

changed? The self-reproach in his expression said it was so. She felt a deep sadness for Sharlyn. "Sharlyn never knew. She loved you."

"She knew ... and she loved me." He stared straight ahead. "She was so fragile. Perhaps if I had cared for her better, loved her better ..."

"What more could you have done, Monte? Can you stop scarlet fever? Can you stop death? Sharlyn's at peace; you need to be, also."

He reached over and squeezed her hand. "Shall we call a truce and enjoy the night?"

"Yes, of course." Abbie wanted to throw her arms around his neck and hold him until the smile was back in his eyes. But he'd been so formal since his return, as though they were truly beginning together with no thought for what had passed before. With the exception of the kiss two months ago by which he had cajoled permission to court her, he had maintained a strained and difficult distance.

Abbie tried for a lighter mood. "You still haven't told me what we're doing. Or was all that to trap me into confessing?"

"It was not, though I daresay your guilty conscience did a good job of convicting you."

"I thought you said truce."

He smiled. "So I did." As they came to the edge of town, he pointed. "Look there."

Abbie stared through the dusk at the crowd gathering outside the hotel. "What is it? What's happening?"

"Theater, Abbie. Theater has come to Rocky Bluffs."

"What theater?"

"A traveling troupe. None other than Miss Carolina Diamond and her Troupe Comique."

"Monte!"

He smiled. "I thought you'd prefer it to tracking rustlers."

Abbie bristled. "And if you keep throwing that in my face, I'll take up with Miss Carolina and her troupe."

He threw back his head and laughed. "Have at it, then. I don't doubt for a moment they'd take you." He pulled the buggy to a stop a good two blocks down because of the crowd of horses, wagons, and buggies.

Abbie alighted, aglow with anticipation. "Why is everyone gathered at the hotel? Surely they're not playing in the restaurant?"

"They're probably waiting to escort them to the saloon. I've heard Miss Diamond is wont to take the arm of some lucky chap and allow him to hoist her right up onto the stage."

"I've no doubt you'll be fighting your way to the front then."

"No, thank you. I've waited long enough to have *you* on my arm." He bent and kissed her fingers. This time there was no mistaking the contact of his lips with her skin, not at all the obligatory courtly bow. Abbie's heart raced. If he had taken her into his arms right there in the street and kissed her, she would not have resisted. But of course he didn't.

Montgomery Farrel was bred of generations of gentlemen, rigid in their honor and respect for the fairer sex. He extended the crook of his arm, and Abbie slid her hand within the protective cocoon as he led her to the saloon. She had been inside two months ago when the political orator had held a rally to propose the cause of statehood. All the town had gone, even Mama.

This time the entire back section had been cleared to erect the traveling stage. In deference to the lady guests, the main shelves of liquor over the bar were hung with fabric, though it wouldn't stop it being served, she was sure. During the political speech the audience had used every dramatic pause to order up.

Abbie followed Monte to a small table directly before the stage. The two chairs were roped together and leaned onto the table. Monte worked the rope free.

"Do you think we should?" Abbie glanced around at the other tables. None were tied.

"It's reserved for us."

Well. But then, she was not used to being formally courted by Montgomery Farrel. That had been Sharlyn's delight. Abbie felt a pang. How bitter she had been. It didn't seem right for her to receive his attention now. She felt for a moment as though the floor would open and swallow her up.

"What is it, Abbie?"

She shook her head. "I'm not used to being fussed over."

Before he could answer, the doors swung open and the uproarious crowd burst upon them. Ethan Thomas proudly sported the jeweled hand of Miss Carolina Diamond on his arm. She literally glittered from head to foot; a sequined headpiece adorned her blond hair, a white sequined gown shirred over ruffled layers of fine, sheer taffeta. Abbie's dress might have been burlap.

"What do you think?" Monte whispered as she passed.

"She's beautiful." Abbie now studied the lady's face. It wasn't really true. She was glamorous, and the clothes sumptuous, but Miss Diamond herself was too hard, too . . . overstated for beauty. Abbie doubted a man in the room would agree with her. The red lips, the eyes outlined and glittering like the rest of her, the beauty mark to the right of her upper lip . . .

Ethan Thomas bent and lifted her into his arms, and she wrapped a hand around his neck, then flounced enough ruffle to reveal both calves as she was swung onto the stage. Applause filled the room. Abbie had to admit this was excitement they hadn't known in Rocky Bluffs. She glanced around and found Clara and Marty Franklin.

She smiled broadly and Clara waved, then raised her eyebrows toward Monte. Abbie hoped he hadn't seen and warned her off with a glare, but Clara laughed. She knew the condition of Abbie's heart at that moment. Monte pulled out the chair and Abbie sat, thankfully with her back to Clara.

Monte took his place beside her, his eyes glowing with the same admiration evident on every face there. Miss Diamond folded her hands at her chest and began to sing. Abbie felt her mouth drop in silent wonder. Carolina Diamond's voice was more rich and clear than the combination of all her jewels. Abbie forgot her initial impression and was swept up in the music.

She noticed the man at the piano, though when he had taken his place, she couldn't say. The song ended, and Abbie clapped vigorously. Turning to her left she saw Judge Wilson with his wife, and beside them, Marcy. She startled to realize Marcy Wilson was not watching the stage but had her eye intently on Monte.

Marcy noticed Abbie and, in typical fashion, put up her nose and turned away. Abbie was dying to know if Clara had seen but didn't dare turn or draw Monte's attention. Instead she stole a glance his way, and he smiled and leaned close. "Not a bad little songbird, hmm?"

"She's wonderful." Abbie didn't have to feign her enthusiasm, for Miss Diamond began to sing again, this time a rollicking, even bawdy, tune. She strode back and forth across the stage, working the crowd with a swing of her hips, a swish of her arm, a flash of creamy neck and more chest than Abbie thought could show without coming loose. She was fascinated. What would it be like to grace a stage with every adoring eye in the room fixed on you alone?

After the second song, the stage emptied, and props were slid into place. Abbie sat on the edge of her seat. She'd never seen a play, not with props and all. The music started up fast, an old man now at the piano. How his fingers could fly! A boy held up a sign painted in gilded letters: *"Watson's Gold"—An Original Comique.* Miss Diamond, now dressed in stockings and layered scarves, played a nymph who led the bemused miners to think of things other than gold.

Monte laughed heartily when the now ragged and starving Watson forsook the glaring vein in the rock wall to follow the nymph to his death. He leaned close and whispered, "Not a bad end, really."

Abbie frowned, and Monte laughed harder. Two of the men juggled knives while the stage was cleared again, then Miss Diamond reappeared, dressed all in black fur except for sheer black sleeves. The dress was fitted to her figure with the front of her skirt cut away to reveal the black stockinged leg beneath her knee.

Abbie stared at the fur. "What animal do you suppose that is?"

Monte never looked her way. "A siren, surely. She's utterly bewitching."

The song was low and sultry, and Carolina Diamond moved her arms in a sleek, suggestive way. Abbie was not surprised that the eyes of the star fixed on Monte and held. He had no doubt drawn them there. She held her breath and watched. Monte was clearly dazzled.

The song ended, the applause thundered, and the players took their bows. Abbie clapped, but with less ardor. Monte made up for her lack. He leaned close to her ear to be heard. "Have you supped? No, of course you haven't. I believe you were washing when I arrived."

Abbie felt the color burn in her cheeks, but he didn't follow up his remark with the expected teasing.

"Let's join the troupe at the hotel, shall we?"

Obviously the sight of her in wet underthings was no competition for Miss Diamond's glitter. Before Abbie could respond, he stood and pulled out her chair. She was crushed against him in the press of the crowd, but he kept her hand firmly in his arm. They had almost made it to the doors when a voice hissed in her ear, "Just try to compete with Miss Diamond, will you."

The jostling of the crowd gave Abbie the opportunity to land her heel squarely on the toe of Marcy Wilson's slipper. It was surely wicked to enjoy the gasp and muffled cry so much. But the taunting words had their effect. She wished Monte would take her to the buggy rather than lead the crowd to the hotel. The restaurant was not large enough for all of them, but Monte had no trouble acquiring a table.

By blind luck or other forces, shortly after Monte had seated her he turned and seated Miss Diamond to his other side. The lead player, who had portrayed Watson, took his place beside her to complete the foursome. He was not tall but well shaped and elegant in motion. He still wore his stage makeup. Abbie could smell the greasepaint.

For some time the two were occupied signing programs until those not actually paying for a meal were shooed out, and Abbie found herself directly opposite Carolina Diamond, still in her black fur and black stockinged legs. Under the chandelier, her made-up features were sharper still, the outline of her lips stark against the pale skin, the black fur exotic and extravagant.

Miss Diamond smiled. "Did you enjoy the show?"

"You have a beautiful voice." That was honest. "I've never heard anything like it." She turned to the male player. "And I enjoyed your performance, Mr . . ."

"Cunnings. Randolf Cunnings. I was introduced at the start, but people rarely notice."

Abbie was surprised. Had he been announced? Was it possible Miss Carolina Diamond had so entranced her she had missed anything else but the woman's dramatic entrance? No wonder Monte was smitten.

Mr. Cunnings stood. "Forgive me, and you are?"

"Abbie Martin." As surely as anything, Monte was out of his senses forgetting himself so much as to neglect introductions.

"And you, Mr. Farrel?" Miss Diamond turned to Monte. "Did we entertain you?"

He reached for and bowed over her hand. "I cannot express the extent."

"Now there's an accent I can't mistake. Don't tell me . . . North, no, South Carolina."

"Madam, you are a marvel. How. . . ?"

She laughed. "Don't ask my secrets. It dissolves the mystery."

Abbie would bet her last dollar Miss Diamond had asked someone. All the town knew from where Monte hailed.

"Well, then . . ." He cleared his throat. "Shall we order?"

"Indeed. I'm absolutely famished." Miss Diamond ran her hand over his arm. "I can't eat a thing before I perform."

"Not nerves, surely."

"Oh yes. To this day I'm petrified the moment my feet touch the stage."

"You hide it masterfully."

"Oh." She gave a little shrug. "With the first note it . . . poof! Vanishes away. Do you know my secret?"

"I thought you weren't telling."

"This one I'll share. I find a good, strong face in the crowd and focus on that. I think to myself, if I can find pleasure on that one face, then I've succeeded." She smiled. "I have you to thank for getting me through tonight."

"Ah." Monte glanced at Abbie. Before she could feign a smile, he turned back. "Let me see if I can hail a waiter."

Hail a waiter? With Rudy Brown hovering behind him, red-faced and nervous as a new fawn? Monte raised his hand and Rudy rushed to his side.

"Mr. Farrel, sir." He turned to Miss Diamond. "Are you ready to order, ma'am . . . miss . . . uh, Miss Diamond?"

"What would you recommend?"

"The game hen with raspberry sauce is fine tonight."

She tipped her head, glittering the thin tiara tucked into her very blond hair. "Hmm. What do you do, Mr. Farrel?"

"I beg your pardon?"

"Your line of work. Your profession."

"At present, I raise cattle."

"Do you provide the beef for the hotel?"

Monte bowed slightly. "Yes, ma'am, I do."

Abbie stared in disbelief. How perfectly she set him up, and how easily he followed. Monte, who saw through Abbie's every move.

Miss Diamond turned to Rudy. "I'd like a steak. Rare."

Rudy looked at Abbie.

She folded the menu shut and held it to him. "I'll take your recommendation on the game hen, thank you." She hoped Miss Diamond choked on her meat. Mr. Cunnings ordered a steak, as did Monte. Abbie fumed as they waited for the food to come.

Mr. Cunnings tried to draw her in, but mainly Miss Diamond spoke of places both she and Monte had visited. Abbie wasn't about to admit she'd only read of them. Miss Diamond had plenty of anecdotes and told of her experiences and the wild enthusiasm of her audiences. "I had a young man follow me from Philadelphia to Chicago and attend every performance in between. It was truly pathetic." She laughed.

Abbie wanted to slap her. Randolf Cunnings was watching,

and she wondered if it was his job to distract her while Miss Diamond entertained her escort. He leaned forward once again to engage her, but the arrival of the food provided a worthier distraction.

The game hen was delicious, tender yet crisp, and the sauce sweetly tangy. The sage dressing and scalloped potatoes, steamed string beans, and apricots made up for a lot. If Monte was fool enough to let their evening together be dominated by that woman, Abbie at least would enjoy her meal. If it were to anyone other than Monte, she would almost find Miss Diamond's blatant ploys amusing.

She would imitate them to Clara, the fingers brushing accidentally against his arm, the fluttering eyelashes, the low, earthy laugh that shook her chest and drew Monte's eyes to her décolletage. And no wonder she put out such effort. Monte was splendid himself. How could she not choose him from all the crowd?

"Is your steak not satisfactory?"

Abbie heard more than courtesy in Monte's tone. His professional pride was also at risk.

"Oh, it's marvelous."

"You've hardly touched it."

"I couldn't eat another bite."

Abbie choked back the snicker with her napkin. Was she playing the southern belle? Too bad she didn't know he spurned the false protests of frail appetites.

For almost the first time, Monte turned her way. "Dessert, Abbie?"

"I'd love a slice of apple cake." She faced Miss Diamond. "You've never tasted anything like the caramel sauce."

"And I surely never will." Miss Diamond spoke in mock dismay. She slid her hands over the fur.

"What animal is that?"

Carolina Diamond showed her teeth. "Panther. Black panther from Africa. Feel it." She held out her arm where the wrist was wrapped with fur around the sheer fabric of the sleeve.

Abbie was certain the woman's perfume wafted up to Monte's

nose. She stroked it reluctantly. *Poor beasts.* "I wonder how many it took to make the whole dress."

"I don't know. Several, I suppose, though they're monstrously big cats. Have you been to Africa, Monte?"

When had they gone to first-name informality? She must have been dozing. But how like Monte to put her at ease.

"No. I haven't."

"Perhaps we'll do a safari someday."

He gave a genteel nod. His expression was unreadable. Abbie's apple cake arrived, and she dug in defiantly.

Monte turned to Miss Diamond. "Are you certain you won't try some? Nothing gives a healthy glow quite like a hearty appetite."

Miss Carolina Diamond's mouth opened and closed. She shook her head slightly and stiffened. Abbie actually felt sorry for her. What a lonely, heartbreaking life it must be to set your hat for a new fellow in each place you went. Sure enough, she probably won plenty of them, but the disappointments must remind her that she was, after all, no better than the rest of them.

The night air felt cold after the stuffiness of the restaurant as Abbie walked beside Monte to the buggy. He released her hand from his arm. "Let me get the top up."

"Oh, leave it down. The night is so beautiful." And she could finally breathe.

He paused. "It'll be chilly."

"That's all right." She walked around to the side and leaned back against the buggy. A profusion of stars lit the moonless night sky. She felt Monte stop beside her.

"Rather takes the glint from Miss Diamond's gown, doesn't it?"

Abbie kept her eyes on the stars.

He turned her face and commanded her view. "I believe I played the fool."

"Not completely. You escaped the web before she sank the poison."

"Are you very angry?"

Angry? What she felt was too confusing to give a name. Part of her wanted to laugh in his face and say she didn't care a fig. Part wanted to run until her lungs cried out. Why, why, why was she standing here hurting for him again?

"Come, Abbie. I've had more than a taste of your temper before."

"I'm not angry."

Monte looked at her a long moment. "I keep company with Marcy Wilson for political reasons, and you put up your nose. I marry Sharlyn because my honor is called upon, and you make my life torture. Now I play into the hands of a skilled temptress right before your eyes, and you say you're not angry?"

"It's not a matter of . . ."

"Have you no affection for me?" His voice was husky, and Abbie's heart beat suddenly against her ribs. He gripped her arms. "Have I estranged you, then?"

The rise of emotion choked her.

"Tell me, Abbie. Tell me you can love me as you once did."

She fought the pressure in her chest. "No, Monte. Nothing is as it was. You've changed . . . and I've changed."

He withdrew his hands, and her arms grew cold.

She searched for the words she needed. "I was a child, full of ignorance and dreams. I'm not a child now." But she felt very young and uncertain.

He smiled wryly. "No, you're not. How I fretted for you to grow up."

Abbie straightened. "I have. And you can't expect me to be as I was, any more than you can again be the man you were two years ago."

The smile wilted, and he turned away. Abbie's heart sank at the defeat in his stance. She had not meant to hurt him. Where was his fight? Had the past year taken more of a toll than she realized? She touched his shoulder.

She had never reached out to him before, and he turned in surprise, then clasped her hands to his chest. "Abbie, I love you. Can you return it in even the smallest way?"

"You know I do. You know I've refused others. I told you there was only one who would claim my heart." She searched his face. "Oh, Monte, could you really think it had passed?"

"You've done a devil of a job concealing it."

"Have I?"

With one hand he raised her chin. "Indeed you have, and I've been ravaged with doubt. Abbie Martin, you're a cruel mistress."

"I'm no mistress . . ."

He pressed her against the buggy. "Marry me." His voice was rough, full of emotion. She had never seen him so, nor were the words the genteel entreaty she had once imagined. They were spoken as though wrenched from him without thought. This again was a Monte she did not know.

Her breath came short and shallow, an ache gripping her chest. How long she had waited, how deeply she had despaired of hearing those words. She fought the ache and searched for an answer, she who had never before failed to say what she thought.

Monte slid his hand from her chin to the back of her neck. His breath was warm on her cheek. "If you refuse me, I'll hound you unmercifully. I'll chase you until you haven't an argument left." He bent and kissed her mouth.

Abbie responded with frightening ardor as though her body and spirit recognized their match. No other kiss, not Blake's nor Cole's, had moved her so. Dear God, did she dare? Was this at last His plan for them? What of all that had passed?

Passed. It was past. She whispered against his lips, "Yes, Monte."

He kissed her again, softly, tenderly, then pressed her head to his chest. The racing of his heart matched hers. She loved this man. Her need to show him rose up, but he stepped back and released her. "I'll speak with your father at the earliest opportunity."

"When?"

"I don't . . ."

"Tomorrow?"

He laughed. "Yes, Abbie, tomorrow, and we'll set a date. Perhaps August..."

"That's two months!"

"If you need longer..."

"Longer!" She almost stamped her foot.

"My dear Abbie..." He pressed her hands together between his. "Plans must be made, your trousseau ordered and fitted, travel arrangements made for your relatives and mine."

She hadn't thought of that. Her sister, Sadie, and Grant. Of course, Grant must come all the way from Boston. She smiled at an impish thought. "Perhaps Gray Wolf will come with his people."

Monte frowned. "I know he saved your life, and I am eternally grateful, but... if it's all the same to you, we'll not have Comanches to the wedding."

"It would be distinctively western."

"And my southern relatives would never get over the shock of it. Especially my sister, Frances."

"Oh, Monte, two months is forever."

"No, Abbie. I've looked at forever. Two months is hardly a breath." He rested his hand on her cheek, and she raised her face. "Oh, Abbie, don't look at me like that. I intend to be a gentleman until August."

"And then?"

He pressed his lips to her forehead before stepping back and lifting her into the buggy, his restraint exemplary. Abbie sighed. She had a sudden urge to run and tell Clara. But that would wait until morning. For now, she savored the strength of Monte's arm around her as they drove. His warmth cut the night's chill.

Four

The following evening Monte rode home through the growing darkness. Sirocco was sure in his step, and Monte gave him his head. It had gone better than he had hoped. Not that he had expected Joshua Martin to refuse him his daughter, but the waters had been muddied. Now he saw again the caliber of man Joshua was.

It felt amazingly good to be once more embraced by the Martins. He would count it a privilege to be part of the family. Abbie came from good, wholesome stock. No bloodlines traced to the founding fathers, no decades of duty and debts of honor. Only honest, hardworking people. It was his good fortune Abbie was also maddeningly lovely.

It warmed him to see the glow in her face and know it was he who put it there. Beyond his hopes, God had restored her affection, he was certain. It had shone in her glance and rung in her voice throughout the meal he had shared at their table.

It had been a little touchy when Monte offered his compliments to Selena, and she suggested Abbie would feed him well. She did not realize that was his cook's job. Wild fowl was not Pearl's specialty, and Abbie had no doubt learned Selena's secret, but Abbie fighting Pearl for kitchen rights was not something he cared to witness.

Still, those things would be worked out. Monte pulled up at the stable, dismounted, and handed the reins to Will. "He's had hay. Just a rubdown and a little mash tonight."

"Yes, sir."

Monte strode to the bunkhouse across the yard and opened the door. The cowboys straightened at his entrance, except for Cole, who sat with a poker hand and a face that matched. "May I have a word with you, Cole?"

"Soon as I fleece this sheep," Cole replied without looking his way.

Across from him Skeeter MacCarthy turned and spat. "All right, I call."

Cole laid down his hand. Three jacks. Skeeter swore and threw down eights and fours. Laughing, Cole scooped the money his way and stood. "Better luck next time, Skeeter."

"No such thing as luck against you."

"Ain't that the truth." Breck Thompson shoved his cards to the center.

Cole swaggered past and joined Monte outside the door. "Mr. Farrel?"

Monte eyed him. Since signing on in his employ, Cole had lost none of his disrespectful pluck. Though he accepted the subordinate position, his maverick attitude rankled. Monte would not let it tonight.

"I remember an evening you informed me that you intended to ask for Abbie's hand in marriage."

"Yeah?"

"I've come to give you the same courtesy."

"I figured you'd be askin'." Cole leaned against the wall.

Monte paused. "I've asked, and she's accepted."

"Shoot, I figured that, too." Pulling a paper from his pocket, Cole shook tobacco from a pouch, then licked the edge and rolled it tight. He struck the match on the wall and lit the cigarette. "You lookin' for congratulations?"

"You know better than that, Cole. I value your skills. I'm asking if this will affect your work for me."

Cole brought up his knee and rested his boot against the bunkhouse wall. "Well, I don't rightly know." He drew on the cigarette again. "I guess we'll wait and see."

Monte nodded. "I appreciate your honesty."

"Ain't no good pretendin'. And I ain't exactly surprised. What puzzles me is why you didn't just marry Abbie in the first place. No offense to the late Mrs. Farrel."

"Well, Cole, God's truth is I did what I had to do."

"Yeah. Sure, marry Abbie. She's so crazy in love with you she'd a spent her life alone, rather'n settle for anyone else."

"You're a good man, Cole."

He tossed the butt and crushed it under his heel. "Anything else?"

"No."

"Then I'll git back to my game. My luck's a whole lot better in there."

Monte headed for the house. Bounding up the front stairs, he opened the door and James came forward to take his hat. "Nice evenin', Mastuh Monte?"

"I'd say." Monte smiled and went to the library. He pulled open the drawer of the walnut desk and took out a sheet of paper. Sitting down, he allowed Abbie's image to form in his mind, her blue eyes with their thick drooping lashes, her mouth soft and full, her silky brown curls in enough disarray to arouse him like nothing else.

In this past year her features had refined from her girlish softness. She was a woman now, and his pulse quickened. How many times had he sat here and forced her from his thoughts? It seemed impossible that he could not only think of her now, but that he soon would have her as his wife.

Dipping the pen, he began to write name after name. Likely they would not travel to the Colorado Territory for the wedding, but they would be invited. This would be no rushed and silent deathbed ceremony. He wanted all the world to know that he was marrying Abigail Martin.

◆◆◆◆◆◆◆

Abbie pulled on the reins and slid to the ground almost before Shiloh stopped, leaving the mare sweating and stamping in the July heat. In the past month she and Monte had covered the ground between their ranches frequently enough to wear a trail in the scrubby golden grasses.

She flung the leather strands around the hitch and skipped up the stairs where Monte stood, tall and darkly handsome, in the doorway. She was bursting with her news. "Grant's coming!"

"And here I thought your exuberance was for me."

Abbie brushed back the curls that clung to her forehead. "Don't tease, Monte. I haven't seen Grant in four years! I can't wait for you to meet him."

"Did you think your brother wouldn't come?"

"Well, they let him finish early on condition he pass at a level of excellence, and he has!"

"Of course he has. If he's anything like his little sister, he's smart as a whip."

"Oh, he's smarter than I am. You'll like him, Monte. I know you will. And he'll like you, too."

"Kind of you to think so." He smiled. "Come in and get yourself cooled off. You're in as much of a lather as your mare."

Abbie's spirits ebbed. "You're not as excited as I wanted you to be."

He ushered her through the door. "James, see that Will tends Miss Martin's horse."

"Yessuh."

Monte stopped at the base of the stairs. "Run up and freshen yourself, Abbie. I'll be in the parlor."

Abbie fought her disappointment as she walked up the stairs into the first bedroom. She hated it when he acted the lord of the manor.

A Negro girl, perhaps a year or so younger than she, rushed in with fresh water and a towel. The water sloshed from the pitcher when she curtsied, then again when she slid the bowl onto the stand.

Abbie smiled. Here was someone after her own heart. "Hello."

The girl curtsied again, wringing her wet hands on her skirt, but she smiled broadly. "Afternoon, Mizz Martin."

"Well, I'm at a disadvantage. You know my name, but..."

"I'm Zena, Pearl's niece. Mistuh Farrel took me on last week."

"Oh. Did you come in on the stage?"

"No'm. Mistuh Farrel's foreman brung me in from Denver, but I traveled on the train all the way from Macon, Georgia."

"That must have been a long and difficult trip."

"Oh, no'm." She squeezed her hands again. "It was worth it. Now I have a real position."

Abbie felt ashamed for thinking ill of Monte. His kindness had brought Zena there. "Well, thank you for the water."

"Yes'm. I wanted a look at you. Aunt Pearl said Mistuh Farrel's goin' marry hisself a real beauty, an' she was right."

Abbie stood still, unsure how to respond.

"You wants me to unbutton you?"

She hid her surprise. "No . . . thank you. I can manage."

The girl backed out, again grinning broadly. Abbie dipped the towel into the cool water and squeezed it out, then applied it to her face. Her hot skin tingled with the chill of it, and she ran it over her neck, as well. Gazing at her reflection, she mused. Soon she would be mistress of this house, and James and Pearl and Zena and Will and all the cowboys would answer to her.

She groaned. Sharlyn, of course, had been born into the southern world of servants and masters, as Monte had. But this was the Colorado Territory, and Abbie knew nothing of all that. No matter. She would learn. She hung the towel on the rack and flipped her hair back, then swung around, her skirts swirling behind. She found Monte in the parlor.

"Better?" He handed her a glass of lemonade.

"Yes, but you needn't scold me. I know when I need a wash." She drank thirstily.

Monte laughed. "I wasn't suggesting any such thing. But your face was flushed, and I didn't want to risk a sunstroke."

"Then thank you for your concern." She drained the glass and set it on the corner table. "Now will you respond to my news?"

"Abbie, I'm thrilled your brother is coming to the wedding. And as far as that goes, my sister and her husband are making the trip also, though Kendal will no doubt have to sedate her."

"Why on earth?"

"I'm afraid I embellished a tale or two when I saw them last, and she believes her very life to be at stake."

"Oh, Monte. How could you?"

"It was altogether too tempting." He reached out for her hands. "But I wish now I hadn't. The trip will not be pleasant for her. If only the railroad were through."

Abbie sighed. "It's close. Sadie's husband, Joe, works for the Denver Rio Grande. He said they're looking to send a spur through anytime now. Why didn't you tell me you hired a new girl?"

He raised an eyebrow. "I didn't know I had to."

"I just mean it was a surprise to meet Zena."

"Ah. Well, Pearl's sister wrote that things were hard, and with Pearl getting up in age . . . and you'll need a lady's maid. Not that Pearl would stand for just any help, mind you, but her own niece . . ."

"That's kind of you, Monte."

"This is a large home." He drew her close. "And soon I expect it will be housing a family."

Abbie raised her eyes to his face. "Oh, Monte, August is too far."

"It's not so far, now. Would you like to walk with me awhile?"

"I would, but I have to go to town. I promised Mama I'd post her letters at once. But you can come for dinner. Mama said to ask."

"I'm afraid not tonight. Cole and I are making preparations for the herd he's taking east."

"Will he be gone long?"

"Does the absence of my foreman concern you?"

She startled at his tone. Why was he so snappish? "I just wondered."

"Several weeks, I'd guess." He walked her back through the hall and out into the dazzling brightness. "Don't rush your mare this time, Abbie. It's too hot to ride her hard."

Abbie bristled. "Thank you, Monte. I do know how to care for her." She started down the stairs, then turned. "Tell Cole I wish him a good journey."

His smile stiffened. "I'll tell him."

She was instantly ashamed. What was it that made them spar? She mounted Shiloh and waved sheepishly. He raised his hand in response. She could feel his eyes on her as she cantered down the drive, and when she turned at the gate, he was still on the porch.

Monte watched Abbie canter off. The horse had mended well, but at times Abbie was careless—even reckless—though it annoyed her to be corrected. Still, it wasn't the horse that had set him off. It was the fear he had felt when she galloped up as though the hounds of hell were on her.

After finding the poisoned calf this morning, he was jumping at shadows. It was no accident. All that he had was in jeopardy. He didn't know why; he didn't know whom. And he didn't want Abbie in the middle of it.

He wearily dropped his forehead against the pillar. Whom should he suspect? Whom could he trust? Cole? The memory of Abbie in Cole's arms still stung. Why would she ask after him? Why not; it was innocent enough. Abbie had no way of knowing the turmoil it stirred in him.

Monte felt an inner probing that he did not want to acknowledge. Yes, he had submitted his will to God's guidance, and by God's hand won back Abbie's affection. But some things a man handled himself. He started across the yard. The sooner Cole was on his way, the better.

Five

Abbie waved away the dust kicked up by the stage as it careened to a halt in the street. Gus always came in with a show of speed, if not comfort. Beside her on the boardwalk, Eleanor Bailey stopped midsentence, mouth open, while her sister, Ruth, fluttered her hand and choked. The memory of Buck Hollister's stage robbery that had terrified their aunt and killed Gus's partner still put them in a tizzy, but Abbie was only interested in seeing the passengers. She raised up on her toes, not caring that it amused Monte. But she could not see in the window.

Gus jumped down from the box, smacked the dust from his shirt, and opened the door. He pulled down the step. A tall man with waxed mustache and sandy hair climbed out. He turned and held a hand to a striking, dark-haired woman.

Abbie squeezed Monte's arm. "I know that's Frances. Her likeness is unmistakable!"

Monte laughed. "You're right. Now behave yourself, and I'll introduce you."

Behave herself, indeed. She'd been looking forward to this almost as though it were her own sister coming from Denver City. She'd wondered about Frances ever since Monte had spoken so heartbreakingly of protecting her during the war. Even now, there was a certain . . . carefulness when he spoke of her.

Monte swept her forward, and the man caught sight of them. "Monte!"

Abbie stared at Frances. She looked like a dressmaker's doll in the newest fashion. Every hair on her head was perfectly coifed, and there was not a wrinkle on her sumptuous dress. She must not have moved the entire trip.

Monte shook Kendal's hand. "I see you've made it safely through with no fire, stampede, or Indian attack." He bent and kissed his sister's cheek. "Permit me to present to you my fiancée, Abigail Martin."

Frances turned, graceful as a doe. "How do you do, Abigail."

"Oh, I prefer Abbie. I'm only Abigail when I'm in trouble."

Monte squeezed her elbow. "Abbie, my sister, Frances, and her husband, Kendal Stevens."

Kendal bowed over her hand. "I'm delighted to meet you."

"And you."

"Yes." Frances waved a delicate ivory fan. "We've been so eager." She looked past her. "What a quaint little place."

Abbie turned. "It's grown tremendously over the last year. What on earth we need with two grocers and three saloons, I'm sure I don't know."

"Competition, my dear," Kendal said. "The lifeblood of commerce."

"I'd think they'd do better going somewhere they were needed."

Kendal chuckled. "Don't have her keep your books, Monte."

"Abbie's not going to run my business, only my home."

Frances fanned herself again. "Then by all means let's hasten out of this scathing sunshine. It's a mercy you don't come out in freckles with no bonnet, Abbie. But then, your complexion is darker."

Abbie put a hand to her cheek. "I hardly notice it, but come stand in the shade. Have you a parasol?"

"In my trunk." Frances stepped under the eaves and made no move toward the trunk. Instead, Kendal searched until he pulled out a ruffled yellow parasol. He snapped it open and handed it to her.

Monte lifted two of the bags into the wagon. Together he and Kendal hoisted up the trunk and tossed in the remaining bags.

Abbie had laughed when Monte brought the wagon instead of the buggy. Now she knew why.

Kendal handed Frances up to the buckboard, and Monte lifted Abbie in beside her, then climbed into the front seat with Kendal. They passed through town, and at the end of the street the wagon lurched, then settled into the twin ruts that led over the prairie. Frances grasped the side of the buckboard. "Is there no road to your ranch, Monte?"

"This is it."

Frances sighed. "You warned us it was rustic. But you never said primitive."

Abbie tried not to stare as they rode. Frances was the most beautiful lady she had ever seen. Unlike Miss Carolina Diamond, her beauty was natural. She looked like the miniature of Monte's mother but more sophisticated and less . . . She couldn't put her finger on the difference. Something disdainful in the expression perhaps.

As they pulled past the gate, Kendal tipped back his hat and appraised the house. He turned to Frances. "Now you don't say primitive, do you, my dear?"

"This almost looks civilized."

Abbie bit her lip. What would Frances think of her family's small, neat farm house? Monte lifted her down from the wagon. Suddenly she spun around. "But where is your daughter?"

Frances stared at her. "Surely you didn't think we could bring her out here."

Abbie stared. "Why ever not?"

"She's with her mammy at my mother's home," Kendal said.

"But you'll be away so long!"

Frances pursed her lips. "Yes. And she'll be far better off in Charleston with her grandmother than out here in . . ."

"I'm sure Abbie's disappointed not to see the child." Monte waved Kendal toward the house. "We'd have both enjoyed meeting the little one. How old is she now?"

"A year and a half in October." Kendal gave Frances his hand at the stairs.

Abbie felt Monte's grip like a vise on her elbow as he breathed in her ear. "Abbie, please. Try not to insult Frances."

She looked up, her mouth falling open. "How on earth did I insult her?" she whispered back. He didn't answer, and drawing a deep breath, she followed him inside.

"It's very like the plantation," Frances said. "Especially this parlor." She stroked the red velvet drapes.

The room was baking from the heat trapped by the heavy velvet even though they were tied back at the sides, but Abbie didn't repeat her advice to remove the drapes. Monte and Frances obviously approved of them. Abbie felt the sweat trickle down the back of her neck. She wanted out of there. "Can I get you something to drink? Your trip was no doubt hot and dry."

Monte turned. "Pearl will see to that, Abbie."

"Oh, I don't mind . . ." His eyes silenced her.

The door opened, and Pearl brought in tall glasses of pale tea with sugared mint leaves and a plate of thin chocolate wafers. Not exactly the oatmeal cookies or honey muffins Abbie might have offered guests at home.

Abbie watched Pearl set down the tray and leave without acknowledgment even from Monte, then realized he was looking at her. What now? Oh goodness, he wanted her to serve. She reached immediately for the tray and handed a glass to Frances and Kendal, then gave one to Monte.

"Thank you." She heard the amusement in his tone, though his expression was merely pleasant. "Perhaps our guests would care for a sweet."

Abbie lifted the plate. As she did, the last glass of tea tipped off the tray. Frances leaped back too late, and it splashed down the skirt of her dress. Abbie felt the blood rush to her face. *Oh heavens!* All the way from Charleston without a wrinkle and now that. "I'm terribly sorry! Let me get a cloth for it."

Before Monte could stop her, she rushed from the room and down the hall to the narrow corridor that connected the kitchen. It was a relief to run. She wished she could keep going out the back door and all the way home.

In the kitchen Pearl spun at Abbie's unexpected arrival.

"I need a wet cloth for Mrs. Stevens' dress."

Squaring herself, Pearl put her hands to her hips. "Mizz Martin. Mr. Farrel uses the bell if he needs he'p. Ain't no cause to run like a chicken on account of a spill."

Abbie stopped short, and the color rose in her cheeks. "I didn't know about the bell. But since I'm here I may as well get the cloth and go before Mrs. Stevens' dress is stained."

"Ah'll see to her, miss. You go on now."

She felt scolded and dismissed. There was nothing for it but to go back to the parlor. Her feet were reluctant. She stood a moment at the door, then squared her shoulders and went in. Only Kendal and Monte were there.

Monte turned from the window. "Frances has retired to change and rest."

Zena came into the room with a towel, dropped to her knees, and blotted the spill from the rug. Abbie wasn't surprised that neither man acknowledged her.

Well, she wasn't so constrained. "I'm sorry I was careless."

Zena's eyes flickered up, then returned to her task without answer.

"Don't worry." Monte raised his glass. "I'll have Pearl fix you another."

He must be mortified, though he didn't show it. And she wished Kendal would stop looking at her like that. The best she could hope for was a graceful exit. "Please don't bother. I think I'll go home now, if that's all right. You must have catching up to do, and Mama's canning today."

"All right." Monte brushed his lips on her hand as he bowed. "I'll call for you tomorrow."

Monte watched her leave. Kendal sent him a crooked grin. "I think your nights will not be dull."

Monte set his tea down and walked to the window. "Abbie is not a southern belle."

Kendal laughed. "You don't have to tell me that or apologize.

58

I find her utterly charming. Frances may have a different opinion, but then, it doesn't really matter out here, does it?"

Monte turned back. "I don't know if it matters. I do know Abbie is in my blood. From the first time I saw her two years ago, she had a hold on me."

"You knew her before marrying Sharlyn?"

Monte felt a shadow of the old shame. "Yes."

Kendal whistled. "Forgive me, Monte, but why did you choose Sharlyn?"

"Her father asked it of me on his deathbed ... for reasons I felt I could not refuse."

"She wasn't compromised?"

"No. But the danger was real."

Kendal shook his head. "Did Abbie know of your feelings?"

"Unfortunately. That's why it's so important to me now to bear with the little infractions. I tell you, Kendal, Abbie is my life."

"I can understand that passion. She is remarkable."

◆◆◆◆◆◆◆

Abbie rode Shiloh along the edge of Pa's ranch. She couldn't go home just yet. Mama would see her humiliation. She stopped the horse and dismounted. The scrub oaks arched twelve feet over the track where she led the horse.

Pa's plot was only forty acres, not a true ranch, really—only enough to keep their few sheep, two horses, the cow, and chickens. Pa had paid a dollar and a quarter an acre, but to Abbie it was worth more than any gold field.

Monte's ranch comprised nearly a thousand acres of grazing land, the two purchased claims, and the open range he used. The house and yard, stable, bunkhouse, and barn occupied a full nine acres. But it lacked the beauty of the foothills.

His was prairie land and trees were scarce, with just a few ponderosas and spiky junipers, scattered mounds of scrub oak, and the cottonwoods that lined the river and surrounded the house. Yet its vastness, bare but teeming with life, the smell of sage, the circling hawks, the broken hills, and arroyos moved her. The mountains might hold her heart, but the plains reflected her spirit.

Soon she would call it home. It was a bittersweet feeling. She sighed. Why couldn't Frances have been like Sharlyn? Or even like Monte? Well, she was in a way. They both carried themselves with impeccable ease and natural poise. But Monte never made her feel . . . low, as Frances had.

She put a hand to her cheek. It was warmed like tallow by the sun. Was she dark and coarse? Frances's skin was a soft pearly white even in August. She frowned.

Beside her a squirrel chattered from the branches of a ponderosa. Abbie raised her chin. "What do you think of this, Frances?" She grabbed up her skirts and ran to the tree. Her muscles tightened and stretched as she mounted higher and higher until the branches could no longer support her. "Bet you can't do that, Mrs. Stevens! I'd like to see you escape a stampede."

Perching on the branch, she felt the breeze in her hair and closed her eyes. *Oh, Lord, I want Monte to be proud of me.* She leaned her head against the trunk. How could she make up to Frances? How could she undo the impression she had made? She started down but her foot slipped, and she slid against the trunk. Crying out, she gripped a branch and stopped her fall, then painfully lowered herself to the ground.

Her knee and chin were scraped, and two fingernails, torn jaggedly, began to bleed. "Oh, God, I know. Pride goeth before a fall." She touched her chin. "A fine display I'll make now, thank you."

She flounced into the yard and stopped at the pump. Working the lever, she forced out the cold water, splashed it over her face, then grimly stuck her head beneath. It served her right.

Inside the house Mama had her back turned, standing at the stove. Abbie wanted to grab her around the middle and bury her face on Mama's chest.

"Monte's sister made it in all right?"

"Yes."

"How is she?"

"Fine. Very fine." Impossibly, unmatchably fine.

Mama turned. "Well, that's . . . gracious, what did you do to your face?"

"I slipped."

"Get the salve from the shelf."

"Yes, Mama."

The sting brought tears to her eyes, but Abbie dutifully applied it, then replaced the jar. Beside it stood the fine cream Pa had given Mama. *For the maintaining of smooth, youthful skin.* Abbie took it down. She dipped a finger in and spread it over her cheek. It was a soft, cool delight.

Her skin felt velvety. She imagined Monte resting his hand there. Had Sharlyn used cream? Of course she had. And she knew better than to let the sun bronze her skin. Abbie looked at her reflection in the polished tin nailed to the wall over the washstand. She jutted her damaged chin. She looked five years old. What a Jonah day.

"Better?" Mama strained the beans and scooped a spoonful into the steaming jar.

"Yes." Abbie tied on her apron.

"You may as well tell me what's on your heart. It'll only trouble you until you do." Mama saw everything.

"I'm afraid I won't know how to be Monte's wife."

"Are you meaning . . . personal things?"

Abbie flushed. "No, Mama. Practical things."

"He'll let you know your duties."

"He just smiles and waits to see if I'll embarrass him. I never knew keeping house for him would be so complicated. I thought it would be like you and Pa. I could keep a fine house for someone like Pa."

"And you'll keep a fine house for Monte. He'll be patient. He loves you so."

"I don't want to disappoint him." Sharlyn had managed his home with perfection. Abbie's throat tightened. She didn't want to compete with that image.

"Don't borrow trouble, Abbie. Today has enough of its own."

Six

The late afternoon shadows stretched across the land as Monte drove the phaeton toward Abbie's homestead. Its springs were good, the ride gentler than the wagon's, and he was glad to see Frances look about her with interest as they headed to Abbie's birthday party.

"This is pleasant over here, Monte. There are trees in the hills."

"Yes, but you can't graze cattle on scrub oak and ponderosas. Cole would have a devil of a time keeping track of the herd on this terrain."

"How does Abbie's father manage?" Kendal asked.

"He doesn't ranch. Joshua runs the newspaper. He's a remarkable man, very quick-witted . . . like his daughter." He winked at Frances.

"I make up my own mind, Monte."

"How well I know that." He waited for Kendal and Frances to climb down, then pulled up to the barn and unhitched Chance. Other neighbors' horses were tethered inside the barn, but they had kept the back stall free for Chance. He was growing accustomed to that space.

Back outside, he saw that Abbie had already shown Kendal and Frances to the refreshment table. Her back was to him as she shared some pleasantry with his sister. It would take more than that to thaw Frances, he was afraid. He caught Abbie's eye, and she hurried to meet him. He squelched the desire to catch her up into his arms and instead brought her outstretched hand to his lips. "You don't look a day over nineteen."

"I'm not yet. Not for another hour. Are you thirsty? There's tea and sarsaparilla at the table."

"All in good time." He tucked a finger under her chin and eyed her. "What did you do to yourself?"

"I slipped."

"Slipped! Fell headlong, more like."

"Don't scold, Monte. I feel conspicuous enough as it is."

He killed his laugh and pressed her hand. "You can't help that, my love. No one with eyes like yours could ever blend into the scenery."

"Well, thank you for the compliment."

"And what is this piece of finery?" He fingered the amethyst brooch at her throat.

"From Mama and Pa. Isn't it lovely?"

"As lovely as the neck that holds it."

She tucked her hand into his arm. "Pa's not home yet. I can't imagine what's keeping him. Would you mind acting as host till he gets here?"

"Not a bit."

While Abbie flitted between the house and yard, Monte introduced Frances and Kendal to the other guests: Ethan Thomas, Frank and Mildred Simms, Becky Linde, and Mary Beth Walker, whose wandering eye made it difficult to know where to look when one addressed her. He couldn't help noticing Frances's increasing disdain. Perhaps it was a mistake to bring her here tonight. It almost made him ashamed of his neighbors.

As the sun crowned the summits and edged behind, it shot fire to the clouds, then disappeared. That at least was a blessing as the occasion had warranted his black coat. He envied Ethan his cotton shirt sleeves. This heat was sharp. Not as pervasive as South Carolina's but more insistent. It didn't linger, though. Already he felt a coolness descending.

Abbie joined them again, as vibrant as always. If she was aware of Frances's mood, she hid it completely. Nor was there the awkwardness of the previous day, but then this was her element, her home, her day. She fairly bubbled with good spirits.

"Oh, Clara, I'm so glad you're here! You must meet Monte's sister." She rattled off the introductions. "And this . . ." she reached a hand to cup the toddler's plump cheek, "is baby Del. Frances and Kendal have a daughter just about Del's age."

"Oh, Del will be thrilled to see someone his size."

Frances stiffened. "We left her in Charleston."

Monte wished Abbie would leave it alone. What was she thinking, bringing that up again? Did she think it unnatural for Frances to have left the child? Abbie didn't understand mammies.

"Oh." Clara shrugged. "Well, Del will just have to wait for Melissa's baby to walk."

Monte didn't miss the glance Clara shot to Abbie, nor the answering rise of Abbie's eyebrows. So she wasn't as oblivious as she let on. Well, she was playing a dangerous game. She left Clara to greet the coming wagon. It was Blake McConnel's mother and sister. Mary McConnel climbed down and hugged Abbie close. "Happy birthday, my dear."

Monte wondered how the woman would feel about their announcement tonight. Had things worked out differently, it might have been her son that Abbie married. He went to the wagon and reached a hand to Mariah, who scuttled down before he could assist her, then stood pressed against the wooden side, shifting her weight from one foot to the other.

It was deucedly uncomfortable, and he was relieved when Abbie swept in and took Mariah's hand. "Come, Mariah, let me introduce you to Monte's sister."

Monte winced.

Mariah shoved her hand out and gave Frances a hard pump, then turned on her heels. "I gotta get the beans." She scurried back to the wagon.

Monte choked, caught between chagrin and the horrible hilarity of Frances's expression as she stared at her hand, then headed for the pump with a look that demanded Kendal assist her. Monte wished it otherwise but knew his duty. He, too, went to offer comfort.

He came up behind as Frances gripped Kendal's arm. "How can he stand it?"

"What?"

"This place, these people? Is that girl simple? Did you hear what she said? 'I gotta get the beans.' My days! I feel contaminated." She lathered her hands furiously.

Kendal worked the pump handle. "It's not so bad. And Abbie is delightful."

Frances held her palms under the flow. "I fail to see the attraction."

"That, my dear, is because you are a woman."

Monte cleared his throat.

Frances faced him. "How do you remain here, Monte? Poor Sharlyn . . . this place alone could cause anyone's death."

He felt it like a slap, and it must have shown.

"I'm sorry." She looked anything but contrite. "It's just . . . so rough and . . ."

"Sharlyn was happy here." He spoke fixedly, containing his anger.

"Of course she was. She loved you. She would have borne anything."

That hit too closely to the truth. His sister's contempt was wearing on him. He'd expected it, but he hadn't thought how it would cloud his own impressions. Monte watched Abbie with her arm tucked through Clara's, giggling. Coiled wisps of hair escaped her ribbon and blew across her face. She brushed the hair back absently but did not bother to contain it, unlike Frances, who regimented every strand.

Laughing, Abbie chattered fiercely and gesticulated. She was a wild thing sprung up on the mountainside, and even as his pulse quickened at the thought, he felt a twinge. Would he ever bring her to his childhood home and present her there? How would women such as Frances receive her? Blast them anyway. He didn't care.

Wes McConnel arrived with the hay wain. Monte hoisted Abbie up and pulled himself up beside her. Frances refused the ride, and in a rare act of defiance, Kendal climbed up without her. Monte couldn't half blame him. If he stayed behind he'd be subjected to a diatribe that no man should have to endure. He sent him a sympathetic smile, and Kendal raised an eyebrow in response.

As the wain started, Abbie wiggled deeper into the hay, grabbed up two handfuls and tossed it into the air. "Don't you love the smell of it, fresh cut like this?" She dropped back onto the heap, oblivious to the straw clinging to her hair and dress.

Monte saw Kendal's eyes on her. He knew what Kendal saw, though Abbie herself was ignorant of her allure. She acted without premeditation, unlike southern girls trained to calculate the effect of every glance. It pleased him to see Kendal's appreciation. Perhaps that would help with Frances, and at any rate, he need hardly feel jealous of his own sister's husband.

Abbie rolled to her elbow. "I wonder what's keeping Pa. He should have been home ages ago."

Monte shrugged. "He won't miss your party, if I know Joshua." The wain dipped, and Abbie jostled against him. Monte caught her arm. "Don't tumble off now. You're battered enough for one day. And you still haven't told me what you did."

"I don't intend to."

"Come, Abbie."

"I spit into the wind."

"What!"

"It's an expression, like laughing at fate or thumbing your nose. It frequently comes back on you."

"Oh?"

"You'll only laugh."

"I won't. My word of honor."

She put her mouth to his ear. "I fell down a tree."

Monte threw back his head and laughed, and Abbie hissed, "Your word is forever tarnished!"

"Forgive me, Abbie. But what were you doing in the tree?"

"Hush! If you think I'll give you one more detail . . ."

At the head of the wain, Marty's voice sang out into the

gloaming and was joined by others as Abbie sank back into the mound of hay. One tune led to another as his clear tenor urged them. Abbie did not sing but closed her eyes and rocked with the motion of the wain.

The first faint star appeared above them, and Monte watched it flicker until it dominated its spot of night sky and shone steadily. He was achingly aware of Abbie beside him. He leaned close. "I wish we were alone."

"It wouldn't do you any good," she replied without opening her eyes.

"Come, Abbie, I begged your forgiveness. I truly meant to not laugh."

They were nearing the house again, and the lanterns had been lit over the tables set out in the yard. The wain lolloped to a stop. Monte leaped down and reached up for Abbie. She placed her hands on his shoulders and slid, landing in a cascade of hay before him.

He did not release his hold. "Forgive me, Abbie?" Pressing her against the wain, he bent his head and kissed her. If he possessed one shred less decorum he would kiss her as he was certain she had never been kissed before. A throat being cleared behind him brought Monte's head up immediately.

Abbie squealed, "Grant!" She dived past Monte and sailed into her brother's arms. Lifted into the air, she squealed again. "Oh, Grant, I didn't know you'd make it here today! This is the finest surprise!"

Behind them stood Joshua. He smiled indulgently when Monte caught his eye.

Grant set Abbie on the ground. "I expect this is the man you intend to marry? Or does he have me to face for stealing a kiss from my sister right out in plain sight?" Grant stretched out his hand.

Monte gripped it. "Sometimes extreme measures are required. It's a pleasure. I've heard much about you—all glowing."

"I'm sure I'll have my earful coming."

Abbie hooked her arm through her brother's. "You must see

Marty and Clara and their little son. She'll be delighted that . . ." Her chatter faded as she dragged him off. Monte watched their retreating backs and felt irrationally bereft. Joshua shrugged, and Monte shook his head, then sought out his sister and Kendal. Frances was seated on the rough bench along the split rail fence, her skirts arranged around her and her plate held precariously. She didn't appear to have taken a bite.

Kendal slouched beside her against the post. "You know, there is an appeal to this place, the way everyone's come together to enjoy the event under the stars. There's something very attractive in its simplicity. I can see why it agrees with you, Monte."

Frances sighed. "I cannot. At least with Sharlyn, you maintained some dignity, some breeding."

"I'm sure he intends to maintain breeding with Abbie, as well." Kendal chuckled, and Monte took his elbow in the ribs.

Frances frowned. "I'll thank you to keep your coarse remarks to yourself."

"I apologize. That was distasteful." But he chuckled again. "I see you've been deposed, Monte."

Monte nodded. "Abbie's brother. She'll no doubt drag him this way in her grand presentation. He's been at Harvard the last four years. Just passed for a lawyer."

"There you see, Frances, there is sophistication in this wilderness."

"Indeed there is." Monte balanced his plate on the fence post. "Abbie is better read than any lady I've known. She speaks intelligently on most any subject."

"That does not mean she can take on the responsibilities of your home."

"No. And I fear she has some to learn in that area, but she's quick and willing. And . . . by far the most entrancing creature."

Frances tossed her head. "I might easily believe you bewitched. You showed good sense when you married Sharlyn, even if it was rushed and mysterious. She was the kind of lady to make a home for someone of your standing, Monte."

"Frances . . ." Kendal frowned.

"Monte and I have always been honest with each other, Kendal. I would do him a disservice if I didn't speak my concerns."

Monte laid a hand on her shoulder. "Indeed you would. But I think you haven't given Abbie a chance. Sharlyn herself was devoted to her. Most of her days were spent in Abbie's company. Were she here to do so, Sharlyn would tell you how wrong you are."

"Would she? When she saw how Abbie plays up to you? It appears to me that she's very brazen—"

"Not brazen, I think." Kendal stroked his mustache. "Just innocent of her charm."

Frances sniffed. "I see you've fallen under the spell, too. But I fear you will regret this hasty decision, Monte."

His temper flared. "There is nothing hasty about it. It's been nearly a year since Sharlyn's death. That's longer than most widowers maintain that status out here."

"I don't expect you to be alone. But I think you should come home and choose a wife, as you did the last time."

"There's no one I would choose over Abbie. Had I my way, she would have been my first wife."

Frances opened her mouth, then closed it.

Abbie approached with Grant still on her arm. "Mr. and Mrs. Stevens, may I present my brother, Grant Martin."

Kendal extended his hand. "I understand you intend to practice law."

"That's right."

"Where?"

Grant glanced at Abbie. "Well, I'm considering Rocky Bluffs."

Abbie gasped. "Here? You're going to stay here?"

He tweaked her chin. "I need to meet with Judge Wilson and confer, but I'm considering it."

Monte leaned on the fence. "You'd be Rocky Bluffs' first lawyer."

"And only." Grant laughed. "But from what I've heard, it's grown enough to support one. I've not decided yet."

Monte touched Abbie's sleeve. "Your father's calling us."

Abbie caught his arm as they walked. "I do."

"You do what?"

"Forgive you for laughing. If it hadn't hurt so much at the time, I might have laughed, too. I'm sure it was quite a spectacle, though only the squirrel who lured me up there observed it. I promise my tree-climbing days are done."

He laughed low. "I'm glad to hear that. It's rather time, don't you think?"

Joshua climbed onto the crate in front of the house and called for attention. "Now, I know you've all probably heard, but this is the official announcement of the engagement between my daughter Abbie and Montgomery Farrel. May their life together be rich and filled with blessing."

"Hear, hear!" Marty yelled.

Monte took Abbie's hand and gave a slight bow. "I know I've spoiled the hopes of many of you, but I don't regret it one bit." He waited through the laughter and cheers. "And you can all come to the wedding." He stepped back and received the congratulations and backslapping from those around him.

There was an appeal to this place, these people. Monte felt more at home in that moment than he had yet. Whatever Frances may think, these people were there to stay, to make something of the town, the territory . . . and maybe in time, the state. While the South was decaying, new life was springing up here. And he was part of it. And so was Abbie.

Frank Simms took up the fiddle, and Monte used the moment to escape. Bending close to Abbie, he whispered, "Come with me."

He clasped her hand and led her away from the lanterns, across the yard to the barn. He eased the door open and pulled her inside.

"Monte, what are you doing?"

He took the lantern from the wall, but did not light it. They moved through the inky space until he felt a stall and got his bearings. "I don't want to be interrupted by anyone seeing the light."

"Interrupted from what?"

"I promised to be a gentleman, remember."

They reached the back of the barn, and he struck a match and lit the lantern, then turned the wick down low. "There, now." He set it on the shelf. "I have something for you." He lifted her chin with his fingers. "Shall I give it to you now?"

"How can I say when you're being so mysterious?"

He pulled a silver-hinged box from his pocket and handed it to her. She ran a finger over the filigreed leaves and vines. "It's beautiful."

"Open it."

Abbie obeyed and found earrings, a single garnet on a gold wire with a teardrop pearl suspended beneath. "Oh, Monte ... they're so fine..."

"They were my mother's. You'll have to have Selena put a needle through your ears to wear them."

Her eyes met his, and her lips trembled.

Monte drew her into his arms. "One week, Abbie..." He found her mouth with his, and she responded.

Suddenly a figure moved behind him, and before he could react they were slammed against the wall. Abbie's jaw smacked Monte's chest as they tumbled down and he fought to break her fall. The lantern toppled and smashed.

He rolled, shielding Abbie from the burst of flame, then leaped to his feet and pulled off his coat as fire rushed up the post and across the hay-strewn floor. The acrid smoke caught his breath as he smacked the coat against the flames. They roared into the adjacent stall and up the far wall. He dropped the coat and gripped Abbie's arm. "Go!"

"The animals!" She choked.

"I'll get them."

"You can't manage, not by yourself—"

"Go."

"No, I..."

He rushed toward the front and shoved her. "Go!"

The door was already open, and she ran through. He turned back. The barn was dry, and there was little time. He plunged into the smoke, opened the stalls, and sent the horses out. Those tethered to the posts he cut loose and shooed. He wrapped his arm across his eyes and fought his way back through the flames. Chance was back there.

Behind him he heard voices, the thumps of bags and shovels and the sizzle of water on flames. It was no good. Even had they a lake, their efforts would be wasted. He had to reach Chance. There. The horse's eyes were wide, nostrils distended. He pulled back his lips and whinnied.

Monte spoke softly. "Steady. Steady."

Chance reared up, both walls of his stall ablaze. Monte gripped the bar. The heat of it seared his flesh as it burst to flame in his hands. Chance screamed, reared up, and his hoof caught Monte in the shoulder.

He went down, only half aware of Chance leaping over him through the smoke. He writhed, kicked at the pant leg aflame, but his hands ... the pain ... then nothing.

Seven

Abbie fought against Kendal's hold. "Let me go!" She wrenched one arm free and beat against him.

"You can't go back. It won't hold now." As his words faded, the corner of the roof collapsed.

"Please, God!"

"Don't faint, Frances! I've only one pair of arms."

Abbie saw her chance. She dropped and twisted. His hold broke, and she ran for the barn. The heat sucked her breath and she fell, regained her feet, and rushed through the door. No vision of hell compared to the raw force inside the barn.

"Monte!" She dropped to her knees and crawled.

Grant loomed up in the smoke, dragging Monte. No! She stood and ran toward them. Others rushed in and pulled Monte free. The smoke. The flames. She hit the floor hard. Someone . . . Grant . . . beat her legs, then pulled her up and ran. The horrible roar that followed sent flames rushing to the sky.

She yanked free of Grant and pushed through her neighbors to Monte's side. The strength left her legs. She dropped to her knees beside him. "Monte?"

He moaned.

Oh, dear God, he was alive. She felt her tears, though she had no knowledge of crying.

Pa spoke at her elbow. "Ethan's gone for Doctor Barrow. Don't try to move, Monte."

Monte rasped, "Abbie?"

"I'm here." She bent close.

He sucked in a strangled breath.

"Here is water for him." Mama handed Pa the cup, and he lifted Monte's head. Monte gulped, then choked and spewed it over his blackened chin. Closing his eyes, he dropped back.

Abbie swiped the tears from her nose. "Can we take him in, Pa?"

"I don't know that we should move him."

People suddenly rushed past, there was a crash, and a flaming geyser shot to the sky. The furious activity ceased. They were beaten. Abbie watched the flames soar and dance with fiendish fury. Held within the break, the fire consumed the barn but did not spread to the house or the land. The walls crumpled. Smoke blotted out the stars. She turned away.

Monte shivered even through the blanket.

"He's cold." She wanted to cover him with her body, hold him to her chest, feel the beat of his heart. "Pa, he's cold."

"All right. Wes, help me lift him." He slipped his arms under Monte's shoulders, and Wes grabbed his ankles. Monte cried out as they lifted him.

"No, stop, you're hurting him!"

Mama put a hand to her arm. They carried him limp and unresisting into the house as Abbie followed weakly. Placing him on the clean sheets Mama spread on the bed, Monte moaned again. His shoulder bled from a gash, but it seemed his hands pained him more. He held them like claws.

Pa tore the shirt free, and Mama pressed a cloth to his wounded shoulder. Without thought, Abbie soaked a towel and laid it across his forehead. A memory of Blake lying just so seized her. *No! Monte won't die!* She felt the hysteria filling her mind. A hand touched her shoulder and she lashed out, then met the eyes of Doctor Barrow. Relief rushed in.

"Joshua, stay. Everyone else out."

Abbie moved one foot after the other. It would be all right now. The doctor knew what to do. Hadn't he nursed her back from shock and pneumonia? He hadn't saved Sharlyn. But Monte was strong!

She could hear voices and commotion outside, but immediately around her all was still. She was in a cottony shell. There was no feeling but a dull numbness and something pressing her chest. Someone took her arm and led her to a chair. It was Kendal.

Frances was seated beside her. "What were you doing in the barn?"

Frances's voice sounded so queer and far away. Something more insistent was trying to penetrate her fog. But she couldn't quite . . .

"Frances." Kendal put a hand on his wife's shoulder, but she shrugged him off.

Her eyes were dangerously bright. "I warned you. I told you what she was. No lady would . . ."

No lady. What were they doing in the barn? Suddenly Abbie remembered the shadowy form that lunged at them. She shot up from the seat. "There was someone in there! Someone hit us, and we fell against the shelf!" She rushed for the kitchen. "Mama, I must get Marshal Haggerty!"

Mama turned from boiling the cloths. "You're not going anywhere."

"Then Grant, one of the men . . ."

"The men are containing the fire, searching for the horses, and taking their families home."

"But Mama, there was someone in the barn. Someone hit Monte and caused the fire. I have to get the marshal before it's too late."

"Listen to me." Mama gripped her arms. "If there was someone, either he's dead in the barn, or he's out there somewhere. And if he had malicious intentions, you're not going anywhere. Do you hear me, Abbie!"

Abbie hadn't the energy to fight. She felt so terribly helpless as she sank to a chair. The voices outside faded and stopped. Grant pushed open the door, spun a chair around, and straddled it. He leaned his elbows on the back and appraised Abbie. "You okay?"

She nodded.

"I didn't mean to hit you so hard, but your skirt . . ."

"I know. Did you get the horses?"

"Most of 'em. A handful headed for home, I guess. We'll find them in the morning."

But the morning would be too late to find the man who hit them. "Grant . . ."

The bedroom door opened, and Pa came out, closing it behind him. "We're ready for the cloths now, Selena."

Abbie leapt up. "Pa?"

"His lungs and throat are damaged, but Doctor Barrow says that should pass. Must have caught a hoof in the shoulder, but the bone is whole. I'm not sure of the burns."

Abbie's chest constricted as Pa took the cloths and returned to the room. Mama held her, stroking her head, and Abbie allowed the touch to soothe her. She turned her face to Mama's neck.

How could God let this happen? Why hadn't Monte come out? Why hadn't someone helped him? She should have stayed, should have helped. What were horses to his life? It was Chance he tried to reach. She knew it. He sent the others out, but Chance would have been behind the fire. Oh, dear Lord . . . why?

"Abbie, offer Frances and Kendal your room for the night." Mama's voice was low, calm. "We'll keep Monte where he is, and the rest of us can sleep in the front room."

Abbie didn't want to move. She wanted Mama to hold her until Monte walked out of the room, strong and whole. She didn't want to think about Kendal or Frances with the accusing eyes. She sniffed.

"Abbie . . ."

She straightened, wiped her tears, then walked to the other room. They sat as she had left them. She steadied her voice. "You're welcome to stay the night here. I don't know if you could find your way back . . ."

Kendal looked up. "Likely not."

"I'll show you to a room."

Kendal took Frances's hand. "Go with Abbie. I'll join you later."

Abbie was surprised that Frances obeyed without argument. She led her to the room at the back. "In the chest at the foot of the bed you'll find a gown to use."

Frances said nothing and closed the door.

Abbie stood staring at the wooden panels. What could she say, what could she do to reach Monte's sister? There was a wall as solid as the wood of the door between them. And now, when they could be a comfort to each other, she felt only condemnation.

Was this her fault? Had she somehow caused it, as the spilled tea, the scraped chin? Who had hit them and why?

Pa stepped into the hall. "He's asking for you."

She rushed past to Monte's side. His face was pale in the dim light. With it washed of the grime, she could see his face was not burned except for the edge of his forehead, which was dressed and bandaged. Also bandaged were his shoulder and his hands that lay above the blanket.

"Oh, Monte," she breathed.

He swallowed, and his voice came out thick and hoarse. "Don't worry. Tell Frances."

"She's gone to bed. I'll tell her in the morning."

He closed his eyes and seemed to try to speak again, but did not.

"I've given him laudanum for the pain." Doctor Barrow snapped the bag shut on the bedside table. "He'll sleep now."

Abbie nodded.

"You can sit with him if you like." He looked up at Pa. "I'll be back in the morning. We'll need to rewrap the burns every day with fresh salve."

The deep voices continued down the hall, but Abbie kept her eyes on Monte. Sleeping, he seemed peaceful. He was alive. She laid her head on the bed beside him. "Thank you, Lord, for sparing his life."

◆◆◆◆◆◆◆

Jip Crocker stared at the crackling embers surrounded by rough stones and spat a long string of brown spittle. He readjusted the lump inside his lower lip and threw a stick at the fire. "What's keepin' the kid!"

Across the fire Emmet guffawed. "Gittin' soft over yer kid brother, Jip? He prob'ly got lost and wet hisself."

Jip kicked a bootful of dirt into the paunchy, pimpled face. "You're a pig, Emmet."

Emmet spit the dirt. "Sheez, I know that. What's funny is you think you're not." He swiped his mouth with his sleeve.

Jip huddled back against the tree. "I knew trouble would come o' this. You shoulda never put him up to it."

"Me? The whelp had his own ideas."

"You dared 'im. I heard you clear as day. Why don't you swipe you a real horse, kid. That's what you said." Jip sent Emmet a killer look. He'd like to squeeze that fat neck till it popped. If anything had happened to Spence, he would. Behind him a twig snapped, and he spun to his feet, his rifle ready in his grip. The boy stepped into the glow of the campfire and tethered three horses to the tree.

Jip caught him by the collar. "Where the heck you been, Spence?"

Spence shrugged him loose and sat down at the fire ring. He grabbed the coffeepot and poured it into a bent tin cup. "Started me a fire."

Jip stuck his nose into the night air and whiffed. "What'd you do thet fer?"

"I was in the barn like Emmet said, waitin' fer night. First I thought it weren't worth it, no corral, one cow, two middlin' horses. Then I saw they was havin' some big shindig. Ever'one brung their horses to the barn. I'd have my pick if I could git out unseen. I settled in fer dark, but then this guy come in actin' real strange . . . didn't light the lantern till he'd stumbled his way to the back in the dark. He was almost on top o' me 'fore he lit up, an' I saw he had his girl with 'im."

"Ya learn somethin', kid?" Emmet poked him with a stick.

Spence shoved the stick aside. "I didn't wait ta see. Any minute they'd'a spotted me. I charged 'em, and they fell aginst the wall. The lantern smashed and flames was ever'where. I got out while he was arguin' with the girl to run."

Spence drank again. "Soon the whole place is goin' up like the Fourth o' July. I figured I better scoot, when all the horses come runnin' one after 'nother. Shoot, I says, this is better'n I planned. I grabbed the ones come my way an' looked 'em over. One wasn't worth nothin' so I left it an' brung these three. An' take a look at the black one. It ain't no common horse."

Jip strode to the horses and ran his hands over the black's coat, then down its legs. The horse shivered and widened its eyes. Then he examined the flank. "This here's the Farrel brand."

"Now, ain't that lucky?" Emmet stood and wiped the dirt from his britches.

Jip spun as another horse entered the circle, this one directed by its master. First Jip could make out nothing but the glow of his cigar. Then the fire lit the edges of his face, the auburn lambchop whiskers and the scar from his scalp to his left eyebrow.

"Captain Jake."

The captain shifted the cigar in his teeth but didn't speak.

Jip cleared his throat and looked from Emmet to Spence. He'd like to knock their skulls together. Why couldn't they keep to the work set for them? He stepped to the campfire. "Coffee?"

The captain swung down from his horse. He let the reins hang and the horse never moved. Military trained. Or something else. Jip had heard yarns of dogs turning tail when Captain Jake came, and other stories, too. Sweat started down his neck.

Captain Jake swigged the coffee, then poured the dregs in the dirt. "You men are a good step from the ranch."

Emmet stood up and hiked his pants. "We got some horses."

Captain Jake did not answer.

"You can look 'em over."

"Whose are they?"

Spence joined Emmet. "One of 'em's got the Farrel brand. It's a . . ."

"And the others?" The captain strode past him to the tied horses. He moved the black aside with a hand on its back, then checked the other flanks. He turned. "Horse stealing's a hanging offense."

Emmet rubbed his chin.

Captain Jake took off his gloves and slapped them against his palm. "I'm a rancher. I don't deal in stolen livestock."

"Then what about them cattle—" the argument died in Emmet's throat.

Jip shook his head. Emmet had more gall than brains.

"Spoils." The captain eyed each of them in turn. "Spoils, gentlemen. I suggest you learn the difference. There's only room for one boss in this territory, and it won't be Johnny Reb."

Emmet shut up. Spence had eyes like an owl. Jip hoped he learned from this.

The captain waved toward the horses. "Turn them loose."

Jip reached for the rope.

"Not . . . the black. That one is commandeered." Captain Jake took the black's rope and drew on his cigar until it glowed red. "I'll expect you at the ranch. Don't make me look for you again." He led the black across the circle, mounted his own horse, and swung them around together. He touched his boots to the horse's sides and disappeared into the darkness.

"Durn him." Emmet spat.

"He's the boss." Jip untied the other two horses and sent them off, then turned to Spence. "Did thet fella make it outta the barn?"

"I didn't wait ta see." Spence's voice cracked.

Another time Jip would have reassured him. Not now. A healthy fear of Captain Jake might keep the kid in line. If only Emmet had brains enough to feel the same. He shook his head. "We better git. Pack it up."

◆◆◆◆◆◆◆

Pain penetrated the woozy lethargy, and Monte cracked his eyes open. The ceiling above seemed low and shrunken as his vision cleared, then blurred and cleared again. This was not his room. He squeezed tears from his eyes and lifted a hand to wipe them clear. What met his face was a white, bandaged mound, and he stared at it, then lifted and scrutinized the other. Memory rushed in. Nerves no longer silenced by the drug began to scream, and he grimaced as he fought back the low moan that would not be contained.

Beside him Abbie raised her head. He turned to her slowly, eyes swimming again. "Abbie." His throat burned. She was seated in a chair directly beside the bed, still dressed in the flame-defiled dress she had worn yesterday. Evidently she had not left his side since his eyes closed last night. He cracked his parched lips, then fought another wave of pain.

"Can you drink, Monte?" Abbie lifted a cup of water.

He closed his eyes. His thoughts were fuzzy, and his tongue felt thick and foul. The skin on the back of his leg and the palms of his hands roared pain to his brain. He opened his eyes and rasped, "Yes, water."

Tucking her arm behind his head, she tipped it forward and held the cup to his lips. He allowed the cool liquid to soothe his tongue before swallowing it down. He did not choke and drank again before closing his lips against any more. Setting the cup down, Abbie gently released his head.

The door opened, and Joshua stepped in with Doctor Barrow beside him. Selena followed with an armful of fresh cloths. "Awake, eh?" Doctor Barrow moved to the bedside. "I'm not sure you're glad for that. Are you in pain?"

Monte nodded.

"We'll need to rebandage your burns."

Monte whispered, "Frances . . ."

Abbie leaned close. "I'll go to her, Monte. I'll tell her not to worry."

He nodded, following her with his eyes as she slipped from the room.

There was no sound yet from the bedroom, so Abbie did not

awaken Frances to deliver Monte's assurances. Instead she washed in the lean-to, pulled on a dress of her mother's, and slipped outside. The ashes and blackened fragments still smoldered.

The horrid smell of burned flesh clogged her breath, and she stared at the mound. Oh . . . sweet, gentle Buttercup. Her breath caught in her chest, but she trapped the tears with an angry sniff. What good was crying? Would it bring anything back? Heal Monte? Help her find the man responsible? Hot anger filled her.

She knew better than to step amid the smoking remains of the barn, but she did it anyway. Kicking aside a half-torched beam, she made her way to the area that had been the back beneath the loft. With the hem of her skirts held up over the devastation, she searched the ground.

There, lying among the ashes, she found what she sought, grabbed it up, and clasped it to her chest. The silver box was blackened, but intact. Like Monte. Injured but alive . . . yes, alive. Even in her fatigue she had been aware of every wheezing breath he took last night. She opened the box and the morning light caught the blood red stones, the white teardrops.

His mother's earrings. She recalled the portrait of the beautiful woman and the softness of Monte's voice when he spoke of her with the low gentleness he reserved for those he held dear. And now his voice was a tortured croak he forced like air through a reed. She closed the box, then retraced her steps.

Pa waited at the edge of blackened ground. "You know better than that."

"I know, Pa. But I had to find it." She held out the silver box, opened to reveal the earrings. "Monte's gift."

Pa brushed her cheek lightly with his ink-stained thumb. "Our guests are awake."

Abbie nodded. Perhaps a night's sleep had soothed Frances. Perhaps their shared concern would unite them. But Frances was paler than before, and blue-gray circles underscored her eyes. Nothing Abbie said changed the tight line of her lips. She refused breakfast, and when Pa said they'd keep Monte, Kendal took her home with Pa's gelding, Sandy, pulling the phaeton.

✦✦✦✦✦✦✦

In the front room of his ranch house, Captain Jake Gifford ran the cloth over the blade of the sword. Its sheen glittered in the lamplight, the filigreed tracery tossing fragments of light to the ceiling. He laid the sword beside the cleaned pistol and the oiled rifle. A man's weapons were his responsibility. Order, cleanliness, and discipline kept a soldier sharp.

Captain Jake stood and examined himself in the mirror. No extra flesh, shoulders back, straight spine. He was a weapon himself, as sharp and deadly as any saber. He would not allow civilian life to soften him, though he must admit he took to the amenities. That was the worst part of the war: the discomfort of it.

He took a cigar from the box on the mantle, snipped the end, and placed it between his teeth. He scrutinized his face. No hint of softness, no glimpse of mercy. He lit the cigar and drew the smoke to his lungs. It felt good to face an adversary again.

Montgomery Farrel. No matter that he had not fought on the fields. Captain Jake knew well enough his efforts to thwart the Union men on his father's land and that of his neighbors. He had heard his men speak of the coward southern boy that gave the soldiers sport. But until he came west, he had not had the opportunity to meet Major William Jackson Farrel's son. His face hardened.

Montgomery Farrel was no coward. It took more courage and strength of will to do what he did for the helpless at home than to go armed to war. Captain Jake did not underestimate him. Underneath his glowing southern charm, he was as uncompromising as his father before him.

Montgomery Farrel was an honorable man. Nowhere had he found anyone who spoke against him. He stood tall in the community, as had his father. His was a voice that held clout, that persuaded, that received respect. A voice to be silenced.

He would take Farrel down. Even were he not the son of Major Farrel, he would take him down—on principle alone. Were it in his power, he would take down every one of those southern slave owners who had . . . Captain Jake tightened his grip on the hilt of his sword.

He turned again to the mirror and studied himself. Sent behind enemy lines in stealth and darkness, had he even once failed to carry out his order? His own troops called him a spy. But it was the other camps, the enemy camps who feared him. They greeted the dawn only to find a man silently slain, the deadly sign that revealed he had been among them, had sniffed out their secrets and left betrayal in his wake.

He turned from the mirror. Betrayal. What to do about Jip Crocker and his kin? He would not tolerate insubordination. On the other hand, their escapade had maimed Montgomery Farrel, no matter unintentionally. Captain Jake drew on the cigar. Very well. For now he would let the incident pass.

He took up the saber and went out to the yard. Farrel's gelding stood tethered to the fence. Captain Jake took another rope, circled the horse's head, and fixed it to the opposite post, trapping the horse in the center of the corral. The animal balked at the constraint, nostrils snorting and eyes widening. Captain Jake came close, sensed the creature's fear, then drew his saber and slit its throat.

He leaped back from the gush of blood, watched the horse buckle and drop, suspended by the ropes. They would have looked for the animal. He could not risk being connected to that business. With the cloth he wiped the blade and sheathed it, then returned to the house. Emmet snapped to attention as he approached the door.

The captain eyed him. Emmet was shifty and unpredictable. Without Jip he would be worthless. He needed a lesson. Let him see what became of his thieving. "There's a carcass in the corral. Burn it. But before you do . . . bring me the head."

✦✦✦✦✦✦

Monte awoke to a room cast in sunset hues. The pain seemed less sharp, his chest less heavy. He breathed without wheezing and felt his mind clear. He turned his head, sensing that Abbie was there. "Evening already?" His throat felt full of rust.

Abbie smiled. "Evening of the third day. Doctor Barrow says no more laudanum."

Three days. No wonder he felt stronger. He tried to smile with cracked lips. "Mighty high price for one stolen kiss." He coughed. "Oh, Monte."

"What was lost?"

She smoothed the coverlet over his chest. "It doesn't matter. You're better, that's all."

"The horses? Chance?"

She shook her head. "He got out of the barn but hasn't been found. All the others but Chance were recovered."

Monte frowned. "He would have gone to my stable."

"Monte, did you see who it was that hit us?"

So that had happened. After the crazy, undefined dreams, he wasn't sure what was real. "No. Not clearly. Perhaps I broke a heart worse than I thought."

"Don't, please."

He forced another smile. The pain was sharpening as his senses wakened, but not unbearably.

"Are you hungry?"

"Famished." He would be lucky to get anything down, but he saw her need.

Abbie sprang to her feet, swept through the door, then called, "Monte's ready for broth, Mama."

Monte stared at the empty doorway. Why was Chance lost? Why Chance alone? A thought pierced his consciousness. Had the attack been intentional? Had his harrasser threatened Abbie's home because of him? She returned with the bowl, set it on the table beside the bed, and tucked in extra pillows to raise him up.

He lifted his hands and stared at the thick bandages. "How bad are they?"

"Doctor Barrow said we'll see tomorrow. The scarring won't be bad if the burns are not too deep." Abbie dipped the spoon into the broth and brought it to his lips.

He recoiled at the thought of being spoon fed. She held it there insistently. He parted his lips, and the broth coursed warmly down his throat and awakened his hunger. She brought another spoonful and another to him. This was not how it was supposed to be. It was his place to care for her, to keep her safe, to . . . She again held the spoon until he accepted it.

"I had to remove a beam to free Chance. It burst into flame in my hands."

Abbie set the bowl down. "You saved all the horses. Not one burned." Her face suddenly crumpled, and tears filled her eyes.

He saw now how thin her cheerful veneer truly was, and that told him more than her words. Was he a cripple? He reached a bandaged hand toward her, touched the back of it to her cheek. "Abbie." He wanted to hold her.

"When you didn't come out, I wished I had stayed in there with you."

"Don't say that."

"It's true."

He pulled her head to his chest. Everything was spoiled. Everything changed. How he wanted her, but . . . "When do the bandages come off?"

"I don't know."

Or wouldn't tell. He released her. "I won't marry you until I'm healed."

She looked as though he had struck her. "Why?"

"We'll wait until my hands are restored."

"Oh, Monte, I don't care!"

"I do." He looked away. Memories of his father returning from the war assailed him. He had put behind him the images of his father, the sleeve that hung slack, the limping gait . . . the broken man.

How could he bring Abbie into the danger escalating around him? How could he keep her safe, with his own body maimed? If his hands did not heal . . . He clenched his jaw. He would not take Abbie as a wife while crippled and dependent.

Eight

Monte stood in the deepening dusk. The September chill seemed premature. Surely autumn had not arrived so soon. It must be that he did not yet gauge the temperature well. Though new skin covered the burns on his leg and back, it was tender still, more sensitive to cold and heat. He went inside to the library and closed the door behind him. He had just settled into his chair when James knocked and admitted Cole.

As always, Cole removed his hat, but it did little to show respect. "How much longer you gonna wait? There's at least thirty head missin'."

Monte straightened. "Good evening, Cole. Pour yourself a drink."

Cole went to the cabinet that held the decanters. He chose whiskey over brandy. Monte was inclined to have one, too, but refrained. He'd come close enough to following his father's footsteps after Sharlyn died. Now, in light of his injury, it was too potent a temptation to take lightly.

Nor did he wish for Cole to see him struggle to hold a glass. Each day proved more strongly Doctor Barrow's fears that the healing would be slow—if it came at all—and that he would never regain full use of his hands. "How do you know the animals haven't strayed?"

"I've looked. Cattle stray, but as a rule they graze close to their home range."

Monte couldn't argue with Cole's expertise. "How are they getting them?"

"Just helpin' themselves. Don't matter how many men're on the herd, if they're ordered not to act." Cole shot the whiskey down his throat and set the glass on a table.

Monte watched him. "I don't want to start anything."

"It's started already. You've watched and you've waited. Now you're givin' 'em leave."

Monte bristled. "What would you have me do?"

"Let the word out to the men they're lookin' for rustlers. They know it already. Tell 'em to shoot what they see."

"And if it's one of our neighbors?"

"You're stuck on that thought. Who do you suspect?"

"I don't—"

"No, you don't."

Monte bridled at the interruption.

Cole leaned on the desk. "Fact is, we got a small operation that only wants stompin', and it's time to stomp it."

Monte stood, then walked to the window. Yes, he had waited, hoped to hear from another rancher that they were likewise besieged, hoped for some sign that the molestation was not directed to him alone. But no word had come. All his feelers had returned empty. The attacks were on him alone. Why?

Perhaps Cole was right. Perhaps it was time to act. All it took was his word. His men would handle the situation while he stayed at the house and waited, while he himself did nothing . . . could do nothing.

"Who's on the herd?"

"Skeeter and Curtis. Breck and Forbes are watchin' the bluff. But it's time . . ."

"I heard you." He turned and fixed Cole in his gaze. "Do you expect trouble tonight?"

"Tonight, tomorrow. Who's to know? The herd's restless, but somethin's movin' in. Could be the storm's got them anxious."

Monte returned to his desk and sat. "Alert the men. Put them on shifts." He could see the relief on Cole's face.

"Yes, sir. You want one kept with Will, also?"

"Why?"

Cole picked up his hat. "Thought I saw someone skulkin' about the other night. I didn't want to say nothin' till I was sure, but it's been botherin' me."

"You think the rustlers are also horse thieves?"

"Might be. Might be they're the ones got off with Chance."

Monte leaned back and rested his hands on his thighs. Unconsciously he stretched the fingers and winced again. "You think they're brazen enough to risk coming to the yard?" He could tell Cole held back what he would say. Would he say they could do anything they liked as long as the cripple refused to act?

Cole shrugged. "Word's gone round about the new horse."

"Abbie's mare."

"How's that?"

"The new Arabian. She's my wedding gift for Abbie." Monte watched Cole's reaction. The man wasn't easy to read.

"Seems to me a weddin' gift wants a weddin'."

That was straight. Cole didn't pull any punches, and right now Monte appreciated that more than the restraint and pitying glances he got from the others. He held his palms out. "You see this?"

"Yeah, I see it."

"When you get a newborn foal that's just struggled to its feet and nuzzled for the first time, you take your hands and go over it, soft and gentle, stroking just so and letting it catch your scent and hear your voice. One spook, one rough or hurried motion, and you've put fear into it. But if you do it right, after that it recognizes your touch every time." He turned his hands palms down. "I'll wait until I have a touch I want her to recognize."

Cole's temple pulsed. He put his hat on. "You don't know Abbie as well as you think."

Kendal knocked on the open door and sauntered in a little unsteadily.

Monte stood. "Put two men in the stable with Will. As many as you need on the herd. We'll see what we catch."

"Yes, sir." Cole strode from the room.

"Trouble?" Kendal went to the cabinet and poured a whiskey.

"It appears we have rustlers. Cole thinks they may also be horse thieves."

Kendal sat and stretched his legs out before him. His fingers worked the waxed end of his mustache. "Doesn't the law handle that sort of thing?"

"If it can. In this case, I have the men to see to it. Marshal Haggerty and Deputy Davis are only two."

"Don't tell Frances of this, will you?" Kendal leaned forward. "Her *nerves* won't take it."

"Perhaps you should take her home."

Kendal sipped the whiskey. "She wants to see you wed or hear that it's off altogether. She'd prefer the latter."

"I'm sorry she feels that way."

Kendal shrugged. "We breed it into them, you know. From the time they learn to distinguish white from black, rich from poor, we set it into their minds to despise those beneath them, those different, just as we do."

"I'm glad I'm removed from that." Monte took his seat again.

"Are you?" Kendal's eyes were bright. "I don't see you so removed. So James and Pearl receive a pension. They're still your darkies, just as they always were. Your hired men jump to your beck. And Abbie now . . ."

Monte didn't like the way he said her name.

" . . . she's a cut above anyone out here. You still skim the cream and throw the rest to the hogs."

Monte frowned. "I admit I am well off. But I don't share your opinions."

"No? Then why don't we invite James in for a drink with us?"

Monte leaned back. "He's an old man. He would not understand a different way."

Kendal threw back his head and laughed. "How well you deceive yourself, my brother by law. But I know better. You would no more drink with a slave than bed one."

Monte seethed. "I find you distasteful." He'd seen Kendal like this before.

"Have you?"

"Have I what?"

"Bedded a slave?"

Monte stood. "You're drunk, Kendal."

Kendal laughed. "You keep a fine whiskey in this house. Whiskey of a quality I've not afforded for some time."

"If you're in financial trouble, we'll discuss it when you're sober. Good night." He left Kendal sitting alone and went upstairs. With both hands he worked the knob until it turned, then entered his room and closed the door behind him.

Kendal was out of his head, was all. They were growing fretful, Frances especially. She took every opportunity to remind him of women back home, women whose beaus and husbands were lost in the war. Some were the sisters and cousins of friends, some the very same he had protected and hidden during the Yankee raids.

He was tired of it. He should marry Abbie and send his sister home. He slowly closed his hands into claws then stretched them out again. They were improving, the skin growing more supple, the nerves less tender.

He walked to the drawer of his dresser, pulled out the jar, and lifted the lid. He rubbed the linament over the scars. The hands were not wholly useless, yet he chafed his infirmity. Why now when he needed to be strong? What was God about?

✦✦✦✦✦✦✦

Abbie stood in the yard in the cool, foggy morning, her shawl snug around her shoulders. She glanced at Monte beside her, but he seemed miles away. He watched, though she wondered if he saw. The men pulled the ropes. The wooden frame swung up perpendicular to the ground. Others sprang forward and braced it firmly.

They cheered, and Abbie clapped her hands. "First wall up! Is there anything like a barn raising?"

Monte's smile was thin.

"All yesterday they built the frames, but it's never so grand as when they stand the walls up. It was good of you, Monte, to provide the lumber. I don't know how Pa..."

"It was nothing."

Abbie almost stamped her foot. They'd spent a month now speaking polite assurances, ever since the morning he'd gone home after the bandages were removed. Where was he? Why had he withdrawn from her?

"What is it, Monte?"

He surprised her by not shrugging off her question. "I wish I could help." His voice was strained.

"You have helped! All the wood and the new cow..."

"You know what I mean. I'm tired of watching." He held his hands up. The red skin was fading but still stretched thick and tight over his palms. The fingers curled in, though less than they had. How helpless he must feel, so used to being in control. But she felt helpless, too ... helpless to reach him, to show her love, her faith that he was still the man he had been.

She took his hands and brushed her lips over the palms. He groaned and grabbed her close with his arms. "Stop, Abbie. You push me past the bounds of decency."

"I won't stop. I don't care that the healing is slow, it will come."

He eased her back, and there was warmth in his eyes. His smile was even amused. Oh, how good it looked.

"I suppose God reports to you now?"

She put up her chin. "If He did, I'd have something to say about His timing."

He actually laughed. Abbie's heart soared.

"I just bet you would." He kissed her forehead. "Let's walk."

Abbie slipped her hand into his arm. The fog was lifting, though no breath of wind stirred. She breathed the dampness. "Why did Frances and Kendal not come this morning?"

Not that Frances would appreciate a barn raising, but she had not left Monte's side since his return home. Not once had she visited without Frances hovering, and Monte had made no move to change it. But James had driven him over today, and having Monte to herself this morning was pure heaven.

"Kendal was not feeling well."

"I hope it's not serious."

"A case of too much whiskey in too short a time."

"Oh." Abbie stepped over the wet gully. "I didn't take him for a drinker." Though she didn't doubt Frances could drive any man to drink.

"I expect he's facing troubles of some sort."

"There are no answers in a bottle."

"I doubt it was answers he sought."

"What then?"

"Escape."

She stole a glance. Had he read her thoughts? She couldn't resist probing. "Escape from what?"

"Abbie, I don't know."

"You must have an idea."

He turned suddenly. "And if I do?"

"Then I want to know."

"I never took you for a gossip."

"It's not gossip when it's family."

He smiled. "You have an answer for everything, haven't you?"

"Not everything."

Monte led her forward again. "I suspect it was the liquor talking more than anything, but I fear he may be in some financial strait. I wondered about his associates when I went there to close on the sale of the plantation." He sighed. "And I'm concerned about his happiness with Frances. There, you can say you knew it."

Abbie felt the blood rush to her face. "I didn't think . . ."

"Oh yes, you did. I know Frances is not easy to live with. But . . ." He shook his head. "I thought they were happy, especially with baby Jeanette."

"Don't get me going on that subject."

He squeezed her hand between his arm and side. "You have been intractable."

"I haven't said half what I think."

"How well I know that. Frances knows it, too."

Abbie sighed. "If only she thought better of me. . . ."

"Now, Abbie."

"Oh, Monte, I'm not blind or stupid. I know what she thinks. It's just that I thought I could . . . I don't know."

"Frances can be petty. Don't take it to heart."

"I don't blame her. She's a fine lady and . . ."

"You are, as well."

Abbie smiled. "That's kind, but you know my shortcomings."

He turned and took her into his arms. "No." He bent close. "I don't know of any." He kissed her for the first time since the fire.

Tears sprang to her eyes, and she clung to him. "Oh, Monte."

"No tears, Abbie. It's not like you."

Maybe not. But how much longer could she hold them back?

••••••••

When Monte returned he found Kendal slumped in a chair in the parlor. The dim noonday light hardly penetrated the velvet drapes. Monte crossed the room and pulled them aside. Kendal raised his head, greeting the light with a groan.

"Where's Frances?"

"Indisposed."

"Shall I get you coffee?"

"That wouldn't be my first choice, but I'll settle for it."

Monte tugged the bellpull on the wall, and James appeared. "Coffee for Mr. Stevens, please, James."

"Yessuh."

A few minutes later Pearl came in with a blue-enameled pot and two cups. She set them on the table and turned to go. "Thank you, Pearl."

"Yessuh."

Kendal's eyes had raised at Monte's thanks, and he grinned. "Determined to prove me wrong, eh?"

Monte shrugged. "Do you mind pouring? It's still a little awkward."

Kendal filled the two cups, then sat back and sipped. He grimaced. "Now that's a rude awakening. Not nearly as satisfying as last night's venture."

"Nor will it carry the price." Monte sipped the coffee and nearly choked. Pearl must have intended to tar Kendal's insides. He set the cup on the table. "So what were you telling me last night?"

Kendal chuckled, but it sounded false. "You should have seen your eyes widen."

Monte waited.

"I spoke with Frances about staying out here."

"What!"

"Why do you think I've tried to make her see the good things? I thought if she . . ."

"Kendal, have you gone mad?"

Kendal dropped his head into his hands. "There's nothing to go home to, you see. I've lost it all."

Monte's stomach pitched. "What? How?"

"My . . . partners. It's far too complicated to give you all the details. Suffice it to say, I was duped."

Monte stood, paced to the window, then back. "Why here?"

"Where else?"

"What will you set up with?"

"Perhaps a loan from my brother-in-law?"

Monte sank again into the chair. "What did Frances say?"

"What do you expect? She'd rather die than live here. She'll go back with my mother and raise Jeanette to be just like her."

"She'll not. Her place and duty is beside her husband."

Kendal smirked. "Tell *her* that."

"I will."

Releasing a deep breath, Kendal said, "Perhaps it's better for her to go. If something happened . . ."

"Frances will not leave you. If you're determined to stay here, she will also."

"And what of Jeanette?"

"What of the children I'll have? What of any of the children being raised here?"

Kendal shook his head. "I'm afraid her mind's made up."

"She's not heard from me yet."

Kendal sagged and looked at him. "Monte, the things I said last night . . ."

"I understand, Kendal. I told you I would forget them."

Kendal nodded. His cheeks were slack and lined, his eyes red rimmed. But there was something more . . . something indefinable but more consuming. Failure. It clung to him. And now Monte wondered about other things. Had the plantation gone down by Kendal's fault?

Others had lost, as well, but Monte had left it to Frances in good shape. Yet not so long after, they had sold it for little enough. What would Kendal do here? Had he the mettle to forge his way in the West? God help him if he did not.

♦♦♦♦♦♦♦

Monte walked alone after leaving Kendal. He would not judge him. It was not his place to condemn. He walked to the cottonwood path behind the house and followed it along the stream. The morning mist had thickened to a solid cap, but no rain fell as yet. The air was chill, but he needed the silence to think.

His duty was clear. He must aid Kendal, but the manner to do so was not so clear. He stooped to pass under the branches and cut up the grassy slope away from the water and the house. He reached and followed the fence line that separated the yard from the back pasture.

The clouds would not hold much longer. That was good. The land needed moisture. The straw-colored grass was brittle underfoot. And the men should have Joshua's barn roofed by now, at least the base wood down.

He looked up. What was that on the corner post? He had not intended to go up that far. He strained to make it out. It was no good. He quickened his pace. As he neared, he narrowed his eyes. He should—it seemed he should know it, but . . .

With a sudden sickening jolt his mind made the leap. He did know it—the shape, the color . . . Dear God, it couldn't be . . . No blood ran from the severed horse head, but the fur was grizzly with it and the eyes had been eaten out of the skull. Chance.

Monte's chest heaved as rage and grief engulfed him.

Here was the reason Marshal Haggerty had found no sign of the stolen horse. Monte's hands clenched. All he had risked, suffered, to save Chance . . . for this! He felt the blood pulsing in his temples.

Teeth clenched, he turned from the head of his horse impaled on the post. He stared at his hands. He could not even hold a shovel to bury it. Who would do such a thing? Who would kill a fine animal only to torment its owner? To terrify him alone? He raised his face to the first drops of rain.

"Whoever it is, Lord, I will not succumb. I will not bend beneath his threats. Reveal him to me, and I will bring him down. He will not drive me from my land!" What else could it mean? No rustler would sacrifice a valuable horse like Chance. This was a warning. He'd seen its sort before.

He needed to find Cole. One of the men could bury the head, but Cole was right. The time of waiting was over. Vigilance and action would put an end to this business. He wiped the back of his sleeve over his face and slowed to a solid stride. And it was time for other things as well. Damaged hands or not, he would get on with his life.

Nine

Abbie could hardly contain herself as she rode to Monte's ranch. That he had sent and not come himself didn't matter at all. Chandler's coming had to mean something, portend some good. Monte had delayed him, but now ... maybe, just maybe, the waiting was over.

Sharlyn's brother. Surely this meeting would be different. How cheerfully Monte spoke of Chandler, of their long friendship. Chandler, whom he had chosen above all his friends here, even above Kendal, to stand up for him at the wedding. Chandler and his wife. She urged Shiloh on, heedless of the dust that rose from the hooves and gathered in her skirts.

She halted the mare at the stable where Will took the reins. She swiped the dust from her skirts and started for the house. *Please, Lord, don't let Maimie be like Frances.* Oh, that was unkind. She crossed the yard and started up the steps. She stopped before the door and looked at the knocker. Heavens, what was she waiting for? She knocked.

James opened to her with a nod. She smiled. "How are you, James?"

"Middlin', Mizz Martin." He ushered her in. She didn't wait for him to show her to the parlor. The door stood open, and she could hear the voices inside and Monte's laughter. Her heart jumped, and she stopped for a moment to listen. He was in rare good spirits by the sound of it.

"Go on in, Mizz. Mastuh Monte's expectin' you."

"Thank you." Abbie drew a deep breath and stepped into the

doorway. Monte's back was to her, but she got a clear look at Chandler. Her chest seized. She had not thought how like Sharlyn he might be, how it would recall to her Sharlyn herself. Fair and slight like his sister, Chandler was as impeccably dressed as Monte but with the same understated ease.

He glanced up and caught Monte's arm. Monte turned. "Ah, Abbie." He came forward, arms outstretched, and caught her hands in his. She was surprised by the firmness of his grasp. If it pained him, he made no sign. "Chandler, permit me to present to you Abbie Martin."

At least he didn't say Abigail. Abbie reached her hand to Chandler.

He grasped it warmly. "How do you do? I cannot tell you the pleasure this gives me."

His vehemence surprised her. She half expected the same shyness as Sharlyn, they were so similar in looks. "It's equally mine. I've looked so forward to your coming." Her voice softened. "Sharlyn was very dear to me."

He pressed her hand. "Thank you. I know she shared your affection."

Behind them she heard motion and turned. Frances was unspeakably elegant in blue silk, her waist corsetted tightly and the skirts billowing to the floor. Abbie's heart sank. Beside her, the petite lady who must be Chandler's wife was equally elegant. Her hair was pulled back from her heart-shaped face and wrapped neatly in a beaded snood, and her dress was impeccable. Abbie was suddenly aware of every dust speck on her plain linen dress, and her thoughtless rejection of corset and bustle.

Maimie clapped her hands together, her face breaking suddenly into delight. "Monte, you should be flogged for withholding. You never said your intended was so lovely."

"Not exactly, my dear." Chandler said. "He held forth at length over breakfast. Only you and Frances were still primping and missed the half of it."

Maimie swept forward, her rose-colored train swishing on the floor. She took Abbie's hands. "I'm so happy to meet you. I see Monte is as fortunate as he deserves to be."

Abbie was surprised by the tears that stung behind her eyes. Maimie's round, brown eyes and frank smile dissolved her unease. Of course she should have dressed for the meeting. But Monte's message had so excited her, she had hugged Mama and run for the barn as she was. Maimie's acceptance was an unwarranted kindness.

She ought to say something, but tears choked her throat. When had she become such a crybaby? "I hope your trip was not too difficult."

"She missed the whole thing with her head in a book." Chandler rested his hand on his wife's back.

"The trip was fine, though I was glad that Monte met us in town, else Chad said we'd have had an Indian guide. Imagine."

Abbie smiled. No wonder Monte got on so well with him. "I'm afraid you'd have looked a long way to find one."

Frances passed by in a swish of silk. "Do sit, Maimie. I'm starved for gossip." She settled onto the settee and patted the seat beside her. "You must tell me everything. You have no idea how I've missed polite company."

Abbie stood frozen. Had Frances poured a bucket of stream water over her head, it could hardly have felt worse. All the elation of Maimie's greeting was lost, and something dangerous stirred in its place. Monte touched her arm and motioned her to the wing chair beside the settee.

Frances hardly looked up. "Maimie, dear, I set to rights the melodeon in the great hall."

Maimie clasped her hands in delight. "Wonderful!"

"I knew you would want to play, though I'm afraid Monte hasn't kept it in the best tune . . ."

"It's a rarity for a tuner to pass through here, and I haven't much use for it." He leaned on the frame of Abbie's chair. She was glad to have him near. It reminded her to guard her tongue.

Frances turned. "I'm certain you play, Abbie?"

It seemed every eye turned to her. Frances had orchestrated that. "No."

"What a pity. Monte loved it so when Sharlyn played, didn't you, Monte? She played almost as well as you, Maimie. Do you remember the duet you played for Mrs. Baldwin's soiree?"

Kendal walked in. He smelled of the stable, and his hair was windblown. "Ah." He reached a hand to Chandler. "Good to see you, man." He bent over Maimie's hand. "You're a muse in pink, Maimie dear." He turned to Abbie, grasped her hand and lingered. "Fresh as a mountain rose."

Abbie felt her cheeks flush. Thankfully Chandler spoke up. "Kendal, where have you been?"

"Enjoying Monte's horseflesh."

"You missed breakfast."

"And I'm famished."

Monte straightened. "I'll order refreshments."

"I've already done so." Frances smiled sweetly. "I ordered early luncheon on the veranda since it's such a pleasant day. I hope you don't mind?"

Monte nodded. "That's fine."

Abbie bit her tongue. Of course it was fine. Everything Frances did was fine. Monte held out a hand and his sister took it, stood, and arranged her skirts. The light played on the silk like gossamer.

Abbie felt like a lump of lead. What was she to do? If Monte was escorting Frances . . . Chandler stepped forward and offered her his arm. "May I?"

Relief washed over her as she stood.

"Maimie and I were so pleased to learn of Monte's engagement. Wild horses could not have kept us away, and only his insistence made us delay."

"Thank you, Mr. Bridges."

"Please. Chandler." He pulled out a chair at the table for her and took the one beside it.

Kendal likewise seated Maimie across from them. Pearl carried out a tray of tiny wild capons boned and roasted with blackberry sauce, while James followed with mashed potatoes, bowls of tossed greens, stewed tomatoes, and fresh rolls. Nothing that needed cutting, Abbie noticed. Monte could not have managed. Either Pearl or Frances had seen to that.

Frances looked at Monte, and he nodded his approval. When James stood beside her, Abbie could hardly tell him what she would like. She was sure every bite would stick in her throat.

She watched Maimie to see which utensil to use when. She was almost certain Maimie intentionally rested her finger on each fork or spoon before lifting it, but she never let on by sharing even a glance.

"I can't get over how clean the air feels out here. Everything seems fresh and new." Maimie took a dainty bite of greens, and Abbie followed.

Monte answered, "It is fresh and new. That is the excitement of it."

"There is much lacking." Frances dabbed her lips. "Culture, gentility, tradition."

"We're making our own traditions, Frances. A new gentility free from the bonds of the past."

"I have yet to see it, Monte dear." She smiled. "What I see is . . . coarse and primitive. Survival, but no more."

Coarse and primitive. Abbie would love to prove her right. The desire to fling her plate down the front of Frances's gown seized her.

Chandler turned to her. "Certainly it's not a matter of survival still?"

Abbie mimicked Frances with the soft linen napkin and laid it in her lap. Wickedness filled her thoughts and found her lips. "Well . . . it is when the Indians attack."

Monte choked into his cup.

"Indians!" Chandler laid down his fork. "Oh, come, Abbie. Have they not been settled on the reservations?"

"Not the wild bands of Comanche, Ute, and Jicarilla Apache, though they rarely come in war paint. It's mainly raids on farms and livestock, though men have been scalped just crossing the street. You see, we've overrun their hunting grounds. They feel it's their right to take what they can. Luckily, this doesn't ordinarily include captives."

Abbie speared a bite of tomato but did not take it. "A worse concern are the bears that come down from the mountains to fatten before hibernation. One year a giant grizzly tried to carry off our hog. You have never heard such a squealing and bawling, but Pa got him—the bear, that is—right between the eyes."

She ran the tomato through the sauce. "The other wild things are more simply a nuisance. Coyotes and mountain lions are frightened by gunshots. If you're a good enough aim you can shoo them away before they eat something they shouldn't."

She took the bite and allowed herself only a quick glance at Frances's pale face.

Kendal banged his hands on the table. "Now tell us about the outlaw, Buck Hollister."

Abbie shrank. Lord only knew how he had heard about that. Well, it served her right. She shook her head. "If it's all the same to you, I can't think of him while eating."

Kendal threw back his head and laughed. He raised his cup. "Here's to Abbie Martin, the new breed of lady!"

Abbie hazarded one look at Monte. She could not guess whether it was pride or fury that lit his eyes. She glanced back at Frances. Perhaps it was, after all, a matter of survival.

✦✦✦✦✦✦✦

Monte rested his hand on Abbie's back as he walked her to the stable. He could feel her spine through the dress and realized what Frances no doubt had noticed at once. No hoop or corset. The new brand of lady. Kendal had hit on it.

Abbie turned so suddenly he stumbled into her. "I'm sorry, Monte."

He tucked up her chin and drank in her eyes. In the daylight, he could hardly believe their blue. "Sorry for what?"

"What I said about the Indians."

He raised an eyebrow.

"And the rest . . . though we did have a bear try to steal our hog once, only it was a runt suckling ... and the coyotes are a nuisance. You've said so yourself. It's just that ..."

"It was time you defended yourself."

"Then you're not angry? You were so quiet."

He did not dare tell her it took all his will not to laugh. Frances would never have borne it. "If you only knew the cruelty of your trick."

"What do you mean?"

"Kendal intends to stay here with Frances."

"What!"

"They are not going home. He claims they've lost everything."

"Oh, Monte, I'm so terribly sorry! I never would have ..."

He put a hand to her lips and drew her into the shade away from the stable door. "I know. Frances will have to learn her place, but ... I would consider it a favor if you didn't scare the breath from her again."

"Of course I won't. I feel dreadful. Oh, when will I ever learn to hold my tongue?"

"What you need is looking after. Someone to keep you in line. I see I'll just have to marry you." He watched his words sink in.

"Monte, do you mean ...?" She quivered in his hold.

"Friday, Abbie. I trust you have your things in order?"

"Yes. And I'll ride today—now—to tell Father Dominic."

"Father Dom ... Abbie, I've already spoken with Reverend Shields." She stared, and he raised his hands helplessly. "I had no idea you'd want the mission priest."

"But Monte, we have to be married in the church."

He suspected she did not refer to the small white building in town. It hadn't even occurred to him that Abbie's ties to the mission went so deeply. A circuit rider would have served as far as he was concerned. But Frances ... She would never forgive him pledging his vows before a Roman Catholic priest.

He groaned inside. Would nothing be easy? "Abbie ..."

"You don't understand. Father Dominic administers all the sacraments. I've been to the mission since I was small. How can I be married by anyone else?"

Monte felt helpless in the wave of her emotion. How could he not have anticipated this? Of course she would expect her priest to marry them. But Frances would never set foot in the mission church, and her behavior today had shown how desperately she needed control. He was walking an impossible line.

Though he made light of Abbie's affront, in truth he was terribly concerned for his sister. Still . . . he would give his life for Abbie. Things had conspired against them for too long now. A sudden urgent longing for her seized him. He took her shoulders, wincing with the grip. "All right, Abbie. Your Father Dominic will join us, but here in the great room. Our guests won't fit in the mission chapel."

Her relief showed in her face, and he kissed her lips, not caring that Will stood in the doorway with her horse.

Ten

Abbie stood transformed before the mirror. The pale gray silk gown pinched in around her corsetted waist, and the white lace overlay billowed to the long train. Monte's taste was exquisite. He could not have chosen a color that better enhanced her eyes and paled her skin.

Mama had pulled her hair into a thick twist behind her head with a fringe of curls around her face. Pa's string of pearls at her throat complemented the pearl and garnet earrings in her ears.

As Mama placed the veil on the crown of her head and pulled the blusher forward, an indescribable thrill passed through her. She was no longer herself. Where was the tree-climbing girl? She felt so beautiful. The thought surprised her.

Mama held her at arm's length. "My little girl . . ."

"Oh, Mama." She squeezed her. "I'm so happy!"

Abbie turned at the knock on the door. Pa stood in his Sunday suit, black-ribbon tie crisp at his throat. He gazed at her. "You're the prettiest bride I've ever seen, along with your mama and sister." His blue eyes swam.

"Pa." Abbie pressed her face to his chest, and he patted her back.

"There's someone waiting for you even more eagerly."

Abbie let go. "I'm ready."

"Here." Mama pressed a handkerchief into her palm. "Sadie sent this."

Abbie recognized her great-grandmother's handiwork. Her

sister had carried the handkerchief on her wedding day. "I wish she could have come."

"She's too near her time."

"If we hadn't delayed..."

Grant pushed in and held his arm for Mama. "At this rate she'll have the baby before you reach the priest." He kissed Abbie's cheek and tweaked her nose, then tugged Mama out to escort her to her place. Abbie held her breath.

She heard the melodeon begin and caught Pa's arm, the same arm that had held her when she took her first tottering steps, that had steadied her on the back of a horse, that had walloped her when her naughtiness deserved it... though never hard enough to feel through her skirts. She felt no shame at the tears in his eyes. He was her pa, the best pa a girl could have. And he knew how happy she was. He knew what Monte meant to her.

He led her down the stairs, through the foyer, and past the parlor to the great hall. The room was filled and some even stood outside the French doors. Abbie saw Mary and Wes McConnel with Davy and Mariah beside them. Mary's eyes were wet with tears, and she nodded her blessing. Reverend Winthrop Shields also nodded from his place in the crowd.

Clara beamed at her from the back where she sat beside Marty with Del in her arms. Face after face passed by, but then she had eyes only for Monte. Had he ever looked so splendid? In his long, cutaway coat and cummerbund, starched white collar, and gray cravat he looked every inch the aristocrat, yet the warmth in his eyes captured her breath.

How could she ever have doubted his love? It was as though the past years never happened. They were alone in this moment as it was meant to be. *Dear Lord, you knew. You made him for me. Let me be worthy.*

She hardly noticed when Pa let go of her hand. Together Monte and Abbie turned to face Father Dominic. The music stopped, but within Abbie it played on and on. She felt buoyant with joy. Monte loved her. She could hear it in his voice as he spoke his vows, feel it in his fingers as he touched the ring to her thumb, *in the name of the Father,* to her first finger, *and of the Son,* the next finger, *and of the Holy Spirit . . . amen.* He slid it home.

Light streamed through the long windows, and her heart raced when he lifted the veil. Looking into his warm, dark eyes, Abbie trembled, unable to believe they were at last man and wife. Monte bent and kissed her, then grabbed her hand and swept her past the cheering crowd. As they went, her eyes landed briefly on Cole standing in the corner, then they were in the hall and through the doors.

The phaeton was at the bottom of the stairs, and Monte lifted her in. "What are you doing? Where are we going?"

He smiled and took up the reins, wrapped the end around his wrist, and slapped the horse.

"What about everyone else?"

"They're not invited."

She saw him wince as the reins tugged, but she said nothing. This was his moment, their moment. The October sun was rich and golden, gleaming on the grass, the horse's sleek back, the ring on her finger. The single gold band was beautiful in its simplicity, and Monte's was identical, save larger for his larger hand. He had smiled when she slid it on, making no sign of pain.

He turned the horse out toward the plain. The wheels bumped and lurched, but the springs cushioned them. They climbed the rise and slowed. The horse tossed its head, and Monte swung around a low clump of scrub oak and reined in.

A harvest smell was in the air, and Abbie wished her corset would allow her to breathe it more deeply. Monte took quilts from under the seat and layered them on the ground.

Then he came back and gave her his arm. She caught up her skirts so they wouldn't drag on the ground. What was he thinking, taking her out here dressed in such finery? Before she sat, he took her arms and turned her away from him. He pointed across the land. "This, Abbie, is the future. Our land, our home. The Lucky Star."

A thrill passed through her. "Oh yes, Monte."

He seated her, and she arranged the bustle and layers of the gown. It was like a frothy pool around her.

Monte smiled. "You look the perfect southern belle."

"I'll try to act it."

His laugh was expected.

"Monte, why did you name the ranch the Lucky Star?"

He pulled off his coat and folded it on the edge of the quilt, then sat beside her. "It was Pearl, really. She always said I was born under a lucky star, and when we came out here, she looked around her and said I'd found it—my lucky star." He took her hand. "Now I believe her."

The quiet enclosed them. With one hand he cupped her face, and she rested her cheek on his palm. She hardly felt the scarring.

"It didn't seem right to know you first anywhere but here."

Abbie felt the ground beneath her, looked up into the mackerel sky, and knew that he was right. This was God's land, their land. Here they would make their life. Here she would give him all she had to give, consummate the love he had awakened.

His voice was thick. "I have never in my life known a love like this. Do you understand?"

She knew what he was saying. There was still apology in him, but there was no need for it. She wrapped her arms around his neck and kissed him as he eased her to the quilt.

♦♦♦♦♦♦♦

"I don't like it." Jip kicked the dirt at his feet and leaned on the split rail of the corral.

"You're squeamish." Emmet spat. "With Farrel married t'day an' his cowboys havin' them a good time, it's the chance we been waitin' fer."

"Maybe."

"We can get in on the herd an' take what we like, make our break from Cap'n Jake, an' clear out."

"It ain't that easy."

"Heck it ain't."

"You don't know the captain. Not like I do, or did 'fore he was a big shot rancher. He's not like other men. He don't..." Jip shook his head.

"He don't what? Bleed?" Emmet laughed at his own joke. "I ain't afeared of him. We can be across the border 'fore Cap'n Jake knows we're gone."

Jip felt the sweat trickle down his neck. Captain Jake knew things other men didn't. The grim reaper. That's what the men of Company D called him. He had the feel of death about him, and one look at him on the battlefield proved he wasn't human. Jip swore he'd seen him smile in the midst of the screams and the dying.

Spence jacked up his pants. "I think we oughta git the horses an' never mind the cattle."

Jip frowned. Spence hadn't any more sense than Emmet.

Emmet knuckled him in the head. "Yup, it's hollow. You know the stable's up right next to the house. They're guardin' them horses like they're yeller gold. We take the cattle. We'll get a good price fer them down in Mexico."

"We'd never make it that far. You know the captain'll be watchin'."

"He'll be coverin' his hide so's no one can connect him with us."

"He'll come after us."

"Let 'im come."

Jip studied the flames. For all his arguments, he'd like nothing more than to cut loose from Captain Jake. He didn't owe him anything. Leastwise not anymore. So the captain had seen him heist the haversack and watch from a fallen comrade. That didn't mean he owed him for life.

Jip tossed a stick at the fire. "A'right, listen up. We'll take a look around, an' if there's no guard on the herd, we git 'em."

"If they're short o' guards we git 'em." Emmet rubbed a purple lump on his neck. "We can take out one or two."

Jip spat, then wiped the brown spittle from his chin with the back of his hand. "Yup, we can take out one or two, an' have a posse on our tail soon's we do. Ain't no use causin' thet kinda trouble. We got lucky no one died in Spence's fire. So far we ain't killed no one. There's no cause ta start now."

"You're soft, Jip. Thet's what it is. You're jest soft."

Jip threw his coffee on the fire and tucked the cup into his pack. With the least excuse he'd show Emmet just how hard his fists and boot could be. "Git goin'."

✦✦✦✦✦✦✦

Stars wavered in the indigo sky as they drove back. Monte rested his hands in his lap. Abbie had insisted on taking the reins, and he allowed her. It wasn't likely he'd deny her anything. He felt more complete, more satisfied than he had ever before. She was meant for him, made for him. All that remained was to make her as happy as he could.

They climbed down outside the stable. "Come." He ushered her inside. Will went out to unharness the horse, and Monte led Abbie to a stall in the back, to the gray dappled mare with the black mane and tail. Her velvety muzzle tossed as they approached, her eyes widened, and she stamped nervously.

Abbie reached a hand automatically to soothe her. The mare shied, then grew curious and sniffled her hand.

Monte smiled. "What will you call her?"

Abbie turned. "She's mine, Monte?"

"She's yours."

"Oh, she's beautiful."

He watched her stroke the mare's neck and smooth the rippled mane. He had chosen well. Give Abbie a choice between this horse or jewels, he knew well what she would take. "She's of the same line as Sirocco."

"Well, since Sirocco means a hot desert wind, I'll name her Zephyr. She looks like a storm, a powerful one." Her eyes shone. "Now I can ride the wind."

Monte laughed. "Soon, perhaps, when she's gentled some. Right now she's still half wild."

"Monte, she's wonderful."

He bent and kissed her forehead. "There's nothing I won't give you, Abbie. Anything that's in my power." He held her close.

"You've given me all I want."

He led her to the house and motioned for her to open the door. "Mrs. Farrel, you may take possession of your home. You are mistress here."

Abbie turned the knob and stopped. "You've no idea how frightening that is."

"Frightening! To the one who faced Buck Hollister, who hobnobs with Comanches?"

"I'd rather face Comanches than Frances, and I don't know what it means to be mistress here."

"It means whatever you want it to. You may do any—" He spun at the gunshot that echoed, followed by another of the same caliber, then answering shots. They were far, but not far enough. His land, certainly. What now? He pushed open the door and turned back to the yard.

Abbie caught his arm. "What are you doing?"

"Go into the house." He shook her loose, ran down the stairs, and across the yard.

Abbie stepped in but held the door and waited, her heart beating her ribs. What would he do? Get his men, of course. They should have heard the shot already. Who was on the herd? Cole? Breck? Monte came out from the bunkhouse alone and ran for the stable. He had a gun belt slung over his shoulder.

No one ran with him. Were they all with the herd? A moment later Monte plunged from the stable, bareback on Sirocco with the rein wrapped on his wrist. He cropped the horse's flank. Abbie stared. She had never before seen him use a crop.

She clutched the doorjamb, then ran for the bunkhouse and pulled open the door. The smell of whiskey and sour breath and something worse assailed her. Snores and grunts. Every bed but one was full. Skeeter hung over the side, head to the floor. They were drunk. Passed out drunk.

She spun as hooves beat the yard. Monte? No. Scotch veered and dropped his rider to the dirt. She ran to where Cole lay. Blood soaked his pant leg. Scotch snorted and tossed his head. Cole tried to sit, then fell back.

Oh, dear Lord. "Be still." Abbie tore open the pant at the thigh. Blood pulsed from the hole. The bullet must have nicked an artery. She pulled up her skirt and tore the edge off her petticoat, then tied it around his thigh above the wound and tugged it tight. "Put your arm around my shoulders."

"Thought you'd never ask."

She heaved him up. Cole was not a small man, and Abbie staggered but eventually got him across the yard and up the stairs. She pushed open the door and helped him inside. Cole collapsed against the wall and sank to the entry floor.

"James! Quickly!"

James came running, half dressed. He must have heard the commotion already.

"Send Will for Doctor Barrow."

Upstairs a door opened. Abbie looked up. Maimie would be welcome, but she saw both Maimie and Frances. If Frances fainted she'd personally slap her.

Maimie tightened her robe and started down with Frances following. Her voice was calm. "What can I do?"

"I need water boiled. Tell Pearl to find clean linen for bandages. He's losing too much blood to wait for Doctor Barrow. The bullet must have caught an artery." She lifted the folds of petticoat pressed to the wound. It spattered the gray satin and white lace of her gown.

Frances muffled a cry as she rushed out the front door. The sound of her retching followed. Abbie felt little compassion for her.

James returned and hovered about until Abbie instructed him, "Get me cushions from the parlor." Did she have to tell him everything? Had everyone gone simple? She'd have to keep Cole where he was. The leg had gushed terribly while getting him inside. "Where are Kendal and Chandler?"

"They gone to town. Playin' cards, Mistuh Stevens said."

Abbie tucked the cushions under Cole's head.

He groaned. "Sure could use some whiskey..."

"Whiskey, James."

He quickly brought her the decanter, then hesitated until Abbie said, "Now see what Pearl needs."

He loped off. She had never ordered anyone about so. Well, as Monte said, she was mistress, and it seemed she'd have no time to work into it gently. She poured a glass of whiskey.

Cole gulped it down. "Guess you didn't reckon on spendin' yer weddin' night with me." His mouth twisted into a crooked grin. "Sure wouldn't mind another glass to kill the pain. Both kinds, if ya know what I mean."

"Don't, Cole."

"You sure are a purty sight with yer hair all down like that." He raised a hand and stroked it.

Frances came in, and Abbie straightened. "You may as well go to bed, Frances. I can handle this."

"So I see."

Abbie heard the stairs creak as she mounted, then the door close behind her. That was one less worry.

"She's a fine 'un, ain't she? Guess I got ya in trouble."

"No more than always."

"Gimme the bottle, Abbie. Don't be shy." He pulled the stopper and drank.

Maimie knelt beside her with a bowl of water and strips of cloth. "Pearl's making coffee."

Abbie bathed the wound, then wrapped the cloth tightly around Cole's leg and tied it off. The bandage reddened. Though she knew it could jeopardize his leg, she couldn't remove the tourniquet until Doctor Barrow could cauterize. She plunged her hand into the bowl and the water swirled red.

Cole closed his eyes. She didn't know what else to do for him. If Chandler and Kendal were back, they could carry him. "Cole, was no one out there with you?"

He spoke without looking. "The men're in bad shape after yer little party. You better git Mr. Farrel."

"He's out there already. Didn't you see him?"

Cole opened his eyes. "No."

"Maimie, will you sit with him?"

"Of course, but..."

"Which way is the herd, Cole?" She pulled the gun from its holster at his hip.

He gripped her wrist. "What're you doin'!"

"Which way, Cole?"

"Farrel will shoot me hisself if I tell you."

"He might not live to."

He locked her eyes with his. She didn't flinch.

"They're runnin' the herd down Templeton Gap. He can't stop them."

She rushed for the stable. Will had gone for the doctor. She flashed a glance at Zephyr but bridled Lady Belle and swung up bareback as Monte had. She kicked in her heels and headed for Templeton Gap.

If Monte didn't know of Cole's condition, he'd have no idea what he was up against. Her chest tightened at the thought of Monte out alone with his hands still stiff and weak. She pictured the reins wrapped around his wrist. If he could not grip the reins, how could he shoot?

She urged the horse faster and shivered. The wind penetrated her wrap, and she wished she had grabbed one of Monte's coats instead. The weather was changing. She strained to see through the darkness. She had to be getting near; she could smell the cattle. Then she heard them.

They were driving along the base of the gap. She could make out two, no three men on horseback. She galloped along the ridge. If she could get ahead ... Where was Monte?

Lady Belle reared, and Abbie seized the mane and clung with her thighs. A hand gripped her arm and dragged her down. Monte hissed, "Abbie! What are you doing here?"

"I came to help."

He caught her arms and turned her back to the horse. "You get right back on and go home."

"I can't leave you here alone. Cole ..."

" . . . ought to be shot for letting you come."

"He is shot."

"What do you mean? How. . . ?"

"In the leg, but it's bad. He made it to the house. I . . ."

A gunshot burst past them and Lady Belle shied, yanked the reins free, and ran. Abbie fell beside Monte as the bullets flew. The squat scrub oaks behind them were no protection but offered concealment. Monte pulled her to the edge of the clump. Below, the panicked cattle charged on, but Abbie could no longer see the men on horseback.

Monte spoke in her ear. "They know where we are. They'll circle around."

Abbie nodded.

"You stay here." He edged forward.

She caught the movement of one man climbing the gap on foot. Did Monte see? The moonlight glinted on the gun in his hand. Monte crouched while she pulled Cole's gun from her pocket and slowly cocked it.

The man came closer. No . . . there were two, one farther down. Where was the third? She turned and searched through the scraggy growth behind her. She saw no one. Abbie strained to hear any sound . . . a twig, a rustle of grass. She looked back to the gulch. The man crept closer.

Monte stood. "Hold it right there."

Abbie saw the flash of gunfire. Monte caught his arm and rolled as the men fired from the gap. Didn't he know this was no time for gentlemen's negotiations? A bullet scattered the earth at Monte's side. He'd never make it back to cover. She raised her gun, aimed for the flashes, and shot. The kickback jolted her arm, but she pulled back the hammer and fired again.

Her bullet hit. The man buckled and fell, screaming, as the other rushed to his side. Abbie froze. It was a horrible sound. Inhuman. The agony in the screams chilled her blood. She pressed her forearms to her ears. Stop. Stop! Time stood still.

A bullet struck a branch at her head, yet she hardly noticed. The third man leaped up from the edge of the gap and shot again.

Dimly she saw Monte rise to his knee. With both hands he held his gun and fired. The man toppled over the edge and rolled.

The last of the trio ran, firing behind him as he went. He gained his horse and veered away. The hoofbeats grew silent. All around was silent.

Monte rasped. "Don't move, do you hear me!"

She nodded, her body quaking. She watched Monte creep over to the man at the edge of the gap. He bent and felt for a pulse, then went down the slope and checked the other, whose screaming had stopped. Neither moved.

Oh, God, what had they done? She wanted to run . . . run away, run to Monte. He came back up the slope and stood over her. She could not move. She needed his strength, his touch. With the moon behind the cloud, she could not see his face.

He took the gun from her hand. "Let's go." His voice was flat, emotionless.

"Are they dead?"

"Yes." He raised her to her feet and led her over the flat and into a gully. Sirocco waited there, and Monte helped her onto the stallion's back. He mounted stiffly behind.

Abbie sank back against his chest. "Why did he scream so, Monte?"

"Where he was hit, I guess."

She closed her eyes against the hot tears. She didn't ask him where her bullet had hit the man. She did not want to know.

The windows of the house were lit up, and Doctor Barrow's horse stood in front. Monte let her down at the stairs and rode on to the stable. She waited, but after a time realized he must be caring for the horse himself. She went in alone.

Maimie and Pearl and James stood like sheep in the corner of the parlor where Cole had been moved. Doctor Barrow was at Cole's side just finishing with the bandage. Beside him the slug lay in a pan. Abbie shuddered at the smell of burned flesh and looked away from the probe cooling on the hearth. Who had held Cole down for the doctor?

Doctor Barrow spoke without turning. "You did a good job on the leg, Mrs. Farrel."

Her throat was too tight to answer.

Cole stirred and opened his eyes. "They were gone?"

She had to speak. She owed him an answer. "No," she whispered. "They were there." Her mouth felt like cotton. "Two of them are dead." She sank to the chair. Maimie hurried over and put an arm around her. Abbie scarcely noticed.

"You shoulda never gone out there." Cole tried to rise, but the doctor kept him down.

"I had to. Monte could not have stood alone."

"I could." Monte came through the door. "Get me something to drink, James. And where the devil is Chandler?"

"They haven't returned from town." Maimie held Abbie's hand. "Shall we send?"

Monte shook his head. He emptied the glass James brought him and turned. "Cole, I hold you responsible for sending Abbie out there."

"I figured that."

Abbie squirmed. "It wasn't Cole, Monte. I gave him no choice."

Doctor Barrow stood. "The leg'll mend. The bullet didn't catch much bone. But he's lucky Mrs. Farrel stanched the blood." He tucked the cooled probe into the bag and turned to Monte. "Let me see that arm."

Abbie stared at the blood on Monte's sleeve.

"It's only grazed. I'll clean it up myself."

Doctor Barrow pulled apart Monte's shirt sleeve in spite of his argument, then swabbed and wrapped the wound. "Now I guess I'd better have a look at the bodies."

Abbie's gorge rose up. Bodies. Dead shells. She thought for a moment Monte would go back out, but he said, "My man's bringing them in."

He must have roused someone before coming inside. Oh, thank God. She needed him.

Cole tried to rise again, then sank back into the cushions. "Sheez."

"You're not going anywhere for a while. You've lost too much blood." Doctor Barrow closed the bag and straightened. "I'll have a glass of that whiskey while I wait. Mr. Farrel, why don't you see your wife to bed."

Abbie leaned on Monte's arm up the stairs. His hold was firm and steady, and she felt weaker than when she had learned he was married to Sharlyn. The sound and smell of death overwhelmed her. The violence, the horror. But once inside the room, he released her.

"They'll expect me to stay here tonight. You have no objections?"

Objections? Abbie's legs felt liquid. Dear Lord, the look in his eyes. "Monte?"

He walked into the dressing room and got out of his clothes. She stood stiffly where he left her. If she moved, if she took a step . . .

He came back in, went to the bed, and lay down. She waited until he turned down the lamp before she undressed and put on her nightgown. She crept to the bed and slid into the sheets. Monte lay on his back, unmoving. She waited.

His words were low and clipped. "I don't need you to protect me, Abbie. I am not so much a cripple that I cannot defend myself."

"I didn't think you were! It's just that . . ."

"You thought you could handle things better than I."

"No . . . no, it's . . ."

"How does it feel to have killed a man?"

Her whole body shook. A wave of nausea rose bitter in her throat and clamped her stomach into a tight ball. She rolled to her side and fought wretched sobs trapped by her will. How could he? She closed her eyes against the tears. She would not cry. She would not let him know how it hurt.

The darkness seemed endless. The screams echoed on and on in her head, and she gripped the pillow to silence them. The grandfather clock in the hall chimed eleven, twelve, then one, two.

Monte lay still, but his breathing was shallow. She was sure he did not sleep. She wanted to bury her face in his chest and feel his arms gentle and strong around her, but she did not move. She kept her back rigidly toward him as weariness overcame her.

◆◆◆◆◆◆◆

Jip dropped from the horse, both of them too exhausted to go on. He balled his fists to his forehead, and buried his face in the ground. He smelled his brother's blood on his hands, on his shirt. His jaw clenched and he groaned. He slammed his fists into the dirt, shouting every vulgarity that presented itself.

Emmet deserved to die. He had started the shooting; he had wanted to kill. But not Spence. Spence was too young to know, too young to choose . . . too young to die. Gut shot! *Oh no, no.* Jip sobbed brokenly. He smeared Spence's blood across his face when he swiped the tears away. He suddenly felt hard and grim. He would pay back the death of his brother if it was the last thing he ever did. And he'd see Captain Jake in hell.

Eleven

When Abbie woke, the space beside her in bed was empty. She looked around the sumptuous room, surveying the fine furniture and the grand mirror that stood in the corner. What was she doing there? She didn't belong in this house, in this bed ... Monte's bed.

The breath left her chest, and she bent forward, holding her stomach. A murderer. She was a murderer. She closed her eyes, whispering, "Dear God, help me." Rolling out of bed, she went to the washstand and bathed. She held out her hands, hands that had killed last night, that ended a life. And Monte hated her for it. Oh, how he hated her.

She walked to the wardrobe, passed over the gowns Monte had commissioned for her, and found her cotton skirt and shirtwaist. She tied her hair back and went downstairs. She heard voices in the morning room but went on to the parlor. Cole lay awake on the settee, his leg up on the end. He looked roguish and uncomfortable.

"How are you?"

"Can't say I haven't been better. How about you?"

She looked away. "I guess the same."

"Look, Abbie, I know how ya feel, but you only did what you had to."

"How do you know what I did?"

"I saw it all over yer face when you come in last night."

Abbie sank into the chair. "I don't even know how it

happened. They shot at us, and I just fired. I just pointed the gun and fired."

"Everyone's got the right to defend himself—or herself—and yer property. You done what you had to."

She dropped her forehead to her hand. "Monte doesn't think so."

"He'll come around."

"I don't think so. I think this will stand between us."

"Don't let it. And don't let him cow you."

She nodded limply. It was easy to say. He hadn't seen the loathing in Monte's face, heard the tone of his cruel words. "Have you eaten?"

"Nope."

"I'll make you breakfast."

"You?"

"It's my kitchen. I'll use it if I like."

He chuckled. "Heaven help you."

Abbie found Pearl in the pantry. "I'll make Mr. Jasper's breakfast. He's hungry now."

Pearl puffed out her cheeks and put her hands to her hips. "Yes'um, Mizz Farrel." She waited without moving while Abbie browned the pork and fried the eggs.

Zena came in. "Aunt Pearl, I . . ." She looked from Abbie to her aunt, then backed out.

It was a mistake. Again. She had forced her way where she didn't belong. She tightened her jaw as she scooped the eggs onto a plate and laid the meat beside them, then smeared a chunk of bread with butter. She poured a cup of coffee and set it all on a tray. Without looking at Pearl, she carried it to Cole. She set the tray on the table, propped him up with cushions, then lifted it into his lap.

"Nothin' like breakfast in bed. You wanna join me? To eat, I mean."

She didn't even blush. She heard hooves and rushed to the window to see Deputy Davis rein in beside the wagon. Monte was there to greet him.

A moment later he entered the parlor. "Deputy Davis needs a statement, Abbie. Will you come outside?" He was gentle and polite, but he did not offer his arm. She followed him out.

"Mornin' Miss Mar . . . Mrs. Farrel." Deputy Davis tipped his hat. "I need a statement about last night's shootin'."

Abbie felt Monte's hand on her elbow as she slowly stepped down. "What do you need to know?"

"Can you tell me what happened? What you saw and did?"

Abbie tried to stop the sudden heaving of her chest, and she looked involuntarily to the bed of the wagon. "Three men . . . were down with the herd, running them off. They shot at us . . ."

"You and Mr. Farrel?"

"Yes."

"And why were you out there, Mrs. Farrel?"

"I . . . needed Monte. I was afraid for Cole. He'd been shot." Monte stiffened beside her. Did he expect her to say she'd gone to protect him?

"And why did you have a gun?"

"I took it from Cole to protect myself."

"Thank you, ma'am. That's all I need to know. It's pretty clear self-defense. I won't ask you to identify the men. Only thing is . . . Mr. Farrel believes one might be the man in your pa's barn the night of the fire."

Abbie turned and found Monte's eyes on her. They told her nothing, and he said no word. She swallowed the hurt. "I'll look." She walked to the end of the wagon. She knew immediately which one she had shot. His belly was caked with blood, and his face was distorted into a freakish grimace. He was young. So young.

She caught the side of the wagon as a wave of horror passed through her. His shape was familiar, and the face under the fair hair could have been the face in the barn, but she had not known he was a boy. Her knuckles whitened on the side of the wagon, and she closed her eyes. "I think it could be."

"Thank you, ma'am. That's all I need. I'm sorry about all that happenin' on yer weddin' day." He tipped his hat.

She left the wagon and walked past the house. Not for anything could she enter those walls and face Frances and Maimie, Kendal and Chandler. Most of all, she could not face Monte. She sped up, and as she rounded the stable, she lifted her skirts and ran. Mounds of pale golden grass muffled her feet as she left the house and all of them behind.

The wind carried a chill that matched the one inside her. The mountain summits were shrouded in gray. How different they looked than yesterday. Everything looked different since yesterday. Everything *was* different. She pushed on and on until she reached the top of a hill and staggered.

She dropped to her knees, and dry heaves shook her, since she had nothing inside. Not even bile. The stone angel over Sharlyn's grave waited, fingers outstretched. She had not intended to end up here but had come blindly. She dropped her face to her hands and wept.

She pictured the face of another boy—Blake's face, as she had swabbed the vinegar water over it and helped his mother prepare the body for burial. Now she had killed . . . same as Hollister. She shuddered. Even Monte blamed her. *Even Monte.*

The little stone angel smiled down at her. The tiny hands stretched out to her. If she could just grasp them and be lifted from this earth, from this loathing. "Oh, Sharlyn, if only you hadn't died. You were so good. You should be here beside Monte. You would have known not to dishonor him. That boy would be alive." But would Monte?

The wind gusted and blew pellets of corn snow. Her hair worked loose and whipped her eyes. She let it fly. "Oh, God, what am I to do?" Her voice was whisked away on the wind, and she knew God hadn't heard. There was nothing she could do.

The cold felt good. Let it numb her. Her neck stiffened with the ice that lodged in the collar of her dress. Her wet cheeks chapped, and her fingers reddened. If she were stone like the angel, she'd feel none of it. Oh, if only she were stone.

◆◆◆◆◆◆◆

Beside Monte, Chandler hollered over the wind buffeting their faces with white pellets. "How far can she have gone?"

"I don't know. With Abbie I never know."

"Perhaps she went to her parents."

"I've sent a man to check, but I don't think so. It's more likely she headed off across the land."

"Surely she knows the area and the weather."

Oh, she knew it all right. But whether she would heed it was another thing. It was his fault. He should have stopped her when she walked past. He should have known, but how could he? He didn't know her at all.

The damaged skin of his hands throbbed from the cold even through the gloves. If the wind would only stop. Where would she go? He scanned the land, shielding his eyes with his arm, then stopped. Of course.

"I have an idea where she might be." He changed course, loping over the ground, then hurried to the hill. The trees at the top waved in the wind, and Abbie huddled beneath, knees wrapped in her arms. Her hair was clotted with corn snow, her skin red and raw.

Chandler came up behind and glanced from Abbie to the angel that marked his sister's grave.

Abbie looked up. Her eyes were red rimmed, her lashes icy.

A pang of remorse stung him, and Monte pulled off his coat and wrapped it around her. "Abbie, what are you thinking? You'll catch your death." He raised her to her feet. "Come on, now."

Between them, he and Chandler shielded her from the wind. But Monte could feel the chill of her skin. What was she doing, sitting there freezing? Did she think to punish him?

Abbie felt the life returning to her fingers and toes as she was hurried into the warmth of the house. Monte led her straight upstairs to her room, then waited outside. A fire burned, and she could smell the pot of cider spiced with cinnamon. She stood near it as Zena peeled the wet clothing from her and rubbed her skin before wrapping her in the robe.

"Lawdy, Mizz Farrel. You's cold as ice."

Abbie wished she could reassure her, but she felt as frozen inside as out.

"If you gets in that bed and drinks yo' cider, you get warm."

Abbie didn't want to get into the bed. She never wanted to get in it again. She wanted her own bed. She wanted Mama and Pa. Her throat tightened. Had they heard? What would Mama think? Oh, what would they think?

Zena pulled the covers up around her. Monte tapped on the door, and Zena admitted him. "She's all dry now."

"Thank you." He waited until Zena left, then came to the bedside and took Abbie's hand between his. "Forgive me, Abbie. I should not have said what I did last night."

"You only said what you thought."

He did not gainsay her. "Nevertheless, I apologize, and I hope you will accept it."

He was formal, sincere . . . but so distant. Abbie felt the lump harden in her throat. "Of course."

He poured a cup of cider and brought it to her. "Drink this, and I'll have Pearl bring your dinner up since you missed it."

"Thank you, but I'm not hungry." Abbie held the cup in her lap.

Monte stood a moment, then nodded and left the room. As the door closed behind him, Abbie set the cup aside and sank into the covers. The tips of her fingers throbbed as the blood returned. She closed her eyes and wept before fitful sleep overcame her.

♦♦♦♦♦♦♦

The fire had burned low and the room was dim when she awoke. The first thing she saw was a tray of soup and bread. She rose to one elbow, and Monte turned from the fire. His presence startled her.

"Ah, you're awake. I trust you're warm?"

"Yes."

"You can manage the soup?"

"I can manage."

He nodded. "Then I'll check in again."

She looked away from his leaving. Duty required his attendance . . . or maybe honor. As it had with Sharlyn. What was it he
had said? Did kindness and faithfulness replace love? The
thought of soup turned her stomach. The cider had been removed. Zena could take the food, too.

She felt desolate. Nothing would bring life back to that boy, nor
to the man Monte had shot, for that matter. And nothing would
restore Monte's opinion of her. She had dishonored him. She rested
her head back on the pillow. Well, they had lived estranged before.
There was some small comfort in its familiarity.

A tap came at the door, and Maimie tucked her head in. "I
hoped you were awake. May I come in?"

"Yes."

She came and sat on the end of the bed. "Are you warm?"

"Yes, thank you."

"I'm so terribly sorry for all of this. If Chad and Kendal had
only been here. . . . Chad feels terrible."

"He needn't."

"Would it help to talk?"

"I don't know." Abbie ran her fingers over the quilted coverlet.
"I . . . I didn't know he was so young. He was only a boy."

"How could you know? Even if you had, you did what you
must."

Did she? Abbie passed a hand over her eyes. "I had a friend . . .
a very dear friend who was killed when he was seventeen. He was
killed for his gold . . . and this one for our cattle."

"No. In defense of your lives."

Abbie shook her head. "I should never have gone out there."

"Then it might be Monte buried today. He tries to hide it, but
I've seen his hands, and I doubt very much he could have fought
them all."

Abbie stared at her.

"It's his pride that blames you, not his heart."

"It doesn't matter which it is."

"Yes, it does. One's pride is more easily mended than one's
heart." Maimie took Abbie's hand between hers. "You don't know

what it was for him not to fight the war."

Abbie searched her face. "He was too young."

"At the start maybe. But later, others as young went to fight. Chad . . ."

"No."

"Yes. And Chad was there when his father pulled Monte's father from the field, bleeding from the ball that cost him his arm. The war did horrible things to our men, but at least they could say they fought for what they believed. Monte was not allowed that."

"I don't understand. Why would he want. . . ?"

"Honor, Abbie."

Abbie wanted to scream. "Who knows how many lives he saved? Surely Frances's more than once. And the girls he hid and the livestock that kept them all alive when the raiders would have left them nothing. . . . Was there no honor in that?"

"But it's not the same."

Abbie shook her head. How could killing men on the battlefield be more honorable than what Monte had done?

Maimie's voice was gentle. "His father was willing to lose his life for the confederacy but not his son's life. Monte honored his father's order, but it cost him dearly."

"How do you know this?"

"Chad. He and Monte were closer than brothers. It nearly killed Monte when Chad went to fight. It was all Chad could do to hold him to his promise. Monte went out last night to fight for his own. He was ready to lose his life if it came to it."

"Oh, Maimie, I'll never understand. I despair of being a good wife to him. I thought to protect him, but I defied him . . . and look what has come of it."

"Monte won't hold his anger forever. One day he'll face the sacrifice you made and love you all the more for it."

If only that were true. Abbie squeezed her hand. "Thank you."

Maimie stood. "If you're feeling up to it, why don't you put on something pretty and come down."

Yes, Abbie thought. There may be no way to change things,

but she would not hide any longer. She had no control over Monte's thoughts and feelings. All she could do was face this. Maimie sent Zena in, and Abbie allowed her to pull the corset tight. She slipped the bustle on and donned a blue velvet dress. Monte had wonderful taste. Zena wound her hair into a chignon, and she hung the earrings from her newly pierced earlobes. At least she would look the part.

◆◆◆◆◆◆◆

Monte stopped midsentence when he saw Abbie gliding down. He was surprised and annoyingly overwhelmed. How could she be so infuriating and so incredible at once?

"You were saying?" Frances touched his arm.

"I'm . . . I'm sorry . . ."

Abbie walked into the great room, and Kendal's jaw fell slack.

Monte met his eye, then turned to her. "Well." He kissed her hand. It was warm and soft. "Feeling better, I see."

"Yes, thank you."

"Wonderful," Chandler said. "Maimie, why don't you play?"

Maimie smiled. "Of course I will."

"Your fingers would be permanently connected if they could," Chandler proclaimed as Maimie began playing a Chopin nocturne.

Abbie turned to Chandler. "That's lovely, isn't it? It stirs my soul."

Chandler bowed. "May I?"

She took his hand. Monte stepped back as Chandler spun her past. His mouth twitched as he watched Abbie murmur something that set Chandler chuckling, then in a lower voice added whatever brought his laugh full force. It was hard to believe this was the same girl who had stood beside him last night with a smoking gun in her hand. Who was this person he had married?

Chandler released her, but before Monte stepped forward, Kendal was at her side. "May I have the honor? A waltz, Maimie."

Chandler took Frances's hand. Monte stepped back again as both couples swept by him. Kendal spun Abbie in wide graceful circles. Did she have to look so deucedly happy about it?

Her lashes drooped, and Monte's fingers tightened into his palms. The pain increased the anger. Kendal pulled her close. Monte stepped in, but Maimie stopped playing, and Kendal bowed and released her.

Frances slipped her arm into Kendal's. "I declare, Abbie, you look as natural with Kendal as you did with Monte's foreman last night."

Abbie flushed. Monte frowned. *What was this?* He turned to her, but she drew herself up.

"If you'll excuse me." She swept out of the room without even a glance his way.

She had to go. One more minute and she'd have clawed Frances. And Monte, with his eyes burning into her, yet so aloof. Abbie pushed the door open and peeked in. Cole was awake.

"Purty music. Puts me in the mind for dancin'."

"I hope this injury won't keep you from it."

"Not much point."

"Nonsense. Every girl will be heartbroken if you don't show up with dancing feet."

Cole shook his head. "You know I don't care about that."

"So you say. I think you're as flattered by the attention as the next man. And you know what else I think, Cole Jasper?"

"What?"

"I think one day you'll settle down and raise sons and . . ."

"You're wrong, Abbie. I had me one notion to settle down in all my life. It ain't gonna happen again."

The look in his eyes silenced her argument. Oh, why had she said anything?

Monte tapped on the door and stuck his head in. "Supper is served, Abbie."

She turned. "I'll have a tray brought in for you, Cole."

"I've already seen to that," Monte said.

Her gown brushed against the doorframe as she passed through. She was surprised Monte extended his elbow. She tucked her fingers into the crook and sat in the chair he held. He lingered a moment, then took his place at the head.

Abbie forced herself to eat. She would not give Frances the satisfaction of costing her appetite. And she'd eaten nothing all day. Laced up as she was, it wasn't long before she was full, though Monte's superb cuisine was lost on her. The conversation was stiff and false, but she smiled and nodded as required.

Monte stood. "I believe I'll retire directly." He bowed slightly. "Good night."

Abbie made her excuses and went up to their room. Monte was not there. She walked around it. It was larger than two bedrooms at home. Home. This was her home, but she was a stranger here.

She looked at her reflection in the long mirror. Not even Frances could fault her appearance tonight. Monte had provided a trousseau worthy of her position. She reached up and let her hair down. Even so she did not know the girl in the mirror.

Monte knocked on the door adjacent to the dressing room. "Come in."

He came to stand behind her. "I wanted to tell you how lovely you looked tonight."

"Thank you."

He reached a hand to her hair. Abbie's heart quickened.

"I didn't get a dance."

"You didn't ask."

"No, I . . . well, I'll be in the next room if you need anything. Good night, Abbie." He kissed the back of her head and left. Abbie dropped her face into her hands.

Twelve

The hand outstretched before her was delicate and long fingered, pale in the starlight, and Abbie studied its form, trying to place it. It seemed familiar as she looked up the arm to her own shoulder. *It's my hand*, she thought with surprise, and looked back at it. The stars glinted on the metal of the gun that it clutched, and with horror she watched the finger squeeze the trigger.

The smell of gunsmoke was acrid in her nostrils. Screams exploded into the night, and a figure staggered toward her. She did not want to look, did not want to see, but a face drew close, and it was the boy in the wagon, spattered with blood and beseeching her. Then it became Blake's face. Abbie cried out and jolted up in bed.

Her forehead was damp, her fists still clenched. Her chest heaved. She pressed her hands to her eyes, but the horrible images remained. "I didn't want to kill him. But I can't undo it. God, I can't undo it." Sinking back down, she buried her head in the softness of the pillow and closed her eyes. If only the rustlers hadn't come. . . .

♦♦♦♦♦♦♦

In the dim that preceded the dawn, Monte crept like a thief into Abbie's room. Her features were soft as she slept, though the bedclothes were tangled as though she had thrashed. A long moment he looked at her, then went to the window. He raised his hands and studied them, slowly squeezing and straightening the

132

fingers, then pressing hard and wincing. The truth was that if Abbie had not fired when she did, he could not have stood against those men. At one time, yes . . . but not now.

Closing his eyes, he remembered the woods that had surrounded the plantation house and the long cut beyond it where he had practiced with a gun in his father's absence. Daily he had honed his skills with bullets from melted farm implements, thinking maybe, maybe he would go yet and fight.

He did not long for bloodshed or imagine glory on the field. But honor had its price. In his sixteenth year, he could have outdrawn most men and fired accurately, as well, but he never had. No one had even known of his skill. When he came to live here where everyone wore a gun, he did also. He was prepared to defend himself and his own, but he had never needed to . . . until now.

Had God made him weak for a purpose? Had He destroyed his human strength to make him know his frailty? Monte chafed at the thought, but it would not go away. Had he taken back the control he had surrendered? But how did a man live in surrender?

He peered through the organdy curtains to the coming day. He pictured Abbie's arm, bouncing with the kickback of the shots. This was not some frail and delicate creature to be protected as Sharlyn had been. He had known how to husband Sharlyn. It had been natural to guard and govern her, and she had responded with feminine tranquillity.

Abbie did not beg his strength. She had done what he should have been able to do, though her whole being trembled afterward as he held her on the horse. His hands had been stiff and awkward in the cold. He could not have taken three. If not for Abbie, he could not have taken them.

She stirred, and he looked back over his shoulder, then left the room.

♦♦♦♦♦♦♦

Abbie washed and allowed Zena to dress her. The house was quiet when she went down except for the faint, soulful humming of Pearl in the kitchen. She would not offend her again by invading her territory. She went instead to the library and breathed in the scent. Three things drew that response: the mountain air, the sage of the prairie, and the leather of books.

Abbie closed her eyes and pictured Pa in his chair, book laid across his knees. A wave of homesickness washed over her, but she couldn't go. She couldn't face them. She opened her eyes. Monte's library was extensive, he being such an avid reader. Dickens, Shakespeare, Tennyson. She pulled down *Idylls of the King*.

Sharlyn had loved that one. Sitting demurely, hands folded in her lap, she had listened with rapt attention as Abbie read to her out in the hills. She did not sense Sharlyn here, not in this room. In other parts of the house, yes, but not here in a room of books. Sharlyn could barely read.

She took the book and went out. Cole glanced up at her entrance and halted the knife on the wood in his hand.

"Good morning, Cole. How is your leg?"

"I'm ready to be up."

"Not according to Doctor Barrow. You have to give the healing time if you want the leg restored."

"Meanwhile, the rest of me is rottin' away."

Abbie smiled. She sat on the chair beside the settee and laid the book on the table. "The doctor said one more day before you try your weight on it. You can manage one more day, surely?"

"I ain't used to bein' coddled, and it's so dim in here I feel like sleepin' all the time."

Abbie looked at the windows. "You're right." She stood, shoved the secretary to the window, and climbed up.

Cole snickered. "You're givin' me more than a glimpse of petticoat, Abbie."

"Then be a gentleman and look away." She balanced herself and lifted the rod, slipping the velvet drapes loose and letting them fall.

Pearl came in with Cole's breakfast tray and gasped. "Mizz Farrel! You get down 'fore you falls!"

"Nonsense, Pearl. I'm not going to fall, and I want these curtains off."

"Them curtains is the crowning glory of this room. You don' know what you's doin'."

Abbie climbed down off the secretary, shoved it over to the next window, then climbed up again. "The lace is perfectly sufficient. The view is the crowning glory of this room."

From the corner of her eye, she saw Pearl's jaw jut, her hands on her hips. "Mastuh Monte had them drapes sent all the way from Cha'leston. You got no cause . . ."

"Honestly, Pearl." Abbie sent the next ones to the floor.

"Them drapes was good enough for Mizz Sharlyn. She knowed what her husband—"

"If Mrs. Farrel prefers the windows without the drapes, we'll have them without the drapes, Pearl." Abbie spun and caught herself when Monte spoke. He walked over and handed her down. "You might ask for assistance the next time. James could manage that better, I think."

"That's debatable." Kendal entered with Frances on his arm. "Redecorating?"

Monte picked up the curtain and handed it to Pearl. "Abbie, Kendal and I are going to Charleston with Chandler and Maimie."

Frances wilted into the chair. "Monte . . ."

"We'll fetch Jeanette, settle affairs, and be back before you know it."

Frances sniffed into her handkerchief. "Please let me come."

He shook his head. "It's better if we go alone. You'll be fine here with Abbie."

That meant she wasn't invited, either, Abbie supposed. She was hardly surprised. He was no doubt eager to put distance between them. She swallowed the ache. "When will you go?"

"We'll be on tomorrow's stage." He turned to Cole. "I wish you were not incapacitated. Breck is a good cowboy, but he lacks your judgment."

"There's nothin' keepin' me from givin' the orders. I'm ready to be up."

"Breck and the men have recovered the herd. They're keeping the animals close for the time being. I've alerted Marshal Haggerty to my absence, and the men can take shifts watching the house."

"We'll keep things in hand."

"Yes. Well." Monte bowed slightly to Abbie. "I've things to put in order now. Kendal."

Kendal followed him out. Abbie glanced at Frances, who looked smugly satisfied even in her misery. Abbie turned and went out. Frances could entertain Cole.

Abbie found Maimie in her room. "I'm sorry you're leaving so soon."

"Oh, come sit, Abbie." Maimie tucked the gloves into the trunk.

"I don't know what I'll do without you. Frances . . ."

"Don't mind about Frances. This has been a terrible shock to her, poor dear. I only hope Monte can salvage something of it all."

"Is it as bad as that?"

Maimie closed the trunk. "Kendal's not to blame. It's all too easy to come to ruin with the Yankee scoundrels preying on decent people. There's no honor, Abbie. And our men don't know how to fight that . . . or even recognize it."

"I wish I understood."

"You do. Honesty, integrity, ingenuity. The honor of the West . . . and you possess them all. Ours is complicated by a chivalry that no longer exists except in men like Monte, Chad, and Kendal. Be patient with Frances."

"Of course I will. But I despair of ever meeting her approval."

Maimie sighed. "You can't blame her. Monte was everything to her, especially through the bad times. In her eyes no one is entirely suitable for him."

"I'm entirely unsuitable."

Maimie pressed her hand. "You're exactly what Monte needs. And Frances, as well, if she only knew it."

Abbie left her to pack. The house was more peaceful with Frances spending the day in bed. At least she could go about without fear of condemnation. Why couldn't she let it go? What did it matter if Frances disapproved?

It mattered because Monte loved Frances. It was another way she had failed him.

"Abbie."

She jumped.

"I'm sorry I startled you." Monte touched her shoulder.

Oh, if only he would hold me.

"I have a favor to ask."

Anything. Doesn't he know?

"Look after Frances. She's not strong, not emotionally. In truth, I'm afraid for her."

"Of course I will. I . . ."

"And another thing. I want you both to stay close to the house. I don't expect trouble, but I've given Pearl and James leave to make any purchases, and the men can see to anything else you need. I've arranged for Breck to keep a man in the house at all times."

Abbie's throat tightened. She wanted to keep him, beg him as Frances had. *Please don't go. Please don't leave with so much unspoken between us.* She nodded.

He bent and kissed her forehead. "James will see us to the stage in the morning."

So she would not even have a good-bye. She refused to cling to him and kept her arms at her sides. "Don't worry about us. We'll be fine."

He almost smiled. "I know you will."

✦✦✦✦✦✦✦

Monte bumped shoulders with Kendal in the stage. He glanced at Chandler and Maimie sitting across from him. They were a glum company, silent and brooding. That was his fault as much as any.

He was more concerned about leaving than he had let on. If not for Frances, he would have left Kendal to settle matters himself, but Monte was determined to salvage what he could for her sake, and time was of the essence. Cole knew what they were up against. He would keep the men lively, and Marshal Haggerty had his eye out for the rustler who got away.

Truth be told, Monte hoped distance would ease his wrath and confusion. He did not want to hurt Abbie, but his chagrin left him no peace. He felt impotent.

Maimie sighed. "I envy you all. I've fallen in love with your West."

Kendal frowned. "I wish Frances felt that way. She thinks I've sentenced her to death."

"She'll recover." Monte watched the endless prairie out the window. Would she? Would any of them?

"I don't know what you said that convinced her to stay. But I am grateful."

Monte nodded. He did not tell Kendal that Frances had clung to him and wept, bemoaned Kendal's failings, and begged to be released from her duty. He had refused, of course. She would see in the end that it was best.

"I so enjoyed Abbie," Maimie said. "She's a wonderful girl, Monte. I know you'll be happy together."

He smiled with his lips. Yes, she was wonderful—wonderful, incredible, and dangerous. She threatened everything he knew, his understanding of the feminine nature, his own manhood, his code of honor as a gentleman. Maybe he was not so removed from the old ways as he had thought.

◆◆◆◆◆◆◆

Abbie wished it was Zephyr she galloped over the field, but it was disobedience enough to be sneaking away. She pulled up and slid to the ground, wound the reins, and ran inside. "Mama?"

The house was empty. Abbie found her in the garden and threw her arms around her, hoe and all. Mama squeezed back. "I was hoping you'd come."

"I would have come sooner, but . . ."

Mama held her at arm's length. "I know about your trouble. It's a terrible business."

She didn't know the half of it. "I don't want to talk about that." She looked at the ground. The garden was nearly finished, the last of the pumpkin vines shriveled and bare, only the potatoes and carrots left in the earth. "Where's Grant?"

"Out riding with Judge Wilson's daughter."

"Marcy Wilson?"

"Yes."

"Oh, Mama."

"He's met with the judge and received a very favorable welcome."

"I just bet." Abbie kicked a wrinkled pod onto the pile of vines Mama had hoed. "I hope he isn't duped by Marcy's pretty face. She hasn't the spirit to match."

"Shame, Abbie."

Abbie turned as the horses cantered to the edge of the garden.

"Abbie!" Grant leaped down and helped Marcy dismount her sidesaddle. "This is a surprise."

She smelled the wind and sweat on him as he kissed her cheek. If Marcy weren't looking so smug, she'd squeeze the breath from him. "Monte's gone to Charleston with Kendal to settle affairs. Oh, Grant, can you believe it—Kendal and Frances are staying."

He pinched her chin. "You know Miss Wilson, of course."

"Hello, Marcy."

Marcy tipped her head adorned in a sweet little riding bonnet. "Abbie."

Grant gathered the reins. "I'll stable the horses. Abbie, show Miss Wilson into the house."

For Grant she would do it.

Marcy lifted her skirts so as not to touch them to the dust and walked beside her. "Your wedding was lovely. I thought maybe it would be a hushed little affair, being Mr. Farrel's second and all. But then, second choice isn't always second rate, is it?"

Abbie didn't dignify her with a response.

"I suppose it was inevitable, the way you pandered to him."

Abbie clenched her skirt. "If Monte fell for pandering, he would have chosen the leech that attached every time he came near. I'm not surprised to find you a poor loser, however. I surely hope you haven't any fantasies about my brother."

Marcy paled. "I was never in the least interested in Montgomery Farrel. And I'm—"

"Oh, stow it, Marcy." Abbie pushed open the door. "But I warn you, Grant is no pushover." She set out milk and molasses cookies.

The minute Grant joined them, Abbie escaped. *Merciful God, open his eyes!* She stalked across the yard, then suddenly stopped short. Is that how Frances felt about her? It turned Abbie's stomach to think of Marcy for a sister. How wretched did she make Frances?

She tried to imagine things from Frances's side and winced. But what could she do? She dropped to her knees beside Mama and worked a potato out of the mound. She brushed it off and dropped it into the bushel. Mama's nails were brown and broken, the knuckles red. Abbie wanted to grasp her hand and kiss it, to tell her how much she missed working beside her, missed the simple, honest labor.

"There's nothing to stop you having your own garden."

Abbie laughed. "Heaven help me if I think something really awful next to you."

Mama laughed with her, then put an arm around her shoulders.

Abbie rested her head. "Pearl has the vegetable garden . . . and the kitchen. I'm not allowed."

"Have an ornamental garden."

"I could." She held Mama's hand between hers. It was warm and dry, the creases more distinct. She stroked the fingers.

"How bad are things?"

Abbie sighed. "What have you heard?"

"Everything from you and Monte fighting off an army of rustlers, to you single-handedly saving the ranch."

"It wasn't like that."

"It doesn't matter. People are more interested in might-have-beens."

"I offended Monte . . . grievously."

Mama nodded slowly. "Well, it's been a difficult time."

"If you only knew. I'll never please Frances, Pearl treats me like a guest or a nuisance. At least when Monte . . . oh, Mama, will he ever forgive me?"

Mama stroked her hair. "So much is bound up in the heart of a man. He loves you, I know that."

"I don't know anymore. I just don't know." She was ashamed of her tears and wiped them away.

"When things seem overwhelming, it's best to take on one problem at a time."

"I wouldn't know where to start."

"Start with Frances."

"Frances? How?"

"Ask her to teach you what she knows, to train you as she was trained."

"Oh, Mama . . ."

"Now listen, Abbie." Mama raised Abbie's chin as she had when she was a child. "As much as you need to learn, she needs a purpose. Think how it would be, uprooted and wondering if all that you know means anything. Sometimes it's easier to be bitter than afraid."

Abbie didn't want to hear it, to think of debasing herself to Monte's sister now that she had just gained the upper hand. "I don't know, Mama. It won't be easy to be alone with her as it is."

"When have the best lessons ever been easy?"

Mama was right, but Abbie was not at all certain she could do it. She rode back to the ranch more discouraged than before. Grant keeping company with Marcy. Mama's directive. Monte gone. It seemed the hole inside would swallow her up. She pushed open the door.

Pearl descended the stairs with a tray. "Mizz Frances won' eat. I done tempted, begged, and hollered till I got no breath left. But she won' eat."

Abbie untied her hat and hung it on the rack. "She'll eat when she gets hungry, Pearl. I'll take my supper in the parlor with Cole."

Muttering, Pearl carried the tray away. Abbie brushed the dust from her dress and went to the parlor. Cole sat in a pile of shavings with his leg up and a herd of miniature animals on the table.

She clapped her hands together. "Cole, they're wonderful!" She dropped down and examined the tiny horse.

"Just keepin' sane. I ain't stayin' on this couch one more day, even if the doc says that artery's gonna burst."

"Don't be crabby, Cole. Did you like the book?"

"What book?"

"The one I brought you. *Idylls of the King*."

He shook his head. "It don't do me no good. I cain't read."

Abbie stared at him. "Not at all?"

"Never had no schoolin'. Not that kind."

She sat down in the wing chair. "Would you like to hear it? It's wonderful—heroes and all."

He set down the knife. "A'right."

Abbie opened the book. " '*Idylls of the King*, by Alfred Lord Tennyson. These to his memory—since he held them dear, perchance as finding there unconsciously some image of himself...' "

"That's poetry."

Abbie smiled.

"Sheez." Cole sank down on the couch and adjusted his leg.

She continued to read and, through her lashes, watched his expressions—sometimes scoffing, sometimes puzzling. " 'Leodogran, the king of Cameliard, had one fair child, and none other child; and she was fairest of all flesh on earth, Guinevere, and in her his one delight...' " She glanced up and bit her lip at the faraway look in his eyes.

Pearl came in with pursed lips, set down the supper tray, and went back out.

Cole chuckled. "You're ridin' herd on a sour bunch, ain't you?"

"I can't seem to please anyone."

"Just keep doin' things yer way. They'll give in sooner or later."

She closed the book and set it on the table. "I'm a stranger in my own home."

Cole looked to the window. "I ain't the one to be hearin' that, Abbie."

"I'm sorry."

He picked up his fork. "Sure do eat good in here. Old Charlie could take some lessons from that huffy cook o' yers."

Abbie smiled. "Sometimes I wish I could take Old Charlie's place, hear the sizzle of a skillet, feel the steam in my face. I wonder what Sharlyn did with herself."

"That's one thing I couldn't figure."

"What?"

"How you and the late Mrs. Farrel got so tight."

"Sharlyn was special."

"I s'pose. Not my type, though. Kinda like them china dolls in the store. You don't wanna touch 'em. Same for that sister. She cleans up real nice, but you wonder if there's blood in her veins."

Abbie giggled.

"The one ta keep yer eye on is that Mr. Stevens."

"Kendal? Why?"

"Cain't say exactly. Somethin' in the eyes."

"Oh, Cole."

"You mark my words. I been around enough ta know. And if you was my wife, I'd keep you clear of him."

A rustle behind her brought Abbie around. Her heart sank. Frances certainly picked her times. "Come in, Frances. I hope you're feeling better?"

"I wondered if we could go into town tomorrow. I want to purchase some things for Jeanette."

"As long as we take an escort, I don't think Monte would mind."

"Good. Well, don't let me detain you." Frances's skirt swirled behind as she left.

Abbie released her breath. She caught Cole's glance.

"I shouldn't've said any of that. Look, Abbie, I gotta git outta here. It's addlin' my wits sittin' around all day. Run down the bunkhouse and get Breck to gimme me a hand, will you?"

"Tonight?"

"The sooner, the better."

Thirteen

Abbie sat up in bed, chest heaving, cheeks wet. Would she never be free of it? The face, the groping hands . . . the screams. If only Monte were there. No. Even if he were, she would be alone. There was only One who was with her always, who knew her innermost thoughts. But she couldn't hear Him anymore.

She slipped out from under the covers. The floor was cold, and she quickly dressed without a corset or bustle. Zena was sleeping, and Abbie wouldn't wake her. She pulled the smart woolen coat over her skirt and shirtwaist, then crept down the stairs.

Matt Weston slept in the alcove off the entry. She crept past him, slowly cracked the door open, and stepped outside into the dark morning. She made her way to the stable. Lady Belle nickered softly, but no sound came from Will's room.

She saddled the mare and led her outside. Enough light shone to guide her way, and its intensity grew with the coming dawn. She crossed the flat grassland with nothing to block the fiery sliver of sun that crested the horizon. She raised an elbow against it but kept on.

The small group of buildings and trees rose up like an oasis before her. She stopped in the mission yard, left Lady Belle at the trough, and slipped like a shadow into the chapel. The brothers had finished the morning Mass, and the chapel was empty. She crept forward and dropped to her knees before the altar.

Candles flickered, sending dancing shadows into the alcove above. She raised her eyes to the wooden crucifix, fixed them on the gaping wound in the side of the Christ. Her mind flashed to

144

the blood-caked torso of the boy. She had put the hole there even as her sin had opened the side of Jesus.

"Oh, God. Sweet Jesus, help me." Her hands trembled. "What was I to do?" She dropped her face and sobbed. Her knees hurt from the stone floor, but she remained, unmoving, draped over the rail. The silence settled upon her.

At the hand laid gently on her head, Abbie looked up to Father Dominic.

"You are in torment, little sister."

"I can never undo what I've done."

"None can." He looked up to the cross above them. "But there is where your sin is hung. There upon the body of our Lord."

"But I've taken a life. The life of a boy not yet a man."

"I have heard."

"I thought it was right to go out there and stand by my husband. I thought . . ." She shook her head, tears starting again in her eyes.

"We can only seek God's way and trust Him to make right our failures."

Abbie's head spun. How could even God make it right?

"Do you seek absolution for your sin?"

She nodded. She spoke the words of contrition and signed herself with the cross. Father Dominic raised his hand in benediction. "*Indulgéntiam, absolutiónem, et remissiónem . . .*"

Abbie felt Father Dominic's presence, but it was the touch of God she needed. As the priest spoke, she opened her heart and welcomed the sweet presence, more real than living flesh. God's peace and forgiveness washed over her.

"*. . . et miséricors Dominus. Amen.*" Father Dominic signed the cross over her, then folded his long hands. "Look to the living and go in peace."

The sun was white in the clear, frigid sky, but Abbie's back was to it as she rode home. She felt charged with new purpose, fresh and vibrantly alive. God was no longer silent but walked with her . . . amazing as that was.

Will came out of the stable. "I thought I'd catch it good. Next time you swipe a horse, wake me."

Abbie almost laughed, it felt so good to be treated like a real person. "I'm sorry. I'll unsaddle her."

"No need." He led the mare inside and loosened the cinch. He looked like a scarecrow in his outgrown clothes. He must have shot up three inches this last year. Who looked out for him?

Abbie followed him in. "How old are you, Will?"

"Thirteen. Fourteen in January."

"Why aren't you in school?"

"Got a job to do." He hoisted the saddle onto the rail.

Abbie rested her elbows on the top of the stall. "How long have you worked for my husband?"

"Since I was seven. I started muckin' stalls under his groom in South Carolina. He died, so I lucked into the job." He took out the bit and removed the bridle.

"But have you never been to school, then?"

"Sure I have. I went a whole year once. I like this better."

"Can you read and write, do numbers?"

"Don't need to." He rested one hand on the horse's back and looked at her.

Abbie wasn't sure she had ever seen his face straight on. But now he held her gaze defiantly.

"My pa was shot in a brawl, and my ma sells herself for money. When Mr. Farrel gave me a room in the stable, it was the nicest place I ever lived. I don't need more than that."

His young face was fierce, daring her to jeer or maybe to show pity. She did neither. "Would you like to learn?"

He stared at her. "I got a job that needs doing."

"I just thought . . ." Abbie rubbed the rail. "Maybe I could teach you. I worked with the children at the mission a long time, and I'm a good teacher."

He took the cloth and rubbed the horse down. "I'll think about it."

She watched him still. He was large for his age, with the kind of looks the eye passed over without a second thought. Nothing to set him apart, and yet . . . she couldn't walk away. "That boy was not much older than you." Her voice was hoarse.

Will glanced up, tossing the straight, mousy hair back from his eyes. "He deserved what he got, if that's what's on your mind. Just like my pa . . . he deserved what he got."

✦✦✦✦✦✦✦

In the Charleston assessor's office, Monte frowned. It was worse than he had imagined, and he glanced at Kendal, who sat crumpled in the chair. He wanted to kick him and say, "Sit up and act like a man!" But Kendal's head was again aching from last night's excess, and Monte wondered if the assessor's words were penetrating his fog. Monte heard, though. They would be lucky to return with the clothes on their backs.

When he stepped outside the door, Kendal at last looked up and stared around him. "One minute you have everything, the next it's all gone."

"You should never have gambled like that on a venture so shady and unpredictable. At the very least you should not have risked Frances's holdings, as well."

"I know." Kendal dropped his head. "That's the worst of it, really."

They walked down the cobbled street and turned onto a crushed oyster shell path.

"I don't mind starting over. It's what it will do to Frances that I fear. She despises me for this."

"It was your responsibility to see to her interests."

Kendal glowered. "I don't need you to tell me that," he snapped, then sagged again. "I can't see her living in a cabin on borrowed land. Maybe if she had Abbie's spirit . . ." Shaking his head, he suddenly swore. "If I ever get my hands on those two . . ."

"I doubt you'll ever see them again. And right now our concern is salvaging what we can from the house before it forecloses."

"Monte." Kendal straightened and stopped. "I will make it back. I will keep Frances in the style she desires."

Monte faced him. "How, Kendal? How can you possibly hope to regain what you've lost?"

"I'm moving to the land of opportunity, remember?"

"That requires work. Real work. The kind of work I think you've never done."

"Nor you, and look where you are."

"You're starting from nothing."

Kendal swallowed and grabbed Monte's shoulder. "If you give me something to work with, Monte—something to get me on my feet—I'll multiply it and pay you back in no time."

Monte walked on. "That would require a substantial investment."

"Yes, but I would make it worth your while, pay you interest on the loan..."

Monte clenched his fists. The pain countered his temper. "You sound like a snake oil salesman, Kendal. I do not require interest from my brother-in-law. Nor will I hesitate to help in any manner that I can. But I must know that you will not again risk what you have so recklessly. It won't come quickly if you hope to gain your feet for good."

"Of course. But with ingenuity and—"

"Common sense and restraint..."

Kendal chuckled. "I'm not a schoolboy."

"I thought different last night."

"I was fortifying myself for today. Now that it's past me, I'll no longer depend on the bottle, no matter how sweetly it beckons."

"I certainly hope you mean that."

Kendal squared his shoulders. "Now, to retrieve my daughter. Mother will be heartbroken, of course, to learn of my intentions. I'll not tell her of the necessity, if you don't mind. It would only cause her to lose sleep."

◆◆◆◆◆◆

The mid-November wind smelled of snow, and Abbie looked up at the lowering sky. What was the weather like in Charleston, and what was Monte doing? She ached for him to come home, then quailed at the thought. Would he still be courteous and distant? That was worse than his anger by far.

She pressed the mare with her thighs, then gripped the horn and leaped the fence. She slowly approached the herd. John Mason turned on his mount, straightened up, and pulled off his hat. "Mrs. Farrel."

Abbie smiled. The cowboys were kind in their respect. *Some of them anyway.* Behind him, Cole rode up and tipped his hat back. His injured leg hung slack, but he managed the horse with no difficulty and pulled up next to her. "What's up?"

"I'm not sure about this, Cole, but last night I thought I saw someone sneak around the back of the stable. I started to follow..."

"You what! Doggone it, Abbie..."

She brought her chin up. "I beg your pardon?"

"Don't play mistress of the manor with me. I'll tan yer backside if you try that again, and Mr. Farrel will thank me for it."

John hid his snicker with a cough.

Abbie fumed. "Do you want to hear what I have to say or not?"

"A'right, tell me."

"I went as far as the corner of the stable, and I swear there was someone disappearing through the corral. I *didn't* follow. But I think someone should stay with Will tonight. I don't like him to be alone."

"Yes, ma'am. But we look after young Will just fine."

"Nevertheless..."

"I'll see to it."

"Thank you, Cole." Abbie turned back for home. He was ornerier than a mule with a toothache. And not only Cole. All the men were on edge, and she was certain they were keeping things from her. What was going on? If the rustlers were gone ... but then whom had she seen? She reined in at the stable and dismounted.

Will took the reins from her and hesitated. "Mrs. Farrel ... I've been thinkin' on what you said the other day. Do you think I could learn a little and still keep up in the stables?"

"I'm sure you could. If you'd keep my secret, I'd love to curry the horses myself. We could make it a trade."

He grinned. "You're sure a lot different than I thought you'd be."

She laughed. "You're not the first to think that. Shall we start today?"

"Yeah."

"Put an *s* on the end."

"Yes . . . ma'am."

She went to the house and found her primer, tucked it under her arm, and returned to the stable. "Let's sit outside in the light."

Will sat down beside her, back to the wall. "I know my letters some."

"Good. Show me what you know, and we'll go from there."

Nearly an hour later Abbie sank back against the stable wall, laughing so hard that tears came to her eyes. "I'm sorry, Will. But you see why it's important to pronounce things correctly if you want it to mean what you thought."

Will shrugged, still grinning. "I wish you'd been my teacher from the start. Maybe I'd've stayed in school."

Abbie smiled. "Thank you, Will."

He glanced up. "Guess I'd better get back to work."

"I'll help."

"There's no need."

"I miss caring for the animals. How will I get to know Zephyr if I never touch her?"

"Suit yourself, then."

Fourteen

Snow blew through a knothole in the stable wall, and Cole turned and stuffed a rag into the gap, then settled back down in the hay and pulled the blanket close. Will's breathing from the room at the back was heavy. Cole rubbed his thigh. The wound was aching from the cold. The small stove that warmed the boy did little out here.

Grunting, he tucked his arms under his head. The soft grating of the door latch brought him up suddenly, and he peered through the darkness. The door cracked, and Cole slid his pistol from its holster. Snow swirled in as the door widened. "Hold it right there."

The figure bolted back out into the night, slamming the door against the wall. Swearing, Cole staggered to his feet and lumbered across the distance. Empty, swirling darkness filled the yard. Sliding the gun home, he limped back in and smacked his palm on the post. "Doggone it!" The horse tossed its head.

Will called out. "Cole?"

"Go back to sleep. Excitement's over." He frowned, then rolled and lit a cigarette. He should have been on his feet. What kind of fool sets an ambush lying down? Well, he'd be ready next time. He blew the smoke and wished he had a whiskey to go with it.

When the sun shone pale into the stable, Cole stood. He brushed the hay from his clothes, strode out to the yard, and washed at the pump. His breath came white as the thin covering on the ground. He shook the water from his hair, then mounted the steps to the house. James admitted him to the library.

Abbie sat penning a letter. She looked fresh and cheerful like he hadn't seen for a while. Not since her wedding, since before the shooting. Maybe she was getting over that business at last.

She looked up. "Cole, you look positively frozen. James, bring coffee, please." She motioned him to stand by the fire.

"You were right, Abbie. There was someone out there last night." He hated to see her smile fade.

"Who do you think?"

"I dunno. He scampered away 'fore I was even on my feet."

She stood and walked to the window. Her voice was small. "Could it be the rustler that got away?"

Had she read his thoughts? Or maybe they just thought alike. "Could be anyone. If he's back tonight, we'll know."

She turned back to him. "Please don't do it alone, Cole."

"I ain't stupid, and I know my limits. Till this leg heals I ain't exactly lightnin' on my feet." He took the coffee James brought and drank. The heat felt good in his belly.

She folded her hands. "I'm taking Frances for tea at Clara's today. Would you escort us to town? Frances is ... concerned about traveling alone."

"Don't she know yet how you can shoot?"

"That's probably what she's worried about—whether her reputation can stand being seen alone with me."

"She don't know what an honor it is."

Abbie smiled. "Thank you, Cole. You always did pay a pretty compliment."

He smacked his hat. "Not that it did me no good. Anyhow, don't you worry none. We'll get this feller and make things safe again."

"Monte is lucky to have you."

"Not near so lucky as to have you." Cole's mouth twisted wryly. "I'm awful useful, but you're a good sight purtier. And don't bother blushin' cuz you know it, too. What time're you needin' my service?"

She raised her chin. "Maybe I'll take Breck. You're too ornery."

"Comes from bein' up most of the night. Now if you'll tell me what time you want to go, I can git some sleep first."

"One o'clock."

Cole replaced his hat and left. *Dang, she is purty with her hackles up.*

✦✦✦✦✦✦✦

Frances was elegance itself as she descended the stairs in tiered layers of white crepe, and Abbie stared. "Frances, that's the prettiest dress I've ever seen!"

"It's just an afternoon gown. But it is rather nice."

"You look just like the miniature of your mother."

Frances stopped. "Do you think so?"

"I do. I've always thought Monte favored her, but you . . . you could be the woman in the picture."

Frances swept past her into the parlor and looked at the portrait in its silver frame. Her voice was soft. "I was so young when she died I don't remember her at all. But I wanted to grow up just like her. Everyone spoke of her beauty and charm . . . usually when I had been less than charming." She cast a slight smile Abbie's way. "I don't believe you would flatter me falsely."

"I wouldn't."

"Then you've paid me the highest compliment."

"I only say what's true."

"That's why Monte loves you." Frances turned away. "He never could stand anything less than the absolute truth." She lifted down the portrait. "Do you know why he married Sharlyn?"

"No."

"I only learned it myself after she died, when Monte came to stay."

Abbie did not press her to tell. She felt a faint disquiet at having Monte's secret opened.

"Her father asked it of him on his deathbed."

"Why?"

"She was entangled in a romance with a man who meant to ruin her family. Monte had given his pledge to marry her when Father went to war, but he never expected it to be called on."

Abbie felt weak. So that was it. What a terrible thing for Monte—torn between a need thrust upon him and the need of his own heart. She pictured Sharlyn, so outwardly frail, yet noble and brave. Would she have been that way had the destructive romance ensnared her?

How like Monte to accept the duty no matter the personal cost. And he had done his best by Sharlyn, though Abbie had resented him for it. How badly she had treated him, how cruelly she had misjudged him. *A matter of honor.* He had tried to make her understand without revealing anything that would dishonor Sharlyn. Her chest tightened.

Frances's eyes glittered. "He kept his pledge . . . but he loved you, didn't he?"

Abbie forced her voice to stay calm. "He was very good to Sharlyn. She was happy."

Frances raised an eyebrow. "I never questioned that. I know my brother. But how that must have tortured him." She replaced the portrait. "My husband . . . has no such scruples."

"Oh, surely . . ."

"You're very naïve. At first I thought you were intentionally enticing him . . . and Monte's foreman, as well. Now I think you don't realize what you do."

Abbie was stunned.

"Well, we should go, shouldn't we? Fetch the foreman."

She wished she'd asked anyone but Cole. How could Frances think . . . and just when she hoped that Frances was opening up to her. How had it twisted again?

Abbie went to the bunkhouse and knocked on the door, but no one answered. She went in. Cole slept, stretched out on his bunk. But for his breathing, the room was silent. She almost turned back, but instead she reached out and touched his shoulder. He sprang up and gripped her wrist. She cried out.

"Shoot, Abbie. Never touch me like that. Feels like someone goin' for my throat."

Abbie's heart pounded. "You scared the wits out of me. I swear you're faster than a rattlesnake."

"Sheez. Next time just kick me." He stood. "Tea time, eh?"

"If you don't mind."

"You're the boss, ain't ya? Leastwise the boss's wife." He snatched up his hat. "You know what I cain't figure? What in God's name I'm still doin' here."

Abbie stiffened.

"I mean it's pure torture every time you sweep by, yer skirts swirlin' just so, and you smellin' so sweet."

"Cole . . ."

"But hang it all, I cain't make m'self leave. Maybe I ain't sure Farrel can take care of you. Maybe I'm just plain stupid."

Abbie spun, but Cole caught her back.

"I'm sorry." He spoke hoarsely. "I always wake up meaner'n a bear in spring. Doggone . . . Abbie, don't cry. I feel so low."

"I didn't mean for . . ."

" 'Course you didn't. It's my own durn fault. Just ferget I said any of that."

Abbie blinked back the tears. "Cole, I . . ."

"Don't say nothin', Abbie. Get yer sweet sister-in-law, and we'll go."

Abbie hurried out. Oh, how could things be worse? Was Frances right? Was it something she did without even knowing?

Frances stood at the door wrapped in her fur-lined cape.

Abbie couldn't look at her. "Cole is bringing the buggy."

He came out of the stable in his sheepskin coat and Stetson. Abbie was sure his bow-legged swagger was exaggerated.

"He is handsome. Did he really propose marriage to you?"

"Yes."

"Does Monte know?"

"Of course."

Cole stopped the buggy and handed them in. He gave Abbie the reins. "I'll ride alongside."

Frances stared at the wet, brown countryside left behind by the melted snow. "I can't believe Maimie liked this dreary place. The sight alone could cause consumption."

"Consumption is healed by this climate. And it's the most beautiful place in the world."

"How would you know?"

Abbie smiled. "Maybe I wouldn't. But no place else matters. This is my home and Monte's. I'll make him happy here."

Frances turned away. "Then I suggest you stay away from Kendal."

Abbie sucked in her breath. "You're wrong, Frances. Kendal loves you. He . . ." She fell silent. What did she know?

Cole pulled his horse even. "Looks like we might get some weather. Don't you ladies dawdle over tea."

Abbie glanced toward the mountains. Already the clouds poured over the summits. "Fetch us from Clara's at three, will you?"

"Yup." Cole circled his horse around the buggy, then rode on up ahead.

"He's devoted, isn't he?"

Abbie refused to answer.

Frances snickered. "At least I won't die of ennui. There's certainly enough intrigue."

Abbie clenched the reins. "There's no intrigue, Frances."

"I don't doubt your fidelity. You're quite simple in devotion to my brother."

"Then leave it alone."

Frances waved her hand. "Fine. You're the lady of the house. I'm simply the poor relation."

Abbie forced her voice to steady. "You are my sister. Nothing more and nothing less, though . . . I hope in time you will also be my friend."

Frances said nothing, and Abbie hid her disappointment. She could have laughed aloud when Clara pulled the door open. Hers was the face of a friend, a true friend who didn't judge or demean her. Abbie wished terribly she had come alone.

Clara bustled them in. "When I saw the clouds I was afraid you wouldn't come. And I have the most delicious scandal to share."

"What are you talking about?"

Clara took their wraps. "Come and sit. Oh, Frances, your dress is marvelous. Tea or coffee?"

"Tea." Frances draped her skirts perfectly about her on the settee, and Clara joined her.

Abbie sat across from them. "So tell."

"You recall the new schoolmarm, Miss Plochman? And how her contract states that no male callers are allowed for the duration of this term and any terms thereafter?"

"Clara, don't tell me she received a caller and it's now considered a scandal."

Clara poured the hot tea into their cups. "Well, you decide for yourself. It would seem Miss Plochman had no intention of rebuffing any male overtures that came her way. Secretly, she's entertained at least seven men in the three months she's been here." Clara handed Frances the sugar bowl.

Abbie shrugged. "I imagine she was beset. Any halfway acceptable female is hard put to ward off the overtures, and she's quite attractive."

"Well, that's not all. This morning when the children showed up for class, there was no Miss Plochman."

"What do you mean?"

"The word is Mitchell Pike crept up to her room at the boarding house and carried her off."

"No."

"They've gone to get married." Clara giggled.

"That's dreadful," Frances said.

"So now the town has no schoolteacher, and it's too late to try the other applicants." Clara looked pointedly at Abbie.

Abbie sipped her tea. Well. She'd even started with Will, and she dreadfully missed working with the children at the mission.

Clara spread her hands. "Someone has to teach the children until they can find a replacement. We can't let them fall behind."

Frances turned to Abbie. "You're not considering..."

"Why not? Clara and Melissa have little babies at home. Neither Mary Beth Walker nor Becky Linde are qualified, and Marcy

157

Wilson would never accept the responsibility. . . ."

"Nor can you! Monte wouldn't hear of it."

"Why on earth not?"

Frances's lips tightened. "You are his wife."

"Under the circumstances, I can't see that he would mind."

"It's not proper for you to take employment."

"It wouldn't be employment. I'd volunteer my services. It's my civic duty." Abbie set her cup and saucer down. "Do you think I'd find Mr. Lowe at the store?"

"I've no doubt." Clara smiled.

Abbie wrapped herself in her cape. "I won't be long." She ignored the protests of her sister-in-law and stepped out into the wind. Here was an opportunity handed her, a God-given chance to serve, and she would not miss it because Frances was too prissy to consider both sides.

Oh, she'd have plenty to say on it, Abbie was sure, but it didn't matter. She'd made up her mind. She hurried to the saddlery. "Good afternoon, Mr. Lowe." The wind banged the door shut behind her.

He rubbed his hands on his vest. "Mrs. Farrel."

"I hear you have need of a temporary schoolteacher."

"That's how it looks."

"I'd like to offer my services to the board."

He set down the saddle he was rubbing. "That right?"

"I'm not officially certified, but my husband is back East for a bit, and I'd be happy to teach the children until a replacement can be found."

"We know how qualified you are, Mrs. Farrel, but I don't know if the board will hire . . ."

"I'm not looking for hire. I'm volunteering."

He rubbed his cheek. "Well, then. I'll bring it to the board members tonight."

"I'll wait to hear."

She had just made Clara's door when Cole rode up. "I know it's early, Abbie, but the wind's whippin' up. I don't think the weather's gonna hold."

"All right. Let me get Frances."

Abbie squeezed Clara's hand. "I'm sorry to run, but the storm's moving in. I'll likely see you soon." She gave her the slightest wink.

Thank goodness the wind made conversation difficult as they rode back.

◆◆◆◆◆◆◆

Mr. Lowe came himself two days later. "You're being hailed as a heroine by the parents."

Abbie offered him a cup of hot coffee. "I'm happy to serve."

"I'm a little concerned about your distance from town. It was a good forty minutes out here today."

"I'm used to the drive."

"I was thinking more of your safety. Suppose we say if it's bad you don't come in."

"I think that's wise."

He smiled. "My son's looking forward to your teaching."

"Thank you."

"The job you did with the foundlings was remarkable."

Abbie frowned. "It was the children who were remarkable. I hope the town children can do as well."

"Er . . . yes, I'm sure." Mr. Lowe took up his hat. "Well, then. You'll start tomorrow? Weather permitting?"

"Tomorrow."

◆◆◆◆◆◆◆

"I won't have it." Cole stood, legs spread in the stable door. "Mr. Farrel said for you to stay put."

Abbie bristled. "Cole, I'm not sixteen. I'll thank you not to use that tone with me."

"Like it or not, your husband charged me with yer care, and you ain't makin' this easy."

"I didn't ask anything of you. I merely informed you that—"

"And I won't have it."

Abbie pulled herself to her full height. "Well, it's not up to you. Please step aside so I can get my horse and be on my way." Didn't he realize she had to do this? Not only could she not bear to be cooped up another day, but she had to serve—whenever the opportunity arose. It was the only way she could live with herself.

"Maybe ya haven't noticed it's snowin'."

"I've noticed. It won't amount to much. It's more a blow and bother."

Will led Lady Belle out to her.

"Thank you, Will." Abbie took the reins and mounted.

"I don't suppose you've given thought to this horse standin' in the weather while you're teachin'?"

"I'm putting her in Marty Franklin's stable."

Cole frowned. "Sheez. If you're stubborn on this, I'll see ya in."

"I can find my own way to town, thank you. I've lived here longer than you."

"That ain't the concern." He said nothing more as they rode into sight of town. Then Cole reined in, and let her proceed alone. She could tell he was anxious to get back. Everyone was anxious. She shook her head and urged Lady Belle to a canter.

By the time she reached Marty's stable, the snow had stopped completely. But with the school at the end of town, the children were all waiting outside by the time she arrived.

"I'm sorry I'm late," Abbie said to the children. "I hadn't counted on the time it would take to stable the horse and walk here. Tomorrow I'll start earlier." She opened the door and waited as they filed past. Parker Bates went to the front and lit the fire in the stove, then ambled to his seat in the back.

Eight little faces and two nearly manly ones looked at her curiously. She knew them all, but the relationship was different now. One of the older boys smirked and whispered to Parker. "Would you share that with the class, Todd Loewe?"

Todd dropped his face and mumbled.

"I don't believe the class heard you. Could you stand and repeat it?"

Todd stood and towered over Abbie, his fourteen-year-old

frame already a match to his father's in height. "I said we're havin' the foundling teacher now."

"Thank you, Todd Loewe. You may sit." Abbie walked forward. "Now, class, who can tell me the correct word for foundling?"

Mary Driscoll raised her small hand. "Orphan, ma'am."

"That's right. Though some people consider orphans an object of sport and ridicule, I'd like to remind each of you that only by God's grace are you not in that position. I pray He will give you compassion for those less fortunate. Now, primer class please open your books and print your letters...."

The day grew dimmer rather than brightening. Abbie hardly noticed, so full was her time. She loved instructing them, listening to them read and recite. All that was missing were the faces of the mission children that she knew and loved so well. She had not been to teach them since before her wedding. Things had become so complicated.

She checked the time on Monte's pocket watch and stood. "You're dismissed. I'll see you all tomorrow." She followed them to the back and helped bundle the little ones. Only a thin layer of snow covered the ground, but it was enough to make tracks, and she smiled when they gleefully did so.

Abbie hurried down the street. The wind was cruel, though dry so far. She saddled Lady Belle, her eyes tearing as she rode. Maybe she should have listened to Cole, but the thought of spending the day with Frances haranguing her ...

She saw Cole riding in and straightened in the saddle. "Business in town, Cole?"

"You know my business."

"Honestly." He was keeping Monte's orders to the letter, as far as he was able. Had Monte reinforced the need? Were things worse than even she knew? Cole turned about and rode at her side. They were halfway home when another horse cantered toward them.

Abbie shielded her eyes and made out the fourteen-year-old orphan from the mission. "Why, that's Silas." She urged Lady Belle. "Silas, what is it?"

"Miss Abbie . . . I mean, Mrs. Farrel. It's Father Dominic. He's . . . he's passed on."

Abbie clutched the saddle horn, and Cole reached for her elbow.

"When?"

"This morning, but . . . it's been coming. And . . . well, Brother Thomas says the brothers have been called back to their order in the East and could you come talk to him."

"*Look to the living*," Father Dominic had said and given her hope. Had he known? Was it near even then? Cole's grip tightened on her elbow. She shook herself.

"Yes, of course I'll come."

Cole held fast. "No, you—"

"Cole, those children need me. Go back and tell Frances where I've gone."

"The heck I will."

"Come, Silas." Abbie turned the mare.

"Mrs. Farrel, yer a regular thorn in my side." Cole drew up with them. "But I reckon the snow might hold off awhile yet."

The children were more solemn than she could have imagined. Poor things. Not only did they have the loss of Father Dominic, but if the other brothers were leaving . . . what would become of them? Abbie didn't want to think how things would change without the mission, but right now her job was to comfort. She opened her arms and they came to her.

They took some small solace in each other before she went to see Brother Thomas. They had laid Father Dominic in the ground behind the trees. Abbie was glad she had not viewed him. Too many dead faces filled her memory, and she chose to remember him as she had seen him last. "*Go in peace.*"

Yes. And he, too, had gone in peace. She returned her thoughts to Brother Thomas and realized with a start what he was saying to her.

"They haven't another to send, and we can't remain here without a priest. The children could come with us. The bishop expects it, but you don't know what things are like in the cities. The sisters do their best, but the homes are filled to overflowing. That's why I hoped you . . ."

He had more confidence in her than Abbie could muster. How could she possibly arrange for eighteen children? Where would she find homes and families? They were already scorned and avoided. Dear heavenly Father, she was only one person.

See to the living.

Yes, but she was already doing that. Wasn't she teaching Will and the town children?

Feed my sheep.

Yes, she could provide shelter and food for some short time, but . . .

Look to the living.

She raised her head. "Yes, Brother Thomas. When you go, the children may stay with me until I can find another way."

"Thank you, sister. You ease my heart."

Abbie stood and walked out. Cole did not say a word on the ride home.

Fifteen

Monte woke at the sound of the brakes and looked out the steam-clouded window. Kendal still slept with Jeanette beside him, and across from them her mammy. It seemed she had only just stopped the child's crying. Rubbing a hand through his hair, he leaned forward and touched Kendal's shoulder. "Denver."

Kendal worked at the crick in his neck. "Where are we putting up tonight?"

"Hightower Inn. We'll get a late supper and start by stage in the morning."

Kendal nudged Mammy, and she lifted Jeanette. He turned as Monte reached overhead for their bags. "Can you manage?"

Monte gripped the handles. "Yes."

The hotel glittered. But what mattered more was that it had two rooms available, one for Mammy and the child, one for Kendal and himself. Top-end rooms, naturally. Monte paid. "Go on up. I'll see about having supper sent."

Kendal lingered. "Couple of fancies there." He nodded toward the ladies on the couch in the corner. "But then you're not in the market, are you?"

"Nor are you," Monte answered without turning.

"Did I tell you Frances locked me out the night before we left?"

Monte turned the bags over to the bellhop and told him where to find the trunks. "You'll be back soon enough."

"You think that'll matter?"

"Kendal, I'm tired and I'm hungry. Take Jeanette up and forget those two in the corner."

◆◆◆◆◆◆◆

Abbie bundled into her coat in the dark. It was long before dawn, but she could not sleep thinking of the men huddled in the stable. It was too cold for a night-long vigil. She lifted the pot of coffee and slipped past John Mason sleeping in the alcove. She made her way through the flurries to the stable. "Don't anyone shoot." She said it just loudly enough for them, then pulled open the door and stepped in.

Cole, Breck, and Skeeter slouched in the back of the stable. "I brought you some coffee."

Breck blew on his hands. "Must be an angel from heaven."

Cole glared as Abbie went forward, set the pot on the ground, and pulled the cups from her cape pockets. The steam rose up when Breck poured.

Cole shook his head. "Guess I gotta escort you back and spoil whatever surprise we had." He started to rise.

Abbie pushed him back down. "I don't need an escort."

"Sure wish you'd stop meddlin'."

"Quit yer complainin'." Breck elbowed him. "This here coffee's puttin' life back in me. Thank you, ma'am."

Abbie turned and slipped out. She closed the door silently. If that wasn't just like Cole to—She gasped as a hand covered her mouth and a frigid gun barrel touched her throat.

"One sound and you're dead. Understand?"

She nodded. She smelled liquor on his breath, but with the cloud cover and no moon she could see nothing of him. His palm was cracked and rough and he was not much taller than she, but his arm was thick and the gun insistent.

He half led, half dragged her away from the stable to the edge of the corral, then bent her down and ordered her through the fence. Gripping the ice-coated rail, she pulled herself through, and he pressed through with her.

"How many men in the stable?"

165

"Who are you?"

"I ask the questions." He tightened his grip on her arm and raised the gun to her face. "How many?"

Abbie brought up her chin.

"Look, lady . . ." He dug his fingers into her arm. "I ain't playin' games."

"I've dealt with worse than you."

He shook her.

She kept silent.

"A'right. You come along with me then. Soon's I have you where you ain't causin' trouble, I'll git back ta business."

"If your business is stealing horses, you ought to ride out right now and forget about it."

"Got a welcomin' committee, eh?" He dragged her on.

"I'm perfectly capable of walking, if you'd stop shoving." Abbie searched the darkness. It was a good while until dawn and the coldest part of the night. She had not dressed for an extended stay. She felt his grip loosen. If she could just . . .

He pressed the gun to her neck. "This here's the business end, lady. Git movin'."

They kept on. Abbie felt a change in the air, and the darkness thinned almost imperceptibly. At last he stopped. "Thet's far 'nough." He sat her at the base of a ponderosa. She knew where she was. This stand of trees was north of the house and a bit west. He pulled a rope from his coat. "Sit up nice an' straight, now, and I won't hurt ya."

"Yes, I know the rules. Do you plan to leave me here to freeze?"

"You got yerself into it."

He tied the rope around her wrists and pulled it tight, then lashed her to the tree. "Why are you doing this? What can you possibly gain?"

"Thet's my business."

"There's honest labor to be found. No one has to steal."

"Ain't nothin' to do with stealin'."

"What then?"

"Avengin'."

"Avenging what?"

"None o' yer business. Now listen, missie, I don't mean ta hurt ya, but if you cause me any trouble, I'll kill ya, got it?"

"Exactly what trouble could I cause tied to a tree?"

"Only the kind I mean to take care of now." He stuffed a rag into her mouth, and she gagged as he tied it. He walked away.

Furiously she pulled against her bonds, but they held fast as she knew they would. She leaned her head back against the tree. *Lord, please . . . help Cole.*

♦♦♦♦♦♦♦

The first paling of the dawn filtered into the stable as Cole rolled a cigarette.

"Farrel would have yer hide if he saw you smokin' in here," Skeeter said.

"Mind yer own business."

"Sure was nice o' Mrs. Farrel ta bring the coffee."

"Durn foolish is what it was."

Skeeter shrugged. "Guess I'm just more appreciative than you."

"Guess you're just stupider. I oughta thrash Mason for letting her slip out when we're waitin' to catch us a horse thief. I don't reckon we'll see hide nor hair of 'im now."

"That's just as good, ain't it? I mean . . ."

"You don't know what ya mean."

"You're awful cranky."

"And don't you ferget it." Cole ground the cigarette butt out with the heel of his boot. He stood and stretched. "I'm gonna have a look around 'fore we call it a night."

He pulled open the door and stepped out. All was quiet. The main house was dark. Abbie must be back in bed. The bunkhouse, the yard . . . he caught the motion only a moment before the handle of the gun crashed against his skull.

He collapsed with a groan. As his own gun was pulled from his hand, a voice rasped in his ear. "Which one o' yer men killed my brother?"

"What're you talkin' 'bout?" Cole gripped his head, felt the lump, and played stupid. The man's breath was foul with liquor. The hammer clicked against his temple. Not enough liquor.

"I know it wasn't you, cuz you was shot. Who was it?"

Cole took a kick in the ribs.

"Who shot the kid?"

So that was it. The boot caught his belly, and he tensed too late. The pain took his breath. The stable door burst open. Skeeter kicked the gun from the man's hand and swung a punch that doubled him.

Breck ran past, grabbed the gun, and spun. "A'right, hold it." He planted his feet and braced his arms. "You okay, Cole?"

Cole rolled to his knees and stood slowly. "Tie 'im up in the bunkhouse."

"You're makin' a big mistake."

"That right?" Cole rubbed his ribs. "Maybe we should just shoot ya."

The man chuckled. "Ya could. But then ya'd never find the young lady till she was good an' froze."

Cole stiffened, then gripped the collar of the man's coat. "What young lady?" he asked, as if he didn't know. "You got one minute ta tell me where she is 'fore I throttle you with my bare hands."

"You ain't gonna kill me. Only I know where I left 'er."

"Start walkin'."

"No, sir."

"You don't value yer life too good." Cole lifted him from the ground by his coat.

"You ... don't ... value hers."

Cole's chest heaved. He could tear this man apart. He could ... The cold cut to the back of his neck. They'd find Abbie. But if they didn't ... He released him. "Wha'd'ya want?"

"The girl fer the man who killed Spence."

"You're crazy."

"Templeton Gap. You got till daybreak. Send 'im unarmed."

"What about the girl?"

"You'll git 'er home alive. It ain't her I want."

Cole kept his face blank. "A'right, git out o' here."

The man went to the edge of the corral and mounted a horse tethered behind the oaks. "Don't follow, or she'll freeze long before we're anywhere near."

Cole clenched his hands and watched until the rider disappeared.

"Guess we're in it now," Breck said low.

Skeeter picked up his hat. "What're we gonna do?"

Cole glanced at him. "I dunno ... yet. First make sure he's really got her." He strode to the house and banged on the knocker to raise the dead, then opened it himself. She hadn't locked it behind her if she went back inside. James hurried forward in his nightclothes.

Cole shoved past, walked to the alcove, and kicked John Mason awake. Then without a word, he took the stairs two at a time to the bedroom. He banged the door.

"What you doin', Mistuh Jazzper? You can't wake the Missus like that."

Cole grabbed the knob and pushed the door open. The bed was empty. He leaned on the jamb and swore.

White-faced, Frances cracked open her door.

"Git yer head back in and keep it there."

She shoved the door closed, and Cole strode down the stairs and back out to the yard where Breck waited.

"Do we search?"

"And git Mrs. Farrel killed?"

"What else can we do?"

"What he said."

Breck stared. "What're you talkin' about? He's got the one who killed his brother."

"He don't know that."

"But who's gonna go?"

"I am."

"He knows it wasn't you. You was shot."

"He won't know it's me. Most likely he'll shoot before he looks close. I'm gonna have me a shave an' git me some bootblack."

"Are you crazy, Cole? You'll git yerself killed!"

"Maybe. Maybe not. Either way he'll let Abbie go."

Breck blocked him. "You're takin' that chance fer Farrel's wife?"

Cole shoved him aside and went to the bunkhouse. Inside, he clipped then shaved his mustache. He hadn't taken that off since he had whiskers enough to grow it. He shaved the rest of his face. "May as well make a job of it, save the undertaker the trouble." He grinned at Skeeter's solemn eyes.

Breck handed him the bootblack. "You really goin', or you got another plan?"

"Ain't no other plan." He smeared the black over his hair and down his side whiskers. "Purty now, ain't I?" He slopped his hands in the wash tub, then shook them dry. "Guess I'll have me some breakfast." He shook the cook. "Git up, Charlie. I need some grub."

Charlie grunted. "Git it yerself, then."

Grabbing him by the shirt, Cole dumped him out of bed. "Don't make me ask twice."

After eating, Cole saddled a spare horse. He would not take Scotch and risk recognition. "You're in charge, Breck. I don't want no one leavin' the yard, goin' for the marshal, nothin' stupid. And keep a watch on them in the house. No one goes anywhere, got it?"

"Cole . . ."

"I know. I'm a durn fool." He tipped his hat at Breck's salute.

♦♦♦♦♦♦♦

Abbie stiffened at the sound of hooves approaching. Her limbs ached with cold, and the folds of her wrap had stiffened under the frost. The gag in her mouth was soggy and foul. Her jaw hurt. Up over the rise a rider appeared, and seeing him in the dawning light, she started. His thick shape . . . and his face. She'd seen the face too often in her dreams to miss the likeness.

He dismounted and began to work the ropes loose. They had

frozen tight. She moaned against the gag.

"Sorry. Cain't risk any noise now. We're changin' camp."

He did not remove the rope from her wrists, and held the end of it as he raised her to her feet. Her limbs were so stiff she staggered, but he held her up and lifted her onto the horse. Abbie's pulse raced. At last. If she just . . .

He put one foot in the stirrup. Abbie kicked in her heels, and the horse bolted forward. The man sprawled to the ground but held the rope. She was yanked from the saddle and fell squarely. She gasped, fighting for breath through the gag.

In a moment he was on her. He sat her up. "Lost yer wind, thet's all." He pulled her to her feet and her chest heaved with returning breath. "Cain't say as I blame ya fer tryin'. Wouldn't do it agin, though." The horse had stopped some yards away. He shoved her up into the saddle.

She could see the rope coiled around his arm. He was no fool. He had anticipated her. He climbed up behind and urged the horse. The sun crested the horizon to her right, dazzling the frost. She knew this ground. They were heading for Templeton Gap. She began to tremble.

"If you're cold, you'll be home soon. If you're scared, I ain't gonna hurt ya, not unless ya make me."

Abbie closed her eyes as they passed the place she had waited with Monte, then dipped steeply into the gulch. She gripped the saddle horn with her tied hands as they went down, then climbed the far side. This rim had heavier growth, and he pulled the horse into a clump of oaks and slid down.

He lifted her off and untied the gag.

"Why have you taken me? Who are you?"

"It wasn't my first intention, if you recall. But turns out fortunate." He pushed her to sit. "In trade fer you, I git the man who killed my brother."

Abbie's stomach pitched. She had guessed they were kin. They were similar, though this one was a man, a good number of years older than the one she shot.

"He was fifteen years old. Jest a kid."

Abbie closed her eyes. She wished she could stop her ears. Fifteen. The screams, the blood, his young face. "How do you know who killed him?"

"I don't. But yer foreman does. I expect you're the missus?"

Abbie felt his eyes go over her.

His voice changed. "Maybe you know, too? Maybe yer fine husband told ya?"

Her chest seized.

"Don't matter. I don't need a name. After today he's a dead man."

Abbie struggled against the rope. "Will killing him bring your brother back?"

"Eye fer an eye."

He pulled a knife from his pocket and ran it over a twig, curling shavings off like wax. Abbie watched them fall. She thought of Cole's little wooden animals. Where was he? What had happened? How could he agree to a trade? He had no one to trade. Was he getting Marshal Haggerty?

The man scanned the gap. "Sure hope they don't try nothin' stupid."

"Why are you doing this?"

"Got to."

Abbie heard the hooves before he did, but a moment later, he tossed the stick and craned forward. A rider came along the gap, riding the base rather than the ridge. Her chest constricted. Cole. Only he rode like he was attached to the horse with every sinew.

The man pulled his gun and eased back the hammer.

She wanted to scream. Instead she whispered, "If it's an eye for an eye, then I'm the one you want."

"Hush, now," he hissed.

"Killing Cole won't avenge your brother."

"That ain't Cole. He ain't dark like thet fella."

"He knows it was my bullet that killed your brother."

She saw his knuckles whiten on the gun.

"I didn't mean to kill him. It was so dark . . ." Tears started in her eyes. "I didn't know he was just a boy. But . . ."

He spun and gripped her shoulder. "You're lyin'! You think I won't shoot a woman."

Abbie didn't dare look back to Cole. He must be in shooting range now.

"You came onto our land to steal our cattle, and you shot first. I did what I had to do, but if you want vengeance, then I'm the one to kill, as God is my witness."

He stared, his throat working, his breath shallow. He brought the gun to her face, the cold barrel inches from her cheek. His eyes burned. He believed her. "I swore revenge on him ... when he died in my arms I swore revenge on him."

"Then have it." Abbie felt suddenly peaceful. She would not go to her grave with Cole's death on her soul.

He grabbed her face and pressed the gun to her temple. Her breath stopped. Every moment lingered. Oh, Monte, if only ...

He groaned and shoved her back. She fell against the branches, her breath rushing in, her mind slowly comprehending. He holstered the gun, looked down at the rider, then once again at her. Then he swore and ran to his horse. He mounted and kicked in his spurs.

Abbie saw Cole stiffen at the sound, but he never looked up. He expected the bullet. The lump in her throat choked her. She made a hoarse croak, scrambled to her feet, and shoved her way through the oaks to the edge of the gap. "Cole!"

He dived from the horse and rolled.

Abbie then slid down the slope, groping with her tied hands. Cole leaped up and ran, grabbed her down, and braced himself over her. He searched the ridge, body tense.

"He's gone." Her voice was hardly a whisper.

Cole did not move. He held her hard to the ground.

"Cole, he's gone." She felt his tension slacken.

He looked at her.

"He left when I ... told him ... I killed his brother."

He searched her face. "What'd you do a durn fool thing like that for?"

"He would have killed you in my place."

Cole sat her up roughly. "You had no business doin' that."

The calm she'd felt with the gun to her head deserted her. "Oh, Cole, why did you come?"

"How'd ya know it was me?"

"I know how you sit a horse."

"Sheez." He searched the upper bank again, then slid an arm under her knees and carried her to the horse. She gripped the horn when he hoisted her up and mounted behind. Relief flooded her, and she blinked back the tears. He turned the horse and started back down the gap.

"Cole?"

"Yeah?"

"Would you mind untying my hands?"

"Yeah, I mind. Tied up you just might stay outta trouble. But I ain't countin' on it."

Abbie leaned back against his chest. "Have it your way then."

He reined in, hooked the reins on the saddle horn, and reached for her wrists. He worked the rope free and tossed it down. She bit back a whimper.

He touched the raw mark on her skin. "I'm sorry, Abbie."

She looked up at him. "You have nothing to be sorry for."

"Don't I?"

His voice was hoarse, and she searched his face, a sudden dull ache inside her. Cole loved her. He understood her. He had risked his life for her. Oh, dear Lord . . . had she made a mistake? Did she misunderstand? Did she think Monte . . . Monte. Oh, it hurt. She needed him. She loved him. And he . . . it didn't matter. She loved him with all that was in her.

Even if he despised her, hated her . . . she would love him. She couldn't help it. They were one flesh.

✦✦✦✦✦✦✦

Monte grimaced as he helped Kendal lift the trunks onto the boardwalk.

"I'll get it, Monte," Kendal said.

"I can manage." Monte reached for the handle of the next

trunk. Though it was painful, there was strength in his hands, if not dexterity. "I don't understand why Abbie didn't send a man out with the wagon as I asked. The wire should have reached her in plenty of time this morning."

"We'll hire a hack and send back for the trunks."

Monte nodded, but that did not explain Abbie's failure. He felt a deep disquiet. Was she punishing him for treating her so poorly? He wouldn't blame her if she were. He should never have left without reconciling. Had he not already caused her enough distress for a lifetime?

Kendal returned with the buggy and handed Jeanette into the back with her mammy. He seemed amazingly cheerful. "You're going to see where Uncle Monte lives, chicken. And you're going to see Mama."

Tear streaked and hollow eyed, Jeanette snuggled into her mammy's chest. She looked about the way Monte felt.

Monte climbed into the front as Kendal took the reins. Their breath misted the air as they drove. He glanced back at the child, nestled closely to the woman's chest. They should have a wrap in this cold, but it wasn't far now.

As they crested the rise, he made out the men standing in the yard. "That's odd. Why aren't they at work?"

"When the cat's away . . ."

"Nonsense. Go." He reached over and slapped the reins. This was trouble and he knew it. Breck and Matt Weston flanked the front door like sentries. What on earth . . .

Monte leaped down. "What's going on?"

Breck stepped forward. "Trouble, Mr. Farrel. That third rustler came back lookin' fer revenge. He's . . . got Mrs. Farrel."

Monte froze. His pulse throbbed in his temple. "Where?"

"Templeton Gap. Cole's . . ."

He didn't wait to hear.

"Monte," Kendal called.

"Take care of the women." He bolted for the stable, but stopped midway as Cole rode into the yard with Abbie cradled against him. Monte's throat tightened.

Cole pulled up beside him, slid Abbie down, then rode on. She stood there, less than an arm's length away . . . yet held back. Dear God, what damage had he done? Slowly he reached out, pulled her into his arms, and smelled Cole's tobacco in her hair. He pressed his cheek to her head. "Abbie, what on earth. . . ?"

"Just hold me."

She was cold and warm at once, her cheek where he kissed it like ice, her chest against his warm and throbbing. God help him, he loved her. *Tell her. Show her.*

Breck cleared his throat. "Uh, Mr. Farrel, if you're not needin' us now . . ."

Monte released her. "Tell Cole I'll see him inside." He led Abbie to the house. In the hall he took her wrap and handed it to James. He glanced at Pearl, and she heaved a sigh of relief. He could hear Frances and Kendal in the parlor with Jeanette. From the sound of it, Kendal would not be cheerful long.

He pressed Abbie's hand. "I'll be up shortly."

He went to the study and in a short while heard Cole's knock. Monte eyed him as he removed his hat and ran his hand through his scrubbed hair, still flecked with bootblack. "Well?"

"The last of them rustlers."

"So I heard. Why was Abbie involved?"

"Well, Mr. Farrel, I reckon it's cuz she's Abbie."

Monte listened to him relate the affair. It chilled him to think what might have happened had Cole not done his part. It chilled him more to think what had made Cole willing to do it. "The man is dead?"

"Nope. He high-tailed it before I got in."

"Why?"

"Abbie told him what she done. I reckon he's no lady killer."

Monte winced. Why had he not prevented this? All of it. He turned to the window. "I don't know how to repay you."

"No need."

"I'm in your debt."

"I just done what I could."

"Do you think this is the end of it?"

"I don't rightly know."

Monte stared at the yard, gray and brown like his soul. He had failed her again. He had not protected her. Because of his pride, he had wounded her, abandoned her, and Cole had been there to assuage the hurt. "That will be all."

He climbed the stairs, knocked on the door and opened before she could refuse him. She stood, clutching the dress to her chest. Zena ducked behind her.

"Zena, leave us."

She scurried out, and he closed the door and turned. In three steps he had Abbie in his arms. He found her mouth hungrily and felt her response. "How many times must I face losing you?"

"Oh, Monte . . ."

He lifted her into his arms.

Abbie lay with her head on Monte's chest. Every deep, satisfied breath he took as he slept was balm to her soul. *Lord, you have restored us, beyond my hope united us. Help me to guard this man's honor as my own.* But as she sank to sleep, she could not help but realize he had avoided any mention of the shooting.

Sixteen

Monte's face was stern. "I'm not running an orphanage."

Abbie hushed him. "It's only temporary."

He motioned toward the door. "There are eighteen scruffy children in my foyer."

"Seventeen. Silas took a room at the boardinghouse." She pressed his hand between hers. "Where else can they turn, Monte? I gave Brother Thomas my word."

"To turn my home . . ."

"Our home. You said as mistress I could do whatever I liked." She rested her hands on his chest.

"That's not fair. And don't use your eyes like that. It's bad enough this . . . volunteering in the town school. . . ."

Abbie caught his face in her hands and kissed him. "I know you won't have me turn them out, so stop your blustering. Where shall we put them?"

"I'll build a new wing."

Abbie clicked her tongue. "Monte . . ."

He released a long breath. "Will the lower guest rooms do?"

"They're used to sharing. Come, I'll introduce you." She tugged him toward the door and caught the knob. "Now, no sour expression."

"You're a minx." He spun her. "And I love you." He kissed her soundly.

Abbie's heart raced. Would she ever have enough of his love?

"Felicity Fenham, Jeremy Smith, Emmy and Pauline Barret . . ." She watched Monte bow over each little hand. How cor-

178

dially he smiled, no hint of his disapproval. Oh, she could hug him herself. "And this is Tucker Finn. He'll have a birthday soon and be six years old."

Monte shook his hand. "How do you do, sir."

"Fine, thank you, sir." Tucker's eyes were sober until Monte ruffled his hair. Tucker displayed the gap in his teeth, and Monte's grin almost matched.

Abbie beamed. "And now, children, I'll show you to your rooms."

She led Tucker by the hand with the others trailing. It shamed her to see the awe in their eyes as they passed through the house. What on earth would she do? Could she find homes, families for them? The townspeople had rejected them once. Would they again?

Mama and Pa would help. Yes. She'd ride to Mama tomorrow. No, she'd be teaching school tomorrow. Well, she'd take them all with her. Thank goodness the brothers had left the wagons with her, as well.

◆◆◆◆◆◆◆

Monte waited outside the door. When it opened he removed his Panama straw hat. "Reverend Shields."

"Mr. Farrel. Come in."

He stepped into the double-roomed house and took a cursory glance. The minister was not as fastidious as he'd imagined.

"This is a pleasant surprise. I've not seen you at services, I don't believe."

Monte turned. "No ... well, my wife is Roman Catholic, you recall. She attends—or did attend—service at the mission."

"A sad business that. The priest dying, I mean, and the others pulling out. But you don't mention your attendance."

Monte half smiled. Was he going to be sermonized? "Ah well, I've made acquaintance with the Lord, but it's a private one."

"A private acquaintance is a doubtful one. Won't you sit?"

Monte took the wooden chair by the wall.

"Coffee?"

"No, thank you."

Reverend Shields sat on the edge of the cot. He had nervous hands, Monte noticed.

"Actually, it's the mission that brings me here."

"If you have questions of conversion . . ."

"No, no. It's about the children."

"Ah yes. The orphans." The minister brushed a hand through his thin blond hair. For all his youth, the good reverend would be bald soon. "I heard they were lodged with you."

"Yes, temporarily. But . . . I was hoping you would help find a solution. Surely there are families . . ."

"It's been tried. Did you not hear the difficulties of my predecessor?"

"Yes, I know. But there must be something."

Reverend Shields stood and walked to the small window. "Every human life is precious, we know. But the sad truth is, not every life is wanted. These poor souls have been cast on the mercy of men who lived . . . a foreign, if holy, life. People don't like what they don't know."

"That's outrageous. They're perfectly normal children." Especially in noise level and food consumption. "Why should not the families here. . . ."

"Are you adopting?"

Monte paused. The minister was clever, for all his washed-out bashfulness. He had caught him squarely. "I've only just married. I would expect with the natural course of things, we'll have children of our own."

Reverend Shields spread his hands. "Everyone has circumstances."

Who was this pup to tell him that? Monte felt a nudge inside. "Very well, I see your point. Is there no assistance you can offer?" He stood.

"I'll see what I can do." The reverend grasped his hand. It wasn't the limp clutch he expected. "And it would be a pleasure to see you and your wife in church on Sundays."

Monte straightened. "Well, there wouldn't be room for her entourage."

The reverend smiled. It was amazingly boyish. "You'd be surprised how tightly we can pack."

Monte left him still smiling. That had not gone as he had hoped. He took the ride home slowly. It was heavenly solitude. Between Jeanette crying, Frances weeping, and seventeen extra mouths and pairs of feet, there was precious little peace at home. If not for Abbie, he would . . .

He sighed. He would watch what he promised hereafter. The day was warm for December, but still a chill breeze caught his collar. He turned it up. Sirocco fought the bit. He wanted to run.

Monte looked at the reins wrapped on his wrist. No more of that. He uncoiled the rein, tightened his hand in the black leather glove, and gave the horse his head.

✦✦✦✦✦✦✦

Abbie clapped her hands together. "You must have gone high to find a fir."

Kendal and James dragged in the tree. "Monte would settle for nothing less than perfection."

Monte laughed. "I was under orders. Call for cider, Abbie."

Abbie tugged the bellpull. "Isn't it funny to have a tree in the house, Jeanette?"

The child gripped her mother's fine chintz dress. Frances bent and extricated the fabric. Kendal had brought every one of Frances's fine gowns back with him. A peace offering, though it didn't seem to appease her.

She smoothed the skirt. "Come, Jeanette. Time for your nap."

Abbie wished Frances wouldn't whisk her off every time she paid her any attention. She was sure the child would feel more at home if they could all reach out to her. And heaven forbid she should play with the orphans. White trash, Frances had called them. White trash! Abbie still shook.

Kendal hammered the crosspieces to the trunk and stood the

tree at the end of the great room. It towered beneath the high ceiling.

"Oh, it's wonderful." Wouldn't the children be thrilled? Of course, they would only be allowed a glimpse when it was lit, then they would be hustled back to bed.

Monte smiled. "I have a surprise for you. I've hired a quartet from Denver. I daresay Marcy Wilson will never quite recover."

Abbie groaned. "You've no idea how difficult it is to keep a civil tongue. How can Grant not see through her as you did?"

"Love is blind."

"Infatuation is blind."

Monte laughed. "It amounts to the same."

James, Pearl, and Zena clipped the tiny candles to the branches. What a lighting it would be! Yet it could hardly compare with her buoyant heart. Abbie was happier this Christmas than she had believed possible. *Look to the living.* Father Dominic's words had filled her with hope. And now her home was filled, her heart overflowing.

Kendal went to the hearth and took down a box. He pulled out a pale sprig.

"What's that, Kendal?"

"Mistletoe."

"That parasite?" Now she recognized the leathery leaves and white berries from her botanical manual. "What for?"

He chuckled. "It's a custom. Quite pagan, I'm afraid. It originated with the Norsemen. Frigga, goddess of love, wished to protect her son, Balder, the sun god. So she drew a pledge from every plant not to harm him, but she overlooked the lowly mistletoe. Loki, god of evil, made an arrow tip of mistletoe which was shot by Hoder, the blind god of winter."

"Was Balder slain?"

"Yes, but Frigga restored him by the power of her love. Her tears became the berries, and in her joy she kissed all who passed beneath the mistletoe. Hung from the rafter, so . . ." He mounted the ladder and secured it. "It brings luck, and no lady caught beneath can refuse a kiss to her captor." Kendal raked her with his eyes.

Abbie looked at it hanging there, and it seemed to suck the joy from her. It wasn't Kendal's story so much as the look in his eyes. If only Frances would show him some small kindness.

But Mama was right. Frances was bitter, so bitter it stung all of them. She felt a guilty twinge. She had not heeded Mama's advice. How could she? But something had to be done. And not only for Kendal's sake.

Abbie swallowed her pride and found Frances in the parlor. "Is Jeanette sleeping?"

"Soon. Mammy's singing."

"Frances . . ." Abbie's tongue stuck, but she forced herself on. "I wondered . . . would you teach me . . . things I need to know?"

"What could you possibly need to know?" Her tightened lips did not help.

Oh, Mama . . . Abbie took a deep breath. "Well . . . how to be a lady."

Frances raised her eyebrows. There was almost a sneer, then she smoothed her features to their serene perfection. "I wouldn't presume."

"There is so much I lack, and . . . well . . ."

Frances's eyes glittered like black ice, frigid and brittle.

Abbie bristled. She'd like nothing better than to shake her. "I apologize. I shouldn't have asked." She swirled her skirts in her wake.

"There's more to being a lady than you know."

Abbie paused at the door. *Guard my lips, Lord.*

Frances continued. "But . . . we could begin with the art of conversation."

Abbie counted ten, then turned back.

"Come, sit." Frances patted the settee beside her.

With stubborn control, Abbie took the seat.

"There are general rules, of course, in how to conduct one's speech and govern one's voice. But you must know that the first rule is silence."

Silence in conversation. Abbie kept her face blank. If Frances were toying, she would not take the lure.

"By that, of course, I mean one should strive to listen more than speak. Always draw out the other person, that they may feel they have participated admirably. No man is interested in your strengths, but there is not a man alive who won't discourse on his. As La Bruyère says, 'The great charm of conversation consists less in the display of one's own wit and intelligence, than in the power to draw forth the resources of others.'"

Abbie felt a stirring inside, her irrepressible desire to learn. There was wisdom in Frances's teaching. She settled into the corner.

"Never quibble or in any way doubt the speaker's sincerity, or speak of things with which others are unacquainted or uninterested. Fluency of tongue and self assurance go a short way when conversing without substance."

Abbie nodded. Of course. Who wanted to discuss things that didn't matter?

"Never pose a direct question. Give an opinion and leave opportunity for the other to respond or not. A gentleman in polite company will avoid asking any question of a lady, and whereas a lady may have an opinion, she will not voice it in his presence."

Frances seemed to take great pleasure in providing that lesson. Abbie frowned. How silly. She and Pa had discussed everything from the time she was small, and Monte had no such qualms. But she listened, learning as much from Frances's delivery as from her words.

It was almost like music—or drama. While she lacked the accent, Abbie could imitate the inflection and expression—though why she'd ever want to, she didn't know. With all the "never do's," she'd be completely tongue-tied before Frances was through.

◆◆◆◆◆◆◆

Abbie winced as Zena tugged the strings of her corset tighter. "If this isn't the most ridiculous thing."

"Just you wait till you sees yo'self in that gown, Mizz Abbie. Lawd, you's gonna be beautiful."

"Well, that's tight enough. Good grief, my lungs can scarcely move. No wonder Frances goes faint at every provocation."

Zena slid the crinoline over her head. Abbie adjusted it and raised her arms for the gown. The emerald silk shimmered as it settled over her figure. Abbie stared at the glass.

Her shoulders were bare, the rim of the V-cut bodice trimmed with red satin roses. A generous flounce of ivory lace gushed from the center of the V where the roses clustered. It was the most exquisite dress she had ever seen, much less worn.

Zena took the brush and worked it through her hair. "This fine, thick hair, these curls . . . they's heaven to arrange."

Heaven for Zena, maybe. Abbie thought her neck would go stiff before it was done, but she had to admit the twists and plaits and ringlets transformed her. She put on the pearl and garnet earbobs.

"You looks like a queen, Mizz Abbie."

She felt like one—or something very near. What would Blake have said? The twinge in her chest told her clearly. But that was in the past. She had grown up and now was Monte's wife. And he had sent to Paris for this silk and stunned Mrs. Munson with the dress order. Abbie wondered how many orders she had turned down to complete his pattern. The fitting alone had taken days, or so it felt.

Monte's eyes showed his approval as Abbie swept into the room. He held her at arm's length. "You take my breath away. You'll have every eye on you tonight."

She smiled. "And you. You look splendid." And he did, in his black coat and satin sash. How was it everything he wore seemed personally designed for him? He was the most handsome man alive.

He reached into his pocket. "Here is something to wear with your dress."

She pulled open the ribbon-tied paper. "Oh, Monte . . ." She caressed the bracelet set with emeralds.

He took it out and clipped it on her wrist. "A perfect fit. You'll have to keep it."

"Wild horses couldn't get it away from me."

He laughed. "I'd hate to see them try."

"And I have a gift for you. In the library." Abbie tugged his elbow, and he followed. She fervently hoped he would like it. It was the first gift she had given him. He untied the string and pulled the paper off the smooth, wooden carving. The horse was rearing, the mane and tail arched and flying.

"It's Sirocco. I commissioned it from Cole."

"Cole carved this?"

"Don't you like it?"

"It's incredible."

Abbie smiled. "When I saw him whittling other animals, I asked him to make a horse for you. I had no idea it would turn out so well."

"I must say I'm impressed. He's a man of hidden talents." He stood the statue on the corner of the desk. "Thank you, Abbie."

Her spirits mounted as she stood in the hall with Monte, Kendal, and Frances to greet the guests. She looked around her at the windows and doors festooned with evergreens, some still bearing their pinecones. She had fallen into a fairy tale and was living it this moment . . . and here was the wicked witch.

Grant came down the hall with Marcy on his arm. Her claret velvet gown with an extravagant bustle perfectly set off her golden curls and green eyes. And she knew it.

Abbie extended her hand. "Marcy Wilson, you look lovely. What an attractive color on you."

"Why . . . thank you."

Abbie received Grant's kiss on her cheek. "And *you* are enchanting," he whispered.

"You must be sure to have the taffy, Grant. Pearl and Zena had a pull just as you and I used to."

"My mouth's watering already. Point me in the right direction."

Abbie laughed. "You're headed the right way."

He clasped Marcy's hand into the crook of his arm and she brushed by, elegantly poised.

Abbie glanced at Monte. "Why are you smiling like that?"

"I confess I overheard you and Frances in the parlor. You *are* a quick study."

"Not so quick as you think. I almost tripped Marcy as she passed." Abbie turned back as he stifled his laugh.

The musicians were playing, and the strains filled the house as the guests continued to arrive. Mama and Pa; the McConnels; Clara and Marty; the Simmses; the ranchers Ephart, Dunbar, and Hodge; Reverend Shields; and Ethan Thomas . . . "Are you certain the house can hold the entire town, Monte?"

"Only our friends and fellow ranchers . . . and hired help." He frowned slightly as Cole walked in with the men behind. All save Cole were slicked and looking bashful. Their suits were a motley assortment of tweeds and broadcloth. But Abbie was glad she had insisted on inviting them, despite Monte's protests.

They were like family. How could they be excluded on Christmas?

Cole was cleaned and combed, his mustache nearly full again, but he had not slicked his hair. He would never slick it again, Abbie guessed, after she'd called him pretty for it. He pulled off his hat and held it to his chest. "Merry Christmas, Abbie. You never looked purtier." He swaggered past.

She felt Monte stiffen beside her. Cole was a rogue indeed. The others filed through the line looking as awkward as schoolboys, but she could sense their high spirits, as well. A dance without cowboys was just no dance at all, whatever Monte may say.

Beside her, Abbie heard Frances gasp. She turned. A man with auburn side whiskers had given James his frock coat and stood at the door in full Union uniform down to the sword at his side. A pale scar ran down his forehead. His features were proud, cold.

"Oh my . . ." Frances swayed. "Take me out, Kendal. I won't stay in a room with a Yankee soldier."

"Monte . . ." Kendal turned to him.

Monte stood still. Abbie's throat tightened at the clench of his jaw. The man was upon them. Monte bowed stiffly. "Mr. Jake Gif-ford . . . Captain Gifford. My wife, Mrs. Farrel."

He bowed. "Good evening."

Abbie nodded. "Good evening."

Monte's tone was even. "Mr. and Mrs. Stevens."

She had to admire Frances. She nodded as required, but froze him to the bone, nonetheless. The moment he passed, she turned. "Take me out, Kendal. I'll spend the evening in my room." She stopped before Monte, and for the first time ever, Abbie saw dis-approval of him, scathing disapproval. "How could you, Monte?"

"I didn't know."

She sagged against Kendal's arm. "You've contaminated your house and your honor."

Abbie felt Monte stiffen, but he said nothing. Kendal took Frances out.

Abbie touched his arm. "Who is he?"

"A rancher." He took her elbow and led her into the great room. "We'll lead the grand march."

"Monte . . ."

"Please, Abbie. If I say more it'll only be ugly."

They lined up and came together to bow and curtsy. She trem-bled for the fierce control in his face. He forced a smile. How she loved his courage. They started down the channel. The couples around them danced with gusto. If anyone was aware of the af-front paid their host, they made no sign. Bright Christmas spirits, hearty smiles, and light steps abounded. She wished she could feel the same.

The music ended and they stood apart. Grant had signed her card for the quadrille and claimed her now, then Davy McConnel the first waltz, and Marty Franklin the caledonian. Abbie noticed Captain Gifford did not dance. He stood mainly at the end with the ranchers clustered about, though she did not see him con-verse once with Monte. Why had he come in uniform like that? Was it intentional, or did he not realize the insult?

Monte claimed her for the next waltz. It would never lose its magic when he took her in his arms and swirled her so. "Oh,

Monte, if I could only breathe we could dance without stopping until the sun comes up."

"I shudder to think how condemned I'd be for keeping you from the others."

"There's no one else in the room when you dance with me."

"Nevertheless, it would be decidedly poor manners." His crooked smile made her heart leap. He seemed recovered, cheerful even, if not entirely himself. Her concern eased. They stopped and did their courtesies.

"If you'll excuse me, my dear." He kissed her hand.

She danced the lanciers with Ethan Thomas, then stood, clapping, as Wes McConnel and Pa did the jig in the center of the floor. The cowboys whooped and whistled.

Abbie stepped back, laughing. They would go until one or the other gave in, she knew. Like two crazy leprechauns they grabbed hands and kicked wildly until both could barely lift their feet, then stumbled to the side, laughing and pounding their backs. Good heavens, they were a pair. Her heart swelled.

Kendal touched her elbow. "I was hoping to find you here."

She turned, and he pointed to the ceiling. She looked up to the white-berried mistletoe, and her chest lurched. "Oh, surely..."

"There's no escape. It's the rules." He claimed her mouth with unexpected ardor. She could taste the brandy on his breath and pulled back.

"Kendal, you snake." Monte scowled and brushed through those standing near. "Turnabout would have me kissing my sister, and that's hardly a fair exchange."

Kendal laughed. "When are things ever fair?" He bowed and walked off.

Monte took her hand and drew her away. "Let's not find yourself there again, my darling."

Abbie swallowed her distaste. "I certainly won't, though I'd swear Marcy's trying her best to lure Grant over." She directed his gaze to where Marcy pouted and tossed her curls at Grant's laughter.

"You have to admit she has style."

"A rattler has style."

He laughed. "Well, I'm signed on Mrs. Franklin's card. I trust you'll manage without me?"

That was the problem with protocol. She had to spend most of the time without the one who mattered. Never mind. Tomorrow was Christmas, and she'd have him all to herself. Abbie's hand was warm where he kissed it.

Cole stepped up and nodded. "I ain't signed on yer card..."

"This waltz is free."

"My lucky night." He held out his arm.

As Cole waltzed her, she caught Kendal watching from where he stood with two men. He responded to what one of them said, but his eyes were on her. She turned away.

"Wish you'd keep clear of him."

Abbie startled. Had she been so obvious? "It's the mistletoe. Some black magic of Kendal's."

"It ain't the mistletoe."

Cole turned so his back blocked Kendal, but her eye caught Captain Gifford.

"Cole, who is the man in uniform? Do you know him?"

"Jake Gifford. Owns a spread southwest of here. Big operation. Runs six hundred head so far. He set up headquarters this spring."

"Does he know... about Monte?"

Cole quirked an eyebrow.

"I mean about being from the South and all. His uniform gave Frances quite a scare, and..."

"I reckon it would." He shook his head. "I'm not familiar with the man, Abbie. It's to Mr. Farrel's credit that he's put that war business behind him. It's a lesser man can't pick up and go on." Cole bowed at the music's end.

Abbie dropped a curtsy. "Thank you, Cole. And Cole... would you keep your ears open?"

He nodded. "And both eyes."

Monte crossed to her. "It's nearly midnight."

"Oh . . . I must get the children."

"Hurry then. I should have hired the men to herd them in."

Abbie clicked her tongue, then left him and passed through the doors. To her surprise, Jeanette's mammy had them all up and dressed, and Jeanette looked like an angel perched on Felicity's knee. "Come. It's time to light the tree."

She stood the children to the side as she and Kendal and Monte took long tapers and lit the tiny candles. Frances would have participated, but for Captain Gifford. Abbie was aware of him at the fringe of the crowd. His presence filled her with foreboding. Something in his stance—in the way he held his shoulders, his hand resting on the hilt of his sword.

She stepped around the tree and stretched up. Kendal took her hand and gave her the needed inch to the candle's wick. His grip was warm and firm, and she wiggled her hand free. James had mounted the ladder and lit the upper candles. One by one the lamps in the room were extinguished until only the tree shone. Marty Franklin sang into the hush, "Silent night, holy night . . ."

Monte rested his hand on Abbie's back. Warmth filled her. It was a blessed night. Monte was beside her, the children's faces glowed, and the Christ Child would visit their home that night. Even though she would tuck the treats into the socks, she never doubted that it was all His gift.

✦✦✦✦✦✦✦

Sitting astride his charger, Captain Jake Gifford brushed his blue sleeves down to the yellow cuffs. He sucked on the thin cigar. What a passion he had for fine tobacco. Too bad the plantations in the South were so decreased. Still, Cuba provided for the lack.

He turned the horse and headed for home in the cold night air. Oh yes, he had enjoyed himself at Montgomery Farrel's Christmas gala. He enjoyed hearing the ranchers praise Farrel's hospitality, geniality, generosity. And he had enjoyed the stir he caused.

It was time to step up his efforts, though he was momentarily hobbled by the loss of Jip Crocker and his unfortunate kin. His mood darkened. Wherever Crocker was, he hoped it was hard and cold.

✦✦✦✦✦✦✦

Monte stood at the window as Abbie slept. He had loved her gently, passionately, but it had not soothed him. Frances's words burned inside. He had not exchanged a single word with Jake Gifford past the greeting, but he indeed felt tarnished.

The war was over. Long over. He had put it behind him. But the swagger of that man. What audacity for a neighbor to enter his home in uniform. And what was the purpose? To challenge him?

For what? Monte's breath fogged on the frosted window. Was Gifford behind the sabotage of the ranch, the fouled pond, the stampede, the poisoned calves . . . Chance? Was it a gauntlet he had thrown down tonight?

Monte looked up to the stars, haloed through the glass. Cole believed their trouble had ended with the last rustler's departure. Certainly the harassment had stopped. But Monte felt uneasy. Too many things did not add up. He rubbed a hand over his eyes and glanced back at Abbie.

In sleep she looked so vulnerable. He ached to keep her safe. He climbed back into the bed and pressed into her warmth. He wished he could find abandon in sleep. Monte sighed. Would life always be a battle?

Seventeen

The afternoon sun dazzled the dusting of snow when Abbie opened the door to Reverend Shields. She scarcely contained her surprise. What could he want the day after Christmas? "Reverend, do come in."

James took his hat and coat, and Abbie showed him to the parlor. She stoked up the fire to chase the chill. "I'm afraid my husband has gone out."

"I'd be glad to give my news to you. In fact I've only just received answer to my inquiry and came as soon as I heard."

"Please sit." Abbie pulled the bell.

"Some time ago your husband asked my assistance with the orphans."

Abbie hid her surprise. Monte had said nothing to her.

"I believe I've found the solution."

"Solution, Reverend Shields?"

He twisted his hands. "Well, yes, of course. They can't all remain here, naturally."

Pearl brought tea and cakes. Abbie poured and offered him a cup. "You've found homes for them?"

"I've arranged an orphan train. At very little cost a Mrs. Beardsly from Denver takes the children from the city to outlying parts and . . ."

"And what, sir? Auctions them off?" He reddened, and Abbie bit off her indignation. "Forgive me, but these are children."

"Mrs. Beardsly disembarks at each township, and people in need of a child choose from those she brings. It's a blessed ar-

193

rangement for all parties. The children have a home, and . . ."

He spoke on, and Abbie sank to a chair. A slave market. People the children had never seen, who want another pair of hands. . . . Oh, little Tucker, and Emmy and Pauline . . . How could Monte have thought . . . well, perhaps he didn't know the means by which Reverend Shields would remove the problem. And the minister—he was so young, so uncertain. But did no one think of the children?

"I'm sorry, Reverend Shields. These children will not be on any orphan train."

"But your husband said . . ."

"Do you know these children? Have you ever seen them?"

"Well, yes, at the Christmas recitation last year . . ."

"Do you know their names? Have you sat beside them and heard their letters and sums? Have you wiped their noses and cleaned their scrapes?"

"Mrs. Farrel. I understand your consternation. I have my own flock."

"Whose flock are these, Reverend?"

He removed his glasses and wiped the lenses, then replaced them. "The Lord's, I suppose."

"And what did he charge Peter?"

"Mrs. Farrel, I've worked hard to arrange . . ."

"I'm sure you did. But Reverend, if you saw these children, spoke to them . . . you must see that sending them to be picked over like—like produce or cattle . . ." She saw something ignite behind his eyes. Maybe it was anger, but perhaps a dose of anger would do him good.

What the minister needed was an awakening. He spoke his message well, as attested by his sermon last Sunday, but now she saw why Monte had brought her there. He was working with the minister to remove the children. Her own anger kindled.

It was time to more than speak the message. It was time to live it. "Have you spoken with the families in town?"

"My predecessor . . ."

"I know all about Reverend Peale. He was a wonderful help to the orphans. Yes, there were some troublemakers who made things difficult. But when his appeal didn't work, he found other ways to support the children—and the brothers in their work."

"I've never opposed . . ."

"But have you risked anything?"

"You forget yourself."

"Maybe I do. No doubt my husband would agree with you. But I know these children. I know which teeth Emmy lost last year. I held Jeremy when Father Dominic set his arm. I won't allow them to be sent off in that way, picked over and rejected. I won't subject them to that."

"Then what will you do?"

Abbie sat back in the chair and folded her hands. "I will accompany you to the homes of our neighbors and friends, your flock. And we will appeal to them to adopt the children."

The minister sat, unmoving. Then he smiled, his face becoming pleasant for the first time. "Very well, Mrs. Farrel. I'll make the appeal with you. And if I lose my congregation, no doubt you and Mr. Farrel and all the children who remain in your home will fill my church in their stead."

Abbie laughed and stuck out her hand. "It's a deal."

◆◆◆◆◆◆◆

With Monte in Denver two days later, it was the perfect opportunity to attempt her plan. Abbie stood in Pa's yard and hugged Mama around the neck. Little Tucker would have the best Mama and Pa alive. He'd be her own little brother. She climbed back up to the wagon with Reverend Shields.

He maintained a straight face. "Where to now?"

"The McConnels. If anyone knows how to rear a boy like Jeremy, it's Mary McConnel. Why, he's Blake all over."

"Don't count on such easy success."

But the reverend shook his head and smiled when she came from Mary McConnel's and nodded the affirmative. She didn't tell him it was her reference to Blake that decided Mary.

"Now, Pauline and Emmy must stay together. Let's try the

Franklins. Clara could use two willing helpers with that rascal, Del, and another on the way."

Clara was easy. Del was fretful with his first molar, and the thought of two little girls to distract him was welcome. Abbie's spirits soared, then plunged when the Simms refused her offer. They were past child rearing and had enough to do with the store. Never mind, there were others.

But the others were not so easily convinced. Many said they'd think on it, but she heard their reluctance. She had chosen families with whom she thought each child would respond well. Those families were her first hope, but if they refused, she would have to look further.

It was obvious this would not be accomplished in a day, and though Reverend Shields was gentleman enough not to press his point, she could see he doubted their ultimate success. What would she do if she couldn't place all of them?

Her back end was tired of sitting, but she was determined to see it through. "Will you attend me again tomorrow, Reverend Shields?"

"If you feel my presence is beneficial, I'll gladly do my part."

She climbed down from the buggy. "I'm certain Monte would appreciate your escorting me in his absence. And your influence is most helpful."

He bent his head. "Then I'll meet you here in the morning."

"Thank you."

◆◆◆◆◆◆◆

The morning came soon enough, and they first made the rounds of those couples who had asked to sleep on it. Abbie's spirits soared when four of them said they'd agreed to take a child. That was more than half of the orphans accounted for, and as she reached the side of the buggy, she glanced expectantly at the minister.

He smiled. "I rather suspect the Lord has his hand in this, Mrs. Farrel."

"I've always believed these children were close to His heart.

And nothing feels so good as accomplishing His plan "

"You are right about that. I've dedicated my life to that practice, but I always thought my strength was in words."

Abbie rested her hand in his as he helped her climb in. "If you'll forgive me, Reverend, out here actions mean more than words."

He dipped his head. "I believe there is need for both." He walked around and joined her.

By the time they had swept the outlying homesteads as far as the Dunbars' ranch, the sun had dropped behind the mountain crests, and the minister stopped the buggy in the yard. There were still three boys without homes. Abbie refused to feel discouraged, but she was at a loss of where to turn next. She was not willing to send even one on that horrible orphan train.

As though reading her thoughts, Reverend Shields spoke gently. "If you're willing, we'll try again tomorrow."

His words surprised her. She'd expected him to say they'd done the best they could and would have to settle for that. "Of course I'm willing, but . . . I must admit I'm not sure whom to try."

"You've thought it through as well as you could. Now we'll leave it for the Lord to say."

She nodded and walked wearily up the stairs. The children greeted her, and she responded with a cheerful smile. She'd not told any of them, yet, that their fate was being decided. She must have a joyful report for all of them before she broached the news.

At first she had approached each family with the prospect of taking the particular child she felt best suited. When she'd exhausted those choices, she'd left it to the couples to indicate their preference for a boy or girl and what age. Now she looked at the three boys unaccounted for—Michael, quiet and studious, and Jacob and Fred, slow with their studies but quick with their hands.

Abbie didn't betray the concern she felt by her expression. Surely the Lord had a place for them, a place specially suited to them. On her knees that night, she turned over her efforts. Abbie could think of no one they hadn't asked whom she found acceptable. Now it was up to God to guide them.

The next afternoon Reverend Shields came for her and drove to town. Whatever they found would be right there in Rocky Bluffs or nowhere at all. Abbie looked about her. She had slept fitfully and was no closer to a solution than when she went to bed. "I'm at a loss this morning. I can't think where to start."

Reverend Shields glanced her way. "You've not tried the Wilsons."

Abbie cringed. That had not been oversight. "I don't dare."

The minister smiled and drove to the end of Wilson Road. He pulled up in front of the judge's fine house. There was certainly room for a child, and she must not let her personal dislike of the judge and his family stand in the way of opportunity for the boys.

"Coming?"

"I think I'll wait out here." She'd be a detriment to the cause. Darla Wilson's feelings for her were mutual.

He hooked the reins. "Then allow me. Any family with only a daughter ought to welcome a studious, comely lad like our Michael. Especially when Mrs. Wilson learns that Mrs. Faulks has taken a son, as well."

He winked, and Abbie raised her eyebrows. When he returned, his smile was broader than she had seen. He climbed up and took the reins. "I suggested the boy might have a leaning to the ministry. She agreed he must, then, have every advantage."

"Why, Reverend Shields . . ."

He bowed. "Mrs. Farrel."

He clicked to the horse. "You say the other two are clever with their hands."

"Yes. And I'd like to keep them together."

"What would you think of apprenticing them?"

She hadn't considered that. "Well, they are ten and twelve. Not so very young."

He pulled up outside the wagon shop. "For some reason, Mr. Garner was heavy on my mind last night."

She climbed down and went inside with him. It seemed this

was the reverend's day, and she allowed him to speak with the bent and gnarled wagonmaker. He wasn't so old, but the rheumatism made him appear so.

He rubbed his chin at the minister's words. "Can't say it wouldn't be good to have some young hands about. Especially when I'm ailing, and the orders won't wait."

Abbie looked around at the orderly shop and felt encouraged. It was a good place for two boys to learn and grow. And Silas was near, working at the livery. She turned back to the men. "They must still attend school."

Mr. Garner appraised her. "Of course. But I will expect them to do their job. It's a valuable skill I'm imparting."

"I know you'll find them hardworking and eager."

They stepped back outside. With Jacob and Fred apprenticed to Mr. Garner, the wagonmaker, Abbie's heart soared. Reverend Shields whistled as he drove her home, then climbed down and assisted her at the stairs. She caught sight of Sirocco in the yard.

"Do stay to supper, Reverend. Monte will be delighted."

"Thank you, I will."

Abbie mounted the stairs and reached for the door. She suddenly spun. "Oh, my goodness!"

"What is it, Mrs. Farrel?"

"Why, we've placed all the children. Every one."

"That was the intention."

"But . . . I had thought Monte and I . . . I intended to keep one for us."

Reverend Shields paused. "Well, I . . . suppose you could speak with one of the kind people who . . ."

"No, no. We've set up their hopes now. I can't go back on the promise."

"With all respect, Mrs. Farrel, Mr. Farrel has hopes for children of his own."

Of course he did. She opened the door. And she would have all the newly adopted in her school in town. She drew a long breath. "Reverend Shields, you've accomplished a great thing."

He bowed. "We have together, Mrs. Farrel."

✦✦✦✦✦✦✦

Monte looked from his wife to the minister. "Every one of them?"

Reverend Shields nodded, and Abbie smiled. An unlikelier alliance he had never seen.

"Well."

Abbie turned in a swirl of skirts. "I'll have Pearl set another place for supper."

Monte stared after her. "Yes, do." Then he turned back to Reverend Shields. "My hat is off to you, sir."

"It was Mrs. Farrel, really. She twists an arm with a silken touch and talks around any obstacle until it vanishes away. One is never quite certain how one got there, but the journey was utterly painless."

Monte smiled. How well he knew.

"She decided in advance the best possibilities for each child, then together we pursued them. Even when she received more regrets than acceptances, she was undaunted."

"A remarkable feat."

"A remarkable lady. With a heart like hers I don't doubt I'll find a willing help in any concern."

Monte chuckled. "No doubt. Mrs. Farrel is not one to contemplate when action will serve. Have you heard she's teaching the town children since the . . . loss of Miss Plochman?"

"Oh yes, I'd heard."

"She's also privately tutoring my stable boy, but don't let on that I know."

"She has a heart for knowledge."

"A heart for many things, not least this territory."

The reverend drew himself up. "That, sir, I can well believe."

Monte stifled his smile. After a few days with Abbie, the young reverend was clearly smitten.

✦✦✦✦✦✦✦

After dinner, Abbie saw the children to bed. They had taken

the news with general acceptance, if some trepidation. It would be an adjustment, but she was certain the families chosen would do their best for them. She tucked the covers up to Tucker's chin.

"Will you really be my sister?"

"Yes, Tucker. My Mama and Pa are going to be yours, too. And my brother, Grant, will be your brother and my sister, Sadie, another sister for you. What do you think of that?"

"Can I still come see you here?"

"Yes, you may. And I'll come see you, too." She turned down the wick and kissed his forehead. "Sleep, now. Tomorrow you all go to your new homes."

She went out and settled into the library. Reverend Shields had gone, and business of Cole's had taken Monte out. She was glad for the solitude. Though the day had been as successful as she could have hoped, she felt a mingled sadness. Things changed so swiftly.

The mission was gone. With the children no longer in her home, it would be truly over. Father Dominic had fulfilled his charge, and she, too, had done her part. But inside it left an emptiness. The board had hopes of a new permanent teacher for the town school come spring, and she would be relieved of that task, as well.

The door opened and Frances came in. Abbie sighed. Frances had a gift for appearing when Abbie's defenses were down, though at the moment she looked more fragile herself. No doubt Kendal's absence at supper disturbed her. Frances went to the shelf and took down a volume of Emily Dickinson, then sat in the leather wing chair.

Abbie glanced up to find Frances watching her with the book unopened in her lap. There was no contempt in her gaze. She looked quite frank and almost vulnerable. Her voice was low.

"I need poetry tonight. I always do when it's cold and dreary in the winter doldrums. Why is that, do you think?"

"Perhaps it brings thoughts of the coming spring and bolsters your hope."

Frances shook her head. "I have no hope."

"You mustn't despair, Frances. I know things seem bleak to you, but it's only a matter of time."

Frances smiled faintly. "I believed I had seen the worst through the war and what followed. But it wasn't. At least then everyone suffered the same. I wasn't alone. Here . . ." She spread her hands.

"But what are you suffering, Frances? Monte and I are happy to have you here, and Kendal is working to reestablish himself. You have Jeanette . . ."

Frances laughed softly. "I should be satisfied. Maybe I am. I don't know anymore. Nothing makes sense to me here."

"You'll get used to it."

"I don't want to get used to it. I want to go home."

What could she say? Frances's honesty deserved no less. "You will make a home here, Frances."

"I don't have what it takes."

"Look at yourself. How long has it been since Kendal produced your smelling salts or calmed a fit of vapors? You're stronger than you think."

Frances ran her finger over the book. "Did you know Sharlyn couldn't read?"

"Yes. I used to read to her."

"Monte detests ignorance."

"He was very patient with her."

"As only Monte can be." Frances laughed, but it was mirthless. "He was always one to overlook another's shortcomings but never his own. Kendal forgets only his own."

"He's trying very hard."

"He brought me here. I shall never forgive him that."

"Oh, Frances, don't say so! He only wants to make it up to you."

"You've no idea what he wants. Nor do I. Do you know why I married him?"

Abbie shook her head.

"He reminded me of my father before the war. Tall and handsome and a little reckless. I had no idea how reckless."

"He'll be more careful now."

"Does a leopard change its spots?"

"People learn from their mistakes."

Frances raised her chin. "Kendal is drawn to unsavory types. Were he not a gentleman, he would be a crook."

Abbie stared.

"Does that shock you? Of course it must. Your only connection to our world is Monte, true and wholly honorable. But I assure you, sometimes pedigree breeds decadence—not overtly, perhaps, but inwardly. Kendal is a gentleman, but he's also a rogue."

"I am sorry." Abbie met her eyes. What she saw made her ache.

"He called your name in his sleep last night." Frances looked away. "I wonder if Monte knows. . . ."

Abbie's chest tightened. Whatever denial she might speak seemed false and dishonest in light of Kendal's recent behavior. Words stuck in her throat. Frances opened the book, flipped the page, and read.

✦✦✦✦✦✦✦

Cole caught Monte by the wrist before he dipped his hand in the water. "It's strychnine. Look at the animals."

Monte stared at the fallen beasts. Eighteen of them collapsed at the edge of the half-frozen water hole. The moonlight shone on their hides. He felt his jaw tighten. "So much for rustlers."

"I reckon you're right."

"Who then?"

"I don't know."

Monte paced. "Have you seen anything like this before?"

"Like and worse."

"For what purpose?"

"Control."

Monte stared at the cow at his feet. He knew what Cole was saying, but he had not thought to find that sort of trouble here.

"I reckon we need more men," Cole tucked his thumbs into his belt, "to watch . . . and take care of business when it comes to it."

Business. Monte toed the cow's frothy muzzle. This was not business. But Cole was right. They could not afford to be careless. He had little spare after guaranteeing Kendal's debts, but there was no choice.

"Take on hands, then. Tell them only what's necessary."

"Yes, sir."

Eighteen

Abbie stared through the canvas flap at the tent city sprung up virtually overnight. The city of railroad men. But not only men—there were gaunt women and even children. A cold January drizzle kept the women and children in the tents, though the hammer blows and hollers of the men never ceased.

Abbie had ridden a good eighteen miles when she learned Sadie was among the workers at the front of the tracks. Within weeks, the rails would be through to town, but she couldn't wait that long to see her sister. Now she was glad she hadn't.

Sadie finished changing the baby, and Abbie turned. At least Joe and Sadie's tent had a wood plank floor and a real four-poster bed with quilts. For a kitchen she had a separate tent with a stove, not merely a fire pit chiseled from the frozen ground. Little Matthew had a bearskin on his cot, and baby Hannah's cradle was piled high with feather ticks and quilts.

"She's like the princess and the pea." Sadie brushed a strand of mousy brown hair from her forehead.

"Are you warm enough?" She couldn't hide the concern in her voice. "Won't you stay with me?"

"Joe needs to be here with the men, even though he is the foreman. The children and I could have stayed in Denver, but I didn't want to be apart."

"No, of course not. But . . ."

Sadie faced her. "I didn't marry into a mansion. But it doesn't mean we're not happy or well cared for."

Abbie flushed. "I didn't mean that."

"Joe's putting enough aside to build us a nice home—maybe when this line is through." Sadie bounced the baby on her hip. "I will be glad when we can settle, though, and stop worrying whether Joe will make it home each night."

"Why wouldn't he?"

"Rail wars. Different lines vying for the same passage. Some crews have seen violence—tracks and supplies blown up, laid again the next day, and blown up again the following night. Actual armies guard the workings day and night."

Abbie stared at her. "Sadie!"

"Don't worry. No one's fighting to get to Rocky Bluffs, being just a side spur and all." Sadie laughed. "And I always thought you'd be the one living the adventure, off with Blake somewhere."

The ache touched her. Abbie took baby Hannah and hugged her neck. It was the first she'd seen of the baby, as she had not seen Sadie since before Blake's death, and they hadn't corresponded as well as they should. How could she relate all the feelings and confusion? She sighed. "Blake was like a brother to me. I loved him as I do Grant."

Sadie smiled with Mama's warm brown eyes. Sometimes even her expressions looked like Mama's—especially now, with her I'm-not-sure-I-believe-you look.

"I miss him, but it was never like that. It was Monte I loved."

"And he's a fine man, Abbie. A true gentleman." She giggled. "Don't."

"I can't help it. My little sister, the ruffian, married to a southern gentleman. How I wish I could have seen the wedding."

"I wish you could have, too, though I assure you I deported myself just fine, thank you." She would not discuss what happened after. If Sadie heard it from someone else, so be it.

Sadie laughed. "I'll check the water." She passed through the back to the other tent and returned with two cups. The coffee steam rose up. "Mmm. Puts heart into one, doesn't it?"

Abbie did not tell her she drank coffee only in the morning. She wondered how long it had been since Sadie had tasted tea. She set the baby down to crawl.

Sadie sipped. "What a treat to be together again. And Grant here, too."

"Oh yes, Grant." Abbie rolled her eyes.

"Now, Abbie . . ."

"I can't help it. I want to kick him every time I see Marcy Wilson on his arm. What can he be thinking?"

"That she has a pretty face, and she does; that her father's the judge; that it's high time he was married . . ."

"Don't even say that!" Abbie set down her cup with a clang on the trunk. "You don't have to live here. Can you imagine having to swallow that pill every time you wanted to see Grant?"

"Have you told him how you feel?"

"Only once. And I don't dare repeat it. Monte says it's a gentleman's natural inclination to defend his own. If I spoke my mind, I might drive Grant to it."

"You know how he defends the underdog."

"Underdog. Marcy's a coyote in pussycat fur. Makes my skin crawl. Do you suppose Grant's kissed her?"

"Abbie!"

Abbie brushed back her hair. "Well, I can't help wondering."

"I'm surprised at you, though why I should be, I don't know. You always did say whatever popped into your head."

"I am trying. Monte's sister, Frances, is taking great delight in pointing out all my improper speech. It's really impossible, you know. She'll never approve of me. What's so funny?"

"When have you ever cared what anyone—especially any lady—thought of you?"

"Of course I care."

"Oh, Abbie. From the time you were small you did whatever pleased you, and the devil take anyone who didn't like it. Remember Marcy Wilson making fun of your short skirt? Did you take it to heart? Indeed not. You intentionally hiked it an inch above your knee and asked Blake if he didn't like it better that way. Naturally, the scoundrel boy agreed he'd like it even shorter, and Marcy was perfectly scandalized. I was, too, but I couldn't bear to scold when you'd held your own so bravely."

Abbie laughed. "I don't remember that, but Marcy has always brought out my worst. It's a gift of hers."

"Then let's not speak of her. Tell me all the news."

"The biggest news is the railroad coming in. People are speculating how it will change things."

"And it will."

"I know. Even seeing the rails across the prairie shook me. It looked so . . . settled."

Sadie smiled. "It's progress."

"Noise and smoke. Hustle and bustle."

"That's not the worst of it. It's the vultures that follow."

"Vultures?"

"Gambling dens and dance halls."

"Not in Rocky Bluffs."

"Just wait and see."

After their visit Abbie rode back through town. She looked at the frame buildings, the folks on the boardwalks, the horses at the posts. The town had a pleasant bustle. She read the signs as she passed: *Peterson's Hardware, Simms General Mercantile, Mrs. Munson Clothier,* and *Men's Haberdashery,* which opened just last week. She passed three saloons, the post office, the hotel, and her pa's newspaper office with the Western Union telegraph inside.

Reverend Shields' small frame church, the school, the frame skeleton of the new courthouse, the scatter of houses on side lanes . . . Rocky Bluffs. It couldn't become a city. Not like what Sadie described. Why did the train have to come through?

She urged Shiloh past the last buildings. Monte expected her home when he returned from whatever business he was conducting. He would not allow her out past dark, and lately he seemed tense and troubled. He didn't tell her why, and she didn't ask. If he wouldn't trust her on his own, she would not interfere.

She sensed he would forbid her going anywhere if he thought she'd listen. He insisted on escorting her to town as long as she continued teaching, and he frowned at her solitary rides. He would not have approved the trip today. The distance to the railroad camp and her detour through town had pressed the limit of the short daylight.

She hurried home, but Monte had not yet returned. She settled down in the library with *Canterbury Tales*. The fire burned warm, and she sank into the leather chair. She looked around at the shelves of books, wooden paneling, and cut-glass lanterns.

Sadie's canvas walls would be wet tonight. But she was happy, she and her husband and her babies. They worked hard and had little, but they were happy. Sadie had always possessed a gift for contentment, and her life was simple, uncomplicated. Abbie sighed.

✦✦✦✦✦✦✦

The noise of new construction and the excitement of speculation filled the streets of Rocky Bluffs. Monte watched the hubbub from Reverend Shields' porch. He leaned against the wall and sipped the coffee the minister had provided. The day was unseasonably warm for February and fair.

"Big things are coming to Rocky Bluffs. With the railroad through, business will flourish, families will settle . . ."

"Vice will reign."

"Oh, come now."

"Look at it." Reverend Shields pointed to the two-story building taking shape just beyond the livery. The new hotel.

Monte knew it was not the lodging that disturbed Winthrop Shields. It was the tent of prostitutes set up behind it. Women waiting to take up residence in the upstairs rooms but already plying their wares in the tent. The objections of the town council did nothing to keep men away—not once word was out.

Across the street, the Gates of Paradise Dance Hall and Gambling Emporium had opened its doors. And just beyond that stood the raw pine railroad station, small but serviceable. Other businesses were coming, but Monte supposed Reverend Shields was right. The railroad was bringing more than progress.

"Still, the transfer of goods will improve. The train coming in this morning begins a new era for Rocky Bluffs. No more freighting by wagon, no more driving cattle over endless miles. Now only to the stockyards to be loaded onto the cars."

"That will help you, I know."

"And others—the smaller ranchers especially, who haven't the manpower for the drives."

"I've heard you're carrying a good number of hands."

"Have you?" Monte shifted on the bench. "Well, there's work to be done."

Monte stood as Abbie bounded up the walk to the porch, two paper-wrapped parcels in her arms. He relieved her of them. "Did you find what you wanted?"

"Yes."

"Will you drop off the cloth with Mrs. Munson?"

"Heavens, Monte. If I can't make a skirt and shirtwaist for gardening . . ." She spun suddenly at the sound of the train whistle. "It's coming."

"Shall we go and see?" Monte glanced at the minister who was beaming at Abbie's arrival. "Reverend?"

"By all means."

Monte held his arm to Abbie, and Reverend Shields followed. They joined the crowd at the end of the street and watched the engine, hung with banners and streamers, chug along the track to a steamy stop before the station.

Monte looked at the townsfolk, alight with excitement. Joshua stood at the front of the crowd, pad in hand. He'd have stories to last him a good while. Beside him Selena hugged Sadie, and Sadie's husband, Joe, stood tall. He and his crew had accomplished the task, bringing the railroad to Rocky Bluffs. The cheers and hoots as the first passengers disembarked rivaled anything Monte had heard.

He glanced at Abbie. She showed none of the gaiety of those around them. He patted her hand tucked into his arm. "Don't fret, Abbie. It'll become commonplace soon enough."

She gave him a halfhearted smile. Over her head he caught the eye of Captain Gifford. Involuntarily, Monte stiffened. Jake Gifford took the cigar from his teeth and nodded. Monte nodded back.

Marv Peterson, newly elected mayor, stepped onto the platform. "Ladies and gentlemen. This is a great day for Rocky Bluffs. . . ."

Abbie squeezed his arm, and Monte leaned his ear close.

"I've seen enough. Let's go."

Monte whispered his farewell to Reverend Shields and led her out of the crowd. "What is it, Abbie?"

"I want to go to the mountains."

"Now?"

"Right now. I want to feel the wind in my face and hear the birds and smell the pine."

"Abbie . . ."

"Please, Monte. Take me. Up behind Pa's ranch, where we picnicked once. Do you remember?"

"Of course I do."

She tugged his hand, and Monte followed. He tossed her parcels under the seat and handed her into the buggy. They drove into the hills and up the pine-clad slopes of the Rocky Mountains. Monte could almost feel her trembling beside him.

When the slope became too steep, he stopped, and she jumped down. "Come with me, Monte." Lifting her skirts, Abbie plunged up the mountainside, panting and stumbling and leaping from one rocky outcropping to another. They were higher than he'd ever gone, and still she kept on.

"Abbie . . ."

She didn't listen. She scrambled over a ridge and cut up the cleft. He could hear water, then presently saw the spring breaking from the rocky wall and cascading down the side. Abbie reached for the jutting rock and dug in the toe of her boot.

Monte caught her arm and held her back. "Stop, Abbie. You can't go up there." He turned her, and there were tears in her eyes. He closed her into his arms. "My darling, what is it?"

"I can't stand it."

He held her while she cried into his neck. He felt as though he held a wild creature, somehow more connected to this mountain than the life he gave her. It hurt. Yet on some level it touched him deeply. "Abbie." He stroked her hair. "Change is inevitable."

"I hate it."

He kissed the crown of her head, raised her face and kissed her wet cheeks, then her mouth, salty with tears. She kissed him back fiercely, and a warm urgency filled him. What was this woman? Would he ever understand her?

He kissed her throat and felt her pulse quicken. Never had he felt more one, yet so vastly different at once. He wanted her. He needed her. And God had given her to him. What he did with her on the mountain seemed more sacred than anything else in this life. She was bone of his bone, flesh of his flesh.

He cradled her head from the rough ground and gave her one last lingering kiss. He ran a finger over her cheek, and she smiled. "That's better." He eased her into his lap and leaned against the rocky mountain wall.

She cradled her head into his neck. "I'm sorry, Monte. I don't know what got into me."

He chuckled. "Don't apologize."

She pinched him. "I mean for leaving town."

He shrugged. "You see one train, you've seen them all. But this . . ." He swept his arm across the expansive view. "Now this is worth seeing."

He watched her take in the scene, her expression so acute it made him ache. He almost wished now that the train had never come. Yet as he looked down over the hills and out to the plain with the single line of track, he was amazed by the emptiness. He tugged a strand of her hair. "I think there's still room."

She turned. "Room for what?"

"Your dreams."

She leaned against him, smiling gently.

He kissed the corner of her mouth. "If we don't go down, we'll lose the daylight."

"I know. Thank you, Monte."

"For what?"

"Understanding."

He didn't tell her that as long as he lived, he'd only scratch the surface.

Nineteen

$\mathbf{M}$onte surveyed the line of fence posts hacked down, the wire trampled and twisted on the ground.

Beside him, Cole rubbed the back of his neck. "Reckon we found our hole."

Breck Thompson rode up beside them. "I make the count sixty-five."

"Sixty-five!" Monte turned in the saddle. "Sixty-five cattle gone?"

"As well as I can make out. The men gathered in the stragglers."

"We can't afford these losses. See that it stops. I don't care what it takes." Monte turned Sirocco and took him through the breach.

"Where're you headin'?" Cole called.

"To see Ephart and Dunbar."

Monte rode hard across the plain. He made Dunbar's ranch within the hour and dismounted at the house. He led Sirocco to the trough, but before the horse finished, the door opened, and Mary Dunbar hailed him.

"Good afternoon, Mary. Is John in?"

"He's out with the men. But I've just baked a winter apple pie."

"That's a worthy temptation, but my errand won't keep."

"Well, I'm sorry to hear that. How's Abbie?"

"Still filling in at the school and getting ready for spring planting. She's planning an ornamental garden."

"I'll have to see it when she's done."

"I'm sure she'd like that." Monte tossed the reins over Sirocco's neck and remounted. "Can you tell me which way?" She pointed and he headed south. Dunbar's spread comprised his 160-acre homestead. It shouldn't be too hard to find the herd.

As Monte approached, John Dunbar pulled the wire tight and hammered in the clamp, then wiped his face with his kerchief and stood. "Monte." He reached up and shook the hand Monte extended. "What brings you down my way?"

"Sixty-five head stolen."

"Stolen?"

"It looks that way. I wanted to see how you and Brock are faring."

"I've lost no stock. I heard about the trouble you had with rustlers before. But I thought you'd run them off."

"I'm not certain it was rustlers."

"Not rustlers—but who else?"

"I don't know. I'd hoped maybe you'd heard something."

Dunbar shook his head. "I spoke with Brock Ephart just last week. He said nothing about losses."

"Well, I guess I'll see if anything's changed since then."

"Good luck."

Monte nodded. What did he expect? He had no doubt as he rode that Ephart would tell him the same as Dunbar. And when he rode south to Hodge's place and on to Bates' Lazy L, he'd hear the same there, too.

It was his ranch alone Captain Gifford wanted to take down, if indeed it were Gifford. Monte shook his head. If it was a fight Jake Gifford wanted, he'd learn what the Lucky Star was made of. And Montgomery Farrel, as well, so help him God. Monte closed his hands around the reins and felt the leather burn as Sirocco leaped forward at his word.

✦✦✦✦✦✦✦

Abbie felt stifled in the cozy warmth of the parlor. Where was Monte? What kept him so late? He was never absent from dinner, certainly not without word.

"Now, then." Frances held herself primly in the wing chair. "If you wish someone to notice you, don't rush at them. Rather position yourself in their way as though by accident."

Abbie walked to the mantle and studied the picture of Monte's father. "That's hardly honest. Why is subterfuge good manners?"

"Because that's the way it's done. Suppose you fling yourself at someone who doesn't want to speak with you. What choice have they? But put yourself in their path, and they can either notice you or change course."

Abbie could just picture Frances changing course. She saw the flicker in her eyes as she said it. *For Mama*, she reminded herself. And she had asked for the help. She sighed. Well, maybe one day all this silliness would come in handy.

"Ladies may show, but never show *off* their children, especially when introducing them to strangers. But then, you don't have to worry about that yet, do you?"

Abbie felt a burning in her chest. Was that an honest observation, or a barb sent right to her heart? The latter she supposed. She bit her lip. Why hadn't she conceived yet? It was surely not for lack of trying. Had Frances any idea how badly she wanted to bear Monte's child?

"Are you listening?"

Abbie startled. "I'm sorry. Please repeat that."

"I said it is unbecoming to exhibit petulance. No matter how angry you might be, your countenance must never show it."

How well Frances obeyed that one. Except for her eyes, she kept her face cool and serene even when Kendal staggered in late or Jeanette had a tantrum.

"Cleanliness of person is required at all times. Slovenly habits destroy character. And if . . ." She looked up at the tap on the door.

Monte came in. He had obviously changed into fresh pants and shirt, but his face was worn and tired. Relieved, Abbie almost hurried to him, then thought better of it and kept her place at the mantle. She was in his path.

He came directly to her, and she felt a rush of warmth. He kissed her forehead. "Forgive my missing supper."

"Where were you? I was worried." And it had been dull and difficult dining alone with Frances and her instructions on table etiquette. Frances was taking smug delight in her training.

"I needed to see some ranchers. It was a good long way." He turned. "Is Kendal home?"

"No." Frances's voice and face were smooth.

It sent a pang through Abbie to see her so. She brushed Monte's arm. "I'll have Pearl fetch your supper."

"Yes, thank you, Abbie."

◆◆◆◆◆◆◆

Kendal staggered back from the brass-edged bar. The room swam, then cleared. He stepped forward and banged his knee on a chair back.

"Watch it, mister."

Kendal steadied himself and passed through the crowd to the doors. They swung open, and he propelled himself onto the boardwalk and grasped the post. He had quite possibly exceeded himself tonight. But he had cause to celebrate. The deal presented him that night would make his fortune ... again. The stars streaked when he looked up, and where was his horse?

A hand gripped his shoulder. "Kendal?"

Kendal staggered as he turned. He couldn't place ... ah yes. Abbie's brother. The lawyer ... though his name eluded him at the moment.

"You're looking a little green."

"I s'pose I yam." Grant. That was the name.

Grant took him by the shoulder. "You won't make it to the ranch in this condition. You'd better stay the night in my room."

Kendal leaned on Grant along the boardwalk to the old hotel. It was quieter than its rival. The way he felt just now, that was fine with him. They crossed the lobby, sidestepping the dining room tables with the chairs upended atop.

"You're up late."

Grant steered him toward the stairs. "I had work to do."

Kendal clicked his tongue. " 'See saw, Margery Daw, Johnny shall 'ave a new master. He shall have but a penny a day, because . . . he can't work any faster.' "

"Something like that."

Kendal slung his arm over Grant's shoulders, and they started up. The stairs would not hold steady. He caught his boot on the edge, and only Grant's strength kept him up. "I think . . . I should not have had . . . that last one. I'm afraid I am . . . inebriated."

"Yeah."

Kendal swayed while Grant worked the key in the door and pushed it open.

"Go ahead and take the bed. But if your stomach wants emptying, hit the chamber pot and not my linens."

"You're a good friend." Kendal staggered to the bed and collapsed. One leg hung over the side, but it was altogether too much trouble to pull it up. He closed his eyes.

Grant sat down on the chair and pulled off his boot. Kendal started snoring before he'd removed the second one. He unbuttoned his vest and tossed it on the bureau, then his shirt and trousers, down to his long johns. With a good tug he freed a blanket from under Kendal and wrapped it around himself, then curled up in the chair.

This wasn't the first time he'd seen Kendal have too much. But he hadn't seen him so badly off as tonight. The man would have broken his neck if he had managed to mount his horse and start for home. Kendal might wish he had, come morning.

Grant pulled the blanket tighter and put his feet up on the end of the bed. Kendal's snoring gained strength. It was going to be a long night.

◆◆◆◆◆◆◆

"No, Kendal." Monte kept his voice low.

"But surely you see the advantage to getting in early. Why, with this information we can purchase railroad land low and sell at tremendous profit. You've already seen the stir the train has made in Rocky Bluffs. That will only continue wherever the rails run."

"I said no."

"The return on your loan would be more than doubled. It . . ."

"It smells."

"What are you suggesting?"

"I don't trust those men. Have you no judgment of character?"

"Of course they seem different. They're English." Kendal rubbed his hand through his hair. Though cleaned and meticulously dressed, Monte saw the bloodshot eyes, the skin of his face, pale and flaccid. If Kendal's head had stopped aching from his excess of last night, it had surely started again from the bite of Frances's tongue.

"Come, Kendal. I've been to England, as have you. Did you at any time have difficulty distinguishing the gentlemen from the lower classes?" Monte stood. "These two . . . they're not one and not the other. They remind me of the carpetbaggers—well dressed and spoken, but inside vulgar and corrupt."

"Some of the carpetbaggers are men like ourselves trying to make their way. We cannot spend the rest of our lives bemoaning the fate of the South."

"I have no intention of doing so. But have you learned nothing from it?"

"I've learned to take my opportunity as it comes."

"So I've seen. And at what price." Let Kendal take offense. "There is honest work and sound investing. Yes, buy land, Kendal. God knows, it's land that matters, the difference between free and bond. Purchase a spread and set yourself up. There's profit in ranching."

"Slow profit."

"Honest profit."

"Meaning?"

"Just what I said."

"Would you accuse me then of dishonesty?"

Monte drew a long breath. "I am not accusing you. But I'll

have no part in this venture. I warn you to stay free, as well."

Kendal's eyes narrowed. "When I need your advice, I'll ask for it."

"Just as you do my money?" Monte watched the blood rush to Kendal's face.

The door opened, and Abbie swept in. Her face was flushed and cold, her hair falling loose. "Oh, Monte, she's wonderful!"

He walked around the desk and took her hands. "Who is wonderful?"

"Zephyr."

"Abbie . . ."

"I know you said she's not ready, but truly, she's as smooth as silk. She carried me like I wasn't there and flew like the wind."

"She's skittish enough to throw you at any provocation, and she doesn't know the land."

"Well, I do."

He frowned. "Abbie, I don't want you to do this again. If you want to ride, take another horse."

Her lip jutted. "Come with me, then, and see for yourself."

Kendal stood. "He'd rather control you, my dear. It's his forte these days."

Abbie spun. "I'm sorry. I see I've interrupted you."

"We were finished," Monte said.

"Indeed we were. If you'll excuse me." Kendal strode from the room.

Abbie turned back. "I'm sorry, Monte. I didn't know you and Kendal . . ."

"It's all right. Listen, Abbie, this has nothing to do with control. Zephyr is not the kind of horse to which you're accustomed. Arabians are very high-spirited. Yes, she can fly like the wind, but she must first know that her wings are clipped."

She raised her hands to his chest. "Don't scold me. It was incredible! It's the first of March, and I've been cooped up all winter."

He took her in his arms. When she looked like that, how could he not? "My wild mountain girl! How can I hope to tame you?"

"I don't want to learn my wings are clipped. I just want to fly."

He shook his head. "Nor does Zephyr. But she will." He brushed her cheek with his fingers. He would not say he wanted her on a horse that would come home should anything happen, nor that he'd prefer she stay close to the house altogether.

He did not expect that Captain Gifford would harm her. But if she happened upon something . . . Monte would put nothing past Gifford, not after Chance. Making Abbie understand that would not be easy. He rested his cheek on her head. With any luck, she would be with child soon. Perhaps motherhood would bring her down to earth.

Twenty

The amber globe of the lamp yellowed the faces across the table from Kendal. They sat in the corner of the hotel, the noise around them sufficient for secrecy. "As I told you, gentlemen, Mr. Farrel is not a risk taker."

"Of course there's risk, Stevens. No venture worth pursuing is without risk." William Emmerson spoke in his horsy accent. Kendal noticed it more since Monte had pointed it out. Perhaps the man was not what he seemed, but who was?

"You're astute enough to see the possibilities, aren't you?"

The possibilities and the consequences. So far they had spoken in vague assurances. Now he wanted more. "I want details."

Emmerson exchanged a glance with Harris next to him. "We handle the details. Less chance of word getting out that way. One slip and our competitors will be on this deal like wasps on a honeycomb."

"Save your blather for the stooges you'll be selling to."

Emmerson narrowed his eyes. "We're only thinking of your welfare. The fewer in the know, the better chance of success. And you want to be part of that success, don't you, Mr. Stevens?"

Kendal sat back in his chair and ran his hand over the waxed end of his mustache. He glanced at Harris, silent as usual. "Maybe I do, maybe I don't. If I'm putting up the earnest money, I need more of a guarantee."

"Such as?"

"First, I want to know the deal."

Again the men shared a glance. "It's very simple, Mr. Stevens.

221

You buy the land low, we sell it high."

"Where and how?"

"Investors from London and New York."

"What's to keep me from doing the same without you?"

"Have you contacts in the North? What entrance do you have, sir, to the monied Yankees, if I might be so bold?"

Kendal's jaw tightened.

"Or perhaps you know of southern gentlemen who came off as well as your brother-in-law?"

That rankled. No one prospered like Monte. "And you have these contacts?"

Emmerson sat back magnanimously. "With our foot in the door, your success is guaranteed. Everywhere the railroad goes the land skyrockets."

"Not everywhere. These plots are stretches of barren country between townships. I checked. I rode them myself."

The man smiled indulgently. "Yes, but that's our little secret."

"What other secrets have you?"

Emmerson cracked his knuckles. Definitely not a gentlemanly sound. "How scrupulous are you, Mr. Stevens?"

"How lucrative is it?" Now he would get some answers.

Emmerson chuckled. "Oh, you won't be sorry."

Kendal leaned back and studied them in silence. So it wasn't on the up and up, as Monte had said. But Montgomery Farrel lived by a code that was as outdated and disarrayed as the southern dreams that had spawned it. Men dealt differently these days, and those with less scruples rose above others more tightly fettered, as he had seen with his last partners. This time he would not go in with his eyes closed. Still, he held his silence.

"All right, Stevens."

Kendal turned to Harris, surprised the man had spoken. Usually he let Emmerson spin the tale.

"We need front money to acquire the titles, pay our travel and expenses, advertise the goods, and pretty up the offering. It's a lay that requires each of us to play our part with discretion. After the sale you receive your share, we receive ours."

"And what's to keep you from disappearing with the lot?"

Emmerson drew himself up. "You have my word as a gentleman."

"Oh, come, Emmerson, even were you a gentleman, I would not take your word."

Sobering, the man asked, "What, then?"

"Your daughter."

Leaning forward, Emmerson glared at him. "What of 'er?" His sudden consternation caused the cockney slip, no doubt.

"Once I hand over the funds she goes into my custody until I receive my portion."

Emmerson glanced at Harris, who sat stone faced, then back to Kendal. "Where?"

"Here at the hotel, in comfortable accommodations. As long as all goes well, no harm comes to her."

Emmerson's fingers tightened on the glass. "Well, I don't . . ."

"Agreed." Harris said.

Kendal waited for Emmerson. His right eye twitched, but he nodded slowly.

Kendal finished his drink. "Very well. It'll take a day or so for me to acquire the funds."

Emmerson stood. He was clearly flustered.

Harris remained seated. "Contact us when you're ready, but . . . time is of the essence."

"I realize that." Kendal stood. He did not extend his hand. Now that they understood each other it was not necessary. He had lain down with the dogs.

When the doors swung closed behind Kendal Stevens, Emmerson turned on Harris. "What d'ya mean by lettin 'im 'ave my girl?

"That's not a concern."

"Well, it's a concern to me. She's but fourteen with no mother to care for her. She's not part of this."

"She is now, if that's what it takes to secure Mr. Stevens. Don't worry, Emmerson. There's more than one dog to set on a man."

"Meaning?"

Harris pulled a crumpled paper from his pocket and licked the end of his pencil, then carefully penned:

Mrs. Stevens
c/o Montgomery Farrel
Lucky Star Ranch

Dear Madame,
Be advised your husband strays.

Emmerson leaned forward. "What does it say?" Harris read it, and Emmerson sputtered, "That insinuates that my Patricia—"

"Insinuates only. I doubt Mr. Stevens goes in for children. And if he does ... well, she's bound to get the education sooner or later. I'll hold this until the time is right, then have it delivered. There is no fury like a woman scorned. We'll get Patricia easy enough."

He drained his glass. "Once we've multiplied Steven's offering, we'll retrieve the girl and be on our way with Mr. Stevens holding the bag." He sent Emmerson a sharp look until the man nodded. No doubt the mention of money went a long way toward easing his fears.

◆◆◆◆◆◆◆

The house was quiet when Kendal went in. He handed James his coat and hat, then made for the study. No doubt Monte had retired with Abbie. Frances would be in bed, not that it meant anything for him. Her intent was clear: to exclude him until he restored their wealth and standing.

And that he would do. He pushed open the door. He would not remain dependent. He would beg, borrow, or steal to get the funds for this deal, and then he would repay his self-righteous brother-in-law every cent. He strode to Monte's desk, pulled open the drawer, and paused.

There was a thick portfolio immediately on top. Did Monte keep his things so carelessly? Glancing up, he listened, then took out the folder. He struck a match to the lamp and swiftly scanned the documents. He looked closer at one and then the next two. "Hmm . . . in Abbie's name . . ." Now, what could he do with that?

He studied the corresponding figures. Well, well, well. If he played his hand right . . . and he was not without charm. Maybe, just maybe . . . He slid the papers back in place and closed the drawer.

◆◆◆◆◆◆◆

Abbie carried Jeanette on her hip through the knee-deep snow and pulled open the stable door. So far, so good. No one had seen her from the house. At least no one had stopped her. She searched in the dim light for the tin tub hanging from the wall, set the child down, and stretched for it.

"I'll help you," Will said, coming out of the back.

"Thank you, Will."

"What's this for?"

"I want to give Jeanette a slide on the hill."

He grinned. "I can do better than that." He went to the back, stooped, and pulled out a wooden toboggan.

"Where did you get that?"

"Made it. I pulled apart some old barrels and refitted the slats. Come on, I'll show you."

Abbie straightened Jeanette's muffler and made sure her mittens were snug, then lifted her and followed Will outside. "How are you enjoying *Robinson Crusoe*?"

"It's a little tough."

"The challenge is good. It sharpens your skills."

"I knew you'd say that."

She scanned the hill as he settled the toboggan. The slope behind the corral looked gentle, but steep enough to afford a good slide as long as they stayed out of the trees to the side. Abbie sat, then gathered Jeanette into her lap.

Will grabbed the back of the sled. "Ready?"

Abbie nodded.

He gave them a shove, then jumped onto the back. The slope

was faster than she thought. She should have tried it without the baby. But Jeanette laughed as she squeezed her tighter. She had never heard Jeanette laugh so. She snuggled her face close. The sled slowed as the land evened out.

"That was wonderful!"

Jeanette clapped her mittened hands and laughed again. It was an incredible sound. What did it matter that Frances would have vapors if she knew? This was the happiest she had ever seen the child.

Abbie grabbed her into her arms. "Let's do it again."

Will tugged the sled. "It'll go faster if we follow the same line, now the snow's packed some."

"I think that's all right. It runs straight."

"Long as you don't lean. Don't want to shoot into the trees there."

Abbie followed his point to the cottonwoods, bare of leaves but bushy with undergrowth. "I won't lean."

The next ride was faster, and the next faster yet. Her cheeks chapped in the cold, and her hair came loose, but Abbie had not been sledding since she and Blake took the hill behind the McConnel's barn. Each time she stood at the bottom, she rebundled Jeanette. "Enough?"

"More."

Abbie laughed aloud. "A girl after my own heart." She couldn't wait to tell Monte that Jeanette had spoken, though he'd laugh when he heard her first word. She trudged to the top, placing her feet in each of Will's tracks.

"Looks like fun."

Abbie jumped. Kendal stood just above them. She would catch it now.

"I hope you don't mind. March snow is the best of the season, and I hated for Jeanette to miss it."

"I'd have taken her myself if I'd known there was a toboggan." Abbie smiled. "She's quite the scamp. Not a bit afraid."

"Mind if I have a run?"

Will shrugged. "Sure, if you want to."

"Keep the child, will you?" He took Jeanette from Abbie and placed her at Will's feet, then motioned. "After you."

Abbie glanced down. "Would you like to ride alone?"

"Now, where's the fun in that?"

Reluctantly she sat, and Kendal shoved off and jumped on. He wrapped his arms around Abbie.

"Don't lean. Kendal, don't lean!"

The sled skewed off the track. The unpacked snow flew up, powdery and choking. The toboggan shot into the air, then plunged into the fringe of cottonwoods. They crushed through the twiggy brush, and Abbie flung up her elbow as they banked off the roots of a cottonwood and flipped over.

Snow stung her neck beneath the scarf and clung to her hair. Lying back, she released her breath.

Kendal leaned over her. "Are you all right?"

"I think so."

"I'm sorry. It was entirely my fault."

She sat up and shook the snow from her hair. Will and Jeanette were lost to view, nor could Will climb down with the child. "Well, no harm done."

She started to rise, but Kendal pulled her up. "Are you certain you're all right?"

"Yes, quite . . ."

He suddenly closed her into his arms and covered her mouth with his.

There was no taste of brandy to excuse him. Abbie pressed her fists to his chest. "Kendal, how dare you!"

"How dare I not? Can't you see I'm sick with wanting you?"

The breath left Abbie's chest.

"My dear . . ."

"You would do well to stop now." She itched to slap him. She felt foul and guilty. If Monte knew . . .

Kendal trapped her against the tree trunk and leaned close. "I can be discreet."

Abbie's hand stung with the blow to his cheek as he staggered back. Her chest heaved. "And I can be dangerous." Will would hear if she screamed, but then Monte would know. What would his honor require? She dared not find out.

Kendal straightened. "I see I've shown an alarming lack of judgment."

"Lack of judgment?" She seethed.

He brushed off his coat. "Will you go to Monte with this?"

"Will I need to?"

He picked up his hat from the snow. "You've made your position clear. It won't happen again."

Will called from the top of the hill.

Abbie glared at Kendal, then called back, "It's all right, Will." She started up. "Bring the sled, Kendal."

Kendal stared after her. His pride stung more than his cheek, but the worst of it was how this might jeopardize his attaining the funds. How could he have judged her so poorly? With what Frances had told him about Abbie and Cole's intimacy, he assumed she would be an easy mark. Oh well. He reached for the sled. He would find another way.

◆◆◆◆◆◆◆

Inside the new courthouse, Abbie turned from the window and faced her brother. "Why do you ask?"

Grant smiled and laid down his pen on his desk. "Because I know you. And I can tell what you're thinking."

"I've not said anything at all against Marcy Wilson."

He stood and came around the desk. "That in itself is evidence enough. I've never known you to hold your tongue so extremely."

"It's not my business to tell you who to court or not to court . . . however much I may wish to."

Grant laughed. "Now we'll get to the truth. Tell me why I should not woo the fair daughter of the judge."

"Oh, Grant!" Abbie stomped her foot. "What can I tell you that you can't see for yourself if you'd just open your eyes?"

"I don't know. I find her intelligent, attractive, and quite charming. I've gathered that you and she have not been close, but then, you are quite different. She is a lady, and you would flee any semblance of such if you could."

Abbie jutted her chin.

"I admit your marriage to Montgomery Farrel has improved your deportment. . . ."

"Oh, you're impossible! Marry Marcy, if you like. But you'll pay the price for the rest of your life."

He caught her arm as she spun past. "Abbie, don't be angry."

Abbie sighed. "I know there are fewer ladies here than in New York, but there are other choices."

"And maybe I'll explore them."

"If you get the chance. Once Marcy attaches she clings like a leech."

"Now, Abbie . . ."

"I won't say another word. Come for supper, and I'll keep any thought of Marcy so far from my mind even you won't know it's there."

"I will, then."

Abbie smiled. "Six o'clock." Her skirts swirled behind her as she swept out the door. She blew him a kiss over her shoulder, then rounded the corner. She caught her breath as she almost landed in Kendal's arms and sprang back.

He frowned. "You needn't look as though you've encountered a rattler in the dust."

"You startled me."

He bowed. "I apologize. Actually I was looking for you."

"What is it? Has something happened?"

"No, no. It's . . . I have a rather delicate matter to discuss."

More delicate than other matters they'd discussed? Abbie flushed angrily. He had made any encounter between them distressing, especially in Frances's presence. "I'm listening."

"Perhaps I could buy you lunch?"

"No, thank you. I'm having lunch with Clara."

Kendal glanced around them, then returned his eyes to her. "First, let me say that I regret my past indiscretion. My conduct was inexcusable, and I can only attribute it to the angst of my current difficulties."

Abbie dropped her eyes. He seemed sincere, and certainly it was a difficult time for him. "I accept your apology."

He hesitated. "The business I would speak of is . . . rather more sensitive."

She waited.

"I need a certain amount of earnest money for a business venture that I think will enable me to set Frances and myself up on our own. But I . . ." He released his breath. "I can't go to Monte with it. I don't want to ask for more than he's already done."

Abbie softened. "You want me to ask?"

"No. That would be one and the same. I don't want him to think that I cannot care for his sister." He took her arm and pulled her aside to the wall as a man started down the hall toward them. Waiting until he had passed by, Kendal said, "You can't imagine how difficult this is for me to ask . . . but . . . I was hoping you could help me yourself."

Abbie stared at him. "How?"

"There are certain stock certificates held in your name."

"In my name?"

"Yes. No doubt Monte has not divulged this to you. He keeps his business to himself, I've noticed. But he has invested in your name as well as his own, and it is this that I'm hoping to borrow against for this venture."

Abbie's stomach tightened. "I don't know anything about this, Kendal."

"It's very simple. You put up your stock as collateral and sign on a loan at the bank for me, and I will pay you back substantially more than you started with when the transaction is completed."

Abbie hesitated. Why could he not go to Monte? Surely they had settled the affairs together, and Monte knew the extent of his need. She should go to Monte herself, but perhaps it was again that southern honor that she understood so little that kept Kendal from seeking the money that way.

He sighed. "I know what you think of me." His eyes fell. "And by God you have every right."

"No, Kendal, it's not that . . ." Abbie's thoughts whirled. What should she do?

"You've no idea what it costs me to beg, but I want a chance to make up to Frances for all the ways I've failed her. This is my opportunity, the one I came out here hoping to find. What little pride I have left forbids my asking Monte, but I throw myself on your generosity. . . ."

Abbie glanced down the hall to Grant's office. Maybe he could help. He would certainly understand the workings of it all and . . .

Kendal cleared his throat. "Forgive me. I'll not trouble you again."

"Wait, Kendal. I . . . all right. I'll help you."

He paused a moment as though uncomprehending, then took her hand and kissed it with a low bow. "You are the finest lady."

If Grant could only hear that. But somehow, it didn't sound quite true. Kendal held out his elbow, and she slipped her fingers through. "I really don't know what's required."

"Don't worry. I have the certificates with me, and it's an amazingly simple process."

As he said, the transaction was completed in less than three-quarters of an hour. They stepped into the street, and Kendal bowed over her hand. "I am forever in your debt." Abbie nodded, then headed slowly for Clara's house.

Twenty-One

That evening Kendal stood, elbow on the mantel, when Emmerson and his daughter entered one of two suites the hotel boasted. He would not be accused of poor hospitality. She was a comely lass, with mousy hair and freckles, but a nice shape and pleasant features. He bowed. "Good evening."

Emmerson brought her forward. "Patricia, this is Mr. Stevens."

"How do you do, Patricia. I trust the accommodations suit you?"

Patricia nodded slightly and glanced at her father. Kendal turned to him, also. "Shall we discuss our affairs in the hall?"

Emmerson nodded, turned to his daughter with a dim smile, then went out.

Kendal closed the door. "Just so there's no confusion, I'll be guarding this room carefully." That was another reason he had chosen the suite with its access only from the hall.

"That's hardly necessary."

"I find it so." He pulled the wallet from his breast pocket. "Here it is in full. Make good use of it, but I warn you, if this does not come out as you say, I will not be easy to reckon with."

"You just see that my girl is safe."

"She'll be my highest priority."

Emmerson stuffed the wallet into his coat in silent response and left.

Kendal returned to Patricia. "I've had supper laid out for you in the other room. You've nothing to fear." She nodded without moving from the spot. He turned. "Well, then, I'll be off to my own supper. Good night."

✦✦✦✦✦✦✦

Sitting on the floor of the parlor, Abbie carefully bent the stand and slid it into the slot, then stood the paper doll on the floor. "There, see?"

Jeanette snatched it up.

"Gently. Don't squeeze."

She watched the little fingers loosen as Jeanette examined the embossed paper of the ruffly hat and petticoat. "Now, then. The blue gown or the red? What do you think, Frances?"

Frances glanced down. "Redheads never wear red." She returned her attention to the fire.

"The blue, then." Abbie cut the paper dress and tucked the flaps over the doll's shoulders. "My, she's pretty."

"Pitty." Jeanette poked one small finger at the doll.

"Come, Jeanette. Time for your bath." Frances swooped over and took the child by the hand.

"No! Play Auntie."

Frances pulled her sternly, and Jeanette dug in her heels.

Abbie handed her the doll. "Go, Jeanette. We'll play again tomorrow."

The scathing look in Frances's eyes was quickly veiled as she took Jeanette out. It hurt less than the child's cries escalating to a tantrum. If only Frances would scoop her up in her arms and smother her with kisses. If only she would smile and say she loved her. No matter how Abbie tried to fill the gap, it was Frances Jeanette needed.

But Frances was untouchable, so removed she hardly seemed alive. And she seemed determined to make Jeanette the same. Abbie stole moments with the child, aching to do more, but Frances always separated them at the first opportunity. Only Mammy was allowed to hold Jeanette and soothe her temper.

Mammy would bathe her now, then tie up her hair in rags and rock her against her breast. For the life of her, Abbie would never

233

understand. And if she did bear children of her own, no mammy of any color would take her place. Abbie closed her eyes and leaned against the settee.

She jumped when Monte stormed into the room in a rare temper and closed the door behind him. "What is it, Monte?" She scrambled up from the floor.

The muscles of his jaw clenched and rippled. "I want to discuss a matter with you."

"What matter?"

"Your loan to Kendal."

Her heart fluttered. "The bank made the loan, Monte. He needed the money for . . ."

"I know what he needed it for. I turned him down."

Her heart sank. Would she never learn?

He paced before her. "Do you know what it means to sign over your stock as collateral?"

"It guarantees the loan."

"Do you know what that means?"

"Not . . . exactly. I believe it means—"

"It means that if Kendal's venture fails, you lose your stock."

Abbie nodded slowly. "He felt very confident—"

"Did you procure the certificates from my desk?"

"I didn't even know they existed. He had them with him."

"Did you not wonder at that?"

"I . . ."

"Why didn't you ask me!"

Abbie started. He had never raised his voice to her, nor to anyone in her recollection.

"I would have told you this 'deal' smacks of infamy! What guile did he use to dupe you?"

"He didn't dupe me, Monte. I wanted to help him. I didn't think—"

"You didn't think to consult your husband."

"Kendal didn't want to—"

"Be turned down again."

Abbie sat down on the settee. "I'm sorry."

Releasing his breath, Monte dropped to his knee before her. "What's done is done. But, Abbie, I must know this will not happen again. I've already stretched by investing in your name. I thought to protect you should anything happen to me and you remarry. But you are to make no financial decisions without me . . . especially if they concern Kendal. Is that understood?"

"Yes."

"Now come. I'm going to teach you somewhat of how the world works."

"A little knowledge can be a dangerous thing."

"Not near so dangerous as ignorance, I think."

♦♦♦♦♦♦♦

The next morning, Monte tapped the bell on the bank counter. "Mr. Driscoll, please."

"Certainly, Mr. Farrel." The teller hurried off.

Mr. Driscoll straightened his vest as he came forward and extended his hand. "Mr. Farrel."

"I'd like to follow up on our previous conversation."

"Ah . . . yes, of course. Come in, please." He ushered Monte into the small office in the back and closed the door. "Cigar?"

"No, thank you."

Mr. Driscoll closed the box and seated himself at the desk, motioning Monte to take the matching brass-studded wing chair across from him.

Monte sat. "When my wife and brother-in-law transacted their loan with you, did Mr. Stevens explain the nature of the business he was pursuing?"

"I . . . ah . . . regret that unfortunate business tremendously. . . ."

"You've already expressed your regrets. I assure you I hold neither you nor the bank responsible. I just want to understand the venture."

"Yes, well, it's . . . ah . . . very sound, I assure you. With the railroad coming through, the land developed along the line will be appreciated considerably. Mr. Stevens is financing the offering for two gentlemen from London working in conjunction with the railroad." He swallowed.

"The Denver Rio Grande?"

"Of course, though as I told you before, I did not require references . . . your standing with the bank and the presence of your wife . . ."

"But the gentlemen, Harris and Emmerson, were referenced."

Beads of sweat stood up on Donahue's forehead. "Well, yes. That is, their references were English, of course."

"But you checked them."

"With Mr. Stevens vouching . . . forgive me, Mr. Farrel, but as he is your brother-in-law I had no reason to doubt his word."

Monte stood. "Let's hope that's an oversight you won't pay for."

He then went directly to Sterling Jacobs' Western Union office in the front corner of the newspaper building. "I'd like to send a telegram to Denver, to the railroad office for the Denver Rio Grande."

"Certainly." Sterling Jacobs took out a pad and pencil.

"And another to New York to be posted to London. Inspector Pierce, Scotland Yard."

Sterling whistled. "No kiddin'?"

From his desk, Abbie's father looked up.

Monte shook his head. "If you don't mind, Joshua, I won't expound for the newspaper just yet."

Joshua cocked his head. "It's been a bit dry lately. I could use a good story."

"I'm hoping very much there's no story here at all. But Inspector Pierce is the one to know if there is."

After writing his inquiries, Monte left. He rode toward the ranch but dismounted out on the range. He walked Sirocco to an upended piñon stump and tied him firmly, then turned and slipped the pearl-handled revolver from its holster.

He centered the gun in his palm and raised it. He aimed for the oaks and fired, winced, then fired again and again, reloading and holstering and drawing. Wood splintered as the small branch shot from the tree. Monte breathed deeply.

◆◆◆◆◆◆◆

Kendal started up the hotel stairs for the eighth day in a row. He knocked, then turned the key in the lock and entered. Patricia sat by the fire, working the sampler as usual. The girl was certainly industrious. Glancing up as he entered, she set aside the sewing.

"And how are we tonight?"

"Fine, thank you." Her accent was clearly cockney.

"I trust you're comfortable?"

"Yes, sir."

"Not lonely?"

"Not too much."

"Good." He glanced casually at her work and nodded. "They've seen to your needs all right?" He always asked this.

"Yes, sir. Very well, sir."

Kendal paused, then followed through with his intention. "Shall I join you for supper?"

Her eyes widened. "If . . . if you like. The food is good here."

"Then I shouldn't miss it." He had already ordered for two, as supper at Monte's had become a decidedly chilled affair not only from Frances, but also Monte since he'd learned of Abbie's loan. He supposed he was lucky Monte hadn't shown him the door, but his disdain and fury were thinly concealed. Well, he'd expected that, but he needn't endure it.

In a moment the tray was brought up to the room. Kendal sat at the small table and motioned Patricia to the chair across. "Please." He would have seated her, but she seemed awkward with formalities.

She sat.

He flipped the napkin open onto his lap. She silently did likewise. He raised his fork and she raised hers. The silence stretched as they ate. It was scarcely better than supping at home. At least with Patricia there was no condemnation. She was certainly not a chatterbox, most likely scared witless by all of this. He could put her at her ease, or at least try. "Tell me of yourself, Patricia.

Your mother is dead?" He flaked the last strip of trout with his fork.

"Yes, sir."

"I'm very sorry. How do you like America?"

"Fine."

"You've no brothers or sisters?"

"My brother died of cholera."

"How very sad." Kendal glanced at her as he chewed slowly. "You and your father, you've not settled anywhere?"

She shook her head. She wasn't making this easy.

He tried a different tack. "Is there . . . a lad you cotton to?"

She dropped her gaze. "No, sir."

He sighed in exasperation. "How was the trout?"

"Good. I don't care much for fish, but this was good."

Kendal pushed aside the tray and stood. "I hope you've not found this time too tedious." There was more of a bite to his words than he intended.

"I don't mind sewing and reading some."

He half-smiled at her misunderstanding. "That's good. I wouldn't want you to be bored or lonely." He noted the flush that came to her cheeks.

He raised her to her feet, suddenly acutely aware of the warmth of her hand. "I wouldn't want you to be unhappy."

She shook her head a little stiffly and glanced back over her shoulder. He followed her gaze. The window was heavily shaded. Kendal's throat tightened. This was a treacherous path.

He reached up and stroked her hair, and she caught her breath. Her lips trembled. The danger beckoned him. He bent low and kissed her.

Her mouth was soft, uncertain. The mouth of a child. He could feel her fear. It was not what he expected, not what he wanted. He drew back, then bowed stiffly, and left.

Downstairs the bar beckoned, and he wasted no time finding a stool.

✦✦✦✦✦✦✦

Monte led Zephyr and Sirocco out to the yard where Abbie stood expectantly. "Before you mount, I'll have your word not to try anything foolish."

"I promise."

He tethered Sirocco to the post and helped Abbie up. Zephyr tossed her head, sidestepped, and flared her nostrils. Cole had worked with her some, but she was still fiery and unpredictable. Monte wished Abbie would wait, but patience did not come easily for her. He handed her the reins.

Besides, they all needed to get out. With the snow melted, the earth smelled damp and inviting, though the air was keen. He mounted Sirocco. "Ready?"

Abbie nodded. He nickered, and Sirocco set the pace. Zephyr vied with him, but Sirocco kept her back. So far Abbie allowed it. Monte glanced over his shoulder and smiled. She drew up beside him, and Sirocco quickened. Zephyr whinnied and broke into a trot.

"Abbie . . ."

Frowning, she reined the horse in. Monte smiled. His wife needed as much training as the horse. They entered the open range and Sirocco fought for his head. Monte looked at the reins in his hand, no longer wrapped on the wrist. It would be painful, but he glanced at Abbie sitting proudly on the equally proud mare. He couldn't hold them all back.

"All right, go then."

With a laugh, Abbie pressed in her knees and Zephyr bolted. Sirocco responded with no urging. Monte watched Abbie's motion on the mare. She sat her well, but then the horse's gait was smooth and even. The ground flew by beneath them until he called, then Abbie reined the mare in, and he allowed Sirocco to circle, establish himself.

"Oh, Monte, I've never felt such freedom!"

He chuckled. "Yes, I know."

They walked the horses down the slope and dismounted at the stream. He kicked away the edge of the ice and the animals drank, then he tethered them with two large rocks and took Abbie by the hand. They walked to the end of the cut, then stood together, the back of her head to his chest.

"Abbie, with you here by my side, I couldn't want for anything else. Do you remember when I told you this place held my destiny?"

"Yes."

"Now I've found it. You and I will raise up generations of Farrels who will tame this land and call it their own."

"God willing."

He stroked her hair. "Yes, God willing."

"I keep thinking to find myself with child."

"It will come."

"It's long in coming."

He turned her to face him. "Are you anxious?"

"Not anxious, really, but surprised. Mama conceived Sadie after two months of marriage. She was only eighteen, and Sadie had Matthew by nineteen."

"No matter, Abbie."

"I know how it was for you to lose your son when Sharlyn died. I want so much to give you children. I've thought of it since the first time you kissed me. Do you remember?"

His chest tightened. "Of course. I carried that moment in my heart through all the time that followed. At first it was a torturous thing, as I'm sure it was for you. I should never have presumed."

"Do you wish you hadn't?"

"I did for a time, knowing that I had hurt you so deeply. Even so, I played it again and again in my memory when I should not have."

Abbie pressed his hands in hers. "Do you think of your child still?"

"I think sometimes of what might have been had he lived, but more than that I think of what will be. Of the children you and I will have."

"I hope so, Monte."

"I know it will be so." He kissed the crown of her head.

Twenty-Two

Monte stared down at the bull. Two seasons ago he'd paid two hundred fifty dollars for it, and now it lay in the dirt, throat sliced. What manner of beast took down a Durham bull and emptied its jugular? He looked out across the land, then again to the ground at his feet. From the tracks, the bull had struggled. Its thrashing destroyed any other marks.

But nothing wild made a clean slice like the one across the bull's throat. Here again was wanton destruction. His stomach tightened. Gifford. He pictured the red lambchop whiskers, the cold, proud expression, the straight military bearing.

That they had served opposite causes was not enough to convict the man, nor the fact that he stood to gain the most should the Lucky Star fail. But something inside told Monte it was Gifford. He turned and walked to Sirocco.

The stallion would not come near the scene and scent of blood. Monte glanced back at the fouled ground, the mound of flesh. Was Gifford capable of such? He was a military man. It would not be the first time he dispatched appropriated stock, but for what? To leave it on the ground to rot? *God, what manner of man have you brought against me?*

Before Monte could mount, Cole rode up with Breck beside him. "Mr. Farrel, we got—" His glance fell on the bull. "Tarnation!"

Breck swayed in his saddle, then dismounted. He stopped beside the bull. "No coyote done this."

"No." Monte calmed Sirocco, who quivered under his hand.

241

Cole turned. "Mr. Farrel, word's gone round that Jake Gifford'll double the wages of any man in our operation who signs on with him."

"Who's going?"

"All the ones that just came on, and Skeeter and John Mason. He's too young to know better."

"Can't fault a man for wanting to improve his lot."

"If you call it that."

Monte straightened the stirrup and tucked in his boot.

"What're you doin'?" Cole questioned.

"I'm going to call on Captain Gifford," Monte replied as he mounted.

"I'm comin' with you."

"It's better if I go alone."

"No, it ain't."

Monte brought Sirocco around. "Trust me in this, Cole. If Gifford wants to kill me, your presence won't change that. And I have to let him know we won't stand for any more."

Cole rubbed his forehead with the back of his sleeve. "Tarnation," he muttered.

Monte urged Sirocco with a word. The horse was fresh and willing, more than willing to flee the scene. They headed southwest for the Double Diamond, headquarters of Captain Jake Gifford. He tethered Sirocco at the post before the long veranda of Captain Gifford's white stucco hacienda. A Mexican woman opened the door but said nothing.

"Good afternoon. Is Captain Gifford at home?"

"*Sí, senor.*" She stood aside.

Monte removed his hat as he went in, then followed her through the large open room. Thick beams spanned the ceiling. Over the fireplace hung a rifle and sword and the head of an elk with a vast rack. Another Mexican girl rubbed oil into the chairs set around the long table. She neither looked nor spoke as they passed. They stopped before a heavy paneled door, and the woman knocked.

"What?"

"A man to see you, *Capitan*."

"Send him in."

She opened the door and backed away. Monte stepped in. The room was small with a single arched window. Other trophies—antelope, elk, even a buffalo—lined the walls. Captain Gifford turned from the window, and Monte caught his surprise before he masked it.

"Mr. Farrel. I didn't expect a social call."

"No doubt it was my men you expected."

Captain Gifford walked to the oak desk. "Cigar?" He held out the box.

"No, thank you."

Gifford clipped the end and lit one for himself. Then he took his seat without offering Monte a chair. "Your foreman's reputation is formidable. I can't do better than men he's handpicked."

"For the Lucky Star."

Gifford shrugged. "It's a free country, even in the territories. I'm taking on hands as I've acquired more cattle."

"Lucky Star stock?"

Captain Gifford drew himself up. "Are you accusing me of thievery?"

"Inquiring only."

"By God, for a reb you've got pluck."

"I know your record, Gifford. Special reconnaissance, captain in charge of 6th Company. Commendations for services rendered beyond your normal duties. I believe that means you were a spy."

"Correct on all counts. I'm flattered."

Monte held his anger in check. "In case you haven't heard, the war's over."

"Oh yes, I'd heard."

"Then have you no honor?"

"Honor? You, the son of William Jackson Farrel, speak to me of honor?"

"What has my father to do with it?"

"Elias Gifford."

Elias Gifford? "I don't—yes, I recall a man of that name. He was . . ."

"My father was an abolitionist."

"He was hung for rape and murder." Monte countered.

"Lies, propagated by your father and the other planters."

It was years ago, but Monte recalled the incident, the daughter of Wallace Bendar found in his field. He remembered the outcry, the horror at the brutality of the crime, the smug denial put forth by the troublemaker Elias Gifford. He now saw a smoldering fury in Captain Jake's eyes that prompted memories of the man on a scaffold, a man consumed by violence.

Did Gifford hold him responsible for his father's just demise? Was that behind the unwarranted attacks? An incident, however traumatic, in which his father had a hand? Of what was the off-spring of Elias Gifford capable? Monte clamped his will over the rage that rose inside. "Let there be no misunderstanding. I expect your harassment to stop."

"Harassment, Mr. Farrel? Business, rather."

"There's room in the territory for both of us."

"Well, now, I don't see it that way. Take that contract you have with Bent's fort."

"What about it?"

Gifford opened the drawer of the desk and pulled out a paper. "Seems the man in charge of purchasing livestock would rather buy from me."

"You undercut me?"

"Only slightly. I served with Lieutenant Beard in '63. In your native state, I believe."

Monte felt the rage pounding in his temple. "If I learn that you have one single head of Lucky Star stock, I'll bring you to court, Captain Gifford."

Gifford leaned back in his chair. "You don't think I'd be that careless, do you? Take that sixty-five head I had driven down to the fort last week. Fine Double Diamond stock, it was."

Monte grabbed him by the collar and dragged him up. "You

set foot on my land, just once, and I'll kill you." He saw the muscles ripple in Gifford's jaw.

"Why don't you have your wife do it for you?"

Monte smashed his fist into Gifford's nose and blood spurted. The door crashed open and three men were on him. He ducked as one swung for his head, but the fist of another caught him in the belly. He doubled and a boot cracked his jaw. The third smacked a stout club across his back. The blows came faster than he could defend, and he collapsed to the floor. Blood ran from his nose and mouth, and he could feel his ribs shift.

Captain Gifford came and stood over him. "Take him where the coyotes will find him."

The men dragged him from the room. Sirocco shied at the smell of his blood when they heaved him over the horse's back. Monte tried to speak to calm him, but they slapped the flank and Sirocco broke away, galloping heedlessly. Monte cried out with the pain in his ribs and clenched one hand in Sirocco's mane, fighting to get upright.

His palms were cracked and bleeding, and the strength left his fingers. Less than a mile from Gifford's ranch, he fell heavily to the ground. Sirocco kept running. Monte lay in the grass. One eye was swelling shut, and every part of him hurt. His breath came sharp and painfully.

God, what can I do against one so evil? I'm only a man. He closed his eyes. He felt utterly helpless.

Trust me.

It was almost as though Monte heard the voice. His mind said he was losing consciousness, but his heart suddenly burned with hope. Even the pain that grew keener every moment did not dim it.

He heard hooves and thought for a moment Sirocco had returned. But when he raised his head, inches from the ground, he saw the pale, heavy hooves of Cole's palomino. Cole jumped down and dropped to his side. "I trust you, Mr. Farrel. It's Jake Gifford I don't."

Monte groaned when Cole raised and half carried him to the

spare horse, tied behind Scotch. "I don't reckon you'll appreciate the ride just now, but it's a sight better than lyin' there till night-fall. Can you hold on?"

Monte nodded. He focused on staying astride, and not crying out with each jolt and jerk. By the time they reached home, he felt numb and exhausted. Cole eased him from the saddle, and he kept his legs with difficulty.

"Go ahead and lean." Cole hauled him to the house.

James opened the door. "Mastuh Monte."

"Monte!" Abbie rushed forward. "Cole, what happened!"

"Had a run in at Captain Gifford's place. Most likely his men." Cole helped him to the sofa.

Abbie turned on him. "Where were you?"

"Waitin' outside."

"Why weren't you with him? How could you let him go in alone?"

"Abbie . . ." Monte flinched from the effort.

"I'll get the doc." Cole put on his hat and left.

Monte turned when Abbie dropped to his side. "It looks worse than it is."

"You don't expect me to believe that." She dipped a towel into the basin Pearl brought and dabbed it over his face.

He could tell by her expression that he'd do better not to speak again. No reassurances would belie what her own eyes told her. He could make out Frances and Kendal standing over him, but his good eye teared as she washed him, and the throbbing in his ribs and head was draining his energy. He fell asleep before the doctor arrived.

♦♦♦♦♦♦♦

Abbie shook as she sat beside Monte after Doctor Barrow left. Fury and fear held sway inside her. They could have killed him. He had slept for two days now, waking only once for water and then drifting back to his heavy slumber. The doctor had wrapped his ribs and treated the cuts, but there was nothing he could do for the internal bruising, save check back as he had just now.

He said it was good Monte slept on his own. He did not want to sedate him. And he felt that there was likely no permanent damage. But why had Monte risked himself? She clenched her hands.

Abbie had not spoken to Cole since he brought Monte in. He of all people should have known. He had told her he'd keep a watch. So what if Monte ordered him away? It was foolishness and stubborn pride. Or maybe it was honor. She flounced up from her seat and paced the room.

Kendal came in. At least he'd been sober since the incident. "How is he?"

"Stronger. Doctor Barrow says he'll mend."

"I don't think I've seen a beating so bad. He must have been outnumbered."

"Of course he was outnumbered. He was alone. By his own order." She spun. "What is it with you men? Why must pride govern your sense?"

Kendal smiled. "Perhaps we haven't enough sense to govern our pride."

Abbie stalked to the sofa and stared down at Monte. The swelling was diminished, though the bruises were dark and ugly. She longed to take him in her arms and love him. Maybe by coming together she could share his pain.

"*Look to the living.*" How could she when life was so fragile and men so stubborn?

Kendal straightened. "I'm going to town. Will you tell Frances if she asks?"

Abbie didn't argue. She hadn't the strength to say he should tell her himself. She nodded and took her place again at Monte's side. He stirred, and she leaned close. "Monte?"

He opened his eyes. The diminished swelling allowed some movement in the bad one. "Well."

"Are you hungry?"

"It seems we've been here before."

"I think you like the attention."

He reached for her hand, and she brought his to her cheek.

"Why, Monte?" Tears stung her eyes.

"Perhaps it was not the best judgment."

"Not everyone is a gentleman. You can't wait for a man like Captain Gifford to remove his coat."

Monte smiled and winced. "Actually, I started it."

"You? Why?"

"I felt he had it coming."

Abbie sank back against her chair. All the times she had seen Monte refrain from action, hold back retribution, control his anger . . . what could have spurred him to attack Captain Gifford? She whispered, "Why, Monte?"

"He's behind all the trouble we've had at the ranch."

"And what is the trouble?"

"The rustlings, the stampede, the poisoned water holes, the slain and mutilated stock. He killed Chance."

Abbie gasped. "How do you know?"

"Never mind that. Where's Frances?"

"In her room."

"I don't want either one of you leaving the ranch."

"You're hardly one to talk."

He raised up slowly. "Don't give me trouble, Abbie."

"Oh no. You find enough of it on your own. Why didn't you take Cole?"

"I thought if I confronted Gifford, we could settle it."

Abbie shook her head.

"At any rate . . ." Monte raised up on his elbow. "At least now we know what we're up against."

"Skeeter, John, and the new men collected their wages."

Monte nodded. "I won't bid for their loyalty."

"That's what Cole said, so I paid them."

There was a knock on the door, and Abbie opened it to find Pearl with broth and bread. She brought the tray to Monte, and Abbie helped him sit.

"Thank you, Pearl." Monte's smile was gentle.

"You get that down, now, Mastuh Monte. Get yo' strength back."

He bowed his head briefly, then raised the spoon and took a sip. He smiled again, and Pearl left them. Abbie sank to her knees beside him while he ate. She did not dare ask him how she could help. But the need to help burned inside. Perhaps Cole . . . no, he would tell her not to meddle.

How could Monte expect her to stay in the house and do nothing? They were down to six men, not counting Will and James. Or Monte. "Have you told the marshal?"

"He's aware of some of it. I alerted him to the missing stock."

"Does he know it's Captain Gifford?"

"I have no proof."

"But, Monte—"

"Abbie, let me handle this my way."

"If he saw you like this—"

"He'd say Captain Gifford defended himself. I went to his home and accosted him there."

"But . . ."

Monte put his hand on her head. "Give me your word, Abbie."

"I won't."

"Then I'll have you guarded day and night."

She stood and stalked to the window. The last of the day's light faded to gray. "Then talk to Pa. And to Grant. And the McConnels and the others."

"I can't defame a man without proof."

"Defame?" She spun. "He tried to kill you."

"No, he didn't."

Helplessness washed over her. What chance had common sense against his southern honor? "I will stay on the ranch unless I've no other choice."

He smiled grimly. "I guess that's the best I'll get from you."

◆◆◆◆◆◆◆

Monte lay awake in the dark. One thing the beating had shown him was that Gifford would not shirk violence. They were all at risk—his men, his family. Monte was not foolish enough to think he had accomplished anything with his threats. Gifford knew he had him by the throat. He had but to hold on, and he'd drain the lifeblood from the Lucky Star.

Where do I turn, Lord?

The other cheek, Reverend Shields would say, as he had spoken eloquently on brotherly love during Sunday's service. Well, Monte had given Gifford both cheeks and the rest of him, as well. Though the bruising was healing, the anger was not.

"Trust me," the Lord had said—if indeed it had been Him. But how? What did Monte know of God and His ways? He rubbed a hand over his face. Gently, so as not to disturb Abbie, he slipped from the bed and pulled on his wrap.

Outside the room, he lit the lamp and went down to the library. He set the lamp on the table. Slowly, painfully he climbed the ladder to the top shelf and pulled out his father's Bible. He ran a hand over the leather, gilt lettered and tooled. Inside were chronicled all the generations of Farrels, but the rest of the book had not seen much use.

The Farrels lived by honor, not by faith. Monte climbed down the ladder and slid it back to the corner. He sat and opened the Bible. God's instructions, Winthrop Shields called it. Monte fanned the pages. Had he years, he would not learn all this book had to say. And he hadn't years. Time was running out already.

He tucked his fingertips in and opened the book. *Ecclesiastes.* He scanned the page. *To every thing there is a season and a time to every purpose under the heaven. A time to be born, and a time to die; a time to plant, a time to pluck up that which is planted; A time to kill, and a time to heal. . . .* Monte frowned as he read. What did it mean? *A time to love, and a time to hate; a time of war, and a time of peace.*

He sat back in the chair and stared at the rows of books on the wall. There was a plan larger than himself. Indeed, what place had he in it at all? Each season would come whether or not the Lucky Star remained. People would be born, people would die. Whether he lived or not was out of his hands.

And yet . . . *A time to love, and a time to hate.* Should he not hate evil when he found it? *A time of war.* Should he not fight that evil?

If he fell, if the Lucky Star failed, who would be next? How would his neighbors stand?

"God," Monte whispered. "I don't know if I've heard you right. But I pledge here and now to stand against the evil Jake Gifford would wrought with whatever weapons I have. Not for myself alone, but for those I love, for my neighbors, and for your righteousness."

◆◆◆◆◆◆◆

Captain Jake frowned at the men who stood awkwardly before him. "I told you to take care of it."

"We flung him on the horse. He was bleedin' bad, and the stallion took off crazy. There's no way he rode it home."

"His man got him home. Cole Jasper. That name mean anything to you?"

The man swallowed. "I didn't see no one around. We figured he'd fall and the coyotes would get him just as you said."

Captain Jake shook his head. "Get out of here. Send Skeeter to me." He ought to learn something from Farrel's man. Something he could use.

Twenty-Three

The day was almost balmy as Abbie strolled arm in arm with Sadie, leading their horses behind. They'd spent the last two days together since Joe's work was completed, and Sadie would leave before the week's end. They had ridden to the edge of Monte's land and dismounted for a walk.

Sadie drew a long breath. "You're very fortunate to have all this, your beautiful home . . . your handsome husband." She elbowed her.

"When he isn't black-and-blue." Abbie spun at the sound of gunshots. Her heart jumped to her throat. The reports brought the sickening feeling of death, the sound of screams, the smell of blood. Unconsciously she pressed her hands to her ears. Her breath came thin and weak.

Sadie gripped her arm. "What is it, Abbie?"

She fought the horror. "I don't know." Her voice was as clipped as her breath.

Sadie clutched her shawl. "Where's Monte? At the house?"

"No. He left for town early this morning." Abbie gathered herself and slowed her breath. This was no time to let past fears disable her. Gunshots meant trouble. "Sadie, do you think you could find Cole? He has the herd just south of here. Send him to me, then wait at the house."

"What are you going to do?"

Abbie swung up into the saddle. There was no time for explanations.

"Abbie!"

252

"I won't get close." Kicking her heels, she swung around. Abbie's heart raced every time the shots sounded, then stopped, then sounded again. They ricocheted off the bluffs with a double report that vibrated in her chest. She slid down from Zephyr but held the reins firmly as she climbed.

Topping the rise, she saw him below, back straight, legs apart, arms ready at his sides. Suddenly he flipped the gun from the holster at his hip and fired, stuffed the gun back, and shook his hand. Abbie didn't need Sirocco near to see that it was Monte.

She watched him reload and repeat the gunplay, the report of the shots echoing off the wall of the bluff to the right. She spun at the sound of hooves behind her as Cole reined in Scotch. His face was thunder and lightning, and Abbie knew he'd lay into her. She hushed him before he began, and he climbed up the rise on foot, then followed her gaze to the range below.

He stared as she had, until the firing stopped. "I'll be licked."

"What is he doing?" Abbie watched again as Monte drew and shot three times, then holstered the gun and gripped his hand tightly, bending low with the pain. He straightened, picked up his hat, and walked over to the horse.

Cole gripped her elbow. "Better git 'fore he sees us."

She nodded and led Zephyr down the slope. Once out of view they mounted. Abbie did not speak. What was Monte doing, shooting like . . . like a gunfighter? A terrible thought seized her. *Please, God . . . he didn't hope to fight Gifford that way!*

The *thunk, thunk* of the hooves on the prairie grass matched the thumping of her heart. A startled cottontail bounded away. A meadowlark sang from a clump of sage. The quiet seemed to have swallowed up the echoes. Abbie glanced at Cole. He glanced back.

"Was he fast, Cole?"

"His draw was. He was slow on the trigger. I guess his hand . . ."

"Why is he shooting like that?"

"I don't know."

Or wouldn't say. She glared. "I have a right to know. Has there been more trouble?"

"No. Things have been quiet since . . ."

"Since Monte nearly got himself killed?" Her fear became anger.

Cole kept his gaze ahead.

"How long are you going to wait and let him face this alone?"

"That wasn't my fault, Abbie."

She huffed and shook her head. She barely heard the rattle before Zephyr reared, hooves pawing the air. Abbie grasped for the saddle horn, but her hand slipped as the horse twisted and bucked. She fell to the ground. In the same moment Cole's bullets blew the snake in half. Zephyr ran.

Cole leapt from the saddle. "You okay?"

She sat up. "I think so." It had not been a good fall. Her ankle throbbed, and her elbow was scraped.

Cole reached a hand to her. She tried to stand, then collapsed with a cry.

"Yer ankle?"

She bit her lip.

"Let's have a look." He raised the edge of her skirt and removed her boot. He ran a hand over the ankle and she winced.

"Tender?"

Before she could answer Sirocco bore down on them and skidded to a stop, and Monte jumped down. "Take your hands off her, Cole." He dropped to the ground beside her, and Cole backed off.

Abbie brushed the hair from her eyes. "Zephyr was spooked by a rattler."

"Are you bitten?"

"No. Cole shot it."

Monte frowned. "I heard the shots. Where's Zephyr?"

"She ran." Abbie touched the swelling around her ankle.

Cole stood. "I'll fetch her back."

"Stable her. I'll take Abbie with me." Monte spoke without looking at Cole.

Abbie saw his jaw tighten as he bent and lifted her into his arms as Cole left them. She knew that look. "He was helping me."

Monte didn't answer. He carried her to Sirocco, lifted her into the saddle, and swung up behind. As he took up the reins, Abbie saw his cracked and bleeding palm. "Monte..." She reached down to it.

He jerked it away. "My hands are fine, Abbie."

His tone hurt and frightened her. "Why are you shooting like that out here alone?"

"I was obviously not alone."

"I heard the shots. I didn't know it was you."

"Then you had less business being there."

"Why are you so angry?"

"How am I supposed to respond when I find Cole with his hands on you?"

"He was checking the injury."

Monte looked away. Abbie shivered. His irrational anger frightened her more than his shooting. And he was excluding her completely. They rode in silence until the house came into view.

He released a slow breath. "Perhaps I overreacted."

Abbie raised her chin. "Not perhaps."

"I apologize. Hearing the gunshots ... and then seeing you down ... I asked you not to—"

"I didn't leave the ranch. Not until I heard *your* gunshots." She could feel the tension in him still. "Oh, Monte, what are you thinking? When did you learn to shoot like that?"

He didn't answer, but his arm around her tightened. He turned his hand on the reins, and she saw the raw and broken skin. His face was firm. "If there's trouble, I'll be the one to handle it ... not Cole, not you, not anyone else."

Abbie trembled.

He pulled up at the stable and took her down. "Will!"

Will rushed out. One look at Monte quenched his questions.

"Did Cole return with Zephyr?"

"No, sir. I haven't seen him."

Monte frowned. "That's what I feared. She doesn't know to

come home." He walked swiftly into the house and laid Abbie on the sofa. "Pearl! See to her, will you?" He strode out.

Abbie sagged. She didn't think his anger was for her this time, but she felt estranged nonetheless.

"Lawdy girl, what you done to yo'sef now?" Pearl's face was a dark cloud.

"It's just a twisted ankle."

Pearl clicked her tongue. "It's swellin' bad." She bustled out and returned with a bandage and her medicine box.

Abbie bit her lip against the thorough ministration of Pearl's hands, firm and insistent. She sank into the couch when it was over.

"You's gotta be mo' careful, Mizz Abbie. Mastuh Monte already lost hisself one wife."

Abbie nodded. A lump came to her throat. It was the first time Pearl had used her given name.

Monte rode away from the house. How could he explain what God had charged him with? How could he tell her the responsibility that rested on his shoulders? He caught sight of Cole, watched him slide from his horse and walk slowly toward the restive mare.

Zephyr tossed her head and stomped, but did not run again. Gently, Cole reached out for her, ran his hands over her neck, then gripped the bridle and relaxed. Monte brought Sirocco over. "Quite a chase."

"Yup." Cole stroked the mare, then led her to Scotch and mounted.

"Cole . . ."

"Don't say nothin'. I know how it looked."

"Nevertheless, I apologize."

Cole grunted. "If you don't know already how Abbie feels about you, you're a durn fool. It ain't like any efforts on my part would change that."

Monte raised an eyebrow. "Are there efforts on your part?"

"No, there ain't. With all due respect, Mr. Stevens is the one you should be watchin'."

Monte eyed him keenly. "I'm aware of that."

Cole turned in the saddle. "You ain't thinkin' of callin' Gifford out?"

Monte stiffened, but there was no judgment in Cole's question, only honest concern. "No. But I won't be caught short. I'd appreciate knowing you're on my side."

"I been here three years. Whose side do you expect I'm on?"

Monte looked out over the land. Perhaps, just perhaps, he wasn't expected to do it alone. He released his breath. "Please excuse my misjudgment . . . with Abbie."

Cole shrugged. "Heck, if I thought there was a chance, you might have somethin' to worry on." He spurred Scotch to a canter, trailing Zephyr behind. Monte watched him go, then smiled. Cole Jasper wasn't exactly the sort he would choose to depend on, but it certainly felt good to know he could.

✦✦✦✦✦✦✦

Abbie felt barely a twinge in her ankle as she stood on the stool to reach the book. It had healed swiftly, as well it should with everyone insisting she stay off it completely. Frances tutored her needlework, and Abbie was sick to death of ripping stitches. Frances had an eye like a hawk for a single crooked or misshapen stitch. And like Cole, Abbie chafed the inactivity. She was ready to be up.

She turned as Frances slipped into the room and closed the door behind. Her countenance was anything but serene.

"What is it, Frances?"

"I need to speak with you."

Abbie replaced the book and climbed down. She waited as Frances walked slowly to the end of the room and turned. Whatever it was, Frances was clearly shaken.

She gathered herself. "I believe Kendal has taken a mistress."

Abbie caught her breath. The feel of Kendal's arms and his kiss rose unbidden to her mind. Did Frances suspect her? Was she here to confront, to accuse? "I know he's been distracted. He's working on a business venture."

Frances sniffed. "That's not what keeps him away." She held out the note, and Abbie took it. *Madame, Be advised your husband strays.*

"Where did you get this?"

"It was delivered to the house."

"By whom? It's unsigned."

"I don't know. It was given to James."

Abbie folded the note and handed it back. How could she deny the possibility? "Who do you suspect?"

Frances shook her head. "I don't know. I thought he could be watched."

Abbie's mouth dropped open. "You're not suggesting that I . . ."

"No. Someone he wouldn't notice."

"Oh, Frances. Are you sure you want to do this? Kendal will be furious if he finds out."

Frances straightened. She was perilously controlled. "I want to know."

Abbie hesitated. If only Frances had treated him more kindly. If only she could have relented, forgiven, reached out to him only once.

Suddenly Frances crumpled. Tears sparkled in her eyes. "I need to know. It doesn't matter the risk."

She loves him. The thought came with sudden clarity. Frances loved Kendal. It was her fear that estranged them, and now his betrayal had brought her to the edge. Oh, Lord, how could they reconcile? Even Monte's pride had been no obstacle compared to what Frances faced if Kendal . . .

She touched Frances's arm. "Grant lives at the hotel. He might know if Kendal frequents . . . someplace."

"Will you talk to him? Will you ask him?"

"Monte . . ."

"I don't want him to know." Her voice broke. "I couldn't bear it."

There it was again. Southern pride demanding silence. Abbie sighed. "All right."

"Will you go now?"

Abbie hesitated, but how could she not respond to the trust Frances placed in her? For the first time since she came, Frances was reaching out—of her own accord. She had made herself vulnerable. Abbie nodded. No sense putting it off. If Grant watched, maybe ... maybe he would find that something else occupied Kendal. She went out and wrapped up in her coat.

Surely even with their difficulties, Kendal would not run out on his wife and daughter, but perhaps he thought no one would know. She felt again the pressure of his hands on her shoulders. *"I can be discreet."* She shook her head. Oh, Kendal.

✦✦✦✦✦✦

Kendal's throat worked as he reread the telegram. Short and to the point. *Deal turned bad. Get Patricia. Pine Creek ford. Thursday by six.* The deal turned bad. His chest felt hollow. He crumpled the paper and dropped it in the yard. He dug his fingers through his hair. The deal turned bad.

Closing his eyes, he tried to think. "Turned bad" could mean any number of things. Perhaps it had not worked out as profitably, or they had to stop before capitalizing on all of it. Perhaps they had overstepped themselves. All these could be remedied.

He smoothed his vest. He still held the trump card. Patricia. They would not dare cheat him as long as she was in his grasp. He would go to town, have a drink, think things through. Maybe he would not bring her to the meeting. Maybe he would hear them out first.

Yes. His tension eased. But he would make sure she was guarded. His bribes to the hotelier had vouchsafed her so far. There was little that could not be gained with a little gold crossing the palm.

✦✦✦✦✦✦

Abbie tethered Zephyr at the new pine courthouse. Grant

hugged her as she entered his office. "Now this makes for a good day. A visit from my sister . . . and the judge's daughter."

Abbie raised her chin. "I'll not comment."

He laughed.

"I've come to ask a favor."

"Anything at all."

"It's rather delicate."

"Oh?"

Abbie walked to the window. "Well, I don't know how to say it nicely. Frances suspects Kendal is . . ."

"Ah. And with good reason."

She spun to face him.

Grant shrugged. "His regular visits to room sixteen."

"Oh, Grant!"

He strode to his desk and tucked some papers into the drawer. "How about lunch? The hotel serves a fine meat loaf."

Abbie nodded as they crossed the street. Her stomach was in knots, but Grant would not talk once he got food on his mind. They took a table and ordered without seeing a menu.

Grant must have understood her need, because as soon as Rudy left to place their order, he leaned close. "At first I assumed he had business, perhaps an associate to meet. But the other night, Monday I guess it was, I met him in the hall on my way up. He seemed . . . agitated, and from behind the door, I heard someone crying."

Abbie closed her eyes. "So Frances is right."

"Well, in a court of law that's extremely circumstantial."

"What else could it mean?"

"Any number of things. But . . ." Grant shrugged. "I allow it is the most likely."

"Can you watch the room?"

He frowned.

"I know it's a dreadful thing to ask. But . . . Frances wants to know."

"I am not a spy. A man's private affairs are his own, however questionable."

Abbie took a bite of meat loaf without tasting it. She should have known better than to ask Grant to skulk around after someone. There was only one way to answer the question; confront it head on. "You're right, Grant. I'm sorry I asked. I'll go up and have a look."

Grant shook his head. "Not a good plan."

"Frances is trusting me. I won't let her down." Abbie wiped her mouth and laid the napkin aside.

"Then I'll come with you." He checked his watch. "But I have to meet a client now. Wait until later."

"There's no need. I'll simply pay a visit." She squeezed his hand, hushed his protest, then headed back to the hotel lobby and up to room sixteen. She tapped lightly on the door. There was no response, and she knocked again. This time there was a soft shuffling inside and the knob turned slowly. The face that appeared was younger than she had expected.

Abbie forced a smile. "Is your mother here?" The girl shook her head. "Your father?"

"No one else."

Abbie's heart sank. Surely Kendal . . . there must be some mistake. "My name is Abbie Farrel. May I come in?"

The girl shook her head and glanced swiftly down the hall. "No, I don't think so."

"If you're worried about Mr. Stevens . . ."

The girl's eyes widened, and the door narrowed. Abbie put up a hand to stop its closing. "Please let me talk to you. I want to help."

"You can't help."

"I can." Abbie stepped between the door and jamb. "You're alone here?"

"Mostly."

"Except when Mr. Stevens comes?"

The girl slowly nodded.

"What's your name?"

"Patricia."

"Now, Patricia, suppose you tell me about Mr. Stevens." Abbie hadn't meant to be so direct, but her growing anger ruled her tongue.

"My father brought me here. I must stay until their business is finished."

Abbie's chest eased. "Your father's in business with Mr. Stevens?" She dared to hope.

Patricia nodded. "Mr. Stevens ... required me to stay as a guarantee."

As awful as that sounded, Abbie felt relieved. If that was all, if he was acting as a guardian over the girl ... "So he comes to check on you?" She expected a quick nod, not the rushing of blood to the face and the mortification in her eyes. Abbie's hope evaporated as her anger rose again.

"Has Mr. Stevens ..."

"Please, I can't talk about it." Patricia squeezed her hands to her cheeks.

It was clear enough that Kendal was not acting the gentleman. Abbie recalled the stinging of her palm against his cheek. She wished he were there to receive it again. Well, she would take matters in hand. "Get your things. I'm taking you with me."

"Oh, but I can't."

"Of course, you can. Whatever business they're conducting does not involve you."

"I don't dare."

"Well, I do. And I'll answer for you when it comes to it." Abbie spun at the sound of Kendal's voice downstairs in the lobby. Another man spoke, and she could not make out Kendal's response. He sounded tense, impatient.

She would not get Patricia down that way. She had intended to take her home, bring the matter to Monte, and even if she must, confront Kendal with it. But not alone. Not here.

She turned to Patricia. The child was quaking. Again her anger gave her strength. "Come quickly." She led the girl by the hand, down the hall past Grant's door to the potted plant at the end. He kept his key there when he didn't want to carry it. With any luck ... she touched the metal nesting in the leaves and hurried to the door.

"This is my brother's room." Stepping in, she saw it was none too tidy. "You'll be safe here. Don't open to anyone. Grant has his own key, but I'll have him knock three times and then once more so you'll know it's him. If you hear any other knock, don't answer. Perhaps you should find a place to hide in case you need to."

Patricia nodded. "Mr. Stevens will be angry."

"Not nearly so angry as I." Abbie turned. "Lock the door behind me." She swept down the stairs, just as Kendal came up.

He raised his eyebrows. "Good afternoon, Abbie."

"Kendal." Abbie composed her features.

He spread his hands and feigned a smile. "What ..."

"I was running an errand for my brother." She didn't bother crossing her fingers. A lie was a lie. She'd confess it to Reverend Shields if he were inclined to listen. "Good day, Kendal." She tossed her cape over her shoulders and went outside.

She crossed swiftly to the courthouse and knocked on Grant's office door. She waited, knocked again, and tried the knob. It held fast. Of course. His appointment. But surely he conducted business from the office. Perhaps he had concluded that and gone elsewhere.

She hurried down the hall to the small courtroom. It was empty. Hastening back, she stopped outside Judge Wilson's door, lifted her hand, and hesitated. She didn't fancy facing him, the way the judge always looked at her as though she were guilty of something. But need drove her. She knocked. He beckoned.

"Excuse me, Judge Wilson." She cleared her throat. "Would you know where to find my brother?"

"Am I your brother's keeper?" His lowered brows alarmed her until he smiled, his goatee poking out stiffly. "A little joke."

Abbie formed a smile. "Yes, sir."

"No, I don't know where your brother is, but if you want to find him, I suggest you check with my daughter. He's not given her a moment's peace since he got here."

Abbie bit her tongue. As though that were Grant's doing.

"Thank you, sir." He nodded, and she backed out. If Grant was with Marcy, she could not speak with him, and in any event, she did not have time to search for him now. Kendal would have long since discovered Patricia's absence. She slipped out of the building and ran for Zephyr.

Sensing her need, Zephyr responded with wonderful speed, and Abbie raced for the ranch. The wind blew against her face, and her hair streamed out behind her as she rounded the hill. Suddenly Kendal's horse blocked her path and Zephyr veered. Abbie felt her hands wrench loose as she fell, and her head hit the ground. Stunned, she found Kendal bending over her.

He looked haggard and disheveled. "Where is she?"

Abbie pressed a hand to her forehead. "What on earth are you thinking, jumping out like that in front of my horse?"

Kendal shook her. "Where is Patricia?"

Her heart raced as she groped for an answer. "What are you talking about?"

Kendal's fingers dug into her shoulders. "The girl, Abbie."

"I must have hit my head harder than I thought. You're not making any sense at all." She struggled to rise.

Kendal held her firmly. "I swear you'll not continue this ruse."

"You're hurting me, Kendal. Have you gone mad?"

"Yes, maybe I have." Crushing her in his arms, he kissed her. Abbie beat her fists against him, and he laughed. "Not nearly so stunned now, are we?"

"Unhand me!"

"When you tell me what I want to know."

Abbie's anger flared. "I expect you have more to tell. How could you, Kendal? She's only a child."

"Oh, she told you about that, did she?"

Abbie's chest heaved with fury.

He shook her. "Where is she?"

"Why do you need her? What part has she in all of this?"

"Collateral."

"Like my certificates? Will you stop at nothing?"

"No, Abbie, nothing. I am holding a two-edged sword. One slip and I'm cut."

"Go to Monte, Kendal. He knows already."

"He doesn't know the half of it. No, Abbie, your husband is too much a man of honor to deal with this. I, on the other hand, have no honor left to hold me back. Nor have I time." His fingers dug into her shoulders like talons. "Where have you taken her?"

Abbie pushed against his chest, but could not match his strength.

His voice was low. "I won't touch you unless you force me to." He took a strand of hair and slowly twisted it around two fingers until his hand reached her neck. "Where is she?" He wrenched her face forward. "I swear I'll take you without a moment's regret."

She cried out as he pulled her close again. "All right! She's in Grant's . . . office." Her breath rasped. "In the courthouse."

Kendal's eyes narrowed. "What does he know?"

"Nothing. He wasn't there. I . . . I couldn't find him; he was out with Marcy." If she buried the lie in truth maybe . . .

He leaned close. "It was foolish of you to interfere."

Abbie trembled. Did he see her lie? Was it written clearly on her face?

"But I suppose I expected no less. In a different world, Abbie, you and I . . ." He released her so suddenly her head snapped back. He stood. "And for your information, I no more than kissed Patricia. I've no need to force any woman, and she was more reluctant even than you."

Abbie couldn't speak. He stood and reclaimed his horse, glanced back, then gave Zephyr a smack that sent her running. She had expected that. Kendal was no fool. He knew she'd go to Monte. And she would still. He had only bought time. She waited until he rounded the hill, then she cut away from the road in a direct line to the ranch.

Twenty-Four

Monte sat in the bank office and fought to control the fury boiling in his chest. Mr. Driscoll wore his most patronizing expression. "I'm terribly sorry. But the matter is out of my hands. The railroad has stepped in to investigate. It appears the business deal your brother-in-law and wife initiated . . ."

"They did not initiate the deal. They were approached. Kendal was approached. Mrs. Farrel had nothing to do with it."

Mr. Driscoll shook his head. "I'm afraid her signature on the loan says otherwise. No doubt you'll clear that up at the inquiry."

"You know as well as I do that my wife—"

"Mr. Farrel." Mr. Driscoll stood. "The good name of this bank has been jeopardized by the shady dealings of Mr. Stevens and his companions. I intend to follow whatever measures are required to clear my reputation. If you are concerned about your wife, I suggest you take her in hand."

Monte stood. Mr. Driscoll had certainly changed his tune now that things had fallen out as they had. He did not need a reply from Scotland Yard. The railroad had responded to his inquiry and stepped in. Abbie's holdings were as good as lost, and God only knew what he would salvage if the railroad sued for fraud in their name.

It was Kendal's affair, not his. Yet honor demanded he stand by him and right the wrong as far as he was able. This was ingrained in him, though it burned. But he would not stand for Abbie to be dragged through it. Her ignorance would cost them dearly, but that did not include her in Kendal's infamy.

Mr. Driscoll knew that, but he was covering his own backside. Monte would find no help there. He took up his black felt hat and left. Kendal must be somewhere in town, and Abbie, as well. He had left Frances alone at the house after divulging as much as he dared of Kendal's scheme. Frances had a right to know. As it was, they would all share the ruin.

He searched each business along the main street but found neither Kendal nor Abbie. He then went to the courthouse, where Marcy Wilson was taking leave of Abbie's brother at the door. Impatiently, he tipped his hat and bowed. "Good afternoon, Miss Wilson."

"Mr. Farrel." She deepened the dimple in her cheek and sashayed past.

"Monte. You're looking better." Grant extended his hand.

Monte shook it. "I'm quite recovered. Have you seen my wife?"

"I left her at the hotel, looking into that matter with Mr. Stevens."

"What matter?"

"With the girl . . . I assumed you knew."

"Knew what, Grant?"

Grant blew a slow breath. "Oh, brother."

Monte listened as Grant explained Abbie's visit. He fought to maintain control. Was Abbie set on destruction? "Where is she now?"

"Monte, I don't know. She can't be there still. Likely you'll find her at home."

Monte turned and strode for his horse. He had not passed her on the road, but he did not limit Abbie to the road. He would find Kendal later. Marshal Haggerty had agreed to question him quietly at the house, though he held warrants for Harris and Emmerson. That would all wait. Right now, Monte's concern was Abbie.

He rode home hard, leaped from Sirocco's back, and bounded up the front stairs. "James!"

"Yessuh."

"Is Mrs. Farrel at home?"

"No, suh."

Monte frowned. As he turned, Zephyr cantered into the yard empty saddled. She had learned to come home—but without Abbie. He remounted and hurried Sirocco to the eastern pasture. He found Cole kneeling beside a new calf entangled in the wire. He reined in. "Have you seen Abbie?"

Cole shook his head.

"Get the men and spread out to Templeton Gap. I'll take the west side."

"Mind my askin' . . ."

"The sky is falling, Cole. And Abbie's in the middle of it."

✦✦✦✦✦✦✦

Kendal clenched his hands. Abbie had lied to him. Patricia was not there. He had searched thoroughly. But he must find her. He stepped out of the courthouse. Activity in front of the marshal's office caught his attention, and he paused, then joined the crowd. The faces on the wanted poster chilled his blood. Harris and Emmerson. The deal had turned indeed. He slunk through the shadows for his horse.

His fear and fury drove him through the deepening dusk to where he'd left Abbie. Of course she was no longer there. Had he not expected as much? Perhaps he had even hoped. He gripped his head between his hands. What was he doing? Where had everything gone wrong? What now? What now!

Pulling the reins, he brought the horse around and searched the ground. Her footsteps showed in the loose gravel at the side. So she had left the road in the direction of the ranch. Still it was a long way. Perhaps he could intercept her.

The westering sun crowned the tip of Pikes Peak and illumined a ghostly half-moon in the pale eastern sky. The light would not hold. Even as he lingered, the edge of sun shrank away. He heeled the horse up the bank and followed her trail.

✦✦✦✦✦✦✦

Captain Jake spurred his charger. The men riding behind

would see that he did not shirk. He would do whatever it took to rid the territory of his rival. With what he had learned from Skeeter, he knew one more blow would sink Montgomery Farrel. And that blow would come at the heart of his operation.

The horses had been moved to the west pasture with the warmer weather. They were accessible now, as they had not been through the winter. Once he had marred the Lucky Star brand with his Double Diamond, he would drive the herd to the fort for the army's use. Lieutenant Beard was eager for horses. Especially fine horseflesh such as Montgomery Farrel raised.

They rode steadily as the night deepened. Soon they would be on Farrel land. Skeeter had directed them, describing where to find the horses, though he did not ride tonight. Captain Jake would not try his loyalty that far. And the kid, John Mason, was too wet behind the ears to be of any use. He was back at the ranch oiling saddles.

The night was clear and keen. They came to the fence line and reined in. Baker dismounted and cut the wire in three sections. They rode through. Captain Jake's charger sensed the herd. He watched the ears raise, the nostrils flare. But the horse made no sound. It was too well trained for that.

Captain Jake caught sight of the grazing animals. They would be guarded, but he could not make out any guards. He motioned his men to circle. As soon as they flanked the herd he would give the signal. He searched the darkness. Surely they would be detected.

Something was not right. It was too quiet. Where were Farrel's men? Was it a trap? Montgomery Farrel would not leave the horses unguarded. But his own men took their positions unchallenged. Captain Jake raised his arm, and they whistled and hollered. The horses shied and started to run. The men held them together and drove them back the way they had come, toward the breach in the fence.

Captain Jake waited for them to pass. His men would drive them to the ranch to be branded at first light while he made an appearance in town to establish his alibi. He cut across the pasture heading east.

◆◆◆◆◆◆◆

Abbie pushed on. Her indignation made her strong. What was happening that Kendal must keep a girl hostage? Even if he told the truth—that he had not forced his attention—she was frightened. He had no business using the child as a pawn.

Abbie would see that he did not continue, but she felt a sinking in her stomach. She had lied to his face. The deception had slipped out in spite of her, a cunning she had not known she possessed. Was it so easy to depart from the truth? Had Kendal taken one step so small?

How much time before he discovered her ruse and returned with a fury? Could she make the ranch before that? Everything in her cried out to run, but she knew if she did, she would soon tire and be forced to stop. It was better to maintain a steady progress.

The darkness was now complete. She thanked God for the stars. Without them she would lose all point of reference on the empty range. She had angled too far east and now cut back slightly west as she kept her northward progress. Pulling her coat close, Abbie kept on. She had to make it to the ranch, find Monte.

The memory of him standing legs apart, Colt blazing, seized her. What would he do? She shook her head. It no longer mattered. He would look for her. Maybe even now he searched. But he would not be alone in that. Kendal had yet to be reckoned with.

She searched the land around her. It was laced with dips and cuts, but none would shelter her, and there were no trees, only scattered low clumps of scrub oak and juniper. " 'The Lord is my light and my salvation...' " She forced herself on. " 'Of whom shall I be afraid?' "

If only she had told Monte. If only Frances ... Oh, Frances. Well, at least she would know Kendal had not taken a mistress ... if he spoke the truth. Somehow Abbie suspected he had. He seemed stripped of his bravado, bared to his essence. Maybe there was still a way for him to make amends. But she did not want to discuss it alone with him in the dark. She had to make it home. Suddenly a horned owl flapped from the grass before her, and she cried out, then shoved her fist between her teeth.

Kendal looked up. Shortening the reins in his hand, he headed toward the cry. Overhead, an owl circled against the star-filled sky. He peered around him with eyes as tuned as the winged scavenger. She was near. The cry could have only been hers. What would he do when he found her?

Monte straightened, head cocked, breath held. He strained to hear it again, but no sound came. Still, he turned his horse and headed in the direction he imagined he had heard the cry.

Cole drew up even and shook his head. "No word from anyone yet. Breck's headed for town."

Monte's jaw tightened. "I thought I heard something over this way." He kicked in his heels and Sirocco sprang forward, Cole on Scotch following right behind.

Lying motionless in the cut, Abbie held her breath until even the sound of Kendal's horse's hooves disappeared, then slowly gave release to her lungs. She forced her trembling to stop and swallowed down the fear. She counted the moments that passed. Her head against the rough ground throbbed.

Kendal had passed, but now he was between her and the ranch. She stood up. Suddenly a horse reared up before her, and she threw her arms over her head. The rider mastered the horse, but her heart thumped madly as she made out the brass buttons and yellow cuffs of Captain Gifford's uniform. His face looked inhuman by the moonlight. Her spirit recoiled.

She turned to run, but he slid from the horse and grabbed her. Abbie cried out.

"None of that." He clamped her mouth with his hand.

She wrenched free and screamed, but he grabbed her by the

hair. She beat him with her fists and screamed again before he got his hands on her throat and squeezed. She ripped at his wrists, desperate for air, but her mind grew fuzzy and her legs gave way.

Monte rode hard. The scream cut short spurred him on, and he unstrapped the gun in his holster. Cole had fallen behind, but Monte could hear him following. Through the darkness he could make out two figures on the ground ahead, and he pulled out his gun and fired into the sky.

One of them leaped up and ran, reached the horse, and wheeled away into the night. The other lay motionless.

"Abbie!" Monte dropped from Sirocco, grabbed her up into his arms.

She choked, then clung to him. "Captain Gifford," she rasped. "It was Captain Gifford."

Cole thundered past them. Monte didn't stop him. If anyone could chase Gifford down, it was Cole. Right now, all that mattered was that Abbie was safe. He pressed her to his chest.

"I'm sorry, Monte."

"Are you hurt?"

"No."

Monte stared up at the sky. Too many emotions clashed inside. "Where is Kendal?"

"He . . . oh, Monte, he didn't mean for it to turn out this way."

"He has betrayed us all."

"Not betrayed, Monte."

"Oh yes. More deeply than you know. One cannot abandon honor without a price. He knew that."

"He lost his way."

"He chose his way." Their breath mingled white in the moonlight. She raised her face, and he stroked her hair, then helped her stand and led her to the horse. "I'll get you home."

She spun. "Home! Monte, we can't."

Monte stared at her, incredulous. Did she know no limits?

"Patricia . . . Grant—we have to go to town. We—"

"Abbie!"

"But . . ."

He grabbed her close. "It's out of our hands, don't you see? The law, the railroad, and Almighty God will take it from here."

◆◆◆◆◆◆◆

Grant stood up from the table and gave a hand to Marcy. She'd seemed impatient throughout dinner, but for the life of him, he couldn't figure what peeved her now. She was harder to understand than any case he'd yet encountered. "Would you care to walk?"

"In the dark?"

"In the moonlight." Why did she make everything he said sound so awkward?

Her eyes went to the stairs. "You could just have me up . . ."

He nearly choked. Did she know what she was saying?

Her dimple deepened. "As long as you're a gentleman."

Grant's heart beat against his chest. He glanced up the stairs. "Uh . . . I don't think my room is exactly presentable."

Marcy laughed. "I didn't expect it would be. What bachelor has time to clean up after himself?" She started toward the stairs.

"Marcy." He caught her arm. "I don't think it's a good idea."

"What's the matter, Grant? Afraid to be alone with me?"

He released his breath. "Well, yes." That and his upbringing, his knowledge of right and wrong, not to mention societal conventions and her father's opinion. Did she want her reputation compromised? And his?

She pouted.

"Marcy . . ."

She hooked her fingers into his vest pockets. "I promise to behave." It was like whiskey to his blood.

"I'm not sure I can say the same."

She ignored him, started up the stairs, and he followed. He dug his key from the plant, opened the door and motioned her inside before anyone below could notice them. He lit the lamp and looked around in surprise. The room seemed strangely tidy.

Maybe he'd kept it better than he thought. He relaxed, then tensed again when Marcy came close.

"You know, Grant, I won't break if you kiss me."

"Oh boy. I have kissed you."

"Ye-es . . ." Marcy ran her fingers up his chest. "I mean really kissed me." She tipped her head up.

"Sheez, Marcy, don't do that." Grant grabbed her close, and she giggled.

"Kiss me, Grant."

He obeyed. Bending low, he kissed her with increased passion, and she melted against him. Her intent was clear, and it burned up inside him. Everything he knew, all he believed melted in the wake of it. She grabbed his shirt and tugged him toward the bed.

They dropped down together, and the bed creaked and sagged. He heard a stifled gasp and froze. It had not come from Marcy. She was as startled as he. Her eyes darted as her breath came quickly. Confused, Grant raised to his elbow and listened, then bent over the side and looked under the bed. The girl beneath began to cry, and he fell off the edge, then scrambled up.

Marcy flew to her feet, her hands at her throat. "Oh . . . I've never . . ." Grant turned to her, and she slapped him smartly.

"What. . . ?"

"Don't even try to explain!" Her face was crimson. "I've never been so insulted! How dare you!"

"I didn't . . ."

She pushed him aside and flung herself out the door. Grant watched her go. Then after a long moment, he turned. "Come out of there, whoever you are."

The scrappy girl climbed out from under the bed. Grant looked her over. "Suppose you tell me who you are and what you're doing under my bed."

"Patricia . . . Emmerson." She cleared her throat. "Your sister said . . ."

"Okay, okay. That tells me everything." Grant shook his head. "I almost believe she planted you there on purpose."

"She . . . said to wait here, that you'd have a special knock, and if I didn't hear it . . . I was to hide." Her face flamed crimson, and she bit her lip.

"Yeah. Well . . . I guess she forgot to tell me." He rubbed his hand over his cheek. He could just shake Abbie. But that was neither here nor there. He studied Patricia. Emmerson . . . the Englishman's daughter? Was that Kendal's game? He hadn't liked the look of those two. His instincts and training warned him against them. But that was hardly this slip of a girl's fault.

"Have you been here since this afternoon?"

She nodded.

"You've had no supper?"

She shook her head.

"Then we'll get you some. I just had the roast beef, and it was passable."

"Thank you." Patricia wrung her hands. "I'm sorry . . . about . . ."

"Yeah." He didn't want to think about Marcy yet. Lord only knew how he'd get past this one. He started for the door and turned back. "What was this knock I was supposed to use?"

"Three and then one."

"Wait until you hear it." Grant started down the hall, then stopped when he saw Emmerson and Harris walk in below. In the shadows of the hall he backed toward his door as Emmerson mounted the stairs with Harris behind him like a wary cur.

Behind them a door slowly opened and Marshal Haggerty stepped out, gun ready. "Stop right there, gentlemen."

Harris spun and fired. The marshal took it square in the chest, staggered and fell. Grant sprang to the banister as Harris and Emmerson jumped the railing and ran. People rushed to Haggerty's side.

Grant ran down the stairs. Someone grabbed his elbow. "Get Doctor Barrow!"

He pushed his way out the door. Only a miracle would save the marshal. A .45 at close range did not leave a man much chance. And somewhere out there were two desperate men . . . three, if he counted Kendal Stevens.

❖❖❖❖❖❖

Kendal heard the horse closing on him. His own mount—Monte's, rather—was spent. If he ran the horse to its death it would be one more debt, but what did it matter? He reined in beside the scrub oak.

The charger that bore down on him was large and powerful. He could see the whites of its eyes in the moonlight, and the sheen of the sword at the hip of its rider. Captain Gifford? What madness . . .

The captain was upon him, then passed. Another pursued him. Cole, leaving the smell of horse sweat and broken sod in his wake. Well, that was a turn. What was Gifford doing here on Monte's land, with Cole in hot pursuit? Kendal rubbed his hand over his forehead. It didn't matter. His only thought now was to get away. Escape. To where? He had not thought to run. A fugitive, with wife and child left behind. Frances.

He slumped in the saddle. It was over. What use in fooling himself longer? He had failed her. There was no hope. Perhaps there never had been. He had lost them. All of them. When Abbie told what she knew, they would align against him. The thought left him empty, hopeless.

He raised his head. The night was silent. The world seemed vast, endless. Where would he go? He had nothing, not even his honor.

Kendal dismounted, attached the reins to the saddle horn, and swatted the horse's flank. It trotted for home. He started on foot for town. What he had in his pocket would get him a drink. The morning could bring what it would.

The lights of town came into view, and he stopped a moment—some sense of self-preservation, perhaps. It waned as quickly as it came, and he took another step. Emmerson lunged from the brush and blocked his way while Harris flanked him.

Kendal stopped. "Gentlemen."

"Where are you off to?" Emmerson hissed.

"I should think that's evident."

"What are you after in town?"

"A drink. Perhaps more than one."

"Don't you know the game is up?"

"You alluded to that in your telegram." Kendal held himself straight. He had half a head on both of them. He had not noticed that before.

"Well, things are worse now. The marshal's dead."

"What do you mean?"

"There's a posse forming . . . for us."

They killed the marshal? Kendal stiffened. "What's that to me?"

Emmerson came up chest to chest. He was shaking. "You're in this as deep as us. Don't forget it."

"I've had no part of murder."

Emmerson gripped his shirt. "You will have, if you mean to double-cross us now."

Kendal heard the cock of Harris's gun. He pried his shirt free. They didn't scare him. What did his life matter now? But he wanted a drink. "Out of my way, Emmerson. You want your daughter back, don't you?"

"Fool! If you walk in there, they'll be on you with a rope."

"And don't think of talking to save your neck." Harris's voice was low, menacing.

Kendal paused without turning. His body yearned for the liquor. One drink. His mouth watered. "Why don't you join me? I'll buy."

"He's daft, off his head," Emmerson muttered.

Kendal looked up at the sound of hooves. They were coming that way. The posse, no doubt.

Emmerson grabbed his collar again. "You get my girl and meet us . . ."

"Where is the money? You must have made something off my investment."

Harris leaned from the horse and held the gun to Kendal's head.

Kendal raised his chin. "Do you think it matters if you kill me?" He felt the man's hesitation. It was terrifyingly heady to taunt death. "I'll take my part of the money now."

Harris clicked back the hammer. "You may not be afraid to die, but we know where to find your wife and child."

Kendal's body went cold. He swallowed against the cleaving in his throat. His legs felt suddenly useless, though he hardly moved. "I don't know where Patricia is. Mrs. Farrel interfered."

"You have till morning to find her." Emmerson released him. "Meet us at the creek down yonder."

The posse was closing. Emmerson mounted, and the two melted into the night. Kendal stood at the edge of the road. He had but to wait and the searchers would be upon him. What then? Do the honorable thing? He narrowed his eyes, gauging the distance, then slipped around the scrub oak and crouched.

The horsemen passed. Kendal remained crouching until the hooves were faint. They must be on their way to the ranch. He could just picture Monte's face, the stern dismay at learning of the marshal's death, the wondering at what part his brother-in-law had played, the honorable agreement to help in any way.

Kendal stood. At least the saloon would be clear. He wouldn't have to wait for a drink. His gait was swift, and he made it to town winded and weary. The light shone from the arched swinging doors where he paused, but inside was quiet.

He put one hand to the wood, then stopped. To his right, Patricia came out the door of the hotel with Abbie's brother supporting her. So Grant had her after all, but what was wrong with the girl? She looked like death. Kendal slipped into the shadow and watched him lift her to the saddle, then mount behind. They left town heading northeast. Patricia would soon meet Frances.

Kendal pushed through the saloon doors. The bartender raised his eyebrows briefly, then recovered himself. Kendal pointed to the top shelf whiskey. The man took it down and reached for a glass. Kendal brushed it away and took the bottle. He paid and left.

✦✦✦✦✦✦✦

Abbie sat down on the edge of the bed. The posse had gone on, Grant had returned to town, and she was weary and shaken. Marshal Haggerty murdered. Kendal missing and his companions on the run. Patricia was in the lower guest room, and down the hall Frances wept.

The clock struck eleven. The deal had been fraudulent, as Monte had suspected. If only she had spoken with him first. She closed her eyes. "Dear Lord, forgive my part in all this. Help us, please." Her voice trembled.

The door opened and Monte stepped in. His shirt was unfastened at the collar, his hair rumpled, his face haggard. There were circles beneath his eyes. Abbie tried to stand, but her legs shook from exhaustion. He sank to the bed beside her, hands limp in his lap. She had never seen him look so defeated.

"Monte . . ."

He reached for her hand and held it without speaking.

Abbie's heart ached. How could they have prevented this, any of it? How much had her silence and lack of judgment cost them? If only she had gone to him with everything—Kendal's affections, his plea for money, Frances's fears . . . She dropped her chin to her chest.

"Don't blame yourself." Monte's voice was gentle.

"I should have told you. I should have told you everything. I was afraid . . . afraid that honor would exact too high a price."

He squeezed her hand. "It might well have." He looked to the ceiling and released a slow breath. "Where is he now, Abbie? Hiding? Running?"

"I don't know."

"What of Frances, Jeanette?" Monte shook his head, and Abbie's heart ached.

She wished she had something to offer him. Hope? Faith? Trust? She had love, but could he accept it? Could he forgive her yet again? He spoke no blame, but it must be there, as it had before.

A knock came on the door, and he opened it. She heard Breck speaking low. Monte suddenly hardened. "No, Deputy Davis is with the posse looking for Harris and Emmerson. We'll have to take care of it ourselves."

Abbie jumped to her feet. "Monte?"

He turned, cold fire in his eyes. "Captain Gifford has made off with the horses."

She felt as though she'd been kicked. How much more? "But he was alone . . ."

"When you saw him, yes. Obviously the deed was done already, while the men were looking for you."

Abbie rushed to his side. "What do you mean to do?"

"Get them back before he's branded and transported them somewhere."

"You can't. You haven't the men."

"Perhaps not. But I have something more."

"What?"

"The right."

Abbie followed him with her eyes as he left. *Dear God in heaven, guard him now.* She dropped to her knees.

Twenty-Five

In the study Monte strapped on his gun. *A time for war.* He went out and gathered Breck and the men in the yard. "How many fresh mounts have we?"

Breck shook his head. "One horse each from the stable, counting your wife's."

"Get them saddled." He watched them go. Matt Weston, Breck, Curtis, Randy Gaines, and Drake. Cole had not returned yet. Monte wished now he had stopped him.

Sirocco was as spent as the men's mounts. Will led Zephyr out, and Monte climbed into the saddle. Well, maybe it was time for the storm. He brought her head around and pressed his knees to her sides. The men followed.

Breck came up even. "Any chance we'll run by Cole on the way?"

"I'm not depending on chance."

"What then?"

"God."

◆◆◆◆◆◆◆

Cole reined in. His chest was pumping almost as hard as Scotch's. Sweat ran down his forehead, and he brushed it from his eye with the back of his arm. He scanned the scrubby growth and ponderosas. Nothing moved. Scotch coughed and shook his head.

Cole stilled him with a hand. He turned and peered behind

him. Nothing. He took off his hat and raked his fingers through his hair, then replaced the hat and dismounted. He couldn't read the ground in the dark, but there were other ways. He listened. No cricket song. Nothing stirred. He climbed back up and nickered to Scotch.

Captain Jake took his hands from his charger's nostrils. The dark had been enough to conceal them in the dry stream bed, but one sound from the horse would have brought Farrel's man onto him. Cole Jasper was a man to be reckoned with.

His reputation in Texas had indeed been formidable. Captain Jake did not underestimate him. He raised to his elbow and sniffed the air, then murmured to the horse. Immediately it rose to its feet with very little commotion.

He stood and sheathed his sword. The sound of Cole's pursuit was past, the night quiet. But still he waited. He needed to think. Encountering Mrs. Farrel had been a shock and a mistake. What on earth was she doing on the range in the dark?

If only she had not recognized him. He felt again his fingers on her throat. He had stopped her air, but the pulse had throbbed still when he had to let go. He looked up. The sky was so clear the stars seemed as deep as the sea, layer after layer of tiny pricks of light. The air was sharp.

He could just keep riding. Any direction, any distance. Taking the reins, he led his horse up the side of the stream bed to the open range. He tossed the reins up and spun as something whooshed in his ears and slid over his head. Rope. It pulled tight on his neck as he grabbed for it. *Jasper.*

Cole yanked hard. Even as the man fell he reached for his gun, but Cole kicked it from his hand and yanked again. Captain Jake clawed and gasped for air. The veins in his head stood up like snakes. He writhed as Cole slid the sword from its scabbard and tossed it in the scrub, then rolled him face down in the dirt. He yanked his hands back and tied them, then loosened the rope on the man's neck.

"Git used to the feel of that. This ain't the last time a rope'll tickle yer neck. On yer feet."

Captain Jake struggled up. Cole tugged as he mounted Scotch.

Captain Jake followed on foot, pulled by the neck. "How did you know I was there?"

"I smelled you."

"It doesn't have to be this way. I have gold. Enough to make you a rich man. You don't owe Montgomery Farrel anything."

Cole touched his spurs to Scotch's sides and the horse broke into a trot. Captain Jake ran behind. He stumbled. "All right! Stop. Please."

Cole drew on the reins, and Scotch dropped to a walk again. "I don't like the sound o' yer voice."

The captain made no response. Cole figured it was about two hours to town—less if Jake Gifford had a mind to talk.

◆◆◆◆◆◆◆

Monte reined in, and the others gathered around him. He could see the horses, penned in the corral behind Gifford's hacienda. He could also see the men with rifles standing watch. The ride had cooled his temper, and he now considered the situation. He did not want to risk his men—or for that matter, those who followed Gifford's orders.

"I count thirteen," Breck said beside him. "Eleven with the horses, and two on the porch."

"And likely more in the bunkhouse."

Breck rubbed his chin with the back of his hand. "Tall order."

"I'm guessing they're waiting for first light to brand them. The house is dark. I'd sure like to know if Gifford is inside."

"I reckon I could manage that."

Monte turned to him.

Breck shrugged. "Plenty of windows. All low down."

"There might be men inside. There are at least two women."

Breck grinned. "My lucky night."

Monte stared at the yard again. They were far outnumbered.

283

The more they knew before anything happened, the better. "All right, give it a try."

Breck walked the horse down as close as he dared, then tied it and continued on foot. Already the night was less deep. The chilled, premorning air stirred, but it was dark enough for Breck to get to the house unnoticed. Monte watched him creep along the side wall and try one window, then move to the next.

He pushed it open and crawled in. Monte held himself ready. At the first sign of trouble they would rush in. But everything stayed quiet. After a time, Breck crawled back through the window and, crouching low, scurried across to where he'd left the horse. He led it, then mounted and rode back.

"The two women are sleepin'. That's all."

"Good work." So Captain Jake had not returned. Perhaps his men would wait for his orders. But Monte couldn't count on that. "All right, circle round. When I see you're in position, I'm riding in."

"Ridin' in?" Curtis raised up in his stirrups. "Out in the open?"

"I must at least give them the chance to release the horses on their own."

Breck shook his head. "Mr. Farrel, with all due respect . . ."

"I won't ambush them."

"Then what chance do we got?"

"What chance have we shooting it out?" Monte held his gaze. "If I give the signal, make as much noise as you can and move about. They may think there are more of us than there are."

"You're makin' yerself a target."

"I don't believe anyone there wants to shoot me. At least not without Captain Gifford's order." Monte raised Zephyr's head. "Go on now."

Monte watched as the men drifted into the darkness beyond the corral. When he guessed they'd had time to seek cover, he started down at a crisp trot. It wasn't long before he was noticed.

"Stop right there."

He slowed but continued at a walk.

"Who are you? What's your business?"

It was one of the men on the porch. He could tell that as he approached. The man stood forward. In the paling darkness Monte could see it was the one who had wielded the stick. He stopped in front of him. "I've come for my horses."

The man guffawed. "He don't learn too good, does he, Dixon?"

The other man joined him. "We shoulda finished him off the last time."

"You ain't got no horses here. You better git back where you come from 'fore you git hurt. Again."

"I'll leave when I have my stock."

The man stepped forward. "Then you're a dead man."

Zephyr reared and caught him in the head with her hooves. The man crumpled. A bullet whizzed past his ear, and Monte fired back and caught the other man in the leg. A shot from the side of the house hit the man in the shoulder and he fell.

Gunfire broke out from the corral, and Monte spurred Zephyr around the side of the hacienda. It was chaos. His men were closing in. He could see them in the dawning light, firing from behind bushes and boulders. The horses rushed frantically in their confinement, and their guards were fighting as hard to avoid being trampled as shot.

Four men came running from the bunkhouse, but their shots were aimed at the men in the corral. Monte stared. It was Skeeter and John Mason, and two of the new men, Landis and Scott. This was help he hadn't expected. It evened the score somewhat and threw the guards into confusion.

John Mason made it to the gate and pulled the slats free. The horses ran out. Monte and his men closed in, and those in the corral dropped their guns and raised their hands high.

Breck came with rope, and they tied them in pairs, then took off their boots and left them sitting. The ground was none too inviting after hosting forty-six horses. Monte took in the scene with satisfaction, but no credit to himself. Through it all he'd felt a presence more potent than his human strength. He whispered a prayer of thanks then surveyed the situation.

John Mason came slowly to him. He pulled off his hat. "Mr. Farrel, I didn't know nothing about stealing them horses. I swear it. I'd've had no part in it, no matter what he offered."

Monte believed him. The young man's throat worked, but his eyes held steady. "Get your horse, John. Help the men round up my stock."

"Yes, sir!"

Monte turned and eyed Skeeter. The man looked chagrinned and uncomfortable.

"Mr. Farrel." Skeeter circled his hat in his hands. "I reckon I'm to blame for some of this. I told Captain Gifford where you kept the horses once the weather warmed."

"Why?"

"Well, I just figured it was my job to answer. I didn't know what he meant to do. Leastwise, I didn't want to know, so I didn't look too close."

Monte considered that. Skeeter could have made excuses, but he didn't. "That's honest, Skeeter."

"I'd sure be obliged to work for you again. At any wage."

"I'll consider that. For now, you can keep watch on the men in the corral." Monte walked around the porch. The man he had shot leaned against the post bleeding from the leg and shoulder. The man Zephyr had kicked still lay in the dirt.

Breck joined him as Monte bent and felt for a pulse. "Well, I suppose one casualty is better than I expected." He thumbed the man on the porch. "Take that one over with the others and send someone for the doctor."

The sky on the horizon was paling to a robin's egg blue. Monte rubbed the back of his neck, then turned as a half dozen horsemen rode in. Ethan Thomas wore a deputy star on his chest. He reined in and dismounted. "Monte."

"Ethan. I see you've been deputized."

Monte waited while Ethan surveyed the yard. "Looks like you don't need us after all."

"There are men in the corral wanting transportation."

Ethan grinned. "Yeah. They'll be wanting it more when the sun comes up and things get ripe."

Monte retrieved his hat from the ground where it had fallen when Zephyr reared. "It seemed appropriate."

"Did you get your horses?"

"The men are rounding them up. How did you know?"

"Cole. He brought in Captain Gifford." Ethan shook his head, chuckling. "Sure was a sight. Gifford was just about played out by the time he staggered in, tied by the neck behind Cole's horse. You know, I never liked that man. Gave me the creeps. Even my dog wouldn't tolerate him, and you know Brutus. He's a sap for everyone."

Monte smiled, and Ethan ran on. "When Gifford confessed to taking the horses, Cole said we'd find you here. Reckon he guessed right, only he thought you'd be mincemeat by now."

"Yes, he would." Monte put on his hat. "If you don't mind cleaning up the mess, it's a long ride home, and I've been up all night."

"We'll take it from here. I must say those horses would have been a sore loss. I'm hoping to have a look at your foals myself come spring."

"You do that, Ethan. I'll make you a fair deal."

"I know you will."

Monte climbed into the saddle. Breck came from the corral and climbed astride his horse. Together they started for home. The miles between seemed long indeed.

✦✦✦✦✦✦✦

Kendal sank down against the back of Monte's bunkhouse and uncorked the bottle. Fully a third of it remained yet, and he swigged a mouthful. The horse he had taken from the livery stood by the corral a short distance away, saddled and ready to convey Patricia.

Kendal frowned and drank from the bottle. He wanted no more part of this business. He had never intended it to go so far.

But Harris and Emmerson had threatened his family. He had no choice but to see it through.

His head sagged against the wall. He was tired, so bone tired even thinking made him groan. And his thoughts were senseless, pointless, futile. He closed his eyes and let his mouth hang open. A little sleep ... just a little ...

✦✦✦✦✦✦✦

Abbie raised her head from her arm on the windowsill. Her neck ached, and her limbs were stiff with cold. But that had not awakened her. The morning sun pierced her swollen eyelids when she opened them, and she couldn't think. Then memory rushed in, and she stared down at the yard.

Horses. One was Zephyr, bearing Monte. She sprang up and ran, her hair flying free and the ribbons on her wrap trailing behind. She yanked open the door as Monte dismounted wearily, and Will led Zephyr away. Without a thought for Breck, she dashed across the porch and down the stairs into Monte's arms.

He staggered back, then wrapped her close. Breck headed for the bunkhouse.

"Come inside, Monte. You're exhausted." She led him up the stairs and sat him on the edge of the bed. She systematically removed his clothes and brought him a damp cloth from the basin.

He smiled. "Let me wash properly. Then I'll tell you what happened so you won't die of wondering."

"I'm perfectly capable of waiting."

He went to the basin and plunged in his arms, then scrubbed his face and neck and toweled dry. He took her hands and kissed her.

"You got the horses?"

"A-ha-ha. I knew it."

"So tell me."

"We got the horses. One of Gifford's men was killed."

"And Captain Gifford?"

Monte pressed her hands to his chest. "Cole brought him in. He's in the jail at this moment awaiting trial. I daresay it won't go well with him, but that cell probably looked like paradise once Cole was through with him."

Abbie closed her eyes with relief.

"Any sign of Kendal?"

"No."

He rested his forehead on hers. "Well, now I must sleep."

She nodded and backed away, but he pulled her close and kissed her again, then let her go. He dropped to the bed like he'd never move again. Abbie leaned against the post and watched him sleep. Her heart rejoiced. He was home safe ... unlike Kendal.

♦♦♦♦♦♦♦

Kendal woke with his face on the ground. The grass and bracken dug into his cheek, and the sun pierced his eyes. His head throbbed and his mouth was foul. He looked around. Everything was quiet, a serene moment when all seemed right with the world.

He pulled himself up and made his way to the stream behind the house. He dipped his hands and splashed his face with the icy water until his senses cleared. The lives of Frances and Jeanette depended on his doing his task, though how he would secure Patricia he didn't know.

He leaned against the gray-brown trunk of a cottonwood and looked at the house. If he could just walk inside, take Frances in his arms, promise her ... promise her anything. If he could hear Jeanette's laughter, watch her tiny hands clap together. He smiled at the thought.

He even hoped for one more chance with Monte, clasping his hand in the man's scarred palm. Kendal had never given him much credit. It was easier to believe things just fell out well for him. But he saw now that wasn't so. Monte deserved what he had. He worked for it.

And Abbie. Better not to think of her. She had given him the benefit of the doubt, time and again kept her faith in him, though God knew he didn't deserve it. Frances had more sense. She saw him for what he was.

It had not always been that way. Once she had cherished the

ground he walked on. They had been happy; he would not forget that. Kendal hung his head. But that had been another life. He had sold it with his soul.

♦♦♦♦♦♦♦

Hearing Frances weeping softly, Abbie left Monte sleeping. She tied up her wrap and went down the hall, then tapped on the door. After a moment it opened. Frances looked as she expected, swollen-eyed and drawn. Her hair was carelessly braided down her back, as though her fingers had forgotten their skill.

She pushed the door wide, and Abbie stepped in. She was surprised to see Jeanette curled into the bedcovers. She was rosy with sleep.

"She was afraid," Frances murmured. "Mammy brought her in."

Abbie nodded.

Frances walked to the chest and lifted the brass-framed picture. She looked at it a moment, then handed it to Abbie. "Our wedding day."

Abbie looked at the stately couple: Kendal in his crisp coat and Frances, young and soft. Abbie was struck by the vulnerable bend of her mouth. It was not tight and bitter, nor were the eyes haughty or angry. Their hands were clasped between them, fingers interlocked.

"It was the happiest day of my life. Kendal was . . . so fine."

Abbie returned the picture to her.

She replaced it in the chest. "Tell me truthfully. Was he faithful to his vows?"

"To the best of my knowledge, yes."

Frances's hand trembled as she fumbled with the tie at the throat of her gown. "I can hardly fault him, if he wasn't. I drove him to all of it." A tear slipped from her eye and trailed down her cheek.

Abbie led her by the arm to the small sofa.

Frances dropped wearily beside her. "I don't know what I hoped for. I don't know if I hoped anything, only . . . to force his hand maybe, to take me home. And now I see he ... could not face that. Of all things he could not bear ... standing as a failure among those he knew..."

"It's too easy to see what's past."

"The past seems less bleak than the days to come."

"We don't know yet what will come."

"What hope is there?"

"God's hope."

"God." Frances shook her head. "He asks too much."

"Only that we forgive."

"How can I? How can I forgive what Kendal has done? He's brought us all to ruin, even Monte."

Abbie's chest tightened. "We don't know that."

"I hoped for plain speech from you."

"I will speak plainly. What God intends through this, I can't see. But I know—I *know*, Frances—that He has a plan if we trust Him."

Frances closed her eyes. "Abbie, I ... I love Kendal."

"And you should. We've all strayed. God help us if love depends on goodness."

Frances smiled faintly. "God help us indeed." She dropped her face into her hands. "It's myself I can't forgive."

Abbie wrapped her arms around the woman, acutely aware of the fragile shoulders that shook with the sobs. When had Frances grown so thin? *How could I have been so blind to her suffering?*

"Oh, Abbie, what can I do?"

Abbie swallowed against the tightness in her throat. "Pray."

✦✦✦✦✦✦✦

When Frances had calmed, Abbie went down. Her limbs felt leaden, but there were others who needed her. She found Patricia in the hall looking dazed and forlorn. "Here, Patricia. This way." Abbie led her outside and pointed. "The privy is there."

Patricia nodded. Abbie watched her cross the yard to the outhouse. She had not spoken since Grant brought her. Was it shock or fear that kept her mute? If only she had not seen what her father or his partner had done.

Abbie recoiled at her own memories that sprung on her unawares: the contorted face, the blood-caked abdomen. She closed her eyes. Oh, Patricia. The poor child was terrified. For the hundredth time Abbie wondered if she had done right to interfere.

She could not blame Grant. He had found Patricia at the stairs when he came back with the doctor. All around her, people railed against Harris and her father. She had stared, stricken, at the marshal's body as Grant led her out. All this Grant had described when he came. He had done well to bring her here, but what would they do now?

Patricia came out and swung the door shut behind her. She stood uncertainly. Abbie walked to meet her, took her by the arm and started for the house.

"Please . . ." Patricia stopped. "May we stay out a minute? I feel . . . queer." Her voice trembled.

Abbie patted her arm, relieved to hear her speak. "Come walk along the stream with me. The air will refresh you." The stream ran freely, and its music was soothing. A blue jay chirped from the cottonwood branches, and a crow cawed loudly in response.

Suddenly a shadow loomed in the trees, and Abbie startled as Kendal stepped free of the growth. He looked as though he had slept in the ditch. His clothes were soiled, his hair tousled, and his expression grim. "Thank you, Abbie. I'll take Patricia now."

Abbie drew herself up. "You'll not, Kendal."

"I must return her to her father."

"She can't go to him. He's running from the law and is at the least an accomplice to murder. If there is decency in you, let this end here."

"I can't do that."

"Why not? If you turned yourself in and testified—I know Grant would defend you. . . ."

"It's too late for that now."

"It's not. Kendal, put things right. Frances loves and needs you . . . so does Jeanette."

He looked away. "That's impossible."

"I know it's so."

"She doesn't know . . ."

"She knows everything." Abbie took a step forward. "Come back to the house. Talk to her yourself. Talk to Monte."

Kendal shook his head. "I can't." He dropped his hands to his sides, then turned from her to Patricia.

Abbie felt the girl shrink behind her. She tried to reassure her with a grip on her arm. One move from Kendal and she'd send the girl running and fend him off the best she could. But she prayed it wouldn't come to that. Somewhere inside him Kendal knew what was right. He must.

Kendal slowly released his breath. "Very well, I'll leave her. But you must tell Monte . . ."

Abbie spun as four horses closed them in. Emmerson and Harris were flanked by two rough men who smelled, even at a distance. She'd never seen them before, but she'd remember them now. One wore a patch on his left eye.

Harris leveled his rifle. "All right, Stevens. You've done your part, now get out of the way."

Abbie held her breath as the patched man also aimed for Kendal's chest. She eased Patricia back behind her.

Emmerson glowered. "Come on, Patricia. We'll be on our way now."

The girl trembled. Abbie's anger kindled. "She'll stay here with us."

Emmerson narrowed his eyes. "I warn you not to interfere. Let her loose."

"I won't."

Emmerson pulled out his gun. "I've nothing to lose by killing you."

The barrel came up, and slowly his thumb pulled back the cock. Abbie raised her chin, though her heart quaked. Would they hear from the house? If she screamed, would they hear? She watched the knuckle of Emmerson's trigger finger whiten.

"No!" Kendal lunged in front of her with the report of the rifle.

Abbie heard the thud of the bullet and screamed as Kendal buckled and fell into the water. Gunfire exploded as she grabbed Patricia and half dragged her to cover. It took only moments to realize the shots were no longer directed at them. The men had turned and were answering gunfire from the trees on the right.

She could see Cole and two others in the undergrowth beyond them. She pressed Patricia down behind the boulder at the stream's edge and crouched. The patched man fell, and Emmerson went down with his horse spurting blood from the chest. He fired, then took a bullet in the throat and collapsed across the beast.

Abbie pressed Patricia's face to her chest. From the corner of her eye, she saw Monte running from the house. He took cover near Cole, and Abbie prayed he would stay there. Harris lunged but was shot from behind. Others must have come from the bunkhouse. The last man looked about him, eyes wild and chest heaving. He stood suddenly, rifle blasting, and Abbie ducked behind the rock as a volley of gunfire erupted. Then it was silent.

She raised her head. Gunsmoke hung in the air with its acrid sulfur smell. For a moment no one moved, then Monte left his cover and dropped to his knees at the water's edge. Grabbing Kendal up, he felt his neck for a pulse, then leaned slowly back, Kendal's body slack in his arms.

Abbie crept to his side.

"Take Patricia in, Abbie."

She didn't want to leave him. She looked at Kendal, soaked in blood from the bullet meant for her, then back to Monte. Tears choked her throat but did not fall. She tried to speak, but there was nothing to say. She obeyed. At the house, she gave Patricia over to Pearl, then found Frances in her room.

Frances must have heard the gunshots. Her head was bowed over her clasped hands as she knelt beside the couch. She did not weep, but Abbie saw her shoulders tremble as she prayed. Slowly she dropped down beside her.

"Frances," she whispered, "Kendal is dead."

✦✦✦✦✦✦

Abbie stood at the window. The house was strangely quiet, and she felt like a shell, emptied and useless. Kendal had been lowered into the ground for taking a bullet meant for her, and the knowledge left her bleak and desperate. Monte came and stood beside her, wrapping his arm about her shoulders.

She leaned against him. "Frances?"

"She's sleeping now."

Frances had not cried when Abbie told her. It was as though the tears had suddenly dried up, left her parched as the brown, barren land outside the window. Even when Monte had come in and taken his sister in his arms, she had not wept. Abbie glanced at him now. How much their lives pivoted around this man. How did he bear up under it?

He spoke low. "I entrusted Frances to him, knowing her fragility. I put her into his arms."

Abbie's chest ached.

"When Kendal first came to court her, he was so beside himself he could hardly speak. I took him aside and told him what to say. I even told him how to propose marriage to her. Oh, there were things we disagreed on, plenty of things. But one thing I knew . . . he loved Frances, and he would do anything for her." His voice broke. "How does that change?"

"Maybe it doesn't. Sometimes loving can hurt as much as hating ever could."

He stroked her arm. "Perhaps they're irrevocably tied together."

Abbie felt the truth of that. Love and hate bound up in the heart together. Had it not been so between them? Had she not felt the extremities of each emotion for Monte? And he for her? Perhaps he did still.

She had betrayed his honor, broken her word, jeopardized their future. She had dishonored, disobeyed, and disillusioned him. Through her silence and bad judgment she had brought everything he worked for crashing down about him. If only she could start again. Her head sank to her chest.

"How bad are things, Monte?"

"No worse than I expected, barring further catastrophe. The railroad made no claim against us. Driscoll dare not do so. And at the very least he now holds stock worth as much as his bank."

Anguish washed over her. "I'm such a fool."

Monte tightened his arm on her shoulders. "At any rate we've both learned something." He turned and cupped her face with his hands. "To trust each other."

"I am so sorry."

"There's no need."

But Abbie felt the need. "Monte ... about the other time ... when the rustlers came ..."

"You saved my life."

Sudden tears choked her throat and stung her eyes.

"I was too stubborn and prideful to admit or even believe it myself. But I acknowledge it now. And I thank you." He kissed her lips, and she let the tears flow.

Twenty-Six

Monte glanced once at Frances before he slid the stone into place. The gray speckled marble looked out of place against the red earth, but it settled in with an air of finality at the head of Kendal's grave. It had lain unmarked for three weeks while the stone was ordered, worked, and shipped. Now the grave was complete.

Death was irrevocable, and it took whom it would. Like his father before him, Captain Jake Gifford had dangled from a rope, kicking out his last moments. Monte had taken no pleasure in the sight, though his presence was required to make the statement that lawlessness would not be tolerated. Reverend Shields and the city council had made strong speeches warning of that, and some who had come in with the train cleared out.

Monte looked up. The breeze blew a strand of hair across Abbie's forehead. Beside her Frances stared down at the stone. She looked strangely strong. How queer for it to come now, her ability to cope.

Slowly Frances dropped to her knees and ran her fingers over the chiseled words. *Kendal Stevens. 1846–1873. There is no greater love than to give one's life for a friend.* Bowing her head, she laid her hand upon the mounded earth. If she wept, he couldn't tell.

He circled Abbie's waist with his arm and waited. At last Frances stood and came to them. Monte took her hands in his. "At the end he knew the price of honor, and he paid it."

She nodded, glancing once again at the stone.

"There's no reason for you to go, Frances. There's nothing for you to go back to, and you're welcome here with us—both you and Jeanette."

She smiled. "I know that, but . . . I don't belong here." She ran her eyes over the graves.

"In time . . ."

She squeezed his hands. "I need time away first. I need the South, the land in which I was born."

The waif, Patricia, had said much the same when Monte sent her back to England in the care of her aunt. But he had hoped to keep Frances close, at least until he was certain she had recovered from her grief. Now he wondered if recovery was possible for her here, where she'd experienced only trouble. He pressed her hand. "I understand."

"At least I'll have the train the whole way this time . . . free from pestilence, fire, and Indian attack." She smiled faintly. "Jeanette and I will stay with Kendal's mother. She's offered us her home."

"I intend to see to your expenses."

"Thank you, Monte." She turned to Abbie. "Thank you for everything. I know I was not kind."

Abbie embraced her.

Monte watched them walk away together, then looked down at the two graves on the hill, the little angel and the monument bearing witness to the lives that had been. His eye rested on the newly chiseled stone. Even with all Kendal's faults and the losses he had caused him, he could not despise him.

Kendal was a man like the rest of them—weak and fallible. But at the end he had shown his worth. In his last moments had Kendal surrendered his will along with his life? For Kendal's sake, Monte hoped it was so, but he'd never know. No . . . not never. One day he would see, when he, too, left this life and stood before God. There was no way but surrender, no strength but God's own, no hope but that won by the Savior. He knew that now, and he could only hope to live by that truth . . . with honor.

♦♦♦♦♦♦♦

Grant strode down the boardwalk and turned at the corner. He headed down the lane, mounted the three stairs that led to the Wilson's front door, and knocked. He had already caught the movement of the upstairs curtain.

Darla Wilson opened the door and frowned down her nose. "I'm sorry. Marcy is indisposed."

Grant removed his hat and held it before him. "I see. Well, I'll just sit here on the porch then, until she feels better."

"I don't think that's wise."

"Oh, Marcy's a hardy girl. She'll recover soon enough."

"*Well*..." Darla turned back in. "Please yourself." The door clicked behind her.

Grant sat on the rocker beside the door and tucked his hat down over his eyes. Rocking gently, he hummed along with the creaking of the boards beneath the chair. Somewhere a dog barked, and a wagon rolled heavily down the street. The shadows lengthened and paled, then vanished with the reds and coppers of the sunset. The evening chill settled over him.

He stood and paced slowly across the porch. He nodded when Judge Wilson came home, scrutinized him, then went inside. The sky deepened and stars dotted it. The crescent moon joined them. Grant rubbed his arms and strode back and forth, then settled again into the rocker. He dozed, felt his chin sink to his chest, then succumbed.

◆◆◆◆◆◆◆

Grant jolted stiffly. He squeezed his eyes against the sunlight until Marcy blocked the rays with her frowning countenance and hands on her hips.

"What on earth are you doing? Have you lost your mind, spending the entire night out here on our front porch?"

"I reckon so." Grant stretched.

Marcy turned to go in, but he caught her arm and pulled her back. "Not so fast."

"How dare you!"

"At least hear what I have to say."

"Whatever excuse you have is of no concern to me." She struggled to free her hand.

"Isn't a man innocent until proven guilty?"

"What more proof could be required than ... than of a woman under your bed?"

"Now see, that's just it. A woman *in* my bed ... now that would be incriminating."

Marcy's face reddened.

"Marcy. She was fourteen years old, and Abbie ..."

"Abbie!" Marcy wrenched her hand away. "I might have known."

"Would you stop and listen? The girl was in trouble. Her father was one of the men who killed Marshal Haggerty. Abbie hid her in my room for safety—only I didn't know she was there. Do you think I'd have carried on as I did if I'd known?"

"I don't know how you'd have carried on." Marcy raised her chin and tossed back her ringlets. Grant guessed she knew exactly the way the sun would catch and shine on them. She walked over to the rail of the porch and leaned against the post.

He followed. "I guess there's only one thing to do." He turned her toward him. "Will you marry me?"

She stared. "Marry you?"

He took both her hands in his. "I'm asking for your hand in marriage." He watched her soften. Tears sparkled in her eyes, but that hardly surprised him. Marcy was not nearly as confident as she made out.

"I ... I didn't think you'd ask. That's why I ... thought if we were alone ... if ..."

"Maybe that little girl was put there to bring us both to our senses. I'm sorry I thought to compromise you." Grant brought her hand to his lips. "But you haven't answered me."

"Yes." Her voice trembled, then her smile broke out broadly. "Yes, I will marry you. Of course I'll marry you! It took you long enough to ask!"

Grant threw back his head and laughed. "Now look here. My back aches, my neck is stiff, and I'm hungry enough to eat a full-grown heifer. I guess I'll run along."

Marcy stuck up her nose. "You'll do nothing of the kind. First you'll come in and ask my pa properly for my hand, and then you'll join us for breakfast. Mother already counted you."

"Oh yeah? You mean you meant to make peace all along?"

"Of course. What kind of ninny do you take me for?"

✦✦✦✦✦✦✦

Abbie slipped her hand into the crook of Monte's arm as he drove the buggy to her pa's house. He lifted her down and rested his hand on the small of her back as they walked to the door. Pa met them there. "Come on in."

Abbie kissed his cheek, then stepped inside. Grant stood in the front room with Marcy beside him. He looked wickedly pleased with himself, and she hid her dismay. It wasn't fair. She'd come with such a good appetite.

Monte bowed over Marcy's hand. "What a delightful surprise."

What a smooth traitor he was. Marcy looked smug over his bowed head. Abbie smiled.

"Come on, everyone," Mama called. "Before the supper gets cold."

They gathered around the table, joined hands and prayed, then took their places. Pa passed Monte the platter of venison steaks. "It's nice to have you all together tonight."

Mama smiled. Grant's eyes twinkled. The hair on Abbie's neck rose. Something was afoot.

Mama turned to Monte. "You saw your sister safely off?"

"Yes. Though I was sorry for her to go."

Grant laid down his fork. "Well, Abbie, you had one sister-in-law leave, so I know you'll be pleased to hear you're getting a new one." He hooked his arm around Marcy's shoulders and grinned.

Abbie felt Monte squeeze her hand under the table. For once in her life she had absolutely no response come to mind.

Monte reached out his hand to Grant. "Congratulations, Grant. You've made a fine choice."

Abbie swallowed. "I'm ... very happy for you both." She couldn't manage more, but Monte made up for her lack.

"When is it to be?"

"The first of June. Marcy needs time to put together her trousseau. We're going to San Francisco for our honeymoon."

"How nice." Abbie forced her eyes to meet Marcy's. "I'm sure it will be lovely."

Grant's eyes softened behind their teasing glint. "It'll be good to get back, too, and settle into our own place. I've purchased the Craddock house in town."

Monte nodded. "Very good. That's a nice place."

Marcy sniffed. "It will be when I redecorate. Mrs. Craddock had the most appalling taste."

Abbie drew herself up. "Then for a wedding gift I'll give you red velvet drapes, brought all the way from Charleston."

Marcy turned in surprise.

"I'll show them to you when we have a chance." She felt, rather than saw Monte's amusement. Only a miracle would get her through the rest of the evening. She hardly heard a word that was spoken and moved automatically through the washing up while Monte visited with Pa and Grant, Marcy sitting like a porcelain doll beside him. She, of course, wouldn't lift a finger to help Mama.

At last Monte stood. "Thank you for a wonderful evening." He extended his hand to Grant. "Again, my congratulations." Bending low, he kissed Marcy's hand and she flushed.

If Abbie didn't get out she'd scream. Her family crowded the door behind them as Monte handed her into the buggy. Marcy leaned into Grant's chest and her dimples deepened. Abbie waved limply as Monte smacked the reins and started home. The creaking and bumping of the buggy hardly penetrated her daze.

Monte glanced at her. "Well ... that was news."

"News! Any simpleton could see it coming. Marcy was bound to have him no matter what."

Monte laughed full out. "My darling Abbie. Life will never be easy for you, will it? What was that you used to play ... the helpless maiden trapped in the jungle?"

"Wild animals I could face. Outlaws and Indians and blizzards ... but this, this is beyond me."

Monte hooked his arm around her shoulders. His eyes shone with pride and amusement. "Abbie, I have come to know above all else that *nothing* is beyond you."

Acknowledgments

Throughout this work there have been many who have stood by me, kept me focused, and more importantly, reminded me to "lighten up." Top on the list are my prayer partners and sisters in Christ, Marianne, Romona, Joey, and Margaret, for all their hours of listening, encouraging, and much laughter. Thank you, ladies.

As always I thank my family. Your faith and understanding bless me daily.

Thanks to my editor, Barb Lilland, who always has an ear ready, a gracious spirit, and a true sense of humor, and to the other hard workers at Bethany House Publishers.

And mostly, thanks to my Savior and Lord for whom it's all done anyway.